Pragmatic Liberation and the
Politics of Puerto Rican Diasporic Drama

Pragmatic Liberation and the Politics of Puerto Rican Diasporic Drama

Jon D. Rossini

University of Michigan Press
Ann Arbor

Copyright © 2024 by Jon D. Rossini
Some rights reserved

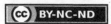

This work is licensed under a Creative Commons Attribution-NonCommercial-NoDerivatives 4.0 International License. *Note to users:* A Creative Commons license is only valid when it is applied by the person or entity that holds rights to the licensed work. Works may contain components (e.g., photographs, illustrations, or quotations) to which the rightsholder in the work cannot apply the license. It is ultimately your responsibility to independently evaluate the copyright status of any work or component part of a work you use, in light of your intended use. To view a copy of this license, visit http://creativecommons.org/licenses/by-nc-nd/4.0/

For questions or permissions, please contact um.press.perms@umich.edu

Published in the United States of America by the
University of Michigan Press
Manufactured in the United States of America
Printed on acid-free paper
First published May 2024

A CIP catalog record for this book is available from the British Library.

Library of Congress Cataloging-in-Publication data has been applied for.

ISBN 978-0-472-07672-7 (hardcover : alk. paper)
ISBN 978-0-472-05672-9 (paper : alk. paper)
ISBN 978-0-472-90441-9 (open access ebook)

DOI: https://doi.org/10.3998/mpub.12652049

The University of Michigan Press's open access publishing program is made possible thanks to additional funding from the University of Michigan Office of the Provost and the generous support of contributing libraries.

This title is freely available in an open access edition thanks to the TOME initiative and the generous support of the University of California, Davis.

In memory of my mother,
Maria Patrocinio Ramona Pilar Miranda y Garcia (1939–2016)
who never accepted her given circumstances.

Contents

PREFACE	ix
ACKNOWLEDGMENTS	xi
INTRODUCTION Given Circumstances, Premise, and Pragmatic Strategies of Liberation	1
CHAPTER 1 From *Palm Sunday* to *REVOLT!*: Rethinking the Political Horizon of Puerto Rican Diasporic Drama	31
CHAPTER 2 Symbolic Action as Pragmatic Politics: Lolita on the Stage	63
CHAPTER 3 Diasporic Return and the Limits of Pragmatic Liberation	94
CHAPTER 4 Before Revolution, Honesty?: The Everyday Pragmatics of Activist Work	124
CHAPTER 5 After the Revolution: Massacres, Collateral Damage, and Moving Forward	156
CONCLUSION The Labyrinth of Free Association and Sustainable Pragmatic Liberation	181
NOTES	193
REFERENCES	223
INDEX	233

Digital materials related to this title can be found on the Fulcrum platform via the following citable URL: https://doi.org/10.3998/mpub.12652049

Preface

This work has come quickly and slowly, moving through several evolutions. In its original form I wanted to think about the real impact of Latine theaters, which evolved into the problems and limits of neoliberal thinking in Latine theater, and then into an increasing recognition of tensions between radical aspirations and everyday lives. In thinking through these tensions across Latine drama, I found myself returning to Puerto Rican diasporic drama. Despite not being Puerto Rican myself I was profoundly struck by the ways the legislative administration of a territorial reality trumps any attempt to dismiss the profound effects of systemic demonstration on the part of reactionaries refusing to accept the existence of systemic problems.

I was also disturbed by my own relative ignorance of the specificities of the Puerto Rican and Puerto Rican diasporic experience that I needed to address as the work shifted away from a general exploration of Latine cultural production to a more specific investigation of the Puerto Rican diaspora. It was a stark reminder not only of the complexity and depth of specific experiences, but also the unintended consequences of potential erasure contained in mostly productive umbrella terms like Latine. This book accounts for too few of the brilliant dramatists in the diaspora, and I look forward to advancing this work. I am excited by the many recent contributions to the study of theater and performance in Puerto Rico and its diasporas by a range of incisive, theoretically sophisticated scholars and will continue to learn from them.

During the review of this manuscript, one reader asked for a clearer answer about my choice to engage specifically Puerto Rican diasporic materials. While I give a brief answer in the text, I wanted to ruminate on this for a moment. This same question arose when an earlier draft of this manuscript went through a workshop process. The Puerto Rican scholars, all pleased that I was specifically attending to this subject, also wanted to know why I was doing this, one asserting the importance of working across identities within Latinidad that are sometimes implicitly imposed as limiting constraints. My own Latine identity is fraught: the son of a first-generation professional Spanish-speaking immigrant mother from the Philippines, it took me a while to process my then so-called Hispanic (Other) heritage growing up in the US

South in the 1970s and 1980s, especially since my father, who had been discriminated against as a young Italian American in Washington, DC and Pittsburgh, tended to minimize his ethnic identity. While my Latine heritage from the Philippines is often considered illegible, the very complexity of when and how making a particular identity claim was a necessary and/or ethical action informs my thinking about the basic structure of pragmatic liberation.

When I was still in graduate school a professor asked me why I didn't use my maternal surname to mark my then Latino identity more explicitly. After considering the question and speaking with my mother, who was always proud of my acknowledgment of Latinidad, though she herself struggled in the gap between being Hispanic and Filipina, she indicated that in her lived space, my full name would be presented as Jon Dominic Rossini y Miranda. This traditional Iberian form held elitist associations that ran counter to the existing assumptions about Latine identity, and rather than reclaim it as a hyphen, which it never was in lived practice, it ended remaining invisible. This, combined with a heritage learning of Spanish that provides me greater comfort in the classroom than on the street, as well as my privileged position as a child of two professionals with graduate degrees from UC Berkeley, placed me outside a conventional narrative of marginalization.

And yet, the very presence of this disjuncture, which explicitly haunted my first monograph's exploration into the legibility of ethnic identity, has not decreased. My entry into Puerto Rican diasporic work, begun in the first chapter of my previous book that explored Miguel Piñero's work, was never previously framed as Puerto Rican diasporic work. However, my increasing understanding of coloniality as an organization of power, and its specific valences in a US imperial context, provide some tenuous historical ground for a connective thread from a contested Hispanic Pilipino legacy to a recognition of similar struggles to understand one's place in the Puerto Rican diaspora. As I consistently remind my graduate students, you make a choice to devote your attention to some things and not to others. You can never be sure it is the right choice, but you can strive to understand the implications and impacts of your choice to the best of your ability and knowledge. In doing so, you should recognize not only its value but its limitations. Hopefully, this book does a reasonable job in this regard, and holds value for those who have more intimate and personal encounters with the materials of this work, not distanced by the tenuous but real connection of sharing space in the world as it exists as we all continue searching for home.

Acknowledgments

This title is freely available in an open access edition thanks to the TOME initiative and the generous support of the University of California, Davis. Learn more at openmonographs.org. This manuscript would not have been possible without two P.L.A.C.E. grants from UC Davis secured by Kimberly Nettles-Barcelón, one to support a manuscript workshop with outside experts and a second to participate in a writing retreat and to work with Elena K. Abbott as a writing coach. I also want to thank the Academic Senate of the University of California, Davis for several Small Research and Travel grants that fostered opportunities to engage relevant questions at major conferences and see productions of theater, including Quiara Alegría Hudes's Elliot Trilogy in Los Angeles.

Patricia A. Ybarra has been a constant interlocutor and source of support for 20 years since we first met at the University of Kansas in 2003. Most recently, for this manuscript she provided an incredibly detailed and careful reading of Chapter 4 on a short time scale, providing a wealth of suggestions I was only partially able to incorporate. Back in 2011 Ramón Rivera-Servera invited me to give a talk at Northwestern University for which I first started talking about some of the issues of liberation and Puerto Rican diasporic drama.

Adam Versényi and Jorge Huerta have been mentors and supporters since my graduate school days in the 1990s, and my former graduate school roommate, Gary Ashwill, himself a stellar researcher in early Cuban league baseball history, took the time to look through and provide feedback on the book's introduction and emerging thesis.

Mark Jerng and Seeta Chaganti at UC Davis served as a wonderful writing group for several years, and although none of this book was composed in that space, the influence of their thinking and our conversations permeates this work. Mark also jumped in several helpful (and reassuring) thoughts at a late moment in the proposal process.

Elena Machado, Jade Power-Sotomayor, Camilla Stevens, and Leo Cabranes-Grant graciously agreed to read the entirety of an early draft manuscript through the P.L.A.C.E. supported workshop process. I could not have asked for a better set of conversations. They not only provided the structure of the book as you see it, but they also advocated for specific threads that have radically deepened my understanding while encouraging me to excise the two pieces I wrote prior to conceiving this structure. I hope those will emerge in revised form soon. Leo insisted that I needed to consider the ELA in its initial formation as a potential gesture of pragmatic liberation; Jade was very helpful in thinking with and through the concept of *bregar*, which she introduced me to; Camilla provided a close reading and insisted on the importance of centering the theater; and Elena reminded me of the circuits of consumption and where value is placed. It was wonderful getting to know them better through this process.

I want to thank the anonymous readers for the University of Michigan Press, as well as a member of the Press Board, who all offered useful and supportive suggestions to make this stronger. I took on as many as I could and believe the work is much stronger for your advice.

In the UC Davis Department of Theatre and Dance, colleagues David Grenke, Lynette Hunter, Margaret Laurena Kemp, and Peter Lichtenfels have over the years provided a broad sounding board for thinking through and with emerging issues of theater and performance. I have appreciated the opportunities to collaborate with David, which has also helped me to a greater awareness of the compositional potentials of language and always encouraged me to engage with the issues most important to me. Lynette has offered a model of consistent and precise thinking, and Margaret has advocated for a clear sense of purpose in the pursuit of that which is most important. More recent graduate students, including advisees Claire Chambers, Sarah Hart, Chris McCoy, Jorge Morejón, and Dennis Somera, as well as current students supporting our Writing Ensemble Exploring Performance, Jamie Davidson, Rosemary Hannon, and Erika Tsimbrovsky, have provided a rich atmosphere for thinking about questions of writing and the idiosyncratic choices we all make in our paths forward. Mike Chin, who also participates in the group, has been a long-time confidante, supporter, and friend. UC Davis Performance Studies colleague Kris Fallon stepped in a timely moment to help with references for Chapter 5.

In the broader profession, the Coloniality of Catastrophe Working Session members at the 2022 ASTR also provided useful feedback on an earlier draft of the conclusion. I also consistently learn from Guillermo Aviles-Rodriguez, Ana Puga, and many others at ASTR. My colleagues in what is now the Latinx, Indigenous, and the Americas Focus Group of the Association for Theatre in Higher Education, including Eric Mayer-García, Carla Della Gatta, Andrew

Gibb, Patricia Herrera, Tiffany Ana López, Courtney Mohler, Noe Montez, Jason Ramirez, Olga Sanchez Saltveit, Daphnie Sicre, and Tamara Underiner have provided support, encouragement, and camaraderie.

Olga and Andy have been especially helpful through virtual connections, with Andy jumping in to provide supportive reads of two chapters and the conclusion in my Writing Together group, which has also most consistently and enthusiastically included Karla Padrón, Beth Levy, and Ryan Lee Cartwright. They and all the other visitors helped sustain my momentum forward in this project.

Finally, I want to thank my friends and family who sustained me as a human during this process, especially Darrin and Natalie Bardin, Heather and Kevin Messall, and Eric and Kelly Christoffersen. My sister Laura has been a constant cheerleader in this process while my brother Tony has reminded me of the importance of making self-sustainable choices. Throughout it all, my wife Paula Ramsay has put up with my angst, procrastination, and excitement about this project for much longer than she would like, consistently offering me the necessary support, belief, and love that made completing this work possible. Thank you for everything.

Introduction

GIVEN CIRCUMSTANCES, PREMISE, AND PRAGMATIC STRATEGIES OF LIBERATION

Start with a conventional climax in the familiar cinematic version of the hero's journey.[1] You know that moment. Everything is lost. We cut to parallel narratives, one after another; each hero losing their fight. The end is near; the enemy is going to win; hope is fading, fading, fading away into nothing. The melodramatic enemy, the clear epitome of evil, takes a moment to verbally gloat over their undeniable victory. But wait . . . (it takes a moment and timing is everything) . . . we can't give up . . . it's not fair . . . things don't turn out that way . . . that's not how the hero's journey is supposed to end. And our patience is rewarded. The familiar sequence begins. The hero is not actually dead, just knocked down. The aid we have given up on is going to arrive. And a reversal begins, inverting our greatest fear and leading to victory. Familiar, satisfying, but not a particularly useful model for seriously considering everyday transformational change.[2]

For a theatrical example of this reversal look at the final moments of playwright José Rivera's 1992 apocalyptic play *Marisol*, perhaps the most recognized Puerto Rican diasporic drama of the 1990s. In the words of the title character, a Nuyorican woman: "Three hundred million million beautiful rebel angels die in the first charge of the Final Battle. . . . There's chaos. There's blood and fire and ambulances and Heaven's soldiers scream and fight and die in beautiful terrible light. It looks like the revolution is doomed. . . ."[3] But, with a shift in lighting, "*a single homeless person*" begins "*throwing rocks at the sky.*"[4] They are soon joined by "billions . . . fighting and fighting as no species has ever fought before. Inspired by the earthly noise, the rebels advance!"[5] The collective human support enables fundamental change: "New ideas rip the heavens. New powers are created. New miracles are signed into law. It's the first day of the new history . . ."[6] ending in a transformation into light at the conclusion of the work. This is revolution, transformation, change from the devastated status quo to a new space of possibility, an exciting gesture toward a new world. And this ending has power: generating a moment of communal dreaming and audience celebration within an imaginary future vision of a different world. Perhaps this is Jill Dolan's "utopian performative," the temporary instantiation of a community through the witnessing of performance.[7]

Certainly, with proper rhythm and sufficient interest in compelling characters this storytelling is moving in the moment; however, Rivera's ending replicates a structure deeply invested in conventional incarnations of the hero's journey. While *Marisol*'s moment of liberation offers a clear social critique, it also presents revolutionary change that too easily transforms into the light of hope. And my suspicion of this "too easy" dramaturgy is reinforced by the fact that as an expression of joy and optimism Rivera posted an excerpt from this ending monologue on his Facebook page to celebrate the election of Joe Biden as US president in 2020, and yet the number of children separated from their families at the US/Mexico border increased in the first months of the Biden administration. As we know too well, a change in political parties with an ostensibly different way of thinking rarely results in radical change. Substantial change is difficult because of the reality of complex, intertwined, conflicting points of view; institutional inertia; and the weight of comfortable habit.

Framing resistance in triumphalist terms in the face of clear and uncomplicated evil, however, tends to obscure this reality, making otherwise complex and difficult choices appear simple. Strident calls for immediate radical transformation make potentially unsustainable demands unburdened by the weight of multiple conflicting contexts. These calls come on the streets, in the media, and in a range of cultural forms. *Marisol*'s ending highlights the seductive pleasure of these rhetorical strategies. In this configuration there is no need to compromise, no need to meaningfully consider the fundamental humanity of the enemy, because they are literally inhuman and actively opposed to humanity as such. These enemies are the villains of superhero drama, the senile and uncaring God who provokes angelic rebellion in Rivera's *Marisol*, or, in the current polarized language of everyday politics, ideological opponents who are callously dehumanized, stripped of rationality, common sense, and good intentions. Even if the enemy espouses nuanced ideological differences to justify their actions, these justifications are too often presented from positions that can be comfortably dismissed by the intended audience because of their "inherently flawed" premise: a view of the world that cannot be shared. They become the ultimate antagonist.

Disturbingly aware of the increasing social degradation eroding our circumstances, Rivera can only provide a satisfying model of change by deploying a *Deus ex machina* in the form of a single homeless person inspiring billions in the blink of an eye, which exposes the limits of conventional revolutionary storytelling. A fundamental shift can only take place when the angels are aided by billions of human allies, something explicitly excluded from their initial revolutionary calculations. Though reliant on an artificial compression of time and space, a kind of wish fulfillment, Rivera's play presents a shift from individual action to collective resistance as a pathway for potential change. The fact that this celebratory transformation occurs only after the death of the title character crucially suggests that the solution may not yet exist in the world we live in. In the face of this recognition, I believe it is important to highlight the political capacity of drama to explore the ambivalences arising in negotiating the disconnects between our aspirational rhetoric and everyday lived practice, our revolutionary ideals and individual complicities, as we fully acknowledge the weight of our complex individual contexts, our given circumstances, in dramaturgical terms. Part of this acknowledgment involves conceptualizing both politics and identity as relational concepts, which I am thinking in part in conversation with feminist theorist Aimee Carrillo Rowe. Carrillo Rowe uses the concept of "be longing" to consider the affiliative desire to belong as a fundamental locus for understanding collective, relational conceptions of the self.[8] Her formulation stresses that a processual state of belonging emerges from one's active desire, one's own longing. Shifting from identities to "modes of belonging,"[9] Carrillo Rowe suggests, "is the aim of a politics of relation. Placing location within the 'clinamen,' the inclination of one toward another, as the basis for community, intimacy, and awareness."[10] She is crucially concerned that though one's position and identity are predicated on a network of connections and relations, too many forms of politics reduce this complexity to an individual subject position. Understanding relational identity requires heightened attention to the extent of the entirety of one's current condition, one's situation, one's circumstances.

This concept of identity emerging in relation to given circumstances is precisely at the center of the creation of dramatic worlds. Remaining aware of the contested nature of relationships and the necessity of constantly negotiating difference, sociologist Chantal Mouffe reminds us, "It is only when we acknowledge that any identity is always relational and that it is defined in terms of difference that we are able to ask the crucial question: how can we fight the tendency towards exclusion?"[11] Concerned about potential exclusion built into the establishment of a democratic polis, Mouffe insists on grounding relational difference in her concept of agonistic politics—the necessarily tensive but not destructive engagement as different groups compete to establish a hegemonic position. This concept has resonated with several scholars writing on theater.[12] Reflecting on her participation in the tensive, multivalent engagement of multiple dramaturgs working on Anna Deavere Smith's one woman play, *Twilight: Los Angeles, 1992*, anthropologist Dorinne Kondo writes:

> I read our backstage drama as an enactment of Chantal Mouffe's politics of agonistics . . . and what I call a politics of affiliation. For Mouffe, agonistics—in which adversaries debate incompatible, even irreconcilable positions, attempting to make their own positions hegemonic—arises from the irreducible differences that ground politics. . . . Mouffe's position contests rationalist perspectives that privilege the liberal humanist subject and the model of power-free communication (Rawls 1999; Habermas 1970). Such liberal schemes exclude exclusion, the passions (is rage not appropriate to encounters with injustice?), and the constitutive, inescapable workings of power relations. Mouffe envisions instead an agonistic politics of shifting hegemonies, since hegemony cannot be wished away. Agonistic politics—conflict among adversaries—contrasts with antagonistic politics: conflict with enemies (Mouffe 2013, 7).[13]

This formulation is crucial because Puerto Rican dramatists writing in the diaspora can ultimately be understood as operating in an agonistic relationship to Puerto Rico's ongoing obscured colonial relationship with the United States as they highlight thematic issues of identity, home, and one's place in the world.[14] Puerto Rico is a US territory, commonly labeled as a "commonwealth," and legislatively understood to be an Estado Libre Asociado (ELA), a free associated state, controlled by Congress where the territory is represented only by a non-voting resident commissioner. While Puerto Ricans have autonomy over their local elections and officials, they only receive US federal voting rights if they leave Puerto Rico and become residents of a state, becoming a part of the diaspora . . . For these reasons, I believe that Puerto

Rican dramatists writing in the United States offer the most powerful example of thinking about a practical politics without abandoning a sustained critique of the inequitable status quo, not only because of a long history of political practice and theory carefully conceived within pragmatic frameworks, but most importantly their multiply anomalous political situatedness: culturally, juridically, and legislatively. Speaking from a complex, explicitly structured set of political marginalities these writers exemplify the important political work being done in theater in scripted form to trace pathways toward real change, the complex ambivalences and conversations that are necessary to advance thinking and begin the movement toward forms of emancipation while continuing to sustain life.

Despite its utopian transformative revolutionary ending predicated on a logic of antagonistic politics, when viewed in its entirety, *Marisol* reflects this practice of exploring the complex ambivalences and collateral costs of change, a particular form of political work I label *pragmatic liberation*. The vast majority of *Marisol* serves as an exploration of the precarity of human existence exemplified through a radical shift in her given circumstances. Thrust outside her comfort zone on the path to heroic change, Marisol is stripped of ideological blindness and forced to come to grips with the insecurity of life on the street, reflecting the lived experience of too many Puerto Ricans on the island and in the diaspora in the face of systemic discrimination and neglect. Her change in condition is especially poignant when placed in the contemporary context of fiscal and climate crisis in Puerto Rico.[15] The intersection of the Puerto Rico Oversight, Management, and Economic Stability Act (PROMESA) of 2016, which led to the imposition of austerity measures through what some consider unconstitutional authority over Puerto Rico's debt, and the continued failure of meaningful federal response to the destruction wrought by Hurricane Maria in 2017 have eerie echoes in the intersections of financial and ecological collapse in the play.

But for the moment, I want to reorient our analysis of *Marisol* to catch the nascent hints of this practice, which I believe is perhaps best illustrated by Puerto Rican diasporic or Diasporican dramatists, though they are certainly not alone in its practice. Though unconventional, analyzing *Marisol* within the framework of the larger structural relationship between the US and Puerto Rico is very effective. In this reading, God's neglect, visible in the environmental degradation and structural injustice that catalyzes angelic revolution, leads to destabilization, and shifts everyone "out on the street," is an unforgiving and implacable authoritarian hierarchy. Awareness of this fundamental inequality highlights both the necessity of striving for change and the intense social disruption generated by revolutionary action. Though Marisol is not enlisted directly in the revolution, she loses what little safety and security she had because of it. While not warning against revolutionary action, the play crucially recognizes its profound collateral impacts. As the angel justifies her reaction to an unsustainable status quo to Marisol early in the play: "You have to fight. You can't *endure* anymore."[16] Marisol's subsequent displacement into the street exposes the fundamental brutality of existing conditions, and the question of endurance is a language invoked often in thinking about the Puerto Rican experience of coloniality. Though the play offers no practical model for how to start and sustain revolution, there is a clear need for change in this future dystopia in which the starting framework, or premise, is disturbingly close to our contemporary present.[17] While coffee is not yet extinct and we have not lost the moon, structural violence attached to the rise of neoconservatives, increased displacement of individuals into problematically housed conditions, and environmental collapse are all part of our lived experience.

Pragmatic Liberation as Dramaturgical Strategy

In the current US environment of polarized and divisive political engagement, I believe more than ever that we must explore questions of social justice and liberation in terms of change that is actionable and sustainable, honoring the reality that active participation in radical change is a long-term sustainable practice for only small minorities of deeply committed individuals and collectives. To practice effective politics in the contemporary moment we need to clearly recognize our given circumstances in the process of envisioning paths toward sustainable change. This process of recognition and analysis is built into standard conventional models of play construction and analysis, and direct engagement with dramatic texts thus provides a useful pathway through which to encounter and reflect on pragmatic politics. The term pragmatic is intended to mark a lived space between the real and the ideal; it is not a capitulation to the status quo or an acceptance of reformist politics.[18] I argue that we must insist on a fundamental distinction between acknowledgment and acceptance in our understanding of pragmatism. While pragmatic gestures may not yield the immediate satisfaction of calls for radical transformation, they enable the much more difficult negotiation of complex landscapes of interpersonal and social relations, acknowledging the potential harm to those who matter most to us that may be generated while working toward transformative change. Pragmatic thinking incorporates practical strategies and small maneuvers that negotiate the challenges of daily life to keep us moving on a pathway toward meaningful change. Pragmatic thinking not only focuses on survival within the framework of the daily struggle of our existing political horizons, it also works to shift these horizons toward better ways of perceiving and being in the world, while continuing to actively acknowledge our given circumstances.

Recognizing that a progressive left political platform of revolution is minoritarian in US political thinking, I argue that "transformation now" is not the only energizing and ethical position to espouse to continue the move toward a more egalitarian future. Drama provides us the capacity to work with and through the tremendous weight of inertia for both individuals and institutions, as well as oppositional perspectives that reflect the ostensibly incommensurable polarizations of the US political landscape. Drama takes the time to excavate ambivalent complexities, providing us the possibility to chart the difficult, deeply conflicted terrain in so many contemporary configurations of the world that acknowledge systemic injustice and oppressive structures of power. It serves as an ideal form to understand that authentically moving forward in a sustained mode of political resistance requires recognizing the limits of transformation and the spaces in which one can intervene. This is the form of political thinking I call *pragmatic liberation*.[19]

Pragmatic Liberation calls out moments where playwrights strategically engage with the limits of individual political action and the challenges of sustaining revolutionary activism despite the best intentions of individuals. Acknowledging the desire for transformative change, pragmatic liberation insists on the necessity of recognizing the limits of radical claims that have not yet done the hard work of laying the ground for transformation as it is happening and possible. However, rather than replacing calls for radical change with examples of reformist politics, I read specific textual moments carefully, reflectively considering politics as relational and arguing that writing, reading, and performing some conventional forms of scripted drama provides access to solutions that are necessary to pragmatically sustain life, even as they continue to work toward larger structural change.

Scripted drama provides an opportunity to rethink the very relations generated by storytelling through connection with, and transformation of, character, by means of expansive use of aesthetic modes, conceptual experiences that extend beyond the confines of tele-visual realism, and language intended as dialogue—carefully crafted, refined, and intentionally reflexive and not merely a representation of everyday talk. In relation to this power of the dramatic, Dorinne Kondo suggests that "Dialogue performs the dialogic relationality of social life, while the script highlights the ways we constantly script each other into roles. Unlike novels, short stories, or poetry, theater requires performers to live, immediately spotlighting the collaborative inter-subjectivity of artistic and scholarly production. . . ."[20] The necessary anticipation of collaborative work both expands the potential sensorial and conceptual inter-relationality and highlights the critical interplay that shapes an understanding of the contours of the script.

In drama's conventional scripted forms, given circumstances is a key starting point for analysis that engages the playwright's dramatic world building. Scholar and dramaturg Michael Chemers explains given circumstances as "the 'who, what, where, when, why, and how' of the action of the play . . . revealed by the setting, the time of day or year, the dispositions and qualities of the characters, or whatever information the playwright gives to direct our analysis in a particular direction."[21] Chemers' formulation centers the intentions of the playwright as world builder and as a precise facilitator of our focus and engagement, but it is also crucial to remember that interpretation and understanding shifts through the practice of realizing a given text in performance. Going on to delineate the familiar structure of dramatic creation within psychological realism, Chemers narrates the character-centered dominant aesthetic of mainstream playwriting:

> [g]iven circumstances give rise to needs; needs incite characters to action. Obstacles appear that block the characters from getting what they want. That generates conflict that is emotionally or intellectually compelling to an audience (but only when the audience cares whether the characters get what they want). The characters develop tactics and strategies to get around those obstacles, and that process puts flesh on the skeleton of the play's action. How characters act to resolve conflicts reveals their traits. . . .[22]

While as a scholar I often find myself pressing at the edges of this model, teaching playwriting has pushed me to partially reconsider this position. Though I will never advocate for a prescriptive or formulaic mode of playwriting, I acknowledge the basic elements of this model as one form of practical reason that allows for thinking through, and with, our varied points of view. But to make full use of this capacity we must pay closer attention and think precisely about the conventional agreements we enter in reading, writing, and creating theater. When these conventions gain the force of prescriptive expectation the result is homogenized, oversimplified storytelling that reduces the precise specificity of diverse experience. This homogenization often arises from an understandable desire for connection as a precursor to understanding that drives the desire for "relatability" as a sign of value for the audience. The challenge is to resist presumptively naturalizing and reducing elements that do not align with our everyday experiences, and to instead attend carefully to sensorial and socio-cultural given circumstances. And we must remember that there are other potential models of understanding the world.

Dramatic writing often centers characters whose unique experiences provide ostensibly different modes of looking at the world, but we must also remember these modes of storytelling are themselves shaped by the limits of points of view imbedded in the implied audiences of regional theater that reproduce and reinforce particular formations of education, belief, class, and access to representation. One powerful alternative model of playwriting pedagogy is the work of Cuban-American playwright María Irene Fornés, highly influential in Latine playwriting practice based on her sustained pedagogical work at INTAR and at Padua Hills.[23] While of the playwrights I focus on in this work only Migdalia Cruz was formally taught by Fornés, her pedagogical practices and thinking were broadly influential in Latine playwriting.[24] Playwright and scholar Anne García-Romero explains, "Fornes guides playwrights through a process that helps them intuitively connect to creating characters rather than teaching her students to build an airtight structure that focuses on conflict and resolution."[25] This practice of centering character creation allows their needs to be explored while recognizing given circumstances as necessary but not deterministic. Her strategy of embracing possibility privileges discovery, not a priori understanding, as the central creative engine of the dramatic world. As García-Romero puts it, "Fornes's environmental pedagogy encourages complexity and mystery, engaging with a juxtaposition of worlds and ideas that emerge organically from the characters' needs. Fornes's method allows character discovery to spontaneously guide the early shape of a play as opposed to predetermining a theatrical narrative."[26] This refusal of determinism is crucial to avoiding the too easy predictability of comfortable storytelling that reflects the limits and constrained presumptions of everyday life.

Even within realism there is the possibility of engaging with and thinking through the very logics and premises of our practice to begin to account meaningfully for existing conditions and their effects. To place this firmly in the space of dramatic worldmaking I return to the words of Puerto Rican diasporic playwright José Rivera, this time in his essay "36 Assumptions About Writing Plays." In number fourteen Rivera reflects on the practice of realism, implicitly gesturing toward his playwriting practice:

> If realism is as artificial as any genre, strive to create your own realism. If theatre is a handicraft in which you make one of a kind pieces, then you're in complete control of your fictive universe. What are its physical laws? What's gravity like? What does time do? What are the rules of cause and effect? How do your characters behave in this altered universe?[27]

Playwrights construct worlds whose logics exist in the space between where things are and where they could be. Embracing a more capacious realism we take seriously the need to conceive of premise, given circumstances, and character as spaces through which existing logics are made visible and shifted toward new possibility. This reflects what I call "expanded realisms," a dominant contemporary writing practice that allows for environments and circumstances beyond kitchen sink realism or social verisimilitude, but which nonetheless insists on characters who mostly talk and act in a recognizable variation of everyday behavior.[28]

Rivera's advice echoes his own treatment of dramatic worlds, emerging in relationship to, but not limited by, the preconceptions that foster hegemonic methods of creation and reception. Individual material conditions, points of view, and belief structures generate substantially different organizational frames for comprehending events and relations. Visceral lived experiences shape the premise and given circumstances from which dramatic storytelling emerges. These expanded realisms contain their own forms of the political along with an exploration of conditions that have enabled alternate modes of political thinking. Engaging these theatrically framed alternatives involves complex cognitive work to briefly, conceptually, witness another world. Whether or not this witnessing ultimately transforms an audience, time is spent engaging the complex paradoxical motivating factors that shape our horizons of understanding. In doing so, we are privy to an understanding that acknowledges failure, both potential and actual, and points toward changes possible in the everyday.

While the dramatization of conflicts often toggles between desires for radical transformation now and more measured consideration of complicities, interconnections, and potential collateral damage, some individuals and collectives gravitate more strongly toward one or the other. The second point of view, which emphasizes the pragmatism of pragmatic liberation is, I would argue, more palpably present for those whose vulnerability is heightened by systemic conditions of discrimination manifest through conditions such as racism, poverty, and colonialism. Here the impulse toward radical action is still present and necessary, but the recognition of potential harm to individuals and communities to which one feels a sense of belonging, combined with differential attitudes toward conditions based on individual interpretations of systemic conditions often promulgates more reflective models of resistance. The intimacy of difference, manifest through familial resistance to one's radical politics, often demands a different set of actions or choices in the face of political disagreement with those closest to you. This resonates deeply with Carrillo Rowe's concept of "be longing," and is echoed in the crucial focus on intimate relationships (platonic, filial, familial, and carnal) in the majority of the plays analyzed in this book. This profound sense of situatedness highlights the human and environmental forms of connection that shape our understanding of the logic of dramatic worlds.

In her famous essay "EF's Visit to a Small Planet," scholar Elinor Fuchs works against the conventional assumption of many dramaturgs who center character psychology as a means of understanding the play as opposed to fully envisioning and embracing the logic of the dramatic world.[29] Her extended series of questions insist on establishing careful and precise attention to how things work in the specific world under investigation. This level of attention and attunement should be valued in examining both dramatic and real-life given circumstances; I argue we must carefully draw attention to micro-variations even when they place significant pressure on the idea that we share a world. These variations, most evident in the shift to indigenous cosmologies, often concern the facticity of spirits and other forms of consciousness beyond the human. Sustaining a variant premise that pushes against historical narratives and conventional wisdom becomes a challenge in both the writing and realization of theater in the face of pressures to conform to an ideal of a shared world mirroring our own. This pressure is lessened when the genre and/or aesthetic of the work explicitly calls for a higher level of theatrical experimentation beyond the premise of a shared real. One's horizon of expectation, political and experiential, too often overtly shape and constrain the contours of reasonable speculation about the socio-cultural and aesthetic expectations of the world, about another's lived experience.

While a great deal of theater, Latine and otherwise, fails to realize its political potential by too comfortably accepting the horizons of individuated neoliberal thinking, these limitations are not inherent in the form of theater but are rather a product of the muting of politics in regional and smaller theatrical spaces, where institutional dramaturgies often shape storytelling to reduce visceral qualities of discomfort. Inequality and oppressions are not merely actions and events but also the product of structures. Unpacking and making these conditions explicit is often accomplished both through forms of resistance and consciousness raising to acknowledge the presence of the condition. In doing so, solutions are typically predicated on notions of changing questions of structure and knowledge, and the change can either be viewed as a product of reformist or more revolutionary thinking. In the best forms of this work an impulse toward storytelling acknowledges the radical complexity of the human experience and invites audiences into revisioning the world, albeit one fully aware of the ambivalent complexities of initiating and sustaining change. I argue that this practice, a politics of pragmatic liberation, more fully acknowledges the ambivalent complexities and limits of relationships in a set of given circumstances that take historical entrenchment, ideological obscuration, and the real challenges of transformation into account.[30]

The dramatist's own given circumstances are also a means of accessing the political, as Fornés reminds us. Often considered resistant to political labels, her dramatic storytelling is deeply invested in forms of liberation, though never in conventional forms. One of her students, Chicanx playwright Luis Alfaro, best known for his powerful solo performance and adaptations of Greek plays, shares the following conversation in a remembrance article reflecting on her understanding of politics. I quote Alfaro's story in full because it clearly illustrates the absorption of politics into the body of the writer as a powerful possibility for playwriting.

> I remember a conversation once about my political activism that could have only happened in Spanish because for me it seemed so vulnerable and pointed. *La Maestra* was intrigued and fascinated by the idea that I would go out in the middle of the night all over Los Angeles in a paper suit, and someone would spray paint the silhouette of my body on a sidewalk, calling attention at the time to the murders of innocent people during the

civil war in El Salvador. I would leave a ghostly image. "You have an interesting voice as a writer, but you have so many concerns . . ." She let the sentence linger in space, almost urging me to catch it. She would continue, "Perhaps you should focus passionately on one, your politics for one, and then come back to writing. I promise you, write about anything, a rock, and it will be political. Let things live in you . . .".[31]

Fornés's key suggestion is offered in deliberate opposition to an intentional writing about politics as a subject, but not a refusal of the possibility of the political emerging out of the lived body of the writer. She is not interested in a programmatic approach that assumes a particular outcome from the representation of politics in the theater. My goal here is to acknowledge the limits of simple representation, arguing that working through difficulty and careful choice of starting points are crucial steps in the creation of work understood to function politically. Here, I align with Fornés's valuation of a different conception or horizon of politics in one's writing that emerges through a profound understanding that permeates the self.

There is a truism in critical writing about US drama and theatrical storytelling in the 20th century that most political work occurs within the domestic family space. This focus on family has tended to privilege the individual exploration of character as the central mode through which to understand individual change as opposed to other more materialist models that provide heightened attention to questions of larger context. The very idea of what constitutes family is a fruitful category to explore; its persistent relevance is predicated on its prevalence—cultural theorist Raymond Williams was correct in his assessment about the shift of European drama primarily into rooms at the end of the 19th century.[32] The advent of naturalism, realism, and the social problem plays of Henrik Ibsen, George Bernard Shaw, and Anton Chekhov invite precise attention to environment in order to understand characters' social position. Intentionally deploying an aesthetic with high levels of verisimilitude, accurate visual representation, these works insist on the invocation of design elements—costume, light, props, scene, and sound—as crucial aspects of given circumstances. Thus, audiences learn to understand the characters by deploying careful semiotic attention to mise-en-scène as well as expositional biography.

However, constricting the aesthetic of realism to its late 19th and early 20th century European roots results in an empty, tired form, referencing social relations of moments very much not our own. This claim, by mid-20th century theater critic Walter Kerr, is developed further in his rejection of the political work of theater through "thesis" plays which function solely to prove a particular point, no matter how complex. As he says, "What is intrinsically wrong with the thesis play is that it puts the drawing board before the drama. It begins at the wrong end of the creative scale. It begins with a firm, fast premise, achieved in the intellectual solitude of the study, and thereafter proceeds to make all life dance to a quite debatable tune."[33] Much contemporary drama can be legitimately critiqued for starting from "firm, fast premise" or from the aesthetics of liberal melodrama and the well-made play, moving toward utopic or socially muted manifestations of revolutionary change. It is dismissed as an insignificant cultural form trapped in the elitism of upper-middle-class privilege and offering overly facile liberalism as political critique. Diasporican Pulitzer Prize winning playwright Quiara Alegría Hudes suggests that,

> Theatre, at least at the upper echelons of the professional field, is frequently elitist, expensive, exclusive, and nondemocratic. Our biggest-budget theatrical institutions purport to encourage equality and champion the underdog, but in fact must appease wealthy patrons and subscribers, disproportionately feature male leadership, and carry stubborn institutional memory beholden to the white aesthetics and values they have built themselves upon for decades.[34]

Despite this powerful and valid critique of White American Theater[35] that facilitates the institutional flattening of what might otherwise be transformational storytelling, I engage scripted drama by Puerto Rican diasporic playwrights intended for US regional and off-Broadway theaters precisely because it is already a fraught space negotiating conventional collaborative practice, pedagogical "rules" of playwriting, and the pressures of institutional dramaturgies catering to relatively exclusive audiences.[36]

When taken seriously, engaged slowly, and generated creatively, premise is a powerful and dangerous organizing principle; it frames engagement with the dramatic world, especially when the terms shift significantly from our understanding and experience of the real one. Premise indicates both where to begin and the path, route, or trajectory along which to proceed. It establishes a kind of promise for the multiple interlocutors who negotiate the dramatic world while providing space for both speculation and understanding. In a sense, the problem of politics is the problem of premise, of the conception of world we are willing and able to see, our current political horizon, our practice of world-making.[37] If, for example, one takes as a basic premise that the violent expropriation of indigenous lands and the institution of chattel slavery (and its later permutations) are the two fundamental economic engines driving the US colonial project and its first century of postcolonial domination, fueling rapid growth in capitalist industrialization, then one would begin from a place in which US exceptionalism, if such a thing ever existed, must be predicated on the economic impact of legalized structures of enslavement and colonialism. It is always important to acknowledge the premise and understand its capacity for shifting our political horizon.

The Given Circumstances of US Puerto Rico Relationality

Puerto Rico has been palpably present in the mainland cultural imaginary over the last few years as a site of crisis and failure—the devastating and sustained consequences of Hurricane Maria in 2017, exacerbated by mainland apathy, racism, and economic corruption, and an ongoing refusal to invest sufficient resources to meaningfully address the infrastructural problems. These conditions are unsurprising given the powerful impact and sustained racist colonial policies practiced by the US Federal Government in relation to this problematically labeled "Free Associated State," an anomalous and hard to grasp "association" whose contours are often deliberately opaque to US citizens except when they are explicitly expressed in neo-colonial economic policies, deliberate and unashamed neglect, disrespect, and structures of culturally constructed models of blame from relevant authorities.

With the acquisition of Puerto Rico at the end of the Spanish Cuban American War the United States was, for the first time, acquiring territory without the end goal of incorporating that territory as a state.[38] Puerto Rico, along with the much smaller Marianas, Guam, and US Virgin Islands, was, through Article IX of the 1898 Treaty of Paris, placed in a territorial status with no meaningful path to independence: "The civil rights and political status of the native inhabitants of the territories hereby ceded to the United States shall be determined by the Congress."[39] The overall question of Puerto Rican status remains in Congressional hands today, shaped by legal precedent in the Insular Cases, the judicial working out of the relational politics of US territorial governance, which has had a profound effect on Puerto Rico's relationship with the United States.[40] Though as US citizens Puerto Ricans do not experience the specific political pressures attached to Latine immigrant populations, their ethnic, cultural, and historical ties to the most populated and most proximate US territory keep them "foreign in a domestic sense."[41] First articulated in the insular case Downes v. Bidwell, this concept has undergirded the conditions of "colonial citizenship" in which access to federal political power is contingent upon location.[42] Law historian Sam Erman argues "Citizenship was no longer either the preeminent constitutional status nor the herald of full constitutional rights and statehood. . . . Territorial nonincorporation sustained colonial governance. Regardless of citizenship, it marked the island as permanently subordinate, and islanders as racially inferior."[43] Though Puerto Ricans resident in a state in the US do have federal voting rights, this geographical contingency implicitly and explicitly sustains their experience as foreign others in the conventional cultural imagination and US political discourse.

The sustained confusion between citizen and foreigner is deliberate, in large part a way of avoiding the problem of officially labeling Puerto Rico a colony, a condition that should no longer exist in the eyes of international governance bodies such as the United Nations. Officially, Puerto Rico is a commonwealth or Estado Libro Asociado (ELA), a "Free Associated State," after a 1952 constitutional referendum locally validated the status quo of what was previously clearly understood as a condition of colonial domination.[44] Acceptance of the ELA condition, which retained the structural function of a colonialist relationship, was validated initially by an aspirational hope of economic empowerment and increased inclusion, an improved quality of life envisioned as a reverse migration of American ideals of prosperity, representative democracy, and economic empowerment. This optimism eventually dissipated in the face of failed projects, sponsored migration, and economic disinvestment, as industrial subventions were shifted to other places to the detriment of Puerto Rico. Though Puerto Ricans accepted their conditions through a local vote, and remain free to determine their local officials, the fundamental issue of territorial administration and US Congressional control is firmly in place.

This continuing condition haunts every instance of the thinking and practice of Puerto Rican politics. In his attempt to consider the policy implications of enacting a change in status to one of the three potentially supported conditions—"a truly bilateral form of association, statehood and independence"[45]—Puerto Rican legal scholar Pedro A. Malavet's *America's Colony* begins with a stringent critique of the fallacy of US exceptionalism,

"Ironically at the start of the twenty-first century, the United States of America, the self-appointed 'beacon of democracy,' is the largest colonial power in the world."[46] He goes on to "identif[y] three flaws in the current U.S.-Puerto Rican regime: (1) the legal and political shortcomings of the colonial relationship on which it is premised; (2) the conflicting legal, political and social constructs of the Puerto Ricans compared with those of the people of the United States as citizens and foreigners at the same time . . . ; and (3) the carefully constructed general ignorance of this relationship among most citizens of the United States."[47] The claim of "carefully constructed general ignorance" indicates the necessity of pro-active engagement with the given circumstances as a means of deconstructing this ignorance and reconfiguring the relationship. Dramaturgically the claim that "flaws" emerge from "shortcomings" in the "premise" of a "colonial relationship" is crucial and resonates with the larger questions of dramatic world building and paths toward liberation.

The quest for sovereignty in Puerto Rico is longstanding, and modern Puerto Rican independence movements trace their beginnings to El Grito De Lares in 1868 and even further back to Taíno and African slave revolts against the Spanish in the 16th century. Anti-colonial resistance by independence freedom fighters reached its highest level of visibility in the 1950s in response to the move to ELA status, whose philosophy of *estadolibrismo* was seen as a pragmatic gesture derailing the larger principle of sovereignty within the framework of economic development. For those deeply invested in independence as the only meaningful form of liberation for Puerto Rico, the 1952 referendum was a calculated betrayal of principle and ethics, as it reasserted and legitimated US domination over the island, ostensibly in exchange for economic and industrial development. For autonomists, still conceptually mourning the failed opportunity that had been offered by Spain to their colony in 1897 through royal decree, there was perhaps a greater possibility built into this "anomalous" state, as cultural and literary critic Ramón E. Soto-Crespo names it.[48] Two events on the mainland, an attempted assassination of President Truman at Blair House in 1950 and a shooting in the US Congressional chambers in 1954 overshadowed the 1950 Jayuya Revolt on the island. While the first act of political violence has not been redeemed outside of contexts in which the fundamental necessity of violence to enact liberation and political change is taken for granted, the second event had an explicitly performative element. As Lolita Lebrón famously states as her purpose in discharging her pistol not at members of congress but at the wooden great seal of the United States in the ceiling, "I didn't come here to kill. I came here to die!"[49]

More recently scholars have been arguing for new modes of thinking about Puerto Rican politics that shift away from a simple distinction between colonialism and nationalism as the framework for political participation. They have recognized that increased human flourishing and a shift away from the violence of colonial practices are key goals and can be shared regardless of one's attitude toward status. In their introduction to *Puerto Rican Jam: Rethinking Colonialism and Nationalism*, sociologist Ramón Grosfoguel, cultural critic Frances Negrón-Muntaner and legal scholar Chloé S. Goeras explain,

> Historically, Puerto Rican intellectuals have adopted one of two discursive poles (supportive of the colonial relationship or anticolonial/nationalist). However, as the island's economy continues to deteriorate, intellectuals and other sectors supporting the colonial status quo have faced a crisis of legitimation. For the first time in fifty years, state intellectuals have publicly accepted that the Estado Libre Asociado . . . is obsolete as an institutional framework to promote the island's economic 'development.' During the 1950s and 1960s, the ELA was able to supply US industries with cheap labor, to grant federal tax exemption to American corporations, and to stimulate free trade between the island and the mainland. Today these incentives have lost all bargaining power.[50]

The existing label for the relationship, the Free Associated State of Puerto Rico, is an interesting site of thinking through and with operations of power in relation to forms of identity and belonging as well as concepts of home and justice. Differential access to power is a pervasive reality that exists not only as implicitly codified practices, but palpably lived experiences in a system built on territorial rules but labeled as a state. Forms of stratification and geographic differentiation are built into the intentional structure, which is perceived in multiple variations: a) as a good that provides a complex relationship to federalism, allowing for some US protections while maintaining a relatively high level of cultural autonomy (*estadolibrismo*); b) as something to be tolerated because there are no better visible conceivable practical alternatives (status quo or possibly an enhanced commonwealth); c) as something to be erased in a movement toward a more normative construct in terms of becoming fully incorporated as a state into the United States (statehood or annexation); or d) as something to be erased in a movement toward a more normative construct of independent action (independence).

Though Maria Acosta Cruz's *Dream Nation* argues that independence is a "symbolic aspiration" for Puerto Ricans that has never captured a wide swath of the Puerto Rican people's attitude in their relationship with the US, the default position of diasporic artists has historically echoed a desire for independence.[51] For some though, even the desire for freedom is itself symptomatic of a misunderstanding of the pragmatic need for survival. Political anthropologist Yarimar Bonilla "suggest[s] that the seemingly exceptional disinterest in 'political freedom' among nonsovereign populations is rooted less in an actual dependence on foreign subsidies than in a political disenchantment with Western categories of sovereignty and freedom."[52] This rejection of a naive conception of freedom within an imbricated structure of global multi-national power suggests less a focus on affective attachment to ideals than on finding ways to exist differently in the world, to understand the politics of relation, both colonial and otherwise. In doing so modes of storytelling tend to focus attention on these connective ties and begin to consider the implication and effects of rupture. This attention enables moving away from simple forms of identification based on status preference "towards a wider analysis of the winners and losers in the relationships of colonialism, globalization, and neoliberalism. Thus, it is not just a matter of who established the colonial relationship but of who is profiting from it today."[53]

Shifting relations to colonialism and a more heterogeneous understanding of its impacts also offer different possibilities for political action, which link the idea of pragmatism to two autochthonous concepts, *jaibería* and *bregar*. In a 1984 essay "Los Paradigmas Políticos Puertorriqueños" journalist and political commentator Juan Manuel García Passalacqua presents his ongoing recognition of the failure to attend to the different experiences of the creole elite and the masses in Puerto Rico in relation to US coloniality. He explores potential synergies between these two groups by demonstrating their varied strategies of accomplishing similar goals of sustaining self-worth and value based on the terms *jaibería* and *dignidad*. He defines *jaibería* as *"la estrategia existencial para sobrevivir en una situación de dependencia y marginación"*[54] ["*the existential strategy for survival in a situation of dependency and marginalization*"]. And he playfully and profoundly claims that "la dignidad de las masas está en su jaibería, y la jaibería de las élites está en su dignidad" ["the dignity of the masses is in their jaibería, and the jaibería of the elites is in their dignity"].[55] Building on the persistence and utility of this strategy, in 1997 Grosfoguel, Negrón-Muntaner, and Goeras further explore this form of pragmatic subversion,

[T]he popular tradition of *jaibería* provides us with an indigenous metaphor for an attitude toward negotiation and transformation. The word *jaibería* has its origins in the term *jaiba*, or mountain crab, who in going forward moves sideways. Within the Puerto Rican usage, *jaibería* refers to collective practices of nonconfrontation and evasion (the *"unjú"* roughly translated as "sure ... no problem"), of taking dominant discourse literally in order to subvert it for one's purpose, of doing whatever one sees fit not as a head-on collision ("winning" is impossible) but a bit under the table, that is through other means.[56]

Like García Passalacqua, who compares the work of *jaibería* to the literary function of the picaro figure, these scholars locate the necessity of this practice within the need for survival and endurance, but also as a response to fundamental asymmetries of colonial power. At the same time, they are careful to acknowledge that it does not necessarily always function in a liberatory fashion, but it is always in the service of the weaker side of a power asymmetry,

It is also important to note that there can be purely complicit uses of *jaibería* that fail to advance any collective agenda. Yet, *jaibería* as a form of complicitous critique or subversive complicity points to an acknowledgment of being in a disadvantaged position within a particular field of power. A nonheroic position, *jaibería* favors endurance over physical strength, and privileges ambiguity over clarity. Although it has been mistaken for docility, it is instead an active, low-intensity strategy to obtain the maximum benefits of a situation with the minimum blood spilled.[57]

Building on the work of Grosfoguel and Negrón-Muntaner, literary and cultural critic Ramón Soto-Crespo highlights the resistant and pragmatic possibilities of *estadolibrismo* itself in its initial formulation in the 1950s. Recognizing that the problematic nature of a Free Associated State does not free Puerto Rico from federal control, he argues it does provide some recourse from the Territorial Clause of the Constitution under which the archipelago had previously been governed. Soto-Crespo argues for the value of non-incorporation as a means of sustaining the Puerto Rican ethno-nation, celebrating the cultural and political savvy of Luis Muñoz Marín, the first democratically elected Governor of Puerto Rico.[58] This sense of sustaining Puerto Rican cultural identification, sometimes referred to as *la gran familia puertorriqueña*, the great Puerto Rican family, encompassing the island and the diaspora, is widely recognized as an achievement of Muñoz Marín, and many voting for the constitution in 1952 saw this as a pragmatic gesture toward liberation with economic benefits. In his work Soto-Crespo moves on to argue for Puerto Rico as a transnational border space. While the logic of Soto-Crespo's border claim is compelling and serves to offer a new configuration of relations between the archipelago and its diasporas, the imposition of PROMESA and the failed federal response to Hurricane Maria, both occurring after the publication of his book, have brought into broad focus the ongoing crisis of colonialism. Increasingly recognized as not a single natural disaster, the conflation of these events is the inevitable outcome of a colonial relation predicated on fundamental and systemic inequalities. Another concern with Soto-Crespo's model is the extent to which migration as an economic escape valve reflects a potential failure to think otherwise about modes of sustaining population on the island, and does not sufficiently account for the ways in which Puerto Rican migrants are continuously placed in conditions that attempt to elide or undermine their status as US citizens.[59] Thus, while possibly true in its initial establishment in the 1950s, the contemporary ELA no longer functions as a form of pragmatic liberation.

However, one practice Soto-Crespo attends to in his description of Muñoz Marín that retains its crucial importance as a form of practicing pragmatic models of liberation is the uniquely Puerto Rican usage of the Spanish term *bregar*, powerfully and thoroughly explicated in an essay by literary scholar Arcadio Díaz Quiñones as a particular mode of conversational negotiation and making do.[60]

> *Bregar* es, podría decirse, otro orden de saber, un difuso método sin alarde para navegar la vida cotidiana, donde todo es extremadamente precario, cambiante o violento, como lo ha sido durante el siglo 20 para las emigraciones puertorriqueñas y lo es hoy en todo el territorio de la isla. Al saludo ritual y cortés "¿Cómo estás?", muchos puertorriqueños contestan lacónica o juguetonamente con una frase aprendida que parece un pie forzado: "Aquí, *en la brega*". No es una forma de ser. Es una forma de estar y no estar, un tipo no preciso de lucha, una negociación entre la ausencia y la presencia. Hay situaciones que se consideran poco propicias o imposibles, y entonces cambia el tono y se escucha la frase: *Yo con eso no brego*.[61]

> [*Bregar* is, it could be said, another order of knowledge, a diffuse method without fanfare for navigating daily life, where everything is extremely precarious, changeable or violent, as it has been during the 20th century for Puerto Rican emigrations and it is today throughout the island terri-

tory. To the courteous ritual greeting "How are you?," many Puerto Ricans reply laconically or playfully with a learned phrase that appears like a forced rhyme: "[I'm] here, *in the struggle*." It is not a way of being. It is a way of being and not being, a non-precise type of struggle, a negotiation between absence and presence. There are situations that are considered unpromising or impossible, and then the tone changes and the phrase is heard: I don't deal with that.[62]

Quiñones himself uses an anecdote from the administration of Muñoz Marín where when placed in the awkward situation of needing to host a ceremony in which a US Admiral was receiving an honor from the government of the Dominican dictator Trujillo, he deliberately served coffee rather than champagne since it would be nearly impossible to perform a toast with coffee.[63] This same choice could easily be described as a form of *jaibería* of the elite in Passalacqua's terms. The careful structuring of the conventional expectations of a social space works to limit action out of the need to maintain dignity in the space.

Discovering the complex flexibility and utility of the specifically Puerto Rican deployment of versions of *bregar* after I had already begun theorizing the concept of pragmatic liberation, my sense of the centrality of Puerto Rican diasporic playwrights was fundamentally strengthened. This complex usage, which occurs both in the archipelago and in the diaspora, exists alongside and informs the creativity of the pragmatic gestures performed by the playwrights in this work. Quiñones, early in his extended account of the multiple complexities of vernacular usage, suggests,

[l]a estrategia del *bregar* consiste en poner en relación lo que hasta ese momento parecía distante o antagónico. Es una posición desde la cual se actúa para dirimir sin violencia los conflictos muy polarizados. En ese sentido, connota abrirse espacio en una cartografia incierta y hacerle frente a las decisiones con una visión de lo posible y deseable. Implica también—es crucial—el conocimiento y la aceptación de los límites. . . . Idealmente, *se brega* hasta encontrar un modo de alcanzar el difícil equilibrio entre elementos potencialmente conflictivos.[64]

[t]he strategy of *bregar* consists of putting in relation what until that moment seemed distant or antagonistic. It is a position from which action is taken to resolve highly polarized conflicts without violence. In that sense, it connotes opening up space in an uncertain cartography and facing deci-

sions with a vision of what is possible and desirable. It also implies—this is crucial—the knowledge and acceptance of limits. . . . Ideally, *it struggles* to find a way to reach the difficult balance between potentially conflicting elements.

The complexities of the colonial condition make acts of revolutionary violence palpably present in the imagination but often less useful in practice, at least in the last three decades of writing that form the heart of this book. And thus, *bregar* models a crucial strategy, not passive acceptance, but an active decision to minimize violence when possible. This is not repudiating revolutionary action, but rather acknowledging that the material conditions of colonialism persist. Acknowledgment of our given circumstances does not mean we must accept them. We must recognize and take into account the material conditions and the existing and varied forms of interconnection in order to fully engage the relationality of politics.

Themes of return and distance, of political freedom and of revolution, and of the transformations of migration and the material conditions of life in the US, are all part and parcel of this larger issue in and around the work of Puerto Rican diasporic dramatists. Their structure of identification has also been radically shaped by a clear understanding of the differential politics of race and identification, and forms of discrimination and systemic racism. These pressures reflect the African diasporic heritage of many islanders that is particularly shaped in the urban contexts of New York, Chicago, and other spaces in the US in which significant numbers of Puerto Ricans have settled. This includes the newest waves of climate refugees, supported by FEMA as a way of finding housing for those impacted by the devastation of Hurricane Maria and other "natural disasters."[65]

In light of this, I want to highlight four basic elements that emerge within the writing of Puerto Rican experience in English for the dramatic stage:

1) an assertion of the need for storytelling that refuses hegemonic narratives or forms to a greater or lesser extent (one might parallel this with the sideways movement of *jaibería*); 2) a sense of collective responsibility even among the most individuated, and a sense that this responsibility is always political but also under negotiation; 3) a recognition that collectivity is never simple or easy and that agonistic relationships are integral to everyday survival, requiring the capacity for *bregar*; and 4) a deep focus on the ethical need to reflect on questions of social justice "*aqui, en la brega,*" that I argue are implicitly predicated on the legislative inequalities enshrined in ELA status.

While some might be tempted to see the exploration of pragmatic liberation as a capitulation to the continuing conditions of colonialism, I understand obscured colonialism as a given circumstance that needs to be understood to recognize the real conceptual work of the plays. I do not believe that the artists and works explored here accept the conditions of the status quo in a naive or defeated sense, but instead recognize that a coming-into-awareness of lived conditions is fundamental to understanding the complex realities of modes of life and survival. One's attitude toward Puerto Rican status, while informing character, is superseded by a fundamental need to improve the conditions of life, the basic resources to sustain life in the face of systemic and structural oppression.

My analysis does not presume that Puerto Rican playwrights in the United States are fixated on and consistently explicitly address the relationship of Puerto Rico and the United States. Instead, I argue that the real, material presence of this explicitly differential power relationship and deliberately obscured colonial structure presents a fundamental backdrop in which it is possible to understand an urgent and necessary desire for revolutionary change combined with a radically pragmatic understanding of potential collateral implications. I believe this situation exists because of an intertwined relational labyrinth that has expanded and increased in complexity through the ongoing process of ostensibly free association. Finding a path through a process of "be longing" to a different form of belonging, of political relationship, necessitates careful attention to the construction of a route that involves meaningfully confronting the challenges along the way, even when the answer yet escapes us in the present.

Modeling Pragmatic Liberation

Puerto Rican diasporic playwright Kristoffer Diaz has been deeply invested in thinking through the limits of politics in a pragmatic configuration through the transformative power of telling a different kind of story. His plays illustrate the possibility of opening minor ruptures in our conception of the world to begin unravelling conventional storytelling and to disrupt the continued power of melodrama as a means of framing politics. His work unpacks the easy language around appropriate political behavior and the possibilities for action in a progressive context, as a way of getting real, of dealing with the multiple concrete and present factors that cannot and should not be dismissed in thinking about moving toward liberation. Perhaps the clearest example of a play illustrating the necessity of thinking through and with pragmatic liberation is his short play *All Ears*, Diaz's contribution to *Every 28 Hours Plays*.

A series of short plays curated by Claudia Alick and the Oregon Shakespeare Festival, *Every 28 Hours* invokes the controversial statistic that every twenty-eight hours a black man is killed by extrajudicial police violence in the US.[66] Diaz's contribution slants away from the affective (and effective) melodrama of individual loss to provide a poignant rendition of the crisis of pragmatic political life in the present, in terms of space, community, and the possibility of transformative politics. Not abandoning politics, the play nonetheless insists that even within the spaces of radical action the family constitutes one form of the limits of radical resistance. What follows is the play in its entirety.

ALL EARS
By Kristoffer Diaz

Unspecified number of actors.

THERE: And I'll be honest with you: I've been fighting this fight for the last fifteen years. And the neighborhood hasn't gotten better. And now I have two kids and they can't sleep at night because of the car stereos and the weed smoke and the police helicopters and the gunshots.

HERE: There aren't gunshots that often.

THERE: There shouldn't be gunshots any often. And look, if you can tell me a way I can stay here and help build this neighborhood or even this block back up from the inside without putting my kids at every day risk, I'm all ears.

Silence.

HERE: Bye.

END[67]

Diaz's concise rendition of the crisis of pragmatic political life in the present points to a sustained desire for the possibility of transforming our lived conditions by working together at the level of local community while crucially refusing to provide a clarion exhortation to change or a romanticized account of the possibilities of coalition building and collaborative transformation. Diaz is not abandoning coalition politics; he is critiquing a demand to keep "fighting this fight" in a mode that is potentially harmful both personally and relationally. Crucially, he acknowledges that family often constitutes one form of limits on radical resistance. "[E]very day risk," the violence engendered by hopeless poverty and the current conditions of illegal narcotic sales is a crucial factor. The exhausting challenge of trying to protect and raise a family while experiencing the dangers that accompany inhabiting and actively working to transform a neighborhood may not be sustainable. I recognize **There**'s decision not as a quick one made in anger or fear, but a necessary choice in the face of the sustained, unrequited labor.

And one of the clearest pragmatic elements of this work is that there is no easy answer. **There**'s invitation for a suggestion is genuine, and the silence before **Here**'s farewell (dismissal) confirms the absence of a viable answer under the current conditions. The uncomfortable silence that follows is at the heart of both the play and a broader concern about forms of political thinking that minimize potential pragmatic limits, including one's control over the environment and the behavior of others. In this latter problematic mode **There** is giving up, selling out, or becoming moderate as they center the logics of conventional parenting. But viewing this as a predictable movement of aging toward moderation and greater investment in the status quo, following familiar stories such as the maturation of the hippies and the conversion to social democracies for radical leftist rebels in El Salvador, misses a basic concern that a call to revolutionary action often refuses to account for the entirety of human complexity. That logic potentially de-emphasizes the lived conditions for human actors over time—"there aren't gunshots that often"—which can often evolve into its own form of exclusive gatekeeping of what constitutes appropriate political action.

The character names and the choices arising from an "*unspecified number of actors*" open up a number of questions about relationships to community and the site in which this conversation takes place. **There**'s insistence on the need to leave may suggest they are already distant from the **Here** arguing for them to stay, or it could be imagined as a single actor in internal conflict. I prefer the more conflicted reading in which **Here** can make the argument precisely because they are not **There**—they don't experience the palpable materiality of everyday risk and their neighborhood advocacy is conducted from a position that does not recognize the immediacy of the risk. There are also multiple possibilities for enactment, ranging from a two-person conversation with one or more listeners, to presentations with choruses speaking each set of lines, or one character being played by an individual and another by a chorus. While "*unspecified*" may be intended as a practical gesture toward shifting production conditions, it enables a wide set of configurations for this political debate. Whatever form the character takes, **There** clearly suggests the limits of some conventional storytelling attached to progressive activist politics.

In thinking through this issue, we must consider the larger context for this work. Generated as a response to the Ferguson Moment, this is part of an explicitly political project engaging the failures that led to the shooting death of Michael Brown at the hands of police by calling attention to the ongoing crisis of police violence, specifically against unarmed black men.[68] In this case, there is a real question about the kind of large-scale societal change that is (im)possible from within the structure of a particular geography. This is a question about location and the difficulties of individually and collectively advocating for change in the face of large-scale systemic, historical forces that perpetuate and foster conditions of poverty and lack of opportunity. I am interested in pragmatically and conscientiously exploring conditions of struggle in which the acts of overcoming, of victory, need reimagining to sustain the possibility of new thinking and forms of transformation.

I come to this subject aslant, moving from the study of literature in an English Department to the study of performance in a Theatre and Dance department. Taking on the teaching of playwriting, I began to think about practices and "rules" to generate dramatic worlds constituted as the given circumstances for characters whose everyday experiences may not neatly map onto our own, but who are presumed to be psychological structures with depth, motivation, and a desire for interaction. These characters exist in the geographies of expanded realisms, in which gaps between the dramatic world and our own, sometimes substantial, can be crucial to the work, whose premises and given circumstances center complex inter-relationalities deeply informed by their specific material conditions. And, I argue, it is through and with them that the horizons of political possibility in their systemic forms become visible and subject to exploration and critique.

I am trying to authentically engage with the intersecting limits as my progressive political framing of issues intersects with my lived practice working in and through institutions that provide me a series of privileges: compensated intellectual labor and the time, energy, and solitude to reflect on the lived conditions not only of our moment, but of the ones before and after, acknowledging the potential violence of private property while nonetheless fundamentally relying on its existence to create the conditions of my work. Though in agreement with the failures of market capitalism (and its fundamental groundings in coloniality and anti-Black racism), I have come to terms with the reality that I am not actively pursuing transformational revolution apart from a pedagogical, scholarly effort to gradually shift the frames of our thinking. In doing so I want to begin shifting the contours of our understanding, the horizons of the possible as politics while staying present with contradictory realities of politics in working toward sustainable change on the human level.

I believe that the study of scripted drama and its manifestations as theater in performance provide useful pathways for thinking through and with these issues precisely because of the process of playwriting itself—the necessity of imagining the creative process as always already a collaborative effort in making a world. My work centers on drama as a powerful site in which the larger structures of politics are negotiated through the lens of individual actors, always necessarily reflecting collective issues of politics. These works offer new ways of being in the world that provide a possible bridge from the present of the now to another present that engages the difficult movement along the path. There is a real need to insist on the difficulty of the labor of transformation, especially considering actions whose viral impact might accelerate transformations whose "time has not yet come." I am not suggesting that reform and radical transformation are not hundreds of years overdue, and structures of anti-black racism, patriarchy, and sectarian dogmatism must certainly be dismantled, but I also acknowledge that the action of emergent revolutionaries is moving in a world where the vocabulary and life practices of some extremely powerful minorities with significant wealth, influence, and rhetorical acumen (though admittedly for some that is much more limited than for others) have seen no value in changing their practices of belief, and perceive much more danger and individual, personal loss.

Not Puerto Rican, my Latino identity rests in a problematic tangent to this space that makes me amenable to acknowledging the paradoxical intimacies of the conflicts over the US/Puerto Rico relationship. I am the son of an Italian/Anglo American academic father (and the grandson of a second-generation Italian American immigrant academic), and more powerfully for my own experience and understanding, of a first generation "Hispanic" immigrant architect mother from the Philippines whose parents maintained a professional, artistic life in a Spanish speaking home. My maternal lineage reflects the broad impact of the last legacies of Spanish colonialism whose "territorial possessions" were ceded to the United States.

This book does not attempt a decolonial solution to the status of Puerto Rico, but rather considers status something to be thought with and through to understand the ways in which Puerto Rican dramatists of the diaspora in the United States have engaged the politics of relationship directly and indirectly in unique and powerful ways. While some works explored have an explicit relationship to factual or probable events of colonial domination and nationalist resistance in the negotiation of Puerto Rican status, these works are a means through which the contours of the politics of relation and the aesthetic strategies that reflect the shifting horizons of the thinking of politics can be investigated.

Moving through a series of case studies to examine and develop our understanding of pragmatic liberation, I focus close attention on key moments within each work. I argue that these moments enable us to acknowledge the complexity of our given circumstances, and this recognition allows us to reframe questions of liberation, autonomy, and connection in newly productive ways. Chapter 1 offers an alternative genealogy for Puerto Rican diasporic drama, focusing on two plays explicitly engaging historical moments of resistance and liberatory action in the island. One covering a single day in a drawing room, René Marqués's *Palm Sunday*, engages the 1937 Ponce Massacre; the second, Nelson Diaz-Marcano's *REVOLT!* a multilayered work sprawling over fifty years explores one legacy of the 1950 Jayuya revolt. Chapter 2 focuses dramatic representations and the catalytic work of revolutionary icon Lolita Lebrón, extending her symbolic importance beyond the fateful day of her shooting in the US Congress through Migdalia Cruz's expansive and playful episodic biography *Lolita de Lares*, Desi Moreno-Penson's more contemporary *Beige*, and a brief glance at *Notes on Killing Seven Oversight, Management and Economic Stability Board Members* by Mara Vélez Meléndez. Chapter 3 moves back to the island as site, looking at two different narratives of diasporic return and the ways they reveal the impacts of the colonial condition. Carmen Rivera's *La Gringa* offers one version of a restoration of the grand Puerto Rican family split by migration, while José Rivera's *Adoration of the Old Woman* is framed by an impending referendum on status to more explicitly address the divisive impact of colonialism. Chapter 4 expands from there to think more broadly through the necessity and limits of activism as a form of liberatory activity in Quiara Alegría Hudes's plays *The Happi-*

est Song Plays Last and *Daphne's Dive* and a young man trying to draw attention to the humanitarian crisis and violence of Hurricane Maria in Nelson Diaz-Marcano's *Paper Towels*. Chapter 5 explores the aftermath of revolution, thinking about the impact of collateral damage and the challenges of sustaining change in meaningful ways through José Rivera's *Massacre: Sing to Your Children*, which charts the moments after the slaying of an authoritarian figure, and Kristoffer Diaz's *#therevolution* in which hipsters deal with the reality of having catalyzed a revolutionary movement. The Conclusion moves speculatively, playing with the metaphor of a labyrinth as a way of unpacking the complexities of moving toward liberation while acknowledging our given circumstances and the potential impact of our actions on those closest to us.

Revolution is always in the wings, surrounded by questions of the relative value of life and liberation, the necessity and costs of violence, the nature of productive resistance, acceptable accommodations and compromises that accompany coalition building, and the challenge of finding consensual pathways for sustaining transformation.[69] However, this is not a book about critiquing historical revolutionary actions and their outcomes, but about reframing and resituating our understanding of the possibility of transformative change. In doing so, it insists on incorporating the lived complexities, ambiguities, and challenges of a struggle between opponents in radically different weight classes, a struggle that seeks to reimagine the human possibilities and power in the act itself, not in the easy conventional dramaturgy of a successful resolution.

CHAPTER 1

From *Palm Sunday* to *REVOLT!*

RETHINKING THE POLITICAL HORIZON OF PUERTO RICAN DIASPORIC DRAMA

In his introduction to *Nuestro New York: An Anthology of Puerto Rican Plays*, John V. Antush claims "The birth of modern Puerto Rican drama in New York might be dated May 7, 1953, the world premiere of *The Oxcart* [*La Carreta*] in the auditorium of the Church of San Sebastian at 308 East 24th Street, under the direction of Roberto Rodríguez Suárez."[1] *La Carreta*, by playwright René Marqués, traces the migratory movement of a jíbaro, a rural laborer, from the Puerto Rican countryside to the city of San Juan and then on to New York City. While the play's premiere may have launched modern Puerto Rican drama on the US stage, *La Carreta*'s importance to the Puerto Rican diaspora truly manifests in its 1966 Off-Broadway production. This version, an English translation directed by Lloyd Richards, starred Raul Julia and, most importantly, Miriam Colón, who reprised her starring role from the 1953 premiere. Colón, who was instrumental in fostering this production and translation, continued sharing the play in English for free during the summer of 1967 through the auspices of what would become the Puerto Rican Traveling Theater (PRTT), a key institution of Puerto Rican theater in New York.[2]

Colón's touring production of *La Carreta*, and the subsequent work of PRTT, had a profound impact on Puerto Rican diasporic drama. According to scholar Jason Ramirez, "This venture, which included dozens of Latina/o actors, designers, and community activists.... nurtured the growth of theatrical artists and audiences who ... saw their first positive Latino representations on Miriam's stage."[3] Colón's vision was grounded in "the transformative magic of the theatre" and the "necessity [of] bring[ing] theatre to the people" to generate "the strongest community bond."[4] Deeply invested in Puerto Rican diasporic communities in New York, PRTT was part of a growing movement of community-based theater engaging questions of community identity and social justice spreading in the second half of the 1960s. This socially engaged theater movement, often represented by El Teatro Campesino, the Chicanx theater in California, emerged in parallel with Teatro Nuevo Popular movements in Mexico, Central America, and the Caribbean.[5] Echoing key values of this work, scholar Elisa de la Roche argues Colón "wanted to promote works that were relevant to the Hispanic community, present them in neighborhoods where community members would get a chance to see them, and provide a source of cultural enrichment for all ethnic groups in New York City by sharing the wealth of Puerto Rican and Hispanic theatre."[6]

Colón's philosophy is consonant with an ongoing political and cultural interest in situating theater within communities that emerged as part of the Little Theater movement of the 1920s and 1930s in the US as well as the contemporaneously emerging desire for a national Puerto Rican theater.[7] Colón's values of relevance and proximity echo the widely-cited formulation of "about, by, for and near" articulated by W. E. B. Du Bois in his 1926 essay "A Little Negro Theatre":

> The plays of a real Negro theatre must be: *One: About us*. That is, they must have plots which reveal Negro life as it is. *Two: By us*. That is, they must be written by Negro authors who understand from birth and continual association just what it means to be a Negro today. *Three: For us*. That is, the theatre must cater primarily to Negro audiences and be supported and sustained by their entertainment and approval. *Fourth: Near Us*. The theatre must be in a Negro neighborhood near the ordinary mass of Negro people.[8]

Du Bois's manifesto serves as a touchstone for thinking about the ways local theater generates, explores, and sustains specific communities. This sense of community as shared culture expressed in and through theater was central to the resurgence of Latine theater not only within the 1960s ethnic civil rights movements but continues as a powerful force and value today.[9] The "about, by, for and near" formulation reflects a strong desire for relational connection accessible through the witnessing of, and participation in, theater that is both meaningfully relevant and proximate.

Unfortunately, the value of the specific and the local has continued to be undermined by egocentric claims of inaccessibility by critics demanding "universal" stories, surprisingly still unaware of the parochial frame of their claims of universality. This concern is exemplified in Pulitzer Prize winning playwright Quiara Alegría Hudes's account of an early post-show talkback in which an audience member insisted her play would be more effective if it were less Puerto Rican.

> "Why limit the story like that?" he asked. On the heels of this comment, an older black subscriber stood, emotional, saying, "We have a right to be here, too! We don't have to explain ourselves! I've been a subscriber here for decades, and I'm sick of apologizing for my existence!"[10]

This presumption of cultural specificity as inherently limiting is symptomatic of the ways in which the stories of communities of color are viewed as fundamentally marginal in the regional theater space described in Hudes's experience. A counter to this problematically pervasive refusal is to insist that meaningful human stories emerge from their unique specificity and precise attention to given circumstances.

The possibility of generating community engagement through theater was framed by Colón's early grant writing as interventions to engage minority communities and minority youth in the established democratic polis, offering one familiar presentation of the political work of theater. She was interested in transforming alienation into productive social activity while centering cultural values. Thus, an early funding proposal highlighted the desire to "promote identification and self esteem in alienated ethnic minorities," "increase understanding and tolerance between the different national and ethnic groups," and "provide constructive outlet for boredom, restlessness, and frustration."[11] This grant language reflects awareness of the deliberate and alienating marginalization sustained by Puerto Rico's obscured colonial relationship with the United States—an affect produced by structural conditions impeding opportunity and countering community rhetorics of hope. This colonial relationship—omnipresent and yet culturally obscured within the United States—created conditions of poverty that were not recognized as the systemic result of rampant discriminatory practices and racism, but rather originally attributed to cultural flaws within Puerto Rican communities. As was common in sociological thinking in the 1960s, the lack of effective pathways for Puerto Rican migrants to enter the American middle class was framed as a "failure" of assimilation and social mobility. The collaborative work of the PRTT during this time, however, increasingly recognized the systemic, political roots of the so-called "Puerto Rican Problem,"[12] and directly opposed problematic psychological and cultural claims that erased the insidious and destructive quality of colonial violence.[13]

This chapter argues that within Puerto Rican drama in the diaspora, the focus on cultural identification and a desire for a sense of home and belonging were fundamental products of the ongoing obscured colonial condition, and that questions of liberation, both literal and figurative, haunt and deeply inform the work. Considered this way, diasporic drama allows us to acknowledge the palpable and continuing structural inequalities that exist within Puerto Rico's ambiguous commonwealth status. In making this argument, I explore pragmatic liberation as a mode of critique and world making, a practice exemplified in the conflicted negotiations with the everyday demonstrated in this drama through various attempts to manage the struggle. Pragmatic liberation acknowledges complicity as well as imbricated and uncomfortable emotional ties across political divides, while nonetheless calling for political action within a sustainable framework as a means of shifting the conditions of the world we share. Recognizing the power of drama to provide the key starting point for pragmatic liberation—deliberate attention to context to fully acknowledge the complexity of one's given circumstances—shows the potential synergies of these forms of writing and politics. One clear parallel exists in the work of the Puerto Rican theater group *El Tajo del Alacrán*. Theater historian Eva C. Vásquez's translation of artistic director Lydia Milagros González echoes this model:

> We were in search of a theatre that would represent the people more authentically and at the same time would be a tool of political struggle for our people. We were always very clear about what we meant by "political." There was no need to affiliate with any organization. We were in conflict with the existing ones. By "political" we conceived the fostering, through the real social conflicts posed by the theatre, of the reality that Puerto Ricans were indeed struggling in a battle of affirmation, were indeed dealing with their real problems within their possibilities, that we were not "weak" or "on our knees", nor lazy or silly as we were taught to see ourselves.[14]

This quote offers a direct critique to playwright René Marqués's well-known and highly problematic figuration of the docile Puerto Rican, a false label conflating a lack of violent action with passive acceptance; it also highlights the fundamental pragmatism of *bregar* as a productive mode of engaging with the specificity of the everyday. In the original Spanish "sí bregaba con sus problemas reales y dentro de sus posibilidades"[15] [were indeed dealing with their real problems within their possibilities], *bregar* is a primary operation of liberation focused on the specific, real, and possible.

A second major example of this institutional work is Pregones Theater, founded in 1979 by Rosalba Rolón and other artists, which continues to sustain the forefront of Puerto Rican theater in New York following a merger with PRTT in 2014. Pregones's investment has historically been in the crucial work of collective creation, with the theatrical language emerging from a collaborative process rather than a central authorial voice. In the conclusion of her study tracing the first 25 years of the theater, Eva Vásquez describes their work as reflecting "the commitment to entertain and educate its audience, but also to ... encourage the development of political activism. ... [W]e see that the unresolved political situation between Puerto Rico and the United States and a predilection for Latin American theatrical aesthetics are the determining factors in choosing the subjects for investigation, experimentation and staging by the company."[16] The group's strategy reflects a desire to deal with real problems, comfortably consonant with an investment in pragmatic liberation in its broadest sense:

> By relinquishing the innate competitiveness of theatre as experienced in the dominant culture, and giving priority to the specific needs of its audience, the troupe has demonstrated its capability to strengthen the support of their work. Pregones embodies its audience, its desires, triumphs, defeats and struggles, making them protagonists eager for artistic representation, not outsiders.[17]

This logic of embodiment centers questions of relationality, and its central focus on specific needs also emphasizes a daily lived pragmatism deeply resonant with the complex adaptive strategies reflected in the multi-faceted concept of *bregar*.

In scholar and filmmaker Frances Negrón-Muntaner's introduction to *None of the Above: Puerto Ricans in the Global Era*, she introduces the idea of "[a] politics of small problems [that] may offer an opportunity to produce more enabling narratives of self and community by seeing through the core assumption that political identities are based on national specificity or legal precedent, not relationships that can be continuously disrupted and reconfigured at multiple levels."[18] Explicating the widespread Vieques protests at the turn of the 21st century which finally resulted in the US Navy's withdrawal from the island, she argues that

> What most local activists agitated for was the immediate resolution to a series of "small problems" affecting their bodies and everyday lives. . . . This is why the movement's success in removing the military from Vieques resulted not in a change in political status but in the navy's abandonment of outdated practices and the consolidation of a global context for Puerto Rican claims on the U.S. state.[19]

To begin thinking about the necessary grounding in the material everyday within the larger framework of political activism, let's start by thinking differently about the trajectory for Puerto Rican diasporic drama. Here we shift from identity as a function of "ethnicity" to focus on the coloniality of politics and the political geography of the US/Puerto Rico relationship to better understand world making in diasporic plays.

Reframing Diasporican Drama

Defining Puerto Rican playwrights doing their work in the continental United States is tricky, reflecting the anomalies of Puerto Rico's relationship to the United States. While after 1917 Puerto Rican writing is not technically "immigrant" writing because of citizenship status, immigrant writing is one framework through which to read *La Carreta*.[20] Critical readings of *La Carreta* historically centered on questions of identity and belonging, and the challenge of establishing a good life. These ongoing, palpable concerns for both artists and audiences are profoundly impacted by colonial citizenship and migration that fundamentally alter material encounters in everyday life in the diaspora. According to Antush,

> *The Oxcart* . . . brought to a boil the simmering awareness that something was radically wrong with the kind of life being sought in Puerto Rico and the United States. . . . On the island *The Oxcart* became the paradigm of a national agony played over and over again like a Passion play. In New York *The Oxcart* became the focal point of a culture in transition from which the first generation of New York playwrights derived their genealogies, their political stance, and their myths.[21]

This interpretive shift, from the agonizing necessity of migration to a new model of identification and resistance for playwrights, anticipates the emergence of a Nuyorican aesthetic in the diaspora.

To understand this shift it is crucial to think more broadly about movement and circulation within the diaspora as both concept and practice. Literary scholars Torres-Padilla and Haydee Rivera follow colleague Eugene Mohr in using "sojourner" to describe Marqués, which they defined as "writers who spent short periods of time in the United States but did not permanently establish themselves there. Many of them returned to the island and became celebrated national authors."[22] The term "sojourner" is useful here because Marqués's work is deeply shaped, as with the rest of the playwrights in this study, by his politics of relation, through a sense of belonging shaped by location. For many critics, this strong sense of locational inflection is modified by a continual process of movement, both literal and metaphorical. For theater scholar Rosalina Perales, writing from the island, Puerto Rican diasporic theater is understood as "crossing over," moving from one space to another.[23] Her language echoes a common narrative connecting the island and the diaspora in a series of metaphors that highlight connection and migratory circulation, such as anthropologist Jorge Duany's famous characterization of a "nation on the move."[24] The quality of this movement, colonial and diasporic, but not transnational in a conventional sense because of the anomalous status of Puerto Rico, provides a framework in which movement itself informs the aesthetic lens.[25]

In an important shift of this sense of movement, performance scholar Lawrence La Fountain-Stokes offers the concept of

> translocality . . . the interlinked experiences of persons in diverse geographic locations, whether in the country of origin or in the diaspora, who nevertheless are in complex and constant daily, weekly, monthly, or yearly contact, be it through travel, migrations, communications, or other forms of exchange; who live in the intimacy of these interactions and of the knowledge they generate; who might not even be living in different sovereign nations, but rather in different locations marked by profound linguistic and cultural differences in the same nation-state, for example as diasporic metropolitan subjects vis-à-vis colonial, insular ones.[26]

La Fountain-Stokes's concept of translocality centers the imbricated intimacies and complexities that help shape "be longing" through various forms of performance that destabilize limited historical forms of coming together. This alternative helps shift the centrality of movement as a descriptor for diasporic Puerto Rican cultural production, since the quality of movement itself is not only figured as a site of tension between individuals on the archipelago and in the diaspora, it is also fundamentally imbricated in the colonial condition.[27] Edgardo Meléndez argues that "Puerto Rico's political relationship with the United States and Puerto Ricans' U.S. citizenship . . . explains the *direction* and *nature* of their migration,"[28] and goes further, suggesting that "by managing migration, the Puerto Rican government played an important role in maintaining U.S. rule on the island."[29] While this act of management can be understood as a pragmatic practice in the face of underemployment, especially during a period of optimism about meaningful US investment in the archipelago's development, its ultimate result is not liberatory. This result is due in large part to its reliance on the behavior of another institution with greater power and over which it has no control. It is important to recognize that not all pragmatism is liberatory. While a series of attempts were made to invest in the Puerto Rican economy, the US has never followed through on sustainable development in the archipelago, maintaining economic precarity on the island through ending favorable corporate tax structures that initially catalyzed industrial and latter pharmaceutical investment.

In New York, continued discrimination directed toward 2nd and 3rd generation diasporic communities catalyzed artistic exploration of Puerto Rican life on the mainland, resulting in a new aesthetic emerging in the early 1970s. While there was artistic innovation in other urban spaces with a significant Puerto Rican diaspora, New York City, especially specific boroughs with a substantial Puerto Rican population, was ripe for writers valuing everyday experience and the innovations in language and aesthetics emerging in these communities. In exploring the fundamentally different experiences of Puerto Ricans on the mainland, they focused on shifting experiences in and through language accompanied by creative code-switching between English and Spanish. Nuyorican aesthetics, emerging from street poets and playwrights in the early 1970s, offered a radical alternative to an often insular and elitist literary, theatrical, and performance culture on the island. Freed from the weight of tradition and impassioned by a lack of storytelling about the New York Puerto Rican experience led to both realistic works engaging lived experience in the underclass as well as experimental works using theatrical form to indirectly account for the colonial condition.

While the work of male playwright/poets Pedro Pietri, Jaime Carrero, and Miguel Piñero was instrumental to this transformation, initially centered on the Nuyorican Poets Café founded by Miguel Algarín and Miguel Piñero, performance scholar Patricia Herrera crucially reminds us that women were also integral to this founding, offering an alternate aesthetic that fostered a different model of "be longing" and communal constitution. Herrera describes these as "*platicás*, a conversational style of writing and performing,"[30] which "carv[ed] feminist spaces for women to not only recount their memories and transmit cultural knowledge, but also to engage women in critically witnessing the lived experience of other women."[31] Centering on crucial figures such as Sandra María Esteves, Herrera's account insists that,

> the performeras' conversational style subverted the male Nuyorican practice of taking up space and volume; instead it cultivated a sense of intimacy arounds social ills that affected women, and it offered generative representations of mothers, young girls, and women. While differing drastically in voice and volume from the militant declamatory approach formalized in *Nuyorican Poetry*, the poetry of performeras fiercely bodied forth revolutionary thoughts of freedom and social justice.[32]

This more specific and intimate attention to "social ills that affected women" reflects one form of liberatory pragmatism structured through conversational dynamics of exchange that reflect potential strategies to negotiate *la brega*. While there were certainly differences in approaches, the crossover between poetry and playwriting reinforced embodied performance and language play as crucial parts of the aesthetic, centering the understanding of identity on specific bodies in particular spaces, highlighting a necessary acknowledgment of given circumstances.

The emergence of Nuyorican and other diasporic aesthetics posed a problem for the ideological project of *la gran familia puertorriqueña*, the unified Puerto Rican "family" connecting individuals on and off the island in a shared, singular culture. Emerging out of *estadolibrismo*, the political compromise that resulted in the referendum establishing the "Free Associated State," it prioritizes autonomy of shared culture to sustain ethno-national identification regardless of location and the value of local governmental control, rather than focusing on larger questions of power and sovereignty.[33] Prior to the 1990s, diasporic cultural contributions were often diminished or overlooked by scholars on the island as a means of implicitly sustaining this construction. Since then, however, a broader critical recognition of diasporic aesthetics and more "trans" connections to and from the island has accompanied a significant growth in cultural production in the diaspora.[34] Literary scholar Marisel Moreno, for example, argues for "a Puerto Rican transinsular literature," "equal positionality of insular and diaspora letters" and "chipp[ing] at the *frontera intranacional* that has been erected between Puerto Ricans on the island and their diasporic counterparts."[35]

Moreno's *frontera intranacional*, intra-national border, is reinforced by the complex politics of relation experienced by Puerto Rican playwrights writing primarily in English where forms of emergent pragmatism seem profoundly located within a particular contemporary arc of the diaspora, mostly over the last 30 years, Recognizing the affective reality of this difference, I de-emphasize the ubiquitous invocation of a connecting bridge, between Puerto Rico and New York, and between the US, Puerto Rico and the rest of Latin America and the Caribbean to highlight the structural differences of geographic change—the specific paradoxes of Puerto Rican diasporic experience, especially federal enfranchisement granted by state residence accompanied by different forms of everyday racism.[36] The on-going shift of Puerto Rican identity between ethnic and national is a poignant demonstration of the complexity of this differential relation. According to Grosfoguel, Negrón-Muntaner, and Goeras, "The ambiguity of this articulation is evidenced by the fact that even when many Puerto Ricans in the United States imagine themselves pragmatically as an 'ethnic group' with no territorial (state) claim in the United States, Puerto Rico is at least claimed symbolically as the territorial site where ethnics become nationals through the magical operation of the air bridge."[37] The "magical operation" integrates ethnic and national identification into culture, manufacturing a symbolic erasure of difference that threatens to elide the structural violence of poverty exacerbated by the ongoing geopolitics of a colonial relationship.

Highlighting articulation, how connectivity is negotiated, is one element of *bregando* in its most basic interpersonal and intersubjective form. Acknowledging the reality that identity is fundamentally relational and situational, the quality and nature of those connections is centered in and through the practice of storytelling, emphasizing both possibility and pragmatic limits. In doing so, storytelling becomes increasingly invested in connectivity as a fundamental issue and material for world building. Like many other marginalized groups, Diasporican playwrights engage the political in relation to their precise position in *la brega*, the struggle, insisting on a need to think about specific material conditions of colonial practice and discrimination.

The threads of Caribbean and diasporic theory that I highlight are more interested in lived specificity to counter real impacts of structural and lived daily violence than in an abstract conception of colonial violence. Though often calling for revolution, the playwrights in this volume do not often explicitly frame their work in decolonial terms, in part because their self-conception includes their voluntary location in the metropolis and consequent closer relationship to full citizenship. Recognizing that citizenship in its various forms is insufficient for sustaining agency and power, the echoes of decolonial thinking within this pragmatic framework are often on the surface domesticated into familiar themes of being in or out of place, of (dis)location. Thus, conversations about structural violence are often framed in attempts to find home and identity, to address loss and family challenges, even as the ever-present colonial condition provides an inevitable political framework for this understanding.

Marqués's *Palm Sunday*: Rethinking the Path

While there is no doubt that *La Carreta*, Miriam Colón, and the work of the PRTT were germinal to fostering Puerto Rican diasporic drama, I want to explore an alternate trajectory by looking at a different play by René Marqués as an inception point. Unlike *La Carreta*, which focuses on the economic and cultural losses generating and driven by migration, René Marqués's earlier play *Palm Sunday* explicitly engages Puerto Rico's colonial relationship with the United States through a retelling of the Ponce Massacre. Written in English in 1949 while Marqués was a Rockefeller Fellow studying at Columbia University with John Gassner and Theodore Apstein, *Palm Sunday* reflects its creative origin prior to Puerto Rico's ELA status but after the passing of Law 53, Ley de la Mordaza, in 1948, which was intended to mute the voice of independence in Puerto Rico.[38] Assuming Puerto Rico's colonial status, it foregrounds the affective and material violence sustained by the colonial relationship.[39] The play has received little critical attention because it was only produced once, in 1956, and was not published until 2019. Conventional in many aspects, it follows familiar tropes of family drama, which had its own set of functions in the late 1950s. According to theater scholar Camilla Stevens: "The family quarrels and failed romances portrayed in these plays evoke the contrasting stances on Puerto Rican political and cultural identity debated on a national level and the use of the space of the house raises questions about what kind of family should embody the nation."[40] *Palm Sunday* takes these questions even further by dramatizing the violent repression of expressions of independence during the Ponce Massacre.

Across his writing Marqués explored a particular form of Puerto Rico nationalism as independence, a white elite model recognizing the imposition of US culture as a betrayal of a home-grown Spanish culture deeply connected to criollo elites. Marqués's more independence-focused drama never achieved significant interest in the English-speaking Puerto Rican community in New York, perhaps because much of the work uses absurdist aesthetics to explicate the colonial condition. Though in his realistic drawing room play *Palm Sunday* Marqués was writing about a historical event, his sojourner status during its creation points to the power of location in the diaspora as a crucial geography from which to critique Puerto Rican politics and history through the theater.

Palm Sunday recreates the events of that Catholic religious holiday in 1937 when Insular police killed 21 people and injured over 200 on March 21 in what is known as the Ponce Massacre. The massacre's ostensible provocation was an unauthorized parade of Revolutionary Cadets, advocates for independence and political supporters of then jailed independence leader Pedro Albizu Campos. After authorities revoked their previously issued permit, the cadets chose to march anyway, defying local authorities and exercising their right to free speech to protest existing conditions in Puerto Rico. The Insular police, a centralized para-military force under the control of a US-appointed police chief, responded with militarized violence: Thompson submachine guns and tear gas. Nelson A. Denis's detailed account of the horrific violence in *War Against All Puerto Ricans* culminates with:

> The police kept shooting and clubbing for thirteen minutes. By the time they finished, nineteen men, one woman, and a seven-year-old girl lay dead; over two hundred more were gravely wounded—moaning, crawling, bleeding, and begging for mercy in the street. The air seethed with gun smoke. Everyone moved in a fog of disbelief as policemen swaggered about and blood ran in the gutter.[41]

Police and legislative authorities in Puerto Rico invested significant energy constructing a narrative in which police were merely responding to violence generated by an unauthorized gathering, but the cover up was thwarted by heroic efforts of Puerto Rican journalists who persisted in refusing the official narrative.[42]

Glaring questions over the facts of the encounter led the US Congress to appoint an eight-member commission, chaired by Arthur Garfield Hays, General Counsel of the American Civil Liberties Union, and staffed by prominent Puerto Rican leaders from the press, education, medicine, law, and culture.

Their report, published May 22, 1937, placed blame squarely on the Insular police and their leadership: "The proper words to describe the conduct of the officers and men would be lack of consideration, lust for blood, and vicious destruction of life."[43] This violent repression stemmed from fear of destabilization brought on by populist independent anger and frustration, following the US government's arrest and imprisonment of Albizu Campos for his revolutionary advocacy and support for striking workers. This action marked a substantial shift in the manner and mode of policing symbolic demands for independence.[44] In addition to incompetent leadership and insecurity, the report also suggests more calculated interest in diffusing the momentum of the independence movement, which was damaged but also radicalized by this act. Confirming the events as a massacre, it unequivocally condemns the culture of repression which led to this violence and offers a record of Puerto Rican protest that vindicates the capacity of individuals to assemble without causing unrest. Along with clear analysis of the events leading up to and on the day, including a wryly understated condemnation of police action, there is forceful argument that divergent points of view can be presented without conflict, as evidenced by several instances of more elaborate actions by Nationalists carried out without violence across the country.[45]

Marqués's dramatic account of the day presents the massacre through a family divided between cultures—the US-born Police Commissioner John Winfield and his Puerto Rican wife Mercedes.[46] Alberto, their son, sits between, resisting his father's values and immersing himself in Puerto Rican culture and identity. Due to Marqués's framing and clear condemnation of a US figure of power, the 1956 production tweaked a central nerve in the operations of the newly established island government. The two-act play is in continuous action, starting at 9:30am and culminating just after 3:30pm with the massacre itself. The action takes place in the 2nd story Winfield "drawing room" containing "[f]urniture [in a] combination of Spanish colonial and modern American comfort"[47] and a balcony overlooking the street. The hybrid cultural mix is inflected by the last lines of the stage directions that highlight the visual imposition of US culture and values: "Across the street is the facade of an old stone building, formerly a family house, now used as United States Government offices. An American flag hangs from a short pole attached to the balcony railing of the old house."[48]

Within this domestic space Marqués marks the cultural difference of this hybrid family in stereotypical affective and communicative terms: Mercedes is "at the piano playing a Puerto Rican 'danza'" with "fire and emotion" and

John is "very much the blond American type. . . . not very communicative; usually self-controlled."[49] Even their son's choice of reading material serves to emphasize these tensions as Alberto daydreams with revolutionary Puerto Rican poet and independence advocate "José de Diego['s] 'Cantos de Rebeldía' in his hand."[50] Marqués also shifts between English and Spanish as a means of marking this difference. The 1956 production text, source for the 2019 publication, reflects the code switching within a mixed household and a potential relationship between language use and ideology. Mercedes and Alberto occasionally speak Spanish among themselves but English whenever Winfield is in the room, though there is no translation as everyone in the play understands both languages.

The audience witnesses increasing conflict between John Winfield's political beliefs and work responsibilities and Alberto's interest in independence, while Mercedes serves as a mediating presence, recognizing some but not all her husband's concerns. The negotiation is punctuated by the arrival of three separate guests who help refract the political picture: Manuel, Alberto's classmate, a Puerto Rican student revolutionary in mourning for his country; Harry Martin, a family friend and "yankee" who explicates the dangerous distortions of colonialism; and the Mayor, a weak, self-interested figure easily manipulated by Winfield. The intensifying conflict highlights how Winfield has been molded by colonialism, twisting him to justify asymmetrical violence to restore an order that was never disrupted. Moving through an explication of motives and justifications for the parade and its cancellation the play culminates with a violent confrontation off stage and a final melodramatic tableau—Winfield cradling his dead son Alberto.

Marqués's premise and given circumstances engage the concrete immediate history of the Ponce Massacre as well as the larger context of Puerto Rico's colonial history. Labeling his fictional family Winfield, evoking the contemporaneous colonial governor Blanton Winship, Marqués points to, but does not always directly map on to, the specific given circumstances of the historical event. Echoing in parts the Hays commission report, Marqués's dramatic retelling predicates US-sponsored violence as a necessary outgrowth of colonialism. Unsurprisingly, this account of the massacre initially encountered informal censorship from theater workers who did not want to participate in the production because of the political nature of the piece. Their primary concern was the negative representation of a US figure of authority at a moment during the mid 1950s when the newly established ELA status was still broadly valued for the economic support that accompanied it, and many still earnestly touted the rhetoric of Puerto Rico as a "showcase for democracy." The controversy went to the highest levels of government, as a letter from Governor Muñoz Marín responding to Marqués's concern about the fear of censorship shutting down a production, insists that though he personally does not find the play particularly useful, there is no reason to fear government reprisal for participation.[51]

Both the play and the Hays report present police leaders as a primary driver of the massacre, and Marqués establishes John's colonial rage as the primary motivation. In the Hays report's account of the massacre, Colonel Orbeta, the Puerto Rican Chief of the Insular Police, convinces the Mayor of Ponce to rescind his initial parade approval, providing rationales that differed widely based on the source. In Marqués's play, the Mayor's initial approval based on the constitutional principle of freedom of speech is rescinded by request of the Governor at John's insistence. Marqués establishes John's explicit intention to both "smash" the nationalists and set up the Mayor to take the fall, establishing John as a figure of absolutes, a product of the colonial condition.[52] In this psychological state John needs his wife to be on his side, in direct conflict with nationalist forces, and sees any questioning of the US presence and domination over Puerto Rico as a personal affront.[53] His anger, centered on the nationalist movement, extends to anyone holding those values, including his son Alberto who claims his father hates Puerto Ricans, which the audience palpably experiences when John, unbeknownst to Mercedes, strikes his son multiple times at the end of the first act. His personal act of familial violence is consistent with his asymmetrical response to the parade's symbolic call to liberation, the use of machine guns and grenades to quell rhetorical defiance, showing the intensity of his connection to the destruction wrought by colonialism.

Despite the Manichean differentiation of colonialism's work, the play recognizes the complex interplay of attitudes underlying the political conflict; Marqués maps this through contrasting figures to Alberto and John. Alberto is an aspirational Nationalist rather than a centrally active one like his friend Manuel, a prize-winning student of Puerto Rican history whose dark suit reflects his mourning for the communal condition of colonial subjection. Recognizing the political symbolism of Manuel's sartorial choice, John treats him discourteously, as "one of them," his enemies.[54] Just as Manuel presents a committed and reflective *independentista* stance as a counter to Alberto's petulant brooding and oppositional defiance of his father, Harry Martin is a yankee with the desire to be "simpático," a refraction of John's position and a recognition of relational choice and not inevitable incommensurability.[55] While Mercedes is pragmatically willing to acknowledge the possibility of a simpático yankee, Alberto is not, insisting that although Harry is a "good man," as a yankee he is ineligible for the label simpático. Alberto's response suggests he defines the term closer to an ally or like-minded than likeable, a mistranslation of the English cognate that reinforces his idealized presumption of radical incommensurability with any political representative of the US. Alberto's idealism parallels his romanticized notions of independence, refusing the dangers of accommodationist compromise but simultaneously invalidating the possibility of genuine rapprochement, ironically echoing John's absolutism and reinforcing the assumption of colonialism as unbridgeable rupture.

The play makes clear that the danger of the absolute position is the impossibility of compromise and the consequent rapid pathway to violence that is implicitly justified by an unbridgeable distance, despite potential evidence otherwise. Of course, this is a controversial position given both Albizu Campos's willingness to explicitly support violence in the service of revolution as well as Frantz Fanon's assertion of the inevitable and necessary violence of revolution in The *Wretched of the Earth*.[56] Absolutism is the direct opposite of a pragmatic approach to liberation, and there seems to be an ongoing tension for Marqués between a longing for an authenticity accessible through a radical rhetoric of decolonial thinking and an ambivalence about the accompanying violence that seems to erupt from this assertion.

One potential opening in this space occurs in more contemporary interpretations of Fanon and decoloniality. In the conclusion to *Subterranean Fanon: An Underground Theory of Radical Change* literature scholar Gavin Arnall reminds us through his analysis of a divided sense of Fanon's own thinking that,

> Fanon holds that it is possible to think universality otherwise, that we need not fear universality as such. This aspect of his thought has been lost among those who equate any universalist project with domination and the erasure of difference. The irony is that such a universal condemnation of universality contributes to erasing the very differences that distinguish oppressive forms of universalism from the universalist demands and formulations that have historically emerged out of the struggle against oppression and represent the greatest threat to the universalizing drives of colonialism and imperialism.[57]

More provocatively for the language of pragmatic liberation, Arnall points to the possibility of emergent questions surfacing from his reading of Fanon in which inherent tensions and multiple answers increase the complexity based on a recognition of the potential emergence of multiple worlds:

> Can we think translation and invention together? In other words, to realize genuine change, could it be the case that some tools must be totally abolished whereas others must be abolished and maintained, negated yet preserved in an elevated form? Finally, the dynamic nature of Fanon's internal division raises the issue of how fluid or mobile we should be when responding to these questions. Can they be answered in an a priori and principled way or must they be continually rethought from within specific conjunctures, such that different historical situations will necessitate different approaches to the master's tools?[58]

This shift away from a fixed Manicheanism is also echoed in the work of Diasporic Puerto Rican cultural theorist Nelson Maldonado-Torres where in his "Outline of Ten Theses on Coloniality and Decoloniality" he first reiterates Fanon's relationship to the concept of coloniality: "[T]he basic coordinates of what for Fanon defines humanity are fundamentally distorted to the point of turning a human being into a promoter of extreme forms of narcissisms, superiority, and self-hate."[59] He goes on to argue that

> Decolonization is not so much about obtaining recognition from the normative subjects and structures, but about challenging the terms in which humanity is defined and recognition takes place. This necessitates the formation of new practices and ways of thinking, as well as a new philosophy, understood decolonially, not so much as a specific discipline or way of thinking, but as the opposition to coloniality and as the affirmation of for forms of love and understanding that promote open and embodied human interrelationality.[60]

Maldonado-Torres's invocation "affirmation *of for*" might push the consideration both of acknowledgment and advocacy, or recognition and action in the reclamation of the possibility of intersubjective relationality that is made impossible in the space of coloniality. This situated and situational call for the fundamental universalist (but not singular or hegemonic) need for interrelationality is framed in inverted terms in the absolutist logic of the play.

It is productive to consider Marqués's discomfort with his reading of the colonial condition and the problematic necessity for unsuccessful resistance in the Puerto Rican context he illustrates in the play, and later in his narcissistic and misogynist essay "The Docile Puerto Rican." I speculate this discomfort emerges from the tension between his recognition of the need to reimagine a world outside of masculinist, colonialist models of resistance and his inability to craft such a possibility. Instead, he defaults to the melodramatic appeals of the doomed parade of the revolutionary cadets.[61]

Revealingly, the challenge and the necessity for resistance is articulated not through Manuel, the native voice of Puerto Rican independence, but through Harry Martin, the "yankee" who recognizes the inherent structural violence of the colonial system as well as the danger and potential necessity of violent resistance, but who in the end does nothing. Responding to Mercedes' cry "But they're talking about fighting!" he replies, "I'm not sure I blame them. Of course they don't have a chance. They want to be heroes—and they can only be martyrs. Very touching, but damned useless."[62] This gesture toward ineffectual martyrdom is a precursor to Marqués's troubling concept of "the docile Puerto Rican." While in his essay Marqués briefly references this play as one example of docility (he uses many of his own works to justify his theory), the play as it exists can be seen as a Janus-faced example of Marqués retroactively refiguring his work within the service of a condemnation of Puerto Rico's problematic idealization of symbolic and failed attempts at revolution that result only in martyrdom.

Ironically, the initial failure here is not idealistic self-sacrifice, but an inability to correctly account for the given circumstances of the current colonial authority, to understand fundamentally the ways in which coloniality collapses the possibility of the intersubjective interrelationality. Mercedes attempts to recuperate this possibility that John continues to refuse through his assertion of asymmetrical violence to repress symbolic protest, reflecting the historical authorities' anxieties about the potential for further unrest related to labor activism. While in his "docility" essay Marqués seems to have shifted the blame to the Puerto Ricans' acquiescence to their colonial condition (shaped in part presumably by the acceptance of the ELA), the play centers on the inevitable impact of colonialism on both the colonizing forces and the colonized; it is deeply concerned with the colonial condition as a symbiotically destructive atmosphere. Martin patronizingly pontificates to Mercedes: "there's something about a colony—any colony—that you don't find anywhere else. People don't seem to act normal. Your people are abnormally sensitive—when they are not just opportunists. My people, on the other hand, become less and less sensitive in this situation."[63]

His claim of "abnormal sensitivity" recognizes the affective and embodied impact of colonial violence and precarity described by Fanon and others but refuses to fully embrace the imbricated exacerbation of this physiological and psychological trauma. Seen in other literary and cultural contexts as a desire for *respeto* or *dignidad* at the center of Puerto Rican culture, it is worth considering whether the centrality of *dignidad* results from the unfortunate necessity of demanding recognition for one's humanity in the face of a structure that refuses to acknowledge it. And furthermore, note the extent to which *dignidad* presents an alternative embodied refusal of failed intersubjectivity—a careful withholding of self. Participation within this structural refusal is precisely what decreases others' sensitivity. And the desensitization, the numbness that stealthily grows in the spaces of colonial power, runs the risk of propagating dehumanization, which is most clearly manifest through the possibility of massacre itself.

The conceptual climax of the play is Martin's long discussion with Mercedes revealing his fears of and for John, establishing the massacre as an inevitable destructive outcome of the colonial relation. Instead of answering the question of source, "weaknesses in our American liberalism or the rotten environment in our American colony?"[64] Martin narrates the good intentions that advance a colonial administrator down the path of corruption: "You decide—naturally!—to fight for the good things these people should have, even if they don't want them. By then, you are not a liberal anymore. You have become—by some evil magic—the exact image reflected in that mirror the natives used to hold in front of you."[65] In John's case this transformation is heightened. Not only does "he [have] the Police Department circulating in his veins," a physiological transformation of the body, "[h]e has grabbed for power and intends to use it in his desperate search for security. That, you know, is going further than even the most reactionary American in the colony has ever gone!"[66] The militarized, violent investment in security is part and parcel, not only of colonial practice, but of a larger expression of the framework of coloniality itself which justifies radically asymmetrical violence against humans who have lost the right to express their desires.[67] Martin's claim of John's exceptionalism operates in contradistinction to his claims about the environmental transformation of colonialism.

Marqués is careful to highlight that this is not a communal or collective sense of security, but rather a concept of order structured from a single point of view; and this absolutist logic is the root of the problem. Despite Martin's ability to "see more than one point of view,"[68] he cannot accept John's descent into violence precisely because of this absolutist response. Encountering the mirror of the Puerto Rican gaze strips away Winfield's illusion of US exceptionalism, but in Martin's account it is not your reflection in the other's gaze but rather in the mediated form of the mirror they hold up for you. While mirrors introduce mediation and distortion, they do not have the agential subjectivity of the colonized. Martin's "evil magic" results in self-transformation, but he refuses the direct agency of the reversed gaze of the colonized, instead relying on the technology of the mirror. The condition of colonial distortion here echoes the Fanonian account of colonial interpellation, but rather than being externally hailed by Althusserian ideological forces, Marqués narrates this transformation as an individual event that occurs when liberalism cannot survive the conditions of colonialism.[69] This familiar progressive critique of the limits of liberal politics voices a continuing tension that haunts the drama of the diaspora, in which the pre-dominant ideology of the local space is manifest as a self-interested liberalism that needs to encounter its own limits as a means of dismantling its hegemony in US thought.

Shifting from the limits of ideology, Mercedes, the optimist, frames Winfield's issue as an internal psychological conflict, recognizing the impact of structural forces but insisting on the possibility of choice. Implicitly agreeing with Martin that his transformation is a direct product of environmental conditions, she suggests that a greater sense of connection, a potential return to the US to reacquaint with his family, might help repair this situation. She frames Winfield's family's dismissal of her as based on fear that their love could not overcome cultural difference and believes the material fact of their continued relationship is grounds for persuasion otherwise. John makes it clear that Mercedes' belief in change is naïve, attributing a static quality to US cultural discrimination toward Puerto Ricans; nonetheless, gives her a voice. And while the presumptive patriarchy of the play diminishes her contributions, her presence also holds echoes within and in fact seems to unravel Marqués's docility theory at the point where he claims the empowerment of the feminine makes it impossible for Puerto Rican revolutionaries to manifest appropriately efficacious violence. This strategy of blaming the emergence of powerful women as a cause and sign of men's docility is not only symptomatic of the ways in which misogyny crosses ideological lines, Mercedes's role also foregrounds the conflict in Marqués's as she complicates the very absolutism he appears to condemn even while asserting its inevitability under colonialism.

Mercedes offers a complex understanding of connection, an imagined community of Puerto Ricans regardless of politics, and her conciliatory attempts offer a pragmatic position pointing toward more radical politics, a future that fosters interrelationality. Her proposed solution to restore Winfield's human connectivity echoes a crucial thread of decoloniality, the valuation of deeper connection and relation as a starting place for humanization. This gesture aligns Mercedes's mediating pragmatism and care with a potential liberation, unrealized as it is within the text. Her high level of clarity and insight is echoed in her distinction between perceived offense and genuine harm; when John, dismissively but not surprisingly, calls her a native, Mercedes insists that the subtext of disgust, rather than the term itself, holds the violence. Her precise recognition of choice and impact reflects an awareness of the given circumstances and a desire to find a means for collaborative coexistence, a gesture of *jaibería*, of moving sideways to move forward; ironically, it is a means of negotiating Marqués deliberately undermines through his use of the clear affective map of melodrama.

As the son of an American father and a Puerto Rican mother Alberto never truly comes to grips with his in-between status, but his marginality is marshaled in direct service of the symbolic right to non-violently call for independence. In predictable melodramatic fashion, when the off-stage shooting starts, the somber nationalist Manuel is among the first marchers killed, the Puerto Rican flag in his hands. Witnessing his death, Alberto, despite his parents' best efforts to keep him away from the violence, manages to jump off the balcony and retrieve the flag only to be mowed down by police wielding machine guns.[70] Marqués uses the primal horror of indirect filicide to intensify his indictment of colonialism, and in doing so, reduce the more radical claim of necessary interrelationality incipient in the play into the recognizable form of intra-familial trauma. The final tableau presents Winfield cradling the body of his son and possibly coming into consciousness of the impact of his absolutist logic and subsequent choices.

As Marqués developed as a dramatist, he became increasingly suspicious of the affective pull of melodrama and martyrdom in the face of colonial power, and yet, in his notorious essay "The Docile Puerto Rican" Marqués argues,

> the Puerto Rican is praised as 'democratic' when he tolerates, with asinine docility, what no civilized person would dream of tolerating in any modern democracy. If "aplatanado" was a stinging ethical barb in the stagnant colonial soul, its newest synonym—democratic—is a narcotic drug mercifully administered to quiet the conscience of the docile Puerto Rican so that he may accept, without scruple, his abject condition.[71]

Condemning the Puerto Rican "Nationalist suicidal impulse," the "martyr complex" which leads to death in events like the Ponce Massacre, he presents *Palm Sunday* as one of several examples employing this frame.[72] Presumably, he would attempt to frame the entire logic of pragmatic liberation as "the psychological synthesis of the weak, timid, and docile man,"[73] but I would argue this as a direct reflection of his own masculine fatalist absolutism unwilling to validate the possibility of other forms of connection as illustrated by all four male characters in the play. The limit of Marqués's political horizon manifests in his claim that increasing attention to the matriarchal has moved away from the productive attitude idea of machismo that might otherwise counter this practice of docility. In doing so he cannot escape the sense of a Manichean zero sum game which refuses the potential sustainable transformation of seeing the world otherwise and the highly productive pragmatic reality of *bregando como necesario*, a necessary making do that, while not always liberatory, is nonetheless a more productive way of shifting toward different possibilities of interrelationality.[74]

While one could insist that Mercedes' pragmatism has no real traction in the work since she is unable to manifest a new form of connection, the total environment allows the audience a way of accessing a more complex counter to Marqués's heavy-handed melodrama. While the tableau of the martyred son provides the final visual image, Marqués's choices with the soundscape at the conclusion of the work point to an alternate sensory experience that offers a different way of thinking. In her study of Marqués's drama critic Bonnie Reynolds shows how symbolic images and sounds layer on top of what otherwise might be purely melodramatic imagery to suggest a complex depth.[75] In this case, the soundscape, which is precisely notated from the beginning of the collapse of the parade music under the hail of gunfire, shifts away from realism into the space of aural symbol, a movement toward mood much like the symbolist dramatists and Anton Chekhov. The parade band is playing and singing and then continues off key, fading after the first barrage of gunfire, before undergoing an aesthetic shift: "*The realistic cries in the street have now become a sort of soft, tragic chorus, without words—just a rhythmic humming, a mournful chant of pain and sorrow. Religious Palm Sunday music begins softly, crescendo to curtain.*"[76] This movement toward the tragic as religious form, moving from a Greek chorus to a Christian religious song, invokes the specificity of the event's historical date. But rather than focus on the redemptive possibility of the Christological parallels of transcendent self-sacrifice, consider the space from which this possibility emerges, a rhythmic humming. This shared choric sonority is affectively expressive, and though it shifts to the recognizably religious, this sonic irruption ensures that the possibility of hope emerges first from a collective chorus without words.

Marqués's figuration of the Ponce Massacre as family tragedy is familiar ground for both US and Latin American theater of the period, but his bilingual intersection of cultures adds an additional layer of conflicted affect to the account. The framework of coloniality leads directly to violence toward both the hated other and those valued most. *Palm Sunday* argues that violence is an inevitable outcome of the colonial condition, and while on one level the play seems to promote the structure of martyrdom as a means of consciousness-raising and individual transformation, Marqués's own beliefs suggest otherwise. In this work consciousness raising is presented not in an exponential growth model, but in single acts of transmission to and from individuals. In this sense, Marqués's family melodrama highlights the potential limits of revolutionary action while insisting on the impact of injustice as a necessary starting point for resistance. Establishing a clear understanding of the roots of violence, the play ultimately swerves away from this. However, I would argue this is not a passive acceptance of the conditions as they exist, but an attempt to find sustainable individual and collective ways to negotiate in and through the struggle that do not rely solely on direct, symmetrical resistance by force. Pragmatic liberation assumes that any liberatory action needs to be taken with awareness of one's given circumstances, especially the impact on one's intimate connections, one's family, both real and metaphorical. John Winfield's melodramatic "punishment" in *Palm Sunday* is a direct condemnation of his failure to consider the immediate impact of actions on the family. In narrating the development and action of resistance the play exposes the limits of conventional thinking and a purely affective mobilization of revolt, while slyly presenting the emergence of individual and collective responses that might sustain pragmatic negotiation through the struggle.

REVOLT!: Continuing the History of Intra-familial Revolutionary Politics

To mark one arc of the revolutionary trajectory of Diasporican drama, I jump fifty years to a play produced in 2018 that continues the history of liberatory sentiment and action foregrounding the intimate and intra-familial tension generated by the struggle for Puerto Rican independence, New York based

Puerto Rican playwright Nelson Diaz-Marcano's play *REVOLT!*[77] Centering the messy intimacy of Puerto Rican independence politics, Diaz-Marcano continues the exploration of the necessity and limits of violence through a historically and geographically expansive play that exceeds the bounds of melodrama to employ the expanded realism of a more epic temporal scope, projections, narrative commentary, and presentation of characters at multiple ages. The premise is that learning history to understand one's familial role serves as a form of pragmatic liberation that enables storytelling as a particular mode of political action. And this sense of family understanding is crucial given the ways in which Puerto Rican cultural nationalism is figured as *la gran familia puertorriqueña*, the great Puerto Rican family, regardless of geographic location in the archipelago or the diaspora. This carefully constructed ideology of one family in the service of sustaining rhetorics of Puerto Rican nationalism highlights the challenges of divided households and fraternal connections that break apart in the face of the possibilities and limits of forms of resistance in the negotiations over the definition of home.

The frame narrative is an explication of The Narrator's complex family history, cobbled together from stories from her mother and letters from her granduncle; she relates the story of her granduncle Quique (whose younger self is called Jose and played by a separate actor) as a way of establishing family ties and history. The historical account begins with Jose and his companion Jonatan (in later life Don Jony) as boys in the late 1930s and moves through their experience of various moments in Puerto Rican history from pre–World War II migration to their return to the island following Albizu Campos's release from prison, with the hope of working toward independence. This enables an exploration of the environment leading to Grito de Jayuya, the abortive military action of the revolutionary independence movement in 1950 betrayed by its own members.[78] The play frames revolution as a family affair, and the ultimate act of betrayal is intimate, selective violence justified as self-interested salvation, as Jonatan betrays Jose's family to save his friend. Jose's refusal to participate in this betrayal of his sister and brother-in-law (one is captured, tortured, and killed, the other shot by Jonatan) leads to his 47-year incarceration sustained by thoughts of revenge, which he finally achieves after his release. Diaz-Marcano carefully allows this to occur in 1998, the 100th anniversary of the US acquisition of Puerto Rico.

REVOLT! echoes the structure of Nelson Denis's *War Against All Puerto Ricans*, a prose historical account which traces the swell and retreat of the Independence movement from the point of view of a sympathetic advocate.

As Diaz-Marcano was trying to connect the parts of his play, a history of this moment of popular revolt, the conflict over its meaning and significance, and the necessity of sustaining vengeance in the present, Denis's book served as a kind of structural outline for many of the key revolutionary events in 1950 as well as the other historical reference points.[79]

One key moment that establishes the protagonist's relationships and attitudes is Jose's early desire to travel to Ponce to participate in the ill-fated Revolutionary Cadets march. Jonatan advises against it, and after his attempts at persuasion are physically rebuffed, he reveals the plan to Jose's older sister Victoria in an act of unsolicited fraternal protectiveness that may have saved Jose's life. Jose's resistance highlights a tension between ostensibly protective betrayal and true responsibility and friendship that moves through the work.

Preventing Jose's journey to Ponce not only ensures his survival, it also explicitly educates him in possibilities for sustaining life under the colonial conditions of Puerto Rico. Rather than merely asserting her age as authority, Victoria shares her understanding of the structures of oppression and repression that are integral to being within a colonized space. Her metaphorical wisdom is offered as a specific strategy for playing Gallitos, a children's game with a long history.[80] Literally "roosters," Gallitos reflects a static kind of "cock fight" in which two combatants compete for dominance by swinging carob seeds with strings attached through holes in their center. You win by striking your opponent's seed with your own in such a way that it will break and fall off the side. Here, Diaz-Marcano uses a game played on stage in real time to manifest the connection between two siblings, through focused, physically intimate, engaged action. Jose loses because of his timidity and Victoria calls out his choice, insisting on the need to stand up in the face of potential risk because "part of being us is taking the hits.... You have to understand that."[81] She wants him to recognize that "Force is not everything. You have to learn to take the hits, learn to take the cracks, and then mold them into you. We take as many as we can, and we make it part of us. That way it doesn't hurt, it motivates you instead."[82]

This education in the need to take both a risk and a stand suggests the importance of finding a way to survive and sustain oneself, even when the terms of engagement are set up as an attempt to destroy the other. While strategy, skill, experience, strength, accuracy, and correct construction all play a role, Jose has not yet learned how to stand and fight, to take the hits in an asymmetrical conflict. Taking the hit and surviving is a form of resiliency, perhaps a necessary survival strategy in a colonized space where the outcome of the game is rigged; it is the first indication of Victoria's pragmatic sense of revolutionary responsibility, which contrasts both her father's drunken radical articulations of nationalism and Jose's own boyish fantasies of an easy revolutionary machismo. At the same time, the need for resiliency is itself a problem because it shifts the responsibility for dealing with colonial conditions from structural violence to an individual's ability to adapt and survive. At its most dangerous the pragmatic power of adaptive survival, the resiliency of a people, becomes a means to excuse and justify further exploitation and colonial violence without recompense, as political anthropologist Yarimar Bonilla has argued in relationship to the post-Maria rhetoric of resiliency in Puerto Rico.[83]

Victoria's wisdom on the nature of Boricua identity holds up even further if we extend it to Jonatan's despair and later fatal betrayal when he and Jose return from the United States to Puerto Rico in 1950. Their return to the island serves to highlight fault lines across conceptions of revolutionary action. The play makes clear the misconception of everyday life in the archipelago that Jose and Jonatan hold based on their experience of everyday discrimination in New York.[84] The changes to the relationship between the US and Puerto Rico had little impact on daily life in New York, where the "Puerto Rican Problem" was a regular news item, reflecting a perception of anti-Puerto Rican sentiment conceived within the same framework as anti-immigrant sentiment directed toward real and perceived impacts on labor.

The key change was the ostensible freedom of a locally elected governor, a shift that would allow the US to claim a level of autonomy for Puerto Rico in the language of a commonwealth relationship to displace scrutiny and resistance from other nations. The approval of this new relationship in the UN was enabled in large part because of a shifting in the voting practices in which the recommendation of a security council member held sufficient weight to overrule objections from a number of hemispheric nations and other new socialist governments around the world.[85] As Denis further describes in *War Against All Puerto Ricans*, which serves in many ways as a primary prose source for the structure and storytelling of some of the key issues of the 1950 revolt,

> As soon as the bill for P.L. 600 was introduced in the 81st U.S. Congress, the State Department began lobbying in favor of its passage. A letter for example, from Asst. Secretary of State Jack K. McFall to Sen. Joseph C. O'Mahoney, the relatively progressive Chairman of the Senate Committee on Interior and Insular Affairs, urged passage "in order that formal con-

sent of the Puerto Ricans may be given to their *present* relationship to the United States" and cited the pending constitution's "great value as a symbol of the basic freedom enjoyed by Puerto Rico, *within the larger framework of the United States of America* (author's emphasis)." Secretary of the Interior Oscar L. Chapman also sent the Chairman the written reminder that "the bill under consideration would not change Puerto Rico's political, social, and economic relationship to the United States."[86]

The explicit admission of the continuation of the status quo, providing merely local autonomy, was further undermined by, at least according to some scholars, the use of FBI files to control the behavior of the newly elected Governor, Muñoz Marín. Marín's victory over the more dynamic independence figure Pedro Albizu Campos resulted in a political shift away from a broad commitment to armed revolution as a means of reasserting rights in the face of presumed capital investment that would improve the everyday lives of Puerto Ricans on the island. As discussed in the Introduction, this was a potential act of pragmatic liberation in the moment, but one ultimately doomed.

As the Radical Nationalist/Independent history of this moment goes, Muñoz Marín was neither committed to the idea of independence nor was he above being sold to the Americans. His leadership instituted in the most radical legislative assault on Puerto Rican identity to date, Law 53, the Gag Law, which made the ownership and display of the Puerto Rican flag illegal. The increased FBI surveillance under the direction of J. Edgar Hoover, and the massive expansion of secret files, are all documented in Denis's account, which takes its title from a quote issued by Chief of Police Riggs, who insisted on declaring a war against all Puerto Ricans. This violent premise of policing in the service of maintaining order and the status quo shared the same dismissive logic that allowed the Ponce Massacre to occur. Apologists for the FBI might assert the necessity of this intervention given that many of the actions of the 1950 revolt and the subsequent and ancillary events on the US mainland were framed as acts of terrorism; however, for most contemporary historians the distinction needs to be made between attempts to secure independence and acts of terrorism, some of which was rectified in the pardoning of the Puerto Rican 5 by President Carter in the late 1970s.

Jonatan's political education accelerates in the US when he realizes his father was disappeared by the FBI in Puerto Rico, highlighting the *carpetas*, the Spanish word for files used to describe the concealed records that various branches of the police held on independence sympathizers, often in explicit coordination with the FBI. Jonatan compares the repression of Puerto Rican independence activists to the internment of Japanese Americans and starts speaking Spanish, moving away from an assimilationist logic to a space of radical independence. His politics shift in large part from personal loss—the death of his American mother and her revelation of his father's fate—moving toward independence, which includes a shift in language practice to Spanish as well as an insistence on returning to Puerto Rico to participate in the necessarily fomenting revolution.

Jose and Jonatan's flight from discrimination in New York encounters a furtive movement, and Jonatan's dream of a popular rebellion supported by a majority collapses in the recognition that the world has changed and that his view of Puerto Rico from the US does not reflect the experience of the average individual on the island.[87] In this environment, the possibility of meaningful revolution is a difficult dream, especially with strong support from federal forces, including the FBI, working to undermine these revolutionary groups to ensure domestic tranquility. As Victoria warns, "People no longer think about independence, but about the economic handouts the mighty government can give them. Marín has them talking about playing ball, giving in into their rules. He won. They won. For now. Gotta be careful."[88]

While "for now" suggests the always speculative future independence, this idealism is partially balanced with a problematic assumption that visibility itself is sufficient to enact, an optimistic ideal that implicitly assumes a broad awareness of structural injustice would lead to calls for change. The fear for the *independentistas* is that the struggle for hearts and minds is the work of rhetorical and economic power—who gets to frame the conversation, who listens to what, and what benefits accrue to an individual for any given choice. For them the essential betrayal of the principle of Puerto Rican freedom occurs through a shift of desire from a general sense of respect to the possibility of economic security in the present, while disguising and devaluing any historical narrative that understands the current economic problems to be the result of extended colonial practice. It is important to remember that pragmatic politics is necessarily liberatory and that one of the challenges is balancing the competing pressures of self-interest and protection for those closest to us.

Jonatan's revolutionary fervor is idealistic, deliberately blind to the conditions of his own involvement based on self-interest where the courage to take revolutionary action toward change is only tenable when he can see a clear pathway to radical transformation. As such, it disappears as quickly when no immediate clear pathway to success emerges; when, in an inversion of their first conflict, Jose wants to stay rather than leave, Jonatan betrays his family to governmental forces in an attempt to save him. The result, Victoria's capture, her husband Tito's murder at Jonatan's hands, and Jose's wounding and incarceration, highlights the problematic logic of Jonatan's attempt at playing savior.

This betrayal is the catalyzing incident for the Quique's (Jose's older self) desire for revenge, only possible in 1998 with his release from prison. His desire for a gun, which is the first major action of the narrative, is initially resisted but broadly accepted once the nature of his specific goal is understood—the fundamental justice of revenge for the death of his family. Quique's need for revenge persists in a time out of joint, marking the sustained weight of betrayal as ongoing feature of the political experience of Puerto Rico. The playwright's choice to place the events in 1998, the same year as the infamous status referendum in which "none of the above" triumphed, as well as the 100-year anniversary of the US acquisition of Puerto Rico, reflects the exhaustion of colonial violence.

The specific temporal choice places this outside of the late 1970s timeframe for the call for liberation for freedom fighters, the Puerto Rican 5 incarcerated in US jails as well as the attention placed on the Cerro Maravilla murders, which exposed to public view the secret files held by Puerto Rican police intelligence.[89] Ironically, Jonatan is traceable because he is celebrated for his work as a police officer, someone who maintains law and order in opposition to the alternative forms of civic participation offered by revolutionary groups such as the Young Lords, whose work is highlighted in the encounter between Quique and Jorge, his nephew-in-law.[90] In a moment in which the very structure of policing itself is under scrutiny for its inherent racism and violence, Don Jony's attitude reflects a refusal to acknowledge the harm enacted by policing. The announcement of his public celebration in the National Puerto Rican Day parade crucially affiliates him with this spectacle that advances questions of culture at a remove from political contestation. By invoking this cultural ritual that stresses the politics of representation and is supported by neoliberal power brokers who work in the interest of Puerto Ricans in New York, the play calls attention to its doubled status as a form of community celebration and a potential counter to forms of liberatory politics.

The last third of the play takes up the lingering effects of the intimate violence and betrayal. In this space, Quique, having survived the carceral space by investing in revenge, moves into present tense storytelling in which different structures of loyalty and the relative importance of risk and sacrifice as sustainable values are placed into question. Jony's betrayals are complete in large part because in the end he wants a world in which it is possible to have authority, power, and control, one in which you can keep those close to you safe, rather than a world in which transformative possibilities remain clearly on the table.

The staging of their confrontation is accomplished by wheeling Jony's restrained body in a wheelchair covered by a Puerto Rican flag. In a pointed reference to the repressive work of the Ley de la Mordaza, Quique briefly savors the spectacle of making Jony's betrayal visible, but he hesitates, they converse, and Quique even engages a spectral figure of his sister in the process. Jony's critique of Quique's intended revenge, "All they will see is another murder and another killer,"[91] reiterates the necessity for establishing the specific frame under which the conditions of transformative revolutionary violence can be seen as such. Jony tries to justify his actions in relationship to a community rather than his own self-interest, but a bifurcated attitude dividing the Puerto Rican community into us and them emerges in his response. More important is Quique's self-recognition of his entrapment: "A whole lifetime gone on the thought of one day being able to put these jump cables on your nipples and let them rip your soul. Tied to this forsaken moment. On an endless loop."[92] Despite this sustained investment in the death and torture, in the end Quique is incapable, or saved from, personally committing an act of dehumanizing violence. His reprieve comes in the form of a conversation with his dead sister, a familial connection, who insists he has more important work to do—writing and sharing his story in letters, enabling it to live and breathe, moving family history forward rather than trapping it in a static loop of revenge. The act of writing, narratively shared, is crucial as a step sideways to sustain relationships despite the inertia of the desire for revenge.

As The Narrator suggests at the end of the play,

> You asked me to come do a presentation about my heritage. About what it is to be Boricua. To tell our history is to dig deep into our roots. Into our own individual stories and share them. It's where the old Puerto Rico exists. It's in our blood that the real history of the island is written. Our strength and honor, it's in our voices. My mother was pregnant with me when he came back. Back from traveling around America looking for himself like a teenager. Looking for the man that was left behind, and stood

him up. Got himself a new purpose. Writing finally got him what he wanted. He got to be heard, but then he realized there was also a part missing. And I got to enjoy him because of it.[93]

While The Narrator extends the experience into the contemporary present, the weight of family history still structures the terms of engagement. The desire to write and tell stories becomes the site and root of Puerto Rican culture in its most authentic and meaningful sense. This pragmatic sense of the insistence on the need for historical context, for a longer form of narration and storytelling in its embodied complexity, makes clear theater's important role in instantiating an audience capable of grasping the implications the very stakes of what is taking place. Radical performance and radical action can reach communities directly impacted by events. And those with shared political horizons can reach understanding because of existing structures of experience and institutional forms of education. But theater's expanded realisms provide a compressed account of a dramatic world with a particular coherence of relation, a particular why that is well served by ambiguous, speculative endings acknowledging both the possibilities and the limits of transformation in the grounded inertia of the real.

And the choice to become a writer, along with the refusal of explicit gun violence suggests that the fantasy of the spectacle of disrupting the Puerto Rican Day Parade with a dead body wrapped in a Puerto Rican flag with Vendio written on it is just that—a powerful and fantastic image whose impact can be retained in the space of the imagination, the space of writing. This is not a refusal of radical revolutionary action, but rather a recognition that the forms of scripted theater itself occupy a default space of explanatory encounter, a need for exposition as an essential component, that provides the necessary limits in which to press questions of the possible. Despite recognition of the ultimately unproductive nature of spectacular violence Jony is still killed, without attention and without attribution, avoiding a saccharine sense of forgiveness and the elision of justice.

The structure of the play acknowledges that the spectacular act of revenge could only be anti-climactic for an audience unless it was staged for an audience already steeped in decades-long repressed resentment—a form of wish fulfillment for already committed revolutionaries. While this could certainly be staged, the realization would move away from the difficult pragmatic realities of surveillance and disappearance—that you always give up something to get away. In this version, fully realizing the desire for revenge would slip into the alternate contextual space of fantasy, giving up the hard-earned lessons of the persistent labor of political work.

This is not to refuse the possibility of the spectacular act (and I certainly must admit a fantastic desire for such things, combined with my current lived refusal to enact them), but rather to recognize that the performative work of such a spectacular act may not effectively disrupt systemic structures of oppression beyond surface transformation. Understanding this requires educating the spectator into the recognizing meaning and possibility; constraints on our horizons of political thinking are more often transformed by changing the story around the staging of the event rather than simply the event itself. Episodic events chart a particular path through historical moments, but these very events are the kernels that carry the structure of theory that opens the autonomous possibilities of Puerto Rico. Here, Diaz-Marcano, taking the feminist idea that the personal is the political, reframes this autonomy in specifically Puerto Rican terms, suggesting that by its very nature as a colonial territory, Puerto Rican identity is always political, whether those conditions are realized or acted upon in explicit ways or not. And more importantly, he offers the critique, very much in the model of the logic of *bregar*, that while spectacular actions of activism may be necessary, the real work of transformation occurs in the storytelling that reshapes the frame and understanding of the possibility of a different form of liberation—away from the static weight of history and toward a new view of relationship autonomously generated through dramatic storytelling.

CHAPTER 2

Symbolic Action as Pragmatic Politics

LOLITA ON THE STAGE

One of the unexpected outcomes of the failed insurrection of January 6, 2021, was a brief media recollection of March 1, 1954, the last time the sanctity of the U.S. Congressional chamber was violently breached by advocates of political change—Puerto Rican nationalists Dolores "Lolita" Lebrón, Rafael Cancel Miranda, Andres Figueroa Cordero, and Irving Flores Rodriguez. While some of the participants in the 2021 storming of the capital were intent on disruptive violence against property and person, to prevent official certification of the 2020 presidential election, others seemed to regard their unlawful entry as a symbolic act of resistance, with little coordination and a great deal of emphasis on the use of costume and props reflecting a cacophony of white supremacist ideologies.

Unlike this mob with heterogeneous intentions ranging from the tactically violent to the carnivalesque, the Puerto Rican nationalists shared a clear intention to focus attention on US colonial rule over Puerto Rico under the problematic status of "free association." Accepting the status quo under another name threatened to conceal Puerto Rico's ongoing colonial condition situation for the average mainland citizen; this action was intended to highlight the problem through a spectacular act of protest. Witnesses reported hearing "Puerto Rico Libre" and "Viva Mexico" as the activists[1] unfurled a Puerto Rican flag and opened fire with pistols from the House Gallery. The shots disrupted a congressional roll call for a contested piece of legislation focusing on Mexican farmworkers.[2] Five members of Congress were injured, one seriously; however, Lebrón carefully framed their act as a symbolic blow against the tyranny of US colonialism, arguing that their goal "wasn't to kill. It wasn't even to scare. . . . It was just to bring the attention of the White House to Puerto Rico."[3] In media interviews and judicial proceedings she deliberately connected their actions to Oscar Collazo and Griselio Torresola's 1950 presidential assassination attempt in conjunction with the short-lived

El Grito de Jayuya. Lebrón later famously claimed "Yo no vino a matar, vino a morir" "I came here not to kill, but to die." Her iconic statement and cool presence made her an enduring symbol for Puerto Rican nationalists and an enigma for the US press; her stated intention was taken seriously enough that she was charged with five counts of assault with a deadly weapon but unlike her companions, not with an intent to kill.[4] Her validated claim situates her action within the framework of pragmatic liberation because of her deliberate unwillingness to inflict collateral violence, grabbing national attention for the cause of liberation without loss of human life. Though certainly not non-violent, Lebrón's actions suggest a model of commitment that recognizes the necessity of struggle, the power of symbols, and the collateral dangers of radical violence.

The most recognized 20th century Puerto Rican freedom fighter, "Lolita" Lebrón was a powerful symbol of resistance not only for independence thinkers and activists in Puerto Rico and its diaspora, but for a range of liberation advocates across the Caribbean, Central and South America. Admired by anti-colonial and anti-imperial liberation thinkers, her investment in spirituality was a point of contention for many deeply focused on changing structural and material conditions. After she was released from prison, an outcome she resisted at times to avoid accepting the legitimacy of US authority over her fate, she continued her activism in more explicitly non-violent terms, serving as an active participant in the resurgent protests over US military bombings of the island of Vieques following the death of Puerto Rican security guard David Sanes Rodríguez.[5] The tension between myth and the reality, and between the call to action and the real impact of the act are crucial questions in pragmatic liberation. The personal complexities that arise precisely because of Lebrón's survival as opposed to an act of spectacular martyrdom, provide a necessary contrapuntal counterbalance to more utopic conceptions of revolutionary action grounded in notions of ideological consistency and purity of purpose.

While theater offers a counter to authoritarian and censorious governmental control, and its potential impact to transform large groups through live, simultaneous reception made it a prime site of censorship in South American and Eastern European countries under authoritarian control, such concerns emerge less frequently in presumptive democracies like the US where theater is rarely imagined or feared as a site of eruptive oppositional political action. The more radical Latin American political theater emerging during the 1960s and 1970s often preferred collectively devised work than plays scripted primarily by individual playwrights. Enrique Buenaventura, Emilio Carballido, and the Peruvian collective Yuyachkani, for example, all saw theater as a site of liberatory politics, but were not interested in traditional stage forms, sensing their potential distance from contemporary political concerns.

This investment echoed the work in the 1960s of the new social movements in Latin America and the civil rights social justice movements in the United States, in which collective theater practices fostered a critical lens on culture, understanding the world not as a fixed system, but as a constructed reality generated and maintained by forms of power: state, institutional, communal, and individual. Much of the theater practice intended to shift state and institutional thinking was predicated on the engagement of the communal and the individual, and at the center of many of these innovative practices is an investment in, and reimagining of, the work of German playwright and theorist Bertolt Brecht. His notion of framing the world in the theater as something that can and should be changed influenced theater practitioners from Luis Valdez of El Teatro Campesino to Augusto Boal of Arena Theatre and forms a central thread of much revolutionary theater thinking. But, as Diana Taylor reminds us in her overview of Brecht's influence on revolutionary theater in Latin America, there is no singular influence or clear direct uptake; rather, there is an adaptation or "transculturation" of the ideas that reflects the deep influence of acknowledging specific local realities in which questions of race, gender, and culture are more important than class.[6]

While the potential to imagine a new world, and the capacity to take action is constantly rehearsed in multiple theatrical spaces, desirable forms of radicality memorably encounter the limits of alternative forms of action and protest when they encounter the danger of explicit violence as the necessary continuation of revolutionary action. This knife edge is a source of frustration for some and a necessary negotiation always. When Augusto Boal was offered a rifle after facilitating a theatrical exploration of revolution, he had to clarify for the eager revolutionaries he was ostensibly educating that this was not his path. He was doing theater, exploring possible pathways for moving but not participating actively in violent revolution.[7] While this encounter certainly changed the way he thought about theater, it is clear that drama is rarely, if ever, capable of sustaining revolutionary action in and of itself. Nonetheless, its liberatory potential is continuously invoked by the possibility that efficacious change can be meaningful when material or symbolic. This tension around the weight and value of the symbolic, the intersection of rhetorical and physical force suggests a more nuanced account of action as such, which is always being negotiated. In this sense, the process of negotiating, of handling, of manipulating, of struggling, of the multiple fields through which *bregar* can traverse in Quiñones's figuration and everyday Puerto Rican practice is crucial. It protects and sustains the complex need for a liberated future, not as an empty exercise of language divorced from action, but as the much more intricate and ambivalent pathway of movement forward that slides around without naively dismissing existing limits. The complexity of this negotiation is often dangerously misunderstood as a pragmatic capitulation, an acceptance of material conditions in the present in exchange for an immaterial future possibility, but this is not the case. Instead, it reflects a basic understanding of embodied performance studies, the simultaneous existence of tension, opposition, and confluence in action, which is the root of drama as a concept.

In *Ricanness: Enduring Time in Anticolonial Performance,* scholar Sandra Ruiz argues that the historical Lebrón "shakes the very leveling ground of democracy, gender, race, sexuality, and humanity, offering her death not as a melancholic, mad subject, but as one compelled by a metaphysical conviction to transcend unsovereign oppression."[8] For Ruiz, Lebrón's historical biography is subject to conventional misogynist tropes of the beauty queen (which she literally was) and the femme fatale (which she was not). Ruiz's reading, deeply inflected by Lacanian psychoanalysis, argues for moving beyond the "dynamic projection [of] Lebrón, the beautiful, mysterious femme fatale and mother of the nation [that] fulfills the fantasy of the body politic, enabling a new metaphysical corporeality through her mortality—a way of being-in-the-world that translates the call for death as an antidote to pathology and suicide."[9] This necropolitical reading situates Lebrón's ability to control the terms of her death as the only power she has access to under colonialism. While her intended martyrdom was thwarted as she was arrested rather than killed after discharging her bullets, there is rhetorical and iconic power in the image of this woman discharging her pistol in Congress, the space that controls Puerto Rican civil rights.

Crucially, the dramatic treatment of Lebrón by Diasporican playwrights deliberately moves beyond this singular moment, delving into alternate aesthetics and modes of historical knowledge to situate her within the longer complex history of Puerto Rican colonialism; in doing so, they validate her catalytic and sustaining role in liberatory action through a lifetime in negotiation rather than transfixing her in place for one political act.[10] Discharging a pistol in public was not the beginning or the end of a story about this revolutionary woman. Lebrón's material and symbolic complexity, explored through dramatic worldmaking, allows for an effective amalgamation of multiple time streams and voices, especially as dramatists craft avatars of radically different historical manifestations that allow not only for polyphonic visions but highlight the shifting complexity of her political thinking. They willingly acknowledge her beliefs that extend beyond everyday experience, incorporating the difficult reality of her consistent spirituality. The plays remind us that her commitment to the decolonization of Puerto Rico was unwavering, but her personal domestic choices were often the subject of critique..

While in the first chapter we experimentally shifted the trajectory of diasporic Puerto Rican drama to highlight attention to revolutionary action in more contemporary work, in this chapter we will analyze the history of Puerto Rican political resistance from the standpoint of an iconic figure who lived in both Puerto Rico and the diaspora. In doing so we focus on two plays emphasizing the complex intersections of her lived biography and her extended, transformative impact and briefly explore a third. The first, Migdalia Cruz's episodic biographical drama *Lolita de Lares* (1995), intersperses moments of her life both before and after her most famous action with key moments of Puerto Rican colonial history using three avatars. The second, Desi Moreno-Penson's *Beige* (2016), centers a young Diasporican journalist negotiating her relationship to identity and politics through multiple manifestations of Lolita Lebrón, both real and imagined. The shared dramaturgical impulse to stage multiple avatars enables a polyphonic presentation of the material and the metaphorical, acknowledging the continuities and shifts in Lebrón's political attitude and actions over time, privileging the pragmatic human reality of change over the static fixity of an ideological symbol. The last and most recent play, *Notes on Killing Seven Oversight, Management and Economic Stability Board Members* by Mara Vélez Meléndez emphasizes Lebrón's continuing catalytic force driving anti-colonial resistance.

Of Lares—Imagining Bodies in the Threads of Revolutionary Geography

The title of Nuyorican dramatist Migdalia Cruz's most explicit play about Puerto Rican liberation, *Lolita de Lares* (*Lolita*) references Lebrón's birthplace, which she shares with the briefly successful Puerto Rican revolution in 1868, El Grito de Lares, foregrounding her connection to revolutionary history through a shared invocation of place. Commissioned in 1995 by the Chicago Latino Theatre Company while Cruz was playwright in residence, the play was also produced in 2016 as a part of UrbanTheater Company's 10th anniversary season, along with José Rivera's *Adoration of the Old Woman*, a play we will explore in Chapter 3.

Moving away from the melodramatic realism of *Palm Sunday* and the clearly framed parallel story structures of *REVOLT!*, *Lolita* employs a range of theatrical techniques to explore the more than 500-year history of Puerto Rico's colonial condition and the multiple complexities of Lebrón's identity. Spanning twelve locations in six cities on both the island and the mainland, the play moves episodically in non-linear time jumps between historical and fictional moments. Cruz employs a chorus of reimagined Vejigante figures and a Dream-Tour Guide to frame broader oppositional viewpoints that shape the complex representational and material histories underlying the continuing colonial condition and Lebrón's decolonial, liberatory position. The play intersperses quick vignettes dramatizing the violent first contact with Europeans with various shifts in colonial power including the economic damage of enforced monocrop agriculture, first coffee and then sugar. Cruz's doubled investment in this history presents it as a continuing violent farce while acknowledging the destructive impact of callous, unreflective operations of power.

Cruz's play offers three different historical avatars to contrast various well and poorly intended attempts to fix Lebrón's identity in place. The play presents Lolita not as an individual, but as a multiplicity of possibilities inflected deeply by the weight of colonial history, recognizing and destabilizing Pedro Albizu Campos's claim of her transcendent impact on Puerto Rican liberty. Moving back and forth between her adult life in prison, Lolita Mujer, her memories as an old woman, Lolita Anciana, and her formative years as a child, Lolita Niña, Cruz pragmatically argues that despite the importance of her action in Congress, change is not generated from a single spectacle, but the full arc of a life in its given circumstances.

The play's movement across historical moments highlights multiple catalysts for fomenting a revolutionary consciousness, showing both the long roots of colonialist economic and military domination, and their manifestations in contemporary cultural attitudes of touristic dismissal. In one explicit scene of education, Ramon Betances and Mariana Bracetti, leaders of El Grito de Lares in 1868, show up as ghostly figures in Lolita Niña's elementary school classroom, replacing the US flag with the Puerto Rican, and framing the displacement of the Spanish authority in Puerto Rico in the interest of securing military advantage for the United States. This education has a temporal urgency to resist the forces of Americanization actively driven through curricular pressure to shift what might otherwise be an independent, nationalist spirit, into something distorted and in the service of a colonial form of extractive and reductive tourism. Betances tells the children that "Lares has its own flag" because "It's the place where the dream of a free Puerto Rico was born."[11] Echoing a fierce view of independence, he centers the autonomy granted by Spain just before 1898, insisting "the Spanish lost. Gave up all its territories in the New World. But the one thing they didn't give was Puerto Rico—because they had already given us our freedom."[12] This language is consistent with Lebrón's own later practice during incarceration of refusing to acknowledge US authority over her to the extent of resisting a prisoner exchange offered by Cuba.

The school children answer their own question about the US acquisition, recognizing Puerto Rico's strategic military importance: "it's a good place to put armies."[13] US military personnel viewed it as a necessary point of control for Caribbean shipping lanes and military investment continued throughout the 20th century.

Lebrón's activism is grounded historically with an account of the devaluation of Puerto Rican life by the US military. The play's anecdote is the tragedy of a young boy killed at the fort when he bites on a bullet left sitting around and the minimal compensation deemed appropriate—two pigs and $500. These 1935 dollars would be worth merely $9500 in 2020. This cavalier attitude of the US military toward Puerto Rico and the disposability of Puerto Rican life are keystones to understanding Lolita Mujer's iconic revolutionary act as well as Lolita Anciana's post-incarceration activism (she was released from prison in 1979 with a pardon from President Carter).

This account of her revolutionary development, less a psychological study than an assemblage of context that generates the conditions of experience on a larger structural and systemic level, provides a counter to some accounts that Lebrón's investment in revolution occurred only after her movement to New York and her encounters there with Albizu Campos. Instead, it acknowledges the reality that she was always in an environment that valued and fostered potential revolutionaries and questioning of the status quo. At the same time, it is clear that Albizu Campos was a deep influence on her thinking, especially as presented in her reaction to his speeches, and some scholars would continue to argue that her actions were done out of love for Campos.[14] While Cruz acknowledges this influence, she labels it "a love of the spirit."[15]

Cruz is deeply committed to fostering cultural knowledge to restore hope for transformation. According to her program note in the 1995 Chicago Latino production "The story of Lolita Lebrón is a story about the survival of dreams in a world that no longer tolerates idealism. Lolita gave me back my dreams, forced me, to look at my own politics, and, most importantly, fed my spirit and my soul. The journey of this play was a journey home."[16] Lolita as a dramatic subject offers the sustainability of the otherwise impossible, the unthinkable. Cruz's language recognizes the metaphorical and material return home as a means of shifting the terms of one's political dreams, as a necessary form of survival intimately attached to spirituality, which the work insists can never be disconnected from Lebrón's legacy.

The play begins and ends with the song "Piedras en mi Camino" [Stones in my Way] to highlight the difficulties of emotional connection and the desire to be driven by destiny toward connection. Lebrón remained an incredibly spiritual woman throughout her life, deeply invested in her Catholicism, which presented a problem for those individuals who wanted her decolonial thinking to be free from religious influence. But for Lebrón, her Catholicism and broader spirituality were part of a larger call toward restorative justice, which was carried out in a principled, daily practice. This configuration aligns with Cruz's own playwriting practice. According to cultural theorist and performance scholar Alberto Sandoval-Sánchez, "[b]y questioning the hegemonic horizon of expectations, she puts forward her own way of doing theatre.... Cruz has redefined Latina/o theatre's ars poetica and ideological framework" by "concentrat[ing] on exploring the human dimension."[17] It is through the act of centering individual daily practices and struggles that Cruz does political work.

He goes on to discuss the ways in which this action becomes a larger claim about the practice of theater and an insistence on an aesthetic that centers those too often marginalized: "For Cruz, Othering the stage means empowering those who inhabit the periphery, particularly Latina women trapped in a patriarchal order where the threat of violence looms. In a world of poverty they struggle to find their place, to find a home, to safeguard their cultural heritage, to stay alive in the most hostile environment at home and in the streets."[18] Furthermore, "in her plays Cruz gives dignity to the poor, to those not having a homeland, and to those having to live dangerously on the wild side, among the wreckage and debris of capitalist imperialism."[19] The centering of empowerment and dignity is understood primarily as a question of access to material resources, culture, place, home and homeland. Cruz herself insists, "For me, the search for home is continual, and a major preoccupation in my life and in the lives of my characters."[20]

The language, and associated effects and affects of the search, are another way of expressing necessary action within the operations of coloniality, the continuing dynamics of power generated by the project of coloniality/modernity. In his "Outline of Ten Theses" Nelson Maldonado-Torres defines "[m]odernity/coloniality [as], in fact, the catastrophic transformation of whatever we can consider as human space, time, structure, culture, subjectivity, objectivity, and methodology, into dehumanizing coordinates or foundations that serve to perpetuate the inferiority of some and the superiority of others."[21] It is the fundamental axis of sustained inequality. Cruz's pragmatic response to this condition is to assert the fundamental humanity of Lebrón as integral to her political meaning and action. In doing so, the necessity of her political position is made crystal clear, but this is never done in the absence of humor and the full spectrum of human emotion. Epic struggles are everyday struggles negotiated in unique and creative ways, with a sense of playful sideways motion as a means of shifting the terms of oppression.

This practice is illustrated in a brief moment repeated at the beginning and at the end of the play, set in 1979 in the disorientation of her release from prison. A "wacked out woman" makes a joke: "What is Puerto Rican luggage?" to which Anciana responds "Two plain brown shopping bags?" before being warned about government deception and then pondering "I wonder how long it'll take to get home," though in the repetition she leaves out the last three words, expanding the journey into a larger question of waiting for future transformation.[22] This exchange poignantly captures the absence of home and access to resources. On a simple yet profound level, her representational project serves as its own form of liberatory pedagogy by providing an impetus to begin a path toward accessing historical knowledge for a Diasporican population discouraged from acknowledging the complexity of their history because of the ongoing project of historically deliberate obfuscation.

In an interview posted on Tumblr from the cast of the 2016 production, Tamika Lecheé Morales who played the role of Lolita Anciana suggests:

> What I loved the most after reading the script was how motivated I was to research Lolita and the colonization of Puerto Rico and as I did I was shocked to learn the history of "The Gag Law" (La Ley de La Mordaza) that they placed on Puerto Rico for nine years which suppressed the independence movement in P.R. Not only were Puerto Ricans not allowed to talk or

write about an Independent Puerto Rico after being conquered and ruled by Spain for some 400 years+ but they couldn't even hang a Puerto Rican Flag in their home or they would be arrested and thrown in prison and how this incited The Nationalist Party. All of this could have easily been included as well but again Migdalia chose to reflect on what makes Lolita human like the rest of us and not on the one act that many believe define her.[23]

For Morales, playing Lebrón was a pathway to learn not only about her but her life context, to resituate her as a humanized political figure as opposed to a distant cultural icon. One of the powerful consistent realities of theatrical practice is not only the pedagogical and political impact on audiences, which can often be inconsistent and difficult to document, but on individual actors who participate in a deep and sustained engagement with imaginative and material worlds of the play. The affective transformation enabled by theatrical interaction becomes a real and often deeply sustained transformation for the political understanding of the individual actors working on the project. And while this transmission of knowledge is a much slower, less exponential form of dissemination, its slow and steady progress also works in cycles that enable multi-generational engagement, which can permeate a larger infrastructure of theater making.

A broad sense of the importance of learning history through productions is sustained in both offerings of the work in Chicago. Scholar and dramaturg Priscilla Page suggests that,

> Taken together, the 1995 Latino Chicago production and the 2016 Urban Theater production demonstrate sustained efforts by Latina/o/x theater artists to engage in creative activities that serve to educate themselves and their audiences in culturally-specific places of their own making. Their autonomy as artists match the liberatory aspirations of characters like Lolita, Betances, and Campos who they portray on their stages.[24]

And earlier she suggests, "This production served an act of remembering for the cast members, the company, and the playwright. Many of them shared that it was a point of entry into Puerto Rican history that they had not been taught elsewhere."[25] This form of embodied pedagogy deeply resonates with Lebrón's lifelong commitment to drawing attention to the history and situation of Puerto Rico.

The connective tissue in the play is at moments associative through objects and concepts facilitated by Vejigantes, a chorus of figures whose trickster qualities offer themselves as malleable figures. The desire for coffee as a culturally soothing practice leads to the account of the violent eradication of sugar and capital investment in coffee (and then subsequent disinvestment). The framing of Albizu Campos's speech in Spanish with the English of the Governor's authority extracting coffee sets up the lack of attention paid to the conditions of independence. According to Priscilla Page, writing before she witnessed a performance of *Lolita de Lares*, "She depicts dreamlike worlds and the emotional connections between her characters drive the action. Each world that she creates for these characters to inhabit demands a fluid and malleable stage space."[26] The Vejigantes help move beyond the secular history into a larger spiritual and cultural vision that transcends material conditions as they move in and through the expansive spaces of the work.

Labeled Azul, Tinto, Blanca, and Estrella, Cruz's Vejigantes reference elements of the Puerto Rican (and US) flag in a shift from their historical colors of red, yellow, and black. Associated with festivals in Loiza and Ponce, the Vejigantes are also recuperated as figures of Puerto Rico, not as the conquered moors and demons they were originally imagined and replicated in versions of the Fiesta de Santiago, but rather as figures of resistance, a means of creating a cultural and spiritual connection to Puerto Rico's African roots.[27] As described for a visual art exhibition at Taller Puertorriqueño in Philadelphia in 2013,

> Some explain their inclusion in the religious festival as a symbol of the ongoing battle of good over evil. . . . Loíza's population (primarily of African descent) views the vejigante as a strong, and unapologetic character with a history of survival and a connection to Africa . . . "this figure that is such an integral character in these festivals has become an iconic symbol that unifies and identifies the people of Puerto Rico" as a nationalist hero; a character that brings into focus issues of Latino identity; a creature that is used as a surrogate to discuss the life and death struggle of living with AIDS; For these artists, the vejigante has evolved into . . . the living incarnation of the Puerto Rican spirit with all its vigor, resilience and jubilant ferocity.[28]

In Cruz's deployment the Vejigantes are "masqueraders who hold the key to history, but can only sing or talk in rhyme."[29] Representing fragmented elements of Puerto Rican nationalism they extend beyond temporal and causal logics of realism into surrealism and stylized action. In one historical scene they symbolically destroy an indigenous Taíno with a crucifix wielded by a Spanish priest, who transforms into a bureaucrat while burying the Taíno in a cabinet and drowning his sorrows in rum. In other scenes they reference the bureaucratic violence of extraction in the service of wealthy comfort and unthinking demand, and the costs of increasing industrialized agricultural monoculture. The primary thread of their contemporary interaction is with the representational politics of the DreamTour Guide (DTG), initially presented as a dismissive flight attendant who continues to provide an exoticized version of Puerto Rico, ignoring conditions in the service of an idealized tourist narrative. Here, the Vejigantes' interventions derail canned speeches, drawing attention to the oversimplification and ridiculous logic that sustains the tropicalization of the tourist gaze while eliding the reality of ongoing colonial violence. In one spiel DTG describes the jibaro, for many a humble, agrarian peasant and a symbol of traditional Puerto Rican culture as a comforting source of simple acceptance and welcome: ". . . Lord!—the salt-of-the-earth jibaros—are so open and kind they'll ask you if you need help even before you realize you're lost. . . ."[30] But DTG's easy confidence collapses the minute her eyes are covered by Vejigante Estrella:

> See what I mean. See. See. I can't see anymore. I—I—I wish I knew who I was. Jibaros know who they are, because their life's so—well—because—well, they have no money to dream with. And dreams without money are—well, darn powerless. They have powerless dreams and that's well—it's kind of swell because they know they won't get anything. So, it's pure—yeah, pure (DREAMTOUR GUIDE *struggles to regain her composure as* ESTRELLA *finally uncovers her eyes.*) And, lord, how they love to dance.[31]

The ungrounded fragility of her touristic narrative is exposed by the simple act covering her eyes which also reveals her true blindness, the highly truncated limits of her political horizon. The experience of physical contact is processed as blindness, clarifying that she exists in a space of perceptual confusion relative to the Vejigante's existence. DTG's blindness, here a temporary condition generated by unrecognized and misperceived external forces, carefully mimics the blindness engendered by the colonial condition itself, the ways in which free association truncates the perception of both colonizer and colonized. Incapable of perceiving the source of her blindness, confusing an external imposition for a physical condition, suggests her distance from understanding. At the same time, the shift from a metaphorical use of "see" to a more literal one reinforces the careful connection between visual signs and meaning. The necessity and fragility of the visual surface, of the limited view shaped by the guide for the tourist, is implicated as part and parcel of the colonial project.

This critique is neither surprising nor particularly revelatory in context; what is more compelling is the anxiety produced by awareness of a lack of vision combined with a desperate attempt to maintain a facade of composure. Here, blindness leads to a more pointed recognition of the social injustice of inequitable power. And, in her search to justify the continued inequality, she stumbles toward something that will allow her to sustain the facade. She replicates the historical sociological reframing of a fundamental lack of opportunity as a lack of motivation and easy contentment. In this racist rhetorical gesture, the body of color has less and smaller dreams and is therefore happier and without care.[32] Her resolution, that they love to dance replicates a stereotypical expectation for performing brown and black bodies, mistakenly dismissing the agency and social performance enabled by embodied movement while invoking too familiar colonial tropes.

Importantly the play offers a form of redemption for this most explicit agent of extraction, though one still very much aware of the institutional restraints designed to preclude revolutionary action. The play has established the DTG as a doubled figure of a young nationalist Agnes, who recognizes Lolita Anciana in a Puerto Rican supermarket at the beginning of Act 2. In that exchange Lolita poetically asserts the possibility of radical transformation, shattering time and engaging memory.

DTG's return to a more authentic identity, a figure who speaks Spanish and has a complex relationship to the history of Puerto Rico not sanitized by pre-existing structures of colonial logic, is activated by participating with the Vejigantes in an act of cannibalism, consuming a figure of Uncle Sam earlier in the act, not as a form of incorporation but as a dismissal of power.

By consuming one's enemy, goes the old Carib logic, one gains their power and power over them. And it is important to consider the specifically American and Caribbean roots of the logic of cannibalism within the European imagination to see this as a particular form of radical reclamation both of indigenous history and of a different relationship to power/knowledge. Cannibalism as a gesture of freedom emerges elsewhere in Cruz's playwriting, as scholar Armando Garcia, in writing about the characters Cruz's play *Fur* reminds us, the protagonist "turns to cannibalism as the only expression of freedom available to her."[33] In talking about Cruz's characters Armando Garcia suggests, "Her account of their sociality is not about their position at the margins of US society. Rather, it is about social relations between people whose lives are organized primarily by race, unfreedom, and histories of colonialism."[34] This analysis insists that the concern is not merely a question of position but of coloniality itself which serves as a structure of social relations.

In this case, DTG's hunger to consume Uncle Sam enables a radical transformation, which initially results in Agnes being lost and then eventually brought into the revolutionary fold. This shift back and forth between the radical poles of a callously distanced DTG and a revolutionary nationalist encountering Lolita in everyday life at the grocery store suggests that every woman who recognizes Lolita has a potential for leadership and liberation. The ongoing difficulty is made clear by the explicit choice to replicate the action of visually transforming Agnes back into the DTG, but this transformation does not prevent her inclusion in the final tableau, as she is gathered into the center by the other actors, insisting on a necessary form of difficult inclusion that recognizes the potential fragility and protean nature of the revolutionary actor. It is an invitation to practice calling in rather than calling out as a means establishing interrelationality in a structure moving toward the decolonial. This choice of inclusion supports a necessary pragmatism in the establishment of coalitional connection. With hope, a Vejigante reveals to the DTG that her name is Esperanza, the sustenance of possibility becomes a pragmatic rather than an idealistic act. And while this gesture is deliberately programmatic, it is also offering a model that incorporates change despite the ongoing struggle. In the next section we will explore a more contemporary play that incorporates two temporal instantiations of Lolita Lebrón as catalysts for a young woman's political awakening.

Liberalism and Pragmatic Symbolic Action— Lolita's Shifting Influences in *Beige*

At the heart of Nuyorican playwright Desi Moreno-Penson's work is an exploration of the ongoing personal violent impact of colonialism in everyday life along with the need to move away from conventional rhetorics and thinking in political organization and action. We see this intersecting critique clearly in *Beige*, winner of the 2016 National Latino Playwriting Award, which centers the journey of Soledad Iglesias, a 20-something Boricua journalist catalyzed to political action as a result of real and imagined encounters with Lolita Lebrón. *Beige* continues the exploration of Lebrón's material and metaphorical impact on political awareness, offering a vision of Lolita as both revolutionary icon and breathing human as a means of negotiating pragmatic liberation strategies for resisting patriarchy.

As a playwright, Desi Moreno-Penson is best known for a style she has labeled Nuyorican Gothic, in which Nuyorican lived experiences are framed within the genre of horror; she has also explored the limits of liberalism in other works. We will take a brief glimpse at two of these plays as a means of exploring her approach before turning in greater detail to *Beige*. She describes one of her most visible works, *Devil Land*, "as a dark allegory of post-colonial angst."[35] This phrase, post-colonial angst, is Moreno-Penson's articulation of sustained coloniality, the obscured colonial condition that impacts atmospheric and environmental shaping of Nuyorican lives. *Devil Land* highlights the cultural entrapment generated by internalized colonialism through its physical space—a closed off basement with windows covered to avoid discovery. The work explores untenable and artificial relations emerging from self-hatred and a fear of sexuality. The resolution, in which a young woman frees herself from being kidnapped into a family, invokes spiritualist knowledge and the Taíno pantheon, along with a creature she fashions as Dr. Seuss's Grinch. In this play the artificially generated nuclear family is self-destructive not only because of violence of kidnapping, but also because it begins from a position of colonialist logic, which includes self-hatred and a fear of sexuality.

Not Like Us, a ten-minute play by Moreno-Penson and Noemi de la Puente that also employs images from Dr. Seuss directly comments on the limits of liberal activism by offering a crucial complaint about the failure of a particular breed of activists to recognize their own limitations and self-interest.[36] In this short play Cosita Una and Cosita Dos, thing one and thing two, conduct a series of interviews (they alternate taking on the role of interviewee) of politically active historical and contemporary women, finding them problematic in various ways, simply "not like us." Bouncing between more and less justifiable exclusions, Cosita Una and Cosita Dos isolate themselves from participating in any form of solidarity by being too precise about the terms of engagement, illustrating the self-constructed barriers that accompany the real challenges of engaging in intersectional activist work. The play ends with a large off-stage protest involving all the other women in a clear and pointed critique of the distance between rhetorical and practical inclusion. These more pointed examples of Moreno-Penson's thinking help situate the cultural politics of *Beige*, which integrates elements of both types of work in its exploration of the political education of Soledad Iglesias.

Beige takes place in an abstract space, its primary pieces of furniture several chairs, a stool, a projection screen and a "large cream-colored table" with a "tablecloth" that "strongly resembles the American flag (but it is not)"[37] that enable quick shifts between multiple locations. These visual signifiers set up key issues of identity and relationality. The color of the table, echoing but not exactly repeating the color of the title, points to issues of racialization and colorism within the space of Puerto Rican identity.[38] In the same way that the table is cream colored, but not dark, Soledad has a conflicted relationship to her own Boricua identity represented by the not quite flag. This existential identity crisis highlights the specifically sexist treatment she receives and fully embraces the complex intersectionality of a college-educated Puerto Rican woman journalist negotiating the racist, patriarchal world of magazine publishing in New York. The flaglike tablecloth, close to but definitely not an American flag, invokes the shared color palette of the flag of Puerto Rico, but it is specifically not that either, setting up a sense of abstract possibility in which a suggestive but not complete idea of America covers over the not-quite white material presence of the table itself. In this sense, the ambiguous sense of belonging is held in place in a flexible playing space that opens itself beyond the forms of contemporary realism into spaces of dreams and memory. This aesthetic choice is a crucial reflection of the generalized convention of setting this moment close enough to the reality to maintain a level of clarity for both performer and audience as we move from sparse abstract materiality to a temporally fluid space of mental reverie.

Soledad's own educated answers are placed into question, not only because of her recognition of the continued limits placed on her by patriarchal gatekeepers, but also by her own attempts to police the nature of her actions, her own forms of internalized colonialism that must be uprooted. The play explores her political awakening, following an interview with Lebrón, who exists in the play as Past and Present Lolita. It charts her conflict with three men, fiancé, boss, and brother, who see her political awareness and desire to act in transformative ways as a sign of mental illness. This diagnosis is not without merit, as she talks with visions of Lebrón as she decides her path forward, eventually going to a UN demonstration with a prop gun to spectacularly protest continued US military bombing in Vieques. The play ends with an ambiguous tableau, leaving open the risk and efficacy of her action.

According to Moreno-Penson:

> *Beige* is a surreal tale of self-identity and the sometimes-schizophrenic effects of post-colonialism. The play is set in 2001, very soon after the tragedy of 9/11, and tells the story of Soledad Iglesias, a young Nuyorican journalist who finds herself caught between the reality of her Jewish fiancé and the ideals of the notorious Puerto Rican Nationalist, Lolita Lebrón. Existing at the crossroads of history, reality, and cultural imagination, *Beige* is a cautionary tale of race, Puerto Rican politics, and love. . . . The notion of cultural identity, the intrinsic value of self-worth, it's parallel link to mental, emotional disorders, and the desire to immerse oneself in the dominant culture—thereby eradicating one's own cultural heritage in the process—continues to dominate my thoughts with regards to *Beige*.[39]

At the heart of this play is an exploration (and a necessary suspicion) of Present Lolita's claim that "(said . . . many times before) Cultural identity as far as Puerto Rico is concerned, has always been a political issue."[40] The parenthetical direction indicates not only the performance of a recognizable utterance, but also the simultaneous truth and formulaic emptiness of the claim. In a sense, Soledad's search for home is finding her own personal pathway through this connective tissue, a relationship she takes fundamentally to heart, not only because of the subject of her interview and article, but because it is through the political that she can claim a connection to culture and shared value. While she is clearly discriminated against for her gender and her cultural identity, she reads this initially solely as a gender issue within a basic framework of liberal feminism that sees the nature and crux of her struggle as an individual actor working against the resistance of individual men.

Soledad's process of self-discovery is shaped by her conversations with Lolita both as a living interview subject in 2001 in the months after 9/11, and as a dream figure she communicates with in an "alternate subconscious reality."[41] Through this complex relationship Soledad begins to define herself outside of the expectation and restrictions of men, and in doing so recognizes the revolutionary potential of her dream thinking that is framed by others as a dangerous psychosis. Central to this play is Soledad's revolutionary necessity driven by intersectional experiences of displacement and dismissal and emerging self-understanding through the reclamation of a revolutionary Puerto Rican identity embodied in the figure of Lolita Lebrón.

Moreno-Penson's two versions of Lebrón highlight not only the 1954 shooting but her prominent non-violent protest in support of Vieques activists, reinvigorated in their campaign to stop US Navy bombing on the island after the death of a Puerto Rican security guard, David Sanes Rodríguez from an unexploded munition.[42] Setting this work soon after 9/11 establishes the specific pressures of a heightened sense of belonging and patriotism that was radically fashionable even in liberal spaces that might typically adopt a posture of cynical distance to an earnest communal coming together, while nonetheless recognizing the continued limits of this practice of inclusion. Although not necessarily occurring immediately after 9/11, 2001 included protests at the UN advocating for the US military to leave the island of Vieques; this choice of historical conflation emphasizes the ways patriotic nationalism reinforces patriarchal structures that attempt to limit the horizon of activism. The invocation of Lebrón is heightened in the immediate aftermath of 9/11 because of her initial (and for many people continuing) label as a terrorist. As we have seen, when she was first arrested the mainstream US media labeled her either a terrorist or an assassin, even though some of the more progressive outlets were aware of her designation as a Nationalist supporter of independence.[43]

The men in Soledad Iglesias's life serve as obstacles and catalysts for change, forcing her to recognize the problems in the life she has adopted through their paternalistic refusal to allow her imaginative life of the mind to flourish. She is nonetheless constrained by the stereotypically reductive love of her fiancé, Dennis, who canceled their civil marriage ceremony after learning she was having visions of Lebrón from her brother Ralph. In addition, he has stripped away her identity as Solitude, transforming her into Solly and is happy to feel she "needs" him. Her brother, troubled by this change, insists Dennis understand her name—"Churches in solitude NOT solitary churches, okay"[44]—a poetic shift from solitary as a form of individual isolation, to solitude as the reflective power of being alone.[45] Dennis's easy liberalism has no capacity for dealing with the specifics of the colonial relationship of the US and Puerto Rico, and the appeal of an interview with Lebrón is unthinkable as he sees her solely as a terrorist, refusing the label freedom fighter. In a particularly cringeworthy attempt to ingratiate himself after a failed attempt to speak Spanish he suggests a painfully neocolonial sexual roleplay: "we'll play Spanish-American War ... I'll be the United States and you'll be Spain, remember? First one who cums gets to keep Puerto Rico."[46] His flippant global neoliberalism (Dennis after all writes for *Global Investor*) is not fully replicated by the other male characters, but it nonetheless shapes their horizon of expectation and experience.

While recognizing Soledad as a Boricua, her editor Larry nonetheless traffics in explicit stereotypes, comfortably naming his own harassment from an unquestioned position of power. His demonstrates a lived acceptance of structural racism and sexism that mitigate against progressive meaningful change. Larry's attempts to constrain and delimit both Lolita and Soledad come through his masculinist, misogynist reading of Lolita's initial rise within the Puerto Rican Nationalists in New York, meanwhile insisting that he cares nothing about her history, only her present investment in the Vieques protests. His condescending rendition of history reframes entrepreneurial creativity and pro-active problem solving as personal self-interest:

> ... now, she knew that to get anywhere in the party, they'd have to become friends ... or at least, friendly. Problem is, he never noticed her, which is weird 'cause she was a good-lookin' gal in her day ... won a bunch of beauty contests back in PR, right? .... Now Campos was a BIG coffee-lover, loved the stuff ... liked it sweet, real sweet, extra sweet! But there was never enough sugar at the meetings. It was the 40s, you know ... shit's rationed ... so Lebrón steals sugar cubes from her boss' pantry at the dressmaking factory where she worked, and brings 'em with her to the next meeting. When Campos asks for cup of coffee ... there's your girl; with a big ol' smile on her face, purse wide open, and lots and lots and lots of pretty little white sugar cubes inside! (Laughs) After that, they were the best of friends.[47]

This account highlights Lolita's pragmatic *jaibería* in establishing connection, but does so in a paternalistic, dismissive way, continuing the pattern of masculine dismissal.

While Soledad's younger brother Ralph maintains an anticolonial political and artistic stance, he equally aligns with patriarchal paternalism. Ralph's own explicit performance of supposed resistance insists on a stereotypical barrio history for external consumption, grasping for "street cred"[48] that belies his middle class, suburban home life, and lack of fluency in Spanish. Avoiding college to maintain this role, he claims freedom from the colonizing power and hegemonic reductiveness of institutional learning in his writing. But rather than framing his action as liberatory, the play suggests it as a form of personal marketing, a kind of liberal elitism trafficking in the potential rewards of crafting a particular form of identity. Oddly enough, despite the tension generated by Ralph's choices and his concern about his sister's mental health, in speculating about the potential reality of her visions, he insists that Lolita would be uncomfortable in Soledad's head: "Let's say this is all true, that this is happening . . . think about it; she can't enjoy being inside your head, right? All the clutter, the elitist bullshit—" and suggests that "maybe you should try telling her something that won't piss her off."[49]

This last comment is particularly ironic given the nature of Soledad's first real encounter with Lolita, which occurs in the first scene of play. It is an awkward encounter between a star struck young woman presuming she understands the ground on which she stands and an older woman no longer willing, if she ever was, to accept bullshit from others. In large part authorized and funded based on her contemporary activism around the now more highly visible situation in Vieques, the presumptive narrative Soledad has carried with her from the United States mainland can be summed up in her already crafted title "Puerto Rico: La Lucha (The Struggle) Continues."[50] As a Latina with some Spanglish she provides an immediate translation of the struggle, but interestingly sees the continuation of the work in English.

The power that Lebrón offers emerges in the ways in which her story also operates within the world somewhere between psychosis and an externalized dream. She fundamentally believes in the power of thought as a means of exceeding the horizons placed upon us. In a powerful confessional moment Soledad reveals

> SOLEDAD: but once, when I was still in college, I was taking an exam, I looked down . . . and instead of a pen, I saw an acetylene torch in my hand . . . the kind that welders use . . . (Looking down at her hand; nervous chuckle) . . . I remember I tried to strike it against my desk to light it.
> PRESENT LOLITA: And did you? Did you manage to light it?
> SOLEDAD: I think so . . . but only for a second. (Bad memory) They had to physically remove me from the room. I was disturbing the other students—
> PRESENT LOLITA: But if they hadn't moved you . . . do you think you would've been able to light it?
> SOLEDAD: I don't know. Why do you ask?
> PRESENT LOLITA: (proudly) I've had visions myself. It's exciting. [An ambient sound. On video screen: we see various projections of Taino imagery, complete with symbols, drawings, sculptures, etc.]

SOLEDAD: It wasn't exciting. It was frightening, terrible.
PRESENT LOLITA: (scoffs) Having visions is not terrible.[51]

The image is a powerful one, an acetylene torch that reflects both the potential intense heat and energy released by the torch; her hidden power, combined with Lolita's fascination with the vision, is viewed not as a problem, but as an opportunity. For Lolita, the question is whether she lit the torch and what it might have taken to do so. In a non-traditional figure of personal power, the notion of that searing white light, nearly impossible to view directly, but responsible as well for welding things together, creating connections, presents a powerful image of Soledad's latent potential. Her "bad memory" incorporates the social norms that resist this possibility as interfering with her conventional education in societal expectations. Present Lolita's attitude opens the possibility that Soledad needs to be willing to encounter the power of her visions and recognize them as a potential path for transformation. This comes as she critiques Soledad's double capitulation to the expectations of North American colonial power and masculinist stripping away of her cultural and authentic power rooted in her identity as a woman. Present Lolita acknowledges the ongoing colonial condition "that the UN encourages people to end by any means," simultaneously capturing Soledad's imagination and reasserting the justification for her 1954 act.[52]

The concepts of political action in *Beige* run in interesting parallels to the visions of both Lolita Lebrón and her granddaughter Irene Vilar, whose memoir and reading of her grandmother's work, *A Message to God in the Atomic Age*, highlights Lebrón's symbolic function and sustained religiosity.

> Lolita was to become the legendary woman who stripped herself of all "womanhood." A sense of offering, of sacrifice in all that she said and did, was always there. And her religiosity still amazes and disturbs many. My grandmother obviously saw herself as a martyr for the liberation of Puerto Rico. . . . when I listen to people of my grandmother's generation speak, not only in Puerto Rico or in Latin America but also in the United States, I realize how much they see themselves, many of them, in Lolita's "act." With apprehension, certainly, but also with some gratitude. For she "did it for them."[53]

This sense of identification is paralleled with Vilar's own experiences of mental illness that nonetheless retain a level of forceful power; Vilar talks about the ways that her dreams within dreams were dismissed by her psychiatrist, marking a clear institutional failure to understand the power of revolutionary dreaming. To be a revolutionary at some level is to be crazy, but only to the extent that the expectations of normative behavior make any other outcome impossible.[54] In her play, Moreno-Penson works in a much more psychologically grounded internal exploration of dreams and psychosis as a means of accessing the transformative power of Lebrón's revolutionary faith. In Moreno-Penson's version her religiosity is replaced by a mytho-history of Puerto Rico, a Taino rather than a Catholic imaginary.

Importantly, the only reason that Soledad is funded to interview the living Lolita is because of the media attention given to the protests over Vieques rather than her initial revolutionary act, which had faded from mainstream consciousness. Lebrón, after her pardon by Jimmy Carter in 1979, focused her activism on other forms of restoring Puerto Rican sovereignty, including the removal of the US military and the cessation of military weapons testing in such close proximity to the civilian populations of Vieques.[55] One of the two smaller islands of the Puerto Rican archipelago, until 2003 more than half of Vieques's land was taken up by a military base and weapons range testing live fire ammo. This ongoing testing, which exposed the other residents of the island to chemical and noise pollution and the material risk of unexploded munitions at a level of proximity that reflects the sustained disregard for Puerto Rican quality of life, is presented by most theorists as a condition of colonial citizenship or complete structural disregard.[56] While there were ongoing protests from Vieques fishermen spanning decades, the international community began a resurgence of interest in the project of getting the military off Vieques after "the death of Puerto Rican security guard David Sanes Rodríguez on April 19, 1999, who was killed by an 'errant' 500-pound bomb that was part of the navy's ongoing war games in Vieques."[57]

Despite the potential risks of reporting on the UN Vieques protest, which Dennis is concerned about merely because she plans to attend, Soledad determines to take action, though her path is once again negotiated through the constraints of a male gatekeeper. To get a press pass so she can enter the UN during the Vieques protest Soledad apologizes to her editor Larry, who both hits on her and relates his own experience of racism at Harvard, in the process acknowledging his relative privilege as well as the power of his willingness to endure in these spaces. Despite his hypocritical conflicted relationship to the operations of power, he helps Soledad come to terms with the limited reality of her relationship with Dennis—a relationship that makes no attempt to include her whole self in a deeply human engagement. Her recognition speech to Dennis clarifies this problematic ideal sustained by "nice"[58] liberals:

... you loved the idea, didn't you? Look at us ... we're perfect, aren't we? Progressive, liberal elites ... we lease a Buick LeSabre ... we own a timeshare in the Hamptons ... look at me; it's so GREAT to be a Latina now! I'm accepted, right? I'm the kind of light-skinned girl with good hair and generic speech that softens my Caribbean hips and forgives my African nose—[59]

Explicitly addressing her physical appearance in relation to conventional signs of African diasporic heritage, she condemns the limited acceptance that masquerades as inclusion and love. Her constrained performance of self sustains Dennis's own problematic liberal ideal. And she recognizes that the necessary gesture to counter these constraints and reassert her full self is one that is conceived as mad by the patriarchal establishment—but it is intended as life affirming, not suicidal.

This logic of liberalism is furthered when Soledad argues for a present logic in which she can find an in-between space, an identity she references as beige, which reduces the potential issues of racial discrimination and colorism into a bland "designer neutrality" that avoids colorful displays that have personality, various codes that mark the homogenous boredom of an ostensibly neutral but practically lifeless existence. And going further, she argues for the "recognition" of Latinos, of their weight and presence, that will take place, disputing the more brutal power of colonial forces that shape the reality of Present Lolita's view. This notion of recognition is a key gesture in a form of liberal claims to relationship between self and other, but in the process works to avoid conditions of necessary violence or radical revolution as modes of engaging with "the other."[60]

In many ways connected to larger questions around the politics of recognition and the ways in which that structure is imbricated in larger scale liberal logics, the notion that social power would lead to recognition comes very close to the dark side of Arlene Dávila's claims in *Latinos, Inc.* This work, which shows the ways Latine peoples are constructed as a consumer demographic with significant spending power, is too often used as a way of gaining cultural knowledge about a market group.[61] Recognition has an interdisciplinary conceptual history in literary studies stemming from Aristotle's basic dramatic structure of anagnorisis and is also deployed within the frame of liberal political theory where an end goal of political action is often conceived as some form of juridical or legislative recognition.

In a highly influential essay attempting to retain recognition as a necessary practice within ethical forms of liberalism, Charles Taylor outlines the ways recognition has developed as a resource for contesting cultural claims.

His fundamentally liberal argument is based on the reasonable assertion of "a premise that we owe equal respect to all cultures,"[62] the active practice of developing a potential understanding through a transcultural interchange, or as he frames it, as a Gadamerian

> 'fusion of horizons.' We learn to move in a broader horizon, within which what we have formerly taken as the background to valuation can be situated as one possibility alongside the different background of the formerly unfamiliar culture. The 'fusion of horizons' operates through our developing new vocabularies of comparison, by means of which we can articulate these contrasts.[63]

Disappointingly, Taylor subscribes to a particularly narrow form of liberal equality as a presumptive starting point that comfortably situates him within an oversimplified notion of encounter in a relatively limited way. He implicitly deploys the proximate anxiety of a lack of truth ostensibly predicated by the Derridean practices of postmodernism as an unnecessary foil rather than understanding Derridean practice as insisting on more radical and careful attention to the seeking of a rigorous and sustainable truth, even if that can never succeed. In more recent debates around the value of recognition and its function, philosopher and gender theorist Judith Butler, in an exchange with philosopher Axel Honneth, argues,

> There is a problem of equality that enters into the situation that precedes the scene of recognition, one in which many people, on the basis of their class status, gender, or the forms of racial stratification to which they have been subjected, struggle for recognition precisely by seeking to change the terms by which recognition is conferred. The subject who confers recognition depends upon the availability of terms, and those terms belong to a life of discourse and power that does not exactly parallel the life of the subject. The intersection of the two, however, is obviously crucial to the scene of recognition itself.[64]

This parallels the differently pointed decolonial critique from Lois McNay who insists that Honneth's reliance on a "rational universal" ignores,

> the creation, by capitalism, in its globalizing, neoliberal phase, of new types of social vulnerability and precariousness—many of which dispro-

portionately affect women—suggests that progress is not as straightforwardly cumulative and inevitable as Honneth implies, but rather a far more discontinuous, fragile, and staccato process. Gaps between formal and substantive freedoms may be mitigated in some areas, but, given the pace and unplanned nature of social change, they perpetually resurface in new, unforeseen guises in others.[65]

The simple ethical claim for recognition runs the risk of oversimplifying the complex matrix of subject formation and the structures of power that shape the encounter. While one version of the Hegelian encounter would insist that recognition incorporates a self-limit on the one enacting the recognition, a move that theoretically empowers, this recognition can be seen as problematic, not only because it is held by others in power who define the terms and legibility of recognition, typically in their own interest, but even in less cynical accounts there is still a horizon that reinforces the status quo. Thus, Butler and McNay insist on the necessary uneven and multiple layers of the process of understanding to more accurately attend to the differentials of lived experience.

The presumption that a particular recognition of status is at the heart of freedom and empowerment is precisely the problem with conceiving of a better life in terms of freedom in and of itself, as the question remains— freedom in relation to . . . ? It is in the distortion of the condition of Free, as in Free Associated State, which in part drives the insistence in this work of conditions and languages of liberation. The structures of freedom are to a large extent the products of an attachment to forms of liberal democracy that structure freedoms as individual goods, and the relative expansions of those freedoms in individual terms like Charles Taylor does in reimagining the politics of recognition in relation to issues of multiculturalism. And one might consider a simple model of recognition and its attendant politics of representation as symptomatic of liberal pragmatism. Liberal pragmatism is a familiar dramaturgy in theater and everyday life that minimizes the attention to structural change, emphasizing individual success and highlighting the psychological over the material.

Moreno-Penson's Lebrón insists on the inevitably political nature of identity, which has a deep investment in the political efficacy of visibility but is not as far removed from a simple notion of recognition as she would like to believe. The crucial difference that separates her position from liberal pragmatism is that she insists on the possibility of seizing recognition rather than receiving it, of asserting autonomous power and sovereignty over the self. The question that hangs next to the ambivalent work of this play is whether or not there is a meaningful search for recognition as such, or whether it is more useful to consider access to the conditions of whole life as manifest in the Butler's claims for performative assembly.[66] This rethinking of the conditions of political action and performative assembly toward the conditions of full life makes radicalism not the function of revolutionary action, but the recognition of a different starting point for the engagement with the other, a structure aligned precisely with pragmatic liberation.

Soledad's final solution points to the very condition of pragmatic liberation that becomes the only thinkable way forward for a kind of middle-class activist. Raised within the frameworks of assimilative liberal success, she recognizes the limitations of these forms but is unwilling to accept the conditions of radical violence as the necessary catalyst for revolutionary acts. Her fascination with Lolita, while singular in the play, is much more global; Lolita's impact cuts across both her anti-colonialist and her feminist positions. Rescripting herself as a contemporary copy of Lebrón, picking up Lebrón's own real and stated interest in the liberation of Vieques from the violence of the US military and its live fire exercises, she replicates the action of bringing a gun to a political space to crystallize attention on the issue.

Her process of decision making happens in part through self-reflexive dialogue with Past Lolita, who is explicitly "recruiting" her, arguing for her to use the prop gun and centering the importance of taking action: "I knew that by going through the action. . . . the action . . . it would be enough. (Short beat) It's about making a statement. Action is everything, mija."[67] The claim that action is everything is curious since the action that she is advocating is symbolic, designed to draw recognition and ideally catalyze change, but with no inevitable material consequences. This exchange is part of a larger contestation over appropriate action in the play. Moreno-Penson stages a debate between Past and Present Lolita at the end of the first act, establishing Past as impulsive and Present as more reflective, Past's singular focus resulting in the often-voiced critique of abandoning her children for the sake of revolution. Their debate draws an interesting series of theoretical readings of Lolita and her positionality, from the initial claim by Past Lolita that she died at the time of her action, echoing Ruiz's necropolitical reading, to Present Lolita's ability to materialize her visions on the theatrical stage, a series of rose petals that has a spiritual, potentially Marianist implication. Present Lolita's position is more pragmatic, but pushes the limits of inaction in its concerns:

Living in the world is tough enough without trying to save a small piece of it. . . . A small piece saved for someone who'll one day call you an arrogant whore. The price for being heard is too high. (By now, the shower of petals has come to an end.) The reporter's not like you. She doesn't share your politics. You will not turn her into a Nacionalista. You will not give her a gun . . .[68]

The question of risk is made explicit, along with a fundamental question about saving the world if one will not be valued for it. But more importantly, it is a question of whether moving away from silence and into a speaking position is ultimately worth the risk. While the historical Lebrón remained committed to an ideal of liberation and refused to capitulate to a recognition of US authority, thus lengthening her prison stay despite several attempts to negotiate her release, she nonetheless shifted away from spectacular violence, even symbolic spectacular violence as a meaningful source of consciousness raising.

While Lebrón came to Congress to die but not to kill, Soledad makes a different move, shifting from an understanding of the control over her own death to a symbolic action with a wooden gun. Using a prop gun ideally frees her both from the implication of carrying a dangerous weapon and materially will pass safely through the metal detectors in the lobby of the UN. While her fiancé Dennis can only see her plan as the product of mental imbalance and an unfortunate drive to suicide/self-destruction, Soledad does not intend that ending, though she takes the rather radical step of drugging her fiancé to keep him from interfering. While acknowledging the possibility of death, she holds a greater hope of effective symbolic political action, recalling the vision of Lebrón with a gun and setting that very gun down. The gun in this case is explicitly and intentionally theatrical, not in a sense intended to dismiss its rhetorical force, but as a means of guaranteeing the recognition of its symbolic function. But the presumption of this recognition retains a level of optimistic naivete, while simultaneously connecting her to both Past and Present Lolita, one willing to take a radical risk and the second very clearly advocating against violence.[69]

Soledad has not come to die, she has come to find a way home, to find an authentic relationship to her lived identity. She takes to heart Lolita's claim that Puerto Rican identity and culture is always political by authentically recuperating home through political action. Her re-staging of Lolita's action only goes so far as raising the gun within the frame of the play, accompanied by the projected demand for peace in Vieques. The final resolution is left open. Her a priori stated intention, to set down the gun and ask for peace, reflects a non-violent ideal but also only offers a vague solution to the specific removal of the US military presence from Vieques. It is a relatively easy political position because it does not address the impacts of the legacy of violence; it simply demands a change moving forward. It points toward an alternate futurity of peace that is presumptively outside of the inherent violence built into the structure of "free" association.

The results of Soledad's symbolic action—successful consciousness raising, categorization as terrorist or mentally ill, or death—are withheld in the shift to darkness to end the play. Though the US military left Vieques in 2003, they have not followed through on the necessary investment in environmental decontamination, in many ways echoing the ways Soledad's political gesture is left in limbo.[70] At the same time, Soledad has clearly entered a space of more authentic self-empowerment, exposing the ways in which Dennis's white Jewish masculinist fantasy of a Puerto Rican woman obscured her fundamental humanity, and clarifying how her self-reclamation is premised on the acceptance of and return to a form of wildness, of energetic power, repressed by the status quo. While the ending is not the bright utopia of an immanently successful revolution, it nonetheless sets up a pathway for authentic individual action that moves beyond the space of liberal recognition. Soledad exceeds the limiting frames of liberal recognition to move to a different and potentially more revolutionary way of being in the world based on her willingness to say no, to meet the world on her own terms, inserting sovereignty into the liberal practice of recognition moving it in the direction of liberation. In a profound reflection, John Holloway, suggests,

> We have to look at the people around us—at work, in the street, in the supermarket—and see that they are rebels, whatever their outward appearances. In the world of possible self-emancipation, people are not what they seem. More than that, they are not what they are. They are not contained within identities, but overflow them, burst out of them, move against and beyond them. The rebelliousness that is in us all starts with a No, a refusal of the alien determination of what we do, a refusal of the alien imposition of limits on who we are. From this No there arises also a creative charge, the drive towards determining our own lives, a drive no less ordinary than rebellion itself. We come together to complain and protest, but more than that: at the level of everyday gossip, in the back-and-

forth of friendship, in the comradeship that develops at work or school or neighbourhood, we develop forms of cooperation to resolve everyday problems.[71]

The potential radicality of the no is crucial as it offers a form of refusal which does not have to act in direct forms of opposition or resistance, but which can instead advance sideways, in an unexpected direction, to work toward larger goals.

However, connecting Soledad's transformation to the Vieques protests adds a level of ambivalence. The irony of the successful Vieques protests is that, for some, its emergence as an international celebrity cause generated momentum in a way that ignored the long history of local protest and US apathy. Crucially, the success was accomplished by "put[ting] aside the question of Puerto Rico's status and focus[ing] on the violations of economic, civil, and human rights in Vieques."[72] Though the Vieques "victory" was seen by many as a shift in practice and a potential resurgence for Puerto Rican activism, Juan Duchesne Winter argues exactly the opposite,

> Despite claims that the Vieques saga was fundamentally a victory of the 'Puerto Rican people,' I would argue that it exemplified the success of what can be defined as the 'political activist movement' in Puerto Rico. The political activists succeed not because they threaten dominant power structures but because they are able to secure an outcome that is beneficial to the current political elite, both on the island and in the United States, and to consolidate a political horizon that encompasses the demands already agreed upon. That is, this form of activism confirms the nation-subject, which in turn generates democratic consensus as a mode of consent to existing power.[73]

Based on Winter's argument the question remains: to what extent Soledad's theatrical act is potentially doing otherwise? And furthermore, to what extent does the resurgence of the individual as a potential radical actor in fact carry forward the necessary starting point of pragmatic liberation? Crucially, it must involve careful attention to given circumstances in a manner that moves beyond the acceptance and conventional and imposed political horizons.

This figuration fundamentally embraces the tension between radical action and rhetoric and the choices we can accomplish as individual actors, a tension crystallized in a very recent production that takes up Lolita as a potential pathway to contemporary violent activism. In the May-June 2022 Soho Rep production of *Notes on Killing Seven Oversight, Management and Economic Stability Board Members* by Mara Vélez Meléndez a "trans Puerto Rican woman ... style[s] herself after Lolita Lebrón" and decides to kill members of the PROMESA board.[74] According to Raven Snook's review:

> Like her idol, Lolita packs a pistol to disrupt politics as usual by infiltrating the Wall Street office of PROMESA—the Puerto Rico Oversight, Management, and Economic Stability Act of 2016—with the aim of assassinating those in charge of restructuring the island's unpayable debt. But when she faints on arrival, clearly unready to carry out her bloody plans, a queer Nuyorican receptionist (the persona-shifting, lip-syncing diva Samora La Perdida) offers to prep her for gory glory by serving up drag incarnations of each board member to castigate and kill.[75]

This shift from physical violence to drag send up is not a refusal of radical action per se, but a reconfiguration of radical action as necessary representation. Here the employment of spectacle, while shifting away from the aesthetic of realism, nonetheless retains politically important elements of the real. In Jed Ryan's account of the work,

> The audience is treated to masc and fem [sic] drag versions of PROMESA's Board members, with fantastic costumes and wigs accessorized by our favorite pop tunes. (In a bold move, the Board members' real names and VERY telling real biographies are used, although you can bet that their "real life" personas could never be as fabulous as their fantasy counterparts!) As Lolita and the unnamed receptionist form an idiosyncratic bond, Lolita grapples with just HOW to fulfill her mission. Or should she just walk away? .... I'm going to be bold enough to say that Mara Vélez Meléndez' *Notes on Killing*, in fact, reveals more about the heart and soul of Puerto Rican people than a years' worth of news articles–which is, unfortunately, usually the only way many mainland Americans know anything about the island. The receptionist also comes to their own personal revolution of sorts by the conclusion of *Notes on Killing*, reinforcing one of the statements made in Vélez Meléndez' script: *"The journey to decolonization starts with YOU!"*[76]

Critic Alexis Soloski's ambivalent concluding evaluation both invokes and elides the political import of the work in a neoliberal gesture that the play itself may or may not embrace:

> Few of us can meaningfully affect Puerto Rico's fiscal crisis or its vexed journey toward either statehood or independence. But can we shake it, shake it, shake it, with authenticity? Can we self-govern in our private lives? "Notes" suggests that, with enough glitter, we can.[77]

I would argue that this should not be misunderstood as a reduction of the political to "mere" individual action, but as was the case with Soledad Iglesias, to consider the ways in which the process of decolonizing the self opens up the possibility of sovereignty in local and meaningful ways that can be sustained as everyday action. More important than just the instance of radical action, which admittedly contains its own level of compelling theatricality, is the meaningful presentation and the afterlife. It is crucially important first and foremost to live, rather than fixate on an idealized form of martyrdom. Only by recognizing the real challenges of physical violence and working through the possibility in an aesthetic familiar and joyful for the actors themselves, does the process of decoloniality emerge in this space. The pragmatics of survival are predicated on recognizing the idiosyncratic power and creative potential of each individual, creating space for *bregando* rather than collapsing to an a priori construct of conventionally acceptable forms of radical action. Moving from dramatizations of Lolita Lebrón and her cultural legacy of activism, in the next chapter we next turn to a set of plays that question the relation of pragmatic liberation as catalyzed by the diasporic return to reconsider the weight of familial history in the shaping of political action in Carmen Rivera's *La Gringa* and José Rivera's *Adoration of the Old Woman*.

CHAPTER 3

Diasporic Return and the Limits of Pragmatic Liberation

Carmen Rivera's 1996 play *La Gringa* and José Rivera's 2002 play *Adoration of the Old Woman* (*Adoration*) are surprisingly similar.[1] Both plays deal with the tensions of diasporic return, take place primarily at dwelling places in rural spaces on the island, and center young diasporic women learning about their Puerto Rican roots (the first voluntarily and enthusiastically, and the second not so much). Both female protagonists visit family on the island for the first time, arrive during the winter holiday season, are embroiled in intra-familial historical tensions they are previously unaware of, negotiate relationships with men with different visions for Puerto Rico, and experience the loss of a family member with whom they have developed a relationship during the play.

More importantly for our purposes, however, their similarities emphasize particular choices in each play to address the intimate familial interlacing of Puerto Rican political tensions. Both explore the impact of a member of the diaspora, and both highlight interpersonal and intra-familial tensions that foment and contain liberational aspirations to highlight the central importance of relationality in the structure of pragmatic liberation. While there are key differences in their level of explicit attention to the US/Puerto Rico political relationship and their forward-looking conclusions, at their heart is an affirmation of Puerto Rico as a home and Puerto Ricans as a unified people. For many Puerto Rican playwrights in the diaspora, the necessary and difficult search for home is always inflected by the colonial condition, but potential access to a meaningful personal relationship to the archipelago as home is only available through an expansion of political and cultural awareness manifest through material and spiritual engagement with the island. In both plays, this process of material and spiritual education situates the transformation of individual consciousness as a sustainable, pragmatic step in liberation at multiple scales.

The different political education available on the island for the diaspora is a crucial trope because the political and cultural knowledge of the diaspora has not easily translated back to the island.[2] While clearly visible in these two plays from the late 1990s and early 2000s, it is also a historical reality well exemplified by the Young Lords' mostly failed attempt to export their revolutionary nationalism to the island in the early 1970s. A brief review of this moment is helpful in considering the origins and efficacy of revolutionary political action, the structure of political education, and the material constraints on activist labor.

In *The Young Lords: A Radical History*, Johanna Fernández provides a detailed and incisive account of the successes and failures of the revolutionary group. The New York Young Lords emerged from a shift toward social engagement of the original Young Lords, a Puerto Rican gang in Chicago. Famous for engaging local conditions in highly visible ways with their "garbage offensive" and occupations of local institutions in the service of immediate local needs, they practiced a revolutionary ethos often paralleled with the Black Panther Party. In a chapter entitled "Organizational Decline," Fernández describes in detail the problematic decision to attempt to export its brand of revolutionary activism to the island in March 1971. Her detailed account of the debate around this choice indicates, on the one hand, a resistance based on a distance from the island and its concerns in counterpoint with those who, at the time believed "that the chance of developing a revolution for independence was more likely in Puerto Rico than in the U.S."[3]

In this context, the Young Lords Party (YLP), who initiated their engagement by marking an anniversary of the Ponce Massacre, found that their brand of activism did not necessarily effectively translate to the island. Not necessarily welcome by existing advocates for independence, their arrival was addressed in paternalistic opinion pieces reasserting the island's historical dismissal of the diasporic experience. While they managed to briefly aid in a few local contexts, their long-term impact was unsatisfying. In a rather telling summary, Frank explains,

> The hard work of the Young Lords in Puerto Rico wound up amounting to little growth. There was no significant success—symbolic or otherwise—. . . . Most important, the Young Lords working in Puerto Rico were very aware of the great discrepancy between the drudgery of their unproductive work and progress toward their identified goal—Puerto Rican independence—a reality that produced profound demoralization. . . . It was clear, especially to those in Puerto Rico, that the YLP had failed to

create a plan that fit both its organizational perspective and Puerto Rico's social and political climate. Rather ... the Young Lords had transplanted a method of organizing that had been effective in politicizing an isolated racialized group on the mainland but didn't work in the island context.[4]

This differential sense of organizing, and the general disconnect between island and diasporic sensibilities, continued as a trope until the second decade of the 21st century when the symbiotic interchange that had always been present was more firmly acknowledged in culture and scholarship. One of the interestingly relevant adjustments that the failed Puerto Rican campaign brought to the Young Lords Party that is especially relevant within the context of pragmatic liberation is the growing understanding that in order to organize along class and labor lines, they would need to shift away from a total ideological commitment to the cause that had previously been expected of members, many of whom were students with much more flexible work and life structures than full time employed members of the working class. This acknowledgment that the Party could not demand total participation in their political project was a necessary lesson that continues to be learned in the shift from the ideological fervor of "transformation now" into a more sustainable path to change. While there is a 25-year gap between the Young Lords' actions and the crafting of these plays, the potential of learning through return to the island remains one pathway toward a more pragmatic model of liberation.

La Gringa: Pragmatic Liberation and *La Gran Familia Puertorriqueña*

Carmen Rivera's OBIE award-winning play *La Gringa*, widely acclaimed and well-loved, demonstrates the difficult but productive bridging of island and diasporic cultures. Originally written in English, subsequently translated into Spanish, and more regularly performed in translation, it is published in both languages by Samuel French.[5] The longest running off-Broadway play in Spanish and the longest continuous production of a Latine play running in repertory in the US, it celebrated its 25th anniversary at Repertorio Español in 2021.[6] Carmen's earliest major success, the play is celebrated for bringing to light powerful intra-familial tensions that resonate both within and beyond Puerto Rican communities. Scholar and playwright Jason Ramirez reminds us that "*La Gringa* has also achieved international success, featured in theatre festivals in Bolivia and in Colombia, where Rivera was also an invited keynote speaker, discussing issues of theatrical latinidad, as well as American, Caribbean, and feminist theatre. In 2007, *La Gringa* was one of three Nuyorican plays invited to be part of the International Puerto Rican Theatre Festival, produced by one of the island's best known cultural institutions, El Ateneo Puertorriqueño."[7]

On one basic level, *La Gringa* explores the breakdown and restoration of *la gran familia puertorriqueña*, the ideological center of a cultural nationalism that is deployed to maintain shared identification even in the face of intense migratory movement. This ideological project insists on sustaining Puerto Rican cultural identification beyond the archipelago's boundaries, reinforcing an expectation of connection despite historical tension between island and diaspora. The title of the play invokes a label used to mark diasporic Puerto Ricans as North American foreigners, playing with this naming as a source of tension. *La Gringa* centers personal, psychological, and familial negotiations in which politics is a backdrop, and in which amends can bring a family together through a melodramatic psychological realism with some elements of spiritualism. Discussing Carmen Rivera's politics, Ramirez argues "Strains of her pro-independentista/anti-commonwealth ideology resound throughout her work but there always seems to be a residual contempt for those who are quick to overpoliticize the cause of Puerto Rico as a colonized territory. Instead, Rivera takes up the cause of the displaced Puerto Rican, lacking a homeland on either shore."[8] This point of view is visible in the play's sometimes sideways attention to questions of the political. *La gran familia puertorriqueña* was intended to expand the bounds of Puerto Rican identity beyond the territorial boundaries, to contain and encompass the large and expanding diasporic population. According to sociologist César J. Ayala,

> In 2018, 64 percent of all Puerto Ricans lived in the 50 states and in the District of Columbia, while the remaining 36 percent lived in Puerto Rico. At the turn of the 21st century, the population of Puerto Rico was still slightly larger than the Puerto Rican population stateside. The Puerto Rican population in the continental United States surpassed that of the Island in 2006, the same year in which the 936 tax exemptions to industry expired in Puerto Rico, accelerating the exodus propelled by the loss of manufacturing jobs.[9]

In its initial formation as an ideological pillar of *estadolibrismo*, the philosophy underlying the pragmatic choice generating popular for the ELA referendum in 1952, *la gran familia* was imagined as an umbilical connecting those leaving the archipelago with those staying; in its initial formulation influence flowed in one direction—from island to diaspora. This presumption has shifted over time to increasingly complex thinking about the structure of influence and transformation. While the flexibility of migration enabled by US citizenship and an "air bridge" have allowed for significant circularity for much of the intense periods of Puerto Rican migration, only in the last three decades has the cultural influence of Puerto Ricans returning to the island been considered. Previously, there was a dominant binary logic that centered the need to maintain traditional Puerto Rican culture in the face of the danger offered by US imports, but not the influence of Puerto Rican diasporic return.

Nuyorican sociologist Juan Flores's *The Diaspora Strikes Back* changes the terms of this conversation by considering the forms of "cultural remittance" that accompany the emergence of "Re-asporicans," those who have returned from the diaspora bringing new cultural ideas to island communities.[10] His recognition came from learning the ways that the spaces are interconnected in ways not previously imagined while giving readings in Mayaguez with, among others, Mariposa, the poet who coined the term Diasporican (see below). Scholar La Fountain-Stokes's notion of the translocal, discussed in Chapter 1, also supports a more complex circulation of influence, insisting that communities exist across the island and the diaspora, a reality reinforced both by the trans communities he so deftly investigates and by the activist connections on and off the island that were sustained by resistance to PROMESA, the failure of the response to Hurricane Maria, and #RickyRenuncia.

The translocal as geography, however, is not as palpably present in the work of most Diasporican drama; the connection is still imagined in relation to the static binaries of here and there. The traditional dramaturgy of the outsider disrupting a static space involves the arrival of a diasporic figure who catalyzes a paradigmatic transformation in the existing relationships. Even in works where social media plays a central role Puerto Rico persists as a separate place, often still held as an idealized repository of memory and story. Oscillating between nostalgia and re-enchantment, diasporic return highlights the anxieties of colonial influence in the face of re-encountering fervent desire for true knowledge of one's cultural history. This recognizable tension between home and diaspora and the conventional restoration of familial ties is also a political stance that insists on the necessity of shifting the terms of social relations which frees liberatory potential in an existing situation. Rather than radical transformation, mutual re-education about the reality of given circumstances allows for a movement sideways toward a more sustainable future of meaningful connection.

While there is a strong liberatory undercurrent in *La Gringa*, the most radical calling out in relation to the politics of identity and culture occurs in the two poems presented as a part of the epigraph to the published English version of the work—Mariposa's "Ode to the Diasporican" and Vincent Toro's "Apologia to the Last Cacique." Mariposa's bilingual poem begins with an earnest claim in Spanish about her identification, evident both through visual signs (brown hands and a Puerto Rican face) and a heart full of pride. This assertion of identity directly counters the presumption that a specific geography generates authentic identity, while still insisting on the importance of multiple kinds of spatial experience. Writing in English, Mariposa parallels island and New York geographies, forming a set of substitutions in parallel that establish "Diasporican" identity, a powerful neologism that centers the diasporic condition rather than a specific urban geography that led to the earlier (and still often used) term Nuyorican. Mariposa's poem suggests that her parallel set of experiences is equally valid in this broader construction of Boricua identity. Her claim builds on the existing specificity of the Nuyorican experience, but deliberately establishes it in relation to an island experience, moving away from direct opposition to a form of connection based on equivalency and substitution.

> cause my playground was a concrete jungle
> cause my Río Grande de Loiza was the Bronx River
> cause my Fajardo was City Island
> my Luquillo Orchard Beach
> and summer nights were filled with city noises
> instead of coquis[11]

The claim that geography enables formative experiences that foster identity is reinforced rather than refuted, but Mariposa's poem asserts multiple paths to a singular endpoint, insisting on the fundamental possibility of connection.

Toro's poem is an invocation of Taíno heritage in the present as a way of offering a counter to the psychological damage of the colonial condition. This invocation of Taíno roots and cultural connection is present at one crucial moment of reconciliation in the play but is also part of a larger continuing attempt to change the narrative of Taíno extinction. Beyond Toro's artistic invocation, there is a body of activism and various structures asserting a neglected continuity of culture, knowledge, and practice, genetic evidence of indigenous heritage in Puerto Ricans reflecting a desire to connect to longer histories that are not constrained within a colonial logic. While these projects have a range of manifestations and are both celebrated and contested within the island and the diaspora, they have become increasingly visible; within the dramaturgy in this work there are consistent references to Taíno epistemology and cosmology as points of connection. In her conclusion to *A Contested Caribbean Identity*, anthropologist Sherina Feliciano-Santos explains, "While the national discourse surrounding the historically imagined Taíno/Boricua as romanticized figures, the actual people who identify as Taíno/Boricua today often do not fit the noble (and extinct) figurations of Taíno/Boricuaness as portrayed in school textbooks."[12] The importance of these claims rests in the fact that, "In searching out ambiguity and incongruity, we witness moments when people attempt to make themselves legible to others, audible against a cacophony of voices—moments when unpredictable forms of understanding and transformation become possible."[13] Or, in the lines of Toro's poem "Now I absolve me. I resolve me. I solve & I evolve me/Into the Post Sorta Neo Rican I been born to be."[14] The movement toward legibility is crucial here as it enables choice in action, and with proper understanding, a better one than may have occurred before.

The complex relation to identity is carried through the play by 22-year-old Maria on her first visit to Puerto Rico from New Jersey during the Christmas holidays (the play begins at midnight on the 27th and ends on January 6th) to connect with her family and her cultural history. Recovering from heartbreak that left her questioning her identity (her Italian boyfriend did not see her as Puerto Rican), Maria chooses to travel to Puerto Rico rather than Europe, confusing and surprising her island relatives. Naively idealizing Puerto Rican culture and determined to explore her roots, Maria is initially unable to recognize the tension generated by her utopian view of Puerto Rico. Her desire to connect with Puerto Rico and see everything goes against the experiences of her cousin Iris and aunt Norma who have neither the time nor the resources to play tour guide. Her initial enthusiasm presents as touristic, expressing joy and pleasure equally in popular and colonial history, and her romanticism is exhausting and embarrassing. This problematic behavior is manifest both in her choice of clothing, a jacket with the Puerto Rican flag, which resonates very differently in mid 1990s New Jersey than it does on the island, as well as her exoticization of everyday life through an incessant practice of taking pictures of everything.[15]

Aunt Norma, bitter with feelings of abandonment and betrayal toward her sister Olga, initially assumes Maria's enthusiasm as narrow-minded self-interest; having given up her dreams of becoming a singer, she lives in the family house she built with her husband Victor whose construction was funded by Olga's remittances from New Jersey. Performing the self-constructed role of martyr to the needs and demands of her family, Norma's sisterly resentment is compounded by Olga's insistence on honoring their mother's wish to bury her body with her siblings in Rincon rather than near her living daughter, preventing regular visits. In many ways Norma represents a rigid level of absolutist unchanging belief in her own martyrdom. This focus highlights the intrafamilial tension of migration through a reconsideration of the perceived impact of personal freedom on one's family. Although the play provides the space for reconciliation and forgiveness, this action is deliberately separated from the material conditions of life on the island and in the diaspora.[16]

The play is primarily set in the marquesina, the covered front porch area of the family home in Puerto Rico, but moves into Manolo's bedroom in the house as well as out into Monchi's field and beyond into the family cemetery and El Yunque the rainforest; these different places mark transformation in social thinking and political philosophy as each location has its own cultural logic of politics and relative forms of pragmatism.[17] The house proper, and the kitchen, are dominated by Norma, whose servicial sense, her fundamental construction as one designed to serve, is only inevitable through her particular form of self-imposed martyrdom. Manolo's room is a space of historical discovery and education, while the broader spaces of Puerto Rican land, farm, and rainforest, are removed from the unproductive historical familial tension, and while representing labor and effort in terms of the manual work of harvest or the challenges of travel, there is a privileged, romanticized relation to the knowledge the land provides.

The work, typically received as showing the struggle to bridge the identity gap between island and diaspora, while well-received, exists in the persistent division it is intended to bridge. A telling anecdote that Rivera provides in an interview about the 25th anniversary of the production is that "I had people come up to me and say, you know, 'I really liked the show and I think you're a really good writer, pero para que sepas, tú no eres boricua.' Like they made it a point to say, 'Just so you know, you're not really Puerto Rican.'"[18] While cousin Iris initially presents the possibility of Norma's tension and jealousy passing into a second generation of family, uncles Victor and Manolo welcome Maria delightedly into the household. Iris employs this same policing of identity in the play itself, a form of geographic exclusion that her Uncle Manolo rejects in support of the broader spiritual and cultural connection of *la gran familia*.

Manolo and Victor (Norma's husband) are on board with welcoming and fully including Maria. Manolo's demonstrated ability to invoke and receive the blessing of a Taíno goddess explicitly connects the investment in the ideology of shared culture with a privileged relationship to spiritual access. Victor is an optimist who accepts things as they are, constantly hoping and being disappointed about the potential repair of his truck but continuing life with his family; his static acceptance reflects the careful knife edge between colonial docility and the necessary creativity of *bregar*, of making do within the struggle of daily life generated by the absence of access to appropriate parts.

Manolo, chronically ill for the last five years, forms the primary connective tissue that enables the eventual emotional reunion of Maria, Norma, and Olga. Maria brings recordings of Beethoven and La Lupe to Manolo from Olga, indicating that despite her absence her mother has kept her family very close in her heart as well as marking the ways in which music becomes a means of potentially bridging existing gaps. Norma and Manolo share a lost dream of making art, Manolo cutting short his acting career with the death of his father and Norma forbidden by her mother to try and do something artistic. This historical weight of protectionism and of rejecting artistic performance as a valid pathway show the problematic limits of pragmatic survival in which decisions become assumed to be necessary in an individually limiting and self-perpetuating way.[19] The material limits of employment opportunities in Puerto Rico and the pressure manifest through the "opportunity" to migrate maintains a profound structure of difference and reflects the parallel but different experiences on the island and the mainland.

Maria has her own experience of being forced to sublimate her desire for the theater, replacing it with a choice to double major in Puerto Rican Studies along with the more ostensibly practical subject of Business Administration. While a source of pleasure for Maria, the construction of the field of knowledge of Puerto Rico as subject operates ideally as a decolonial operation, but to the extent to which it is contained within larger discourses of Latin American area studies, it remains within the operations of colonial power. Manolo finds such study ridiculous, "¡¡qué bobería!!"[20] an exclamation Rivera deftly and conventionally translates through Maria's retort: "It wasn't silly. I wanted to learn about my culture, there's nothing wrong with that?"[21] Two key elements of this exchange are Maria's choice to frame her response as a question, looking for approval and Manolo's choice to respond by labeling her "a gringa," which produces another emotional reaction. Since Manolo is the strongest defender of Maria's inherent Boricua identity to members of his own family later in the play, one could argue it stems from his recognition of her precarious insecurity in this exchange. There is a doubled ambivalence about the potential silliness of Puerto Rican Studies. On the one hand, cultural knowledge could be arguably accrued most effectively through experience, but simultaneously the opportunity to take an observer's point of view allows for alternative forms of contextualization. Ideally, both strategies would be integrated to form a complex yet coherent understanding of given circumstances. Yet, ironically, both Maria and Manolo frame Puerto Rican Studies in problematic ways. While better than Manolo's exclamatory dismissal of a field of knowledge, Maria presents it as a pathway to learn about culture, potentially depoliticizing the unique analytic framework presented by Puerto Rico's continued obscured colonial condition.

Maria's farm labor with "el último jíbaro,"[22] Monchi, initially highlights a romantic attitude toward the land but is also the site where the strongest gesture toward decoloniality emerges in the work. University educated, Monchi turns away from engineering and the destructive climate impact of factories toward an embodied relationship with the land and invites Maria to join him in his harvest. His choice is radical, but the mildly patronizing attitude with which his actions are treated by those around him helps to obscure its potential. Rather than claiming a nostalgic return to an authentic relationship with the land, he presents a way of moving forward, of providing for self and community by operating within a different economy. There is a radical decolonial claim operative in Monchi's actions, complete with conventional suspicion of his idealism and willingness to sacrifice a productive job within a capitalist framework.

> We're buying back Puerto Rico. It's more like a corporation but instead of buying stocks, we're buying acres of land. I'm in the east. One is in the north, another in the south and one in the west. We'll keep buying land until we meet in the middle of the island. I already have two and a half acres. It's a hard idea to sell to people.[23]

The real challenge is trying to find individuals willing to participate in this alternate version of pragmatic politics.[24] Ironically, much like farmers in the continental US, local laborers are not interested or meaningfully capable of performing the difficult work of small-scale agricultural farming, thus undermining the alternative collective economy being proposed: "I can't even get people to pick up the vegetables for free. They could be starving and they'd rather buy two plátanos for a dollar in the supermarket."[25] Maria's response to her experience of labor is predictable—she falls in love with the land even as all of those around her recognize her naivete, suggesting the infatuation will dissipate, one more way of obscuring but not diminishing the importance of Monchi's choice.

Part of the back and forth debate between island and diaspora experience is access to privilege, relative cost of living, and clear understanding of the different social conditions and practices on the other side. Employment opportunities, for example, are deeply shaped by not only availability within the labor pool, but also the diversity of employment opportunities. Maria suggests that Iris could find work as a teacher in New York because she is bilingual when she is forced to look for jobs in pharmaceuticals in Puerto Rico, despite concerns about potential social injustice and environmental pollution. This conversation sheds light on a larger problem of the coloniality of Puerto Rican political economy where cycles of temporary tax incentives have led to industrial and pharmaceutical investments that are typically abandoned the moment the incentives disappear, creating an ongoing model of corporate subsidy and extraction rather than generating more stable ongoing employment opportunities. While these foreign businesses are not easily accessible to locals, and while initially it appears that Maria will get a job at her current company, it turns out that jobs in Puerto Rico are designated for Puerto Rican nationals.[26] The question of labor and access to forms of meaningful employment is central to the notion of pragmatic liberation because of questions of value, autonomy, and survival.

Carmen's conclusion is the least ambiguous and most optimistic of the works in this book. One way to understand this conventional familiarity is her deliberate use of the hero's journey.[27] Jason Ramirez highlights two key structural and theoretical elements in the work that might shape this result. In addition to her explicit reliance on the hero's journey for the structure of the second act, she also frames her political engagement through the concept of fantastic realism, based on Argentinian Guillermo Gentile's fantastic theatre, an aesthetic that she wrote about for her MA thesis. Gentile's theory was also deeply influential on Nuyorican playwright Cándido Tirado, Carmen's writing and life partner, and the one who introduced her to his theories. Tirado describes Gentile's work as

> He would say, you know, 'these are the ten [pages] that have transformation. The other has imagination. Imagination is crap. Transformation that's where magic happens . . .' Even when we think there has to be logic, there's no such thing. Logic is the smallest part of the brain. So we're talking about feelings and fantasies and irrational stuff. He said 'that's where the magic happens, that's where life resides in theater.'[28]

Maria's trip to the cemetery and El Yunque, encounters the play shares directly with the audience, contain the clearest examples of what Rivera might call fantastic realism, and center Maria's affective accumulation of a profound relationship with the space.[29] These spaces invoke a spiritual dimension that is central to unleashing liberatory potential. Rather than necessarily proposing a primacy of the indigenous spiritual, it is the necessary co-presence of these connections which allows for a deep human relational politics, serving as the ground for pragmatic liberation. Maria "sense[s]" where her grandmother's grave is in the cemetery, leading Manolo and Monchi and insisting "She's right here,"[30] suggesting a palpable present immediacy of experience and connection. Their subsequent stop in El Yunque emerges out of this recognition of proximate connection; Manolo wishes her to experience the transformative power of Atabey's blessing. Within the world of the play Maria explicitly receives this blessing as a "*DRY rain*" and is gifted with "an amazing sense of inner peace."[31] Monchi's own initial experience of the blessing gave him the strength to begin his decolonial land reclamation and farming project, while Manolo, the conduit for these gifts claims this time "Atabey liberated my spirit. I can go home a free man."[32] Though peace, strength and liberation are all divinely gifted, Maria remains unable to hear the song of the coqui, the ultimate symbol of connection.

In sustaining this condition the play insists that most powerful path to familial reconciliation (and communal integration with the land) is achieved through the embodied experience of music and sound.[33] This sense of integration is a powerful point of initiation for political work within a specifically Diasporican understanding of the weight of colonialism. In this conception home and the deliberate labor of fostering such a space is a necessary precursor to revolutionary action and consciousness. Interestingly, the first point of entry into the musical space of the house is Olga's gift of a classical album to Manolo, but in his subsequent discussion with Maria, he engages her playing the guiro. A traditional percussion instrument, it is an important symbolic image throughout Puerto Rican cultural production because of its long history in Puerto Rican musical practice extending to its contemporary use in both traditional and salsa performance.[34] The culminating transformational bridge building is the family parranda, where Norma participates through the singing of a bomba and Maria once again attempts to play the guiro, after which she can hear the coqui.

This sonorous performance of bridge building resonates as a powerful form of cultural connection. According to scholar and dancer Jade Power-Sotomayor,

> While many Afrodiasporic traditions link dancing to drumming and drumming to dancing, bomba is notable for the particular way the dancer's moves are marked with rhythmic synchronicity by the lead drum. . . . this exchange necessitates a practice of listening that is both resistive and restorative and, as such, maps a relational praxis that effectively reroutes both nationalist filiations and liberal investments in individual agency and liberation.[35]

She goes on to suggest her "valued" personal affective and political experience as "the Diasporican sense of togetherness produced through the communal suspension of time and space, collapsing the ancestral and the immediate, arcing toward and claiming a still-yet-to-be-determined and increasingly threatened future."[36] For Power-Sotomayor the bomba is a powerful cultural act generating the conditions "for Puerto Ricans—specifically Black Puerto Ricans and Puerto Rican women—to be heard, seen, and understood, not just by colonial forces, but by each other."[37] Thus, Rivera's choice of celebratory communal engagement resounds on multiple levels even as it serves as a conventionally satisfying conclusion, predictably interrupted by Manolo's death and a reparative conversation between sisters.[38]

As the reparations to *la gran familia* continue, Maria is in the position of more fully grasping the complex difficulties of living in *la brega*, the limited resources of her island family, while also gaining access to a full Puerto Rican identity authorized by an indigenous spiritual connection. The ongoing popularity of this play is reflected in its comfortable conclusions, but even in those moments Carmen maintains space for a more incisive politics to continue sounding in the world of the play.

Liberation, History, Referendum:
The Speculative Future of *Adoration of the Old Woman*

José Rivera's *Adoration of the Old Woman* (*Adoration*), which premiered at the La Jolla Playhouse in San Diego, California in September 2002, combines the genre of diasporic return with an exploration of Puerto Rico's electoral politics to highlight the material impacts of Puerto Rico's obscured colonial relationship to the United States.[39] In doing so he illustrates the capacity of ambivalent endings to simultaneously acknowledge the necessity of education and self-development in recognizing the potential problems of current status, while explicitly highlighting the cost and failures of revolutionary acts of liberation. As with much of his other work during the first decade of the 21st century, resistance and political revolution maintain close traffic with interpersonal interaction, a familiar model of politics in US regional theater.[40]

His play makes audible the complexities of difference in attitude toward status and social geography, exploring the feasibility of coming together across time and space in a future that is still framed by the pragmatic politics of the shifting US/Puerto Rico relationship. Two of his central characters' experiences extend beyond the typical human lifetime to literally embody history; in doing so, his play rewrites Puerto Rican futurity as grounded in a diasporic return that makes blackness solidly visible within the genealogy of Puerto Rican political and cultural life.

Set in a "near future" Puerto Rico, the speculative play weaves together two narratives: 1) Seventeen-year-old New Jersey Diasporican Vanessa's journey toward liberatory Puerto Rican consciousness alongside Cheo and Ismael, two men with differing attitudes toward status but a shared interest in her; and 2) the haunting persistence of memory and history in contemporary life, manifest through Doña Belén, who is "between one hundred and one hundred and fifty years old,"[41] and her ghostly tormentor Adoración. Taking place entirely in the house and on the porch of the "Old Woman," Doña Belén, the play engages all five characters in parallel discussions of Puerto Rican history. Framed by the anticipation and realization of a status referendum, *Adoration* ends in a majority demand for Puerto Rican statehood, a decision recognized and acted on by the United States, resolving the question of Puerto Rican status but not the pragmatic quest for liberation. Along the way Vanessa shifts her appreciation from two attractive men to family, culture, and history, learning that Adoración, not Belén is her grandmother. Doña Belén forgives Adoración for her adulterous betrayal with her husband, frees herself from haunting and moves on, Cheo gives up on non-violent protest, radicalizes and pre-emptively dies at the hands of the FBI, while Ismael resolves to ensure the US holds itself accountable for its actions. The play comes full circle as Vanessa welcomes back Cheo's spirit into Belén's bed at the end of the play as she continues her education in Puerto Rican culture and history.

This precise description of an age range for Belén has multiple interlocking functions, connecting her to the early days of the US colonial domination of Puerto Rico, and perhaps as far back as the 1868 Grito de Lares. Though her fundamental attachment to a liberated island is clear, her life more than spans Puerto Rico's history as a US territory. Her symbolic function as a living archive of Puerto Rico is made explicit in her post-referendum acknowledgment that "It's not mine anymore, this old island"[42] and her recognition "I'm the last of my kind.... There's nobody like me in the whole world. What I carry in my skin. What I know of life. What I remember of this island. But I'm as fertile as a stone."[43] Her character function as individually embodied memory is sensorially maintained in her skin, but the absence of fertility suggests she cannot figure as a space of direct legacy, that the paths of transmission of knowledge must take place otherwise, thus insisting on both reproductive and non-reproductive genealogies of cultural memory.

Belén's longevity also reinforces the continuity of patriarchal forms of oppression even as the terms of colonial power shift. Alive at the moment of transition to US authority, she describes witnessing her grandfather mowed down by US troops after discharging his gun into his foot, a prescient but problematic critique and foreshadowing of the self-destructive weight of history. Though adored, this figure is also haunted: emotionally by her extremely long life, seven miscarriages, and husband Toli's untimely death; and explicitly, by Adoración, a verdant and sexualized ghost who shares her bed and shared her husband in life. Belén is only freed from this weight by death, in the process forgiving both Toli and Adoración, acknowledging the pain she inflicted on others—"The worst pain—the pain of extinction,"[44] and apologizing to Adoración for "t[aking] your daughter and kill[ing] you with my words."[45]

Her relationship to Adoración prevents any easy romanticization of Belén's symbolic role as the font of history. While she holds memory in her body, in her skin, that memory is also structured through the experience and use of information that serves to conjoin and separate—language itself becomes one site through which Belén enacts revenge on Adoración. She recounts her tension with Adoración in an atmosphere reminiscent of Lorca's rural tragedies. Adoración goes out to the men, serving them as the heroes they are for bringing back food, but her behavior, judged unseemly by other women, also eventually leads to an adulterous relationship with Toli and pregnancy. Adoración is shunned, labeled a mulatta whore, extending toward the racist, colorist legacy of the Spanish erasure of African heritage in Puerto Rico.[46] The historical moment gestures toward the agricultural changes associated with the first colonial governor of Puerto Rico, the so-called Green Pope, who took the opportunity of the destruction of infrastructure caused by the 1899 Hurricane San Ciriaco to set up a monoculture of first coffee and later sugar production to maximize profits for investors during the first decades of the 20th century. These poor working conditions contributed to the social unrest and labor activism expanding into the 1930s that encouraged the beginnings of "sponsored migrations" to the mainland and fostered increasingly visible calls for independence which crystallized under the leadership of Pedro Albizu Campos.[47]

Though Belén's labeling follows a familiar judgmental trope whose racist melodramatic roots are never fully excised from the work, in her final extended monologue Adoración provides Vanessa and the audience access to the truth that has been obscured through the centering of Belén's version of history. She offers a familiar tale of pregnancy ending masculine desire. Belén's jealousy names her "*whore*. Over and over—in front of God, Mary, the entire town. Soon I was known as the Mulatta Whore of Las Arenas. When Don Toli started saying it too—the words were like knives right into my body!" The explicit misogyny emerges simultaneously with the creation of life, and it is the moral restrictions on life giving that become the source of a historical lie on which a future is written. The violence of the language is equated with physical violence and leads to death. "My baby was born. And the dirty words of Las Arenas killed me." She goes on to reveal that she, not Belén, is Vanessa's great grandmother. As she spitefully recounts the betrayal: "It was what the old witch wanted more than anything. To make life. . . . She never had that. All her stillborn hopes are buried under a Ceiba tree in Las Arenas. Each branch of the tree is another dead hope. My one baby—my girl—walked away from all that death. To think, to pray—and maybe, somehow, if there's justice, to remember the passage from my body into the humid air."[48]

Adoración affirms the power of life and the power to give life through a personal record of the visceral trauma of language. Her extended account insists on the danger of extinction and erasure and a hope for the memory of life itself. This need for sustaining life in whatever form and the "dead" and "stillborn hopes" echoes both the lost possibilities and the ways in which the problematic erasure of history falsifies a genealogy of knowledge and understanding. Only with the recuperation of a true history, with all its violent blemishes and ugly truths, is there a possibility of moving "into the humid air." This gesture acknowledges the complex histories of violence, and while Belén's act of reparation is individual, it is a necessary step in moving forward into new possibility by confronting one's historical truth. This act of honest acknowledgment and sharing of information becomes the means through which relation is formed, not in the absence but in the full presence of it, and as we shall see, this shifting relationship does not disconnect Vanessa from Doña Belén, but instead allows her to become a new surrogate, bringing her diasporic experience into the space of a new Puerto Rican history.

The Ceiba tree, a powerful symbol of memory and violence, echoes across multiple sites of the circum-Caribbean and gestures toward a larger connection with indigenous knowledge, a connection José gestures toward without providing detailed dramaturgical attention. For the Mayans the Ceiba was explicitly a living thing bridging the realms of life and death. This larger spiritual, historical legacy exceeds the bounds of Spanish and later US colonial violence. There is a Ceiba tree in Ponce that dates back five centuries to the colonial encounter, and the trees are widely recognized sites of Taíno ritual transmission, which despite the narrative of extinction, is sustained in forms of tradition knowledge passed down through, often women's, bodies.

Though controversial, many assert that a Taíno legacy remains in clear unbroken lineage, carried through the continued practice of the areíto as a dance/performance form and the prevalence of indigenous genetic markers in the Puerto Rican population. Tony Castanha argues that the continuity of practice and knowledge in rural indigenous spaces is maintained by the figure of the rural peasant, the jíbaro as the clearly connected legacy descendant of Taíno knowledge.[49] Academic and political resistance to these claims emerge from two different perspectives. On the one side there is an insistence on widely recognized empirical evidentiary markers in the face of a widely accepted narrative of eradication and extinction. A more complex concern is the extent to which figures of the Taíno and the jíbaro are at times deployed in a version of cultural nationalism that privileges its construction by a white elite.[50] This invocation of a longer history that extends the horizon of politics beyond 500 years of colonialism is crucial, though the way it is deployed matters deeply. A parallel structure exists in the relationship of Belén and Adoración. The need to rewrite a history originally conceived in the service of moral whiteness exposes the fundamental sterility of that historical narrative, eliding both indigenous and African contributions to the history of Puerto Rico, which offer a different model of the survival of life and knowledge.[51] Rivera here suggests both the potential death lingering in the weight of history and the desire, even among those who represent the desire to sustain traditional models of Puerto Rican culture, to free themselves from its weight by creating a new way forward. In doing so, the concept of independence takes on the familiar neoliberal concerns of freedom from oppression and the abstract question of sufficient autonomy is entangled in the material specificities of individual experience, resulting in a familiar tension between rhetorics of idealized transformation and a necessarily pragmatic liberation that acknowledges the basic conditions of sustainable survival—of life with hope—in the face of continued colonial violence.

Vanessa's mother Celia's survival allows a counter narrative of liberation in the broadest sense, working against the conservative structures of power that desire independence but require the violent erasure of performances of racial and sexual difference. Interestingly, this personal, familial history of usurpation and erasure echoes in loose fashion the colonial claims of Spain and the United States, in which both manifest forms of oppression and violence that homogenize codes of morally acceptable behavior and erase the conditions of racial and sexual difference in everyday life performance. Naming Adoración a "Mulatta Whore"[52] conflates a long history of class and racial difference policed through moral surveillance and the deployment of destructive stereotypes through the communal operation of shame. In this world, the information, the rumors, are acts of violence, of knives piercing, transforms the possibility of intimacy, desire, and love, into a space of violent public rejection.

Ironically, it is her very fertility that, in Adoración's view, destroys a relationship that even Belén eventually admits was based on love. Here Puerto Rico is a space in which memory and history are held through and beyond conditions of life and death. Belén's status as a problematically static historical figure critiques the danger of a singular repository of historical knowledge, archive, or narrative, erasing the truth; instead, there is a necessary shift to empowerment through more fluid, open disseminations of historical and future possibility. In this sense it is fundamentally important that Adoracíon is fertile while Belén is not.

One important choice in Patricia McGregor's INTAR production not made in the La Jolla premiere was to cast Danielle Davenport in the role of Adoración. This visual introduction of blackness within the Puerto Rican family acknowledges the color semiotics of identification, indelibly marking the genetic source of the protagonist as Afro-Latina. This casting decision was repeated in the 2016 UrbanTheater production with the casting of Melissa DuPrey. These casting decisions are crucially significant choices in refusing the historical erasure of blackness within the space of Puerto Rican thinking of racial history and were importantly enacted in specifically Latine theater spaces. While the revelation that Adoración is the source of the future, that Vanessa is her descendant, highlights the sustained and overlooked presence of blackness, too often elided in accounts of Puerto Rican history, the narrative itself runs the risk of replicating the problematic figure of 19th century US melodrama, the tragic mulatta. This figure also verges on the stereotype of desirability and fertility because of the play's deliberate contrast with Belén, reflecting a very rural Catholic Hispanic model of policing through shame.[53] The affective pleasure of the conventional habit of women's self-sacrifice is disrupted by Adoración's revenant presence. Her voice and agency resist the problematic reductionism that could have left her a martyr or an unrepentant villain.

In a familiar critical failing, the UrbanTheater production was called out for an absence of magical realism, but this very claim is worth considering because the existence of a ghost in and of itself existing in the same material conditions as everyone else in the space is precisely the form of magical realism that has the most political power as an analytic and aesthetic tool. In this logic, Puerto Rico is a space where ghosts are living and palpably present, at least for the women who sleep in the bed in this house.[54] The specter retains the power to intervene, and the history is only hidden for a time, significantly emerging in the aftermath of the change in Puerto Rico's status. From this reading, the epochal political shift is a necessary precursor to displace the sterile weight of a self-righteous demand for independence. The rigidity of history itself becomes the failure, but this simple contrast is inflected by the very title of the work itself.

Based on the literal action of the play centering these characters, the title might have been "Adoración's Haunting of Doña Belén." But *Adoration of the Old Woman* removes Belén's proper name and shifts from a proper name in Spanish to an action in English. Regardless of this shift, "of" is retained as the relational connector. This is not merely overattentive grammatical quibbling but a meaningful concern of the grammar of relationality—the relationality "of" Puerto Rico and the US. "Of" points both toward and from, often insisting obliquely on origin or possession without being direct or precise.

The action of adoration is also fascinating in relational terms. Adoración/ *Adoration* is the action of *adorar*/ to adore: "to revere or worship someone considered to be of divine nature"[55] but also extreme forms of love, desire, and veneration directed to other people and objects. This ambiguity deftly expresses the complicated relationship of Puerto Rico's condition. Directed toward Belén, it is an act performed by the work, the playwright, or the two contesting voices over Puerto Rican status, Ismael and Cheo, toward an embodied history that exists prior to the establishment of the current politics of relation with the US. If, on the other hand, adoration is Belén's action, then the focus is on an independent Puerto Rico that specifically holds a connective tissue across generations and political difference, that disappears with the incorporation of Puerto Rico at the end of the play leaving education and the development of consciousness as pathways forward to retain the sovereignty of Puerto Rican culture. In this second version, Belén's role as the container of history disappears in the face of incorporation. A new form of connective history needs to emerge beyond structures of loss, to reimagine a new future for Puerto Rico in which it is possible for the coqui to sing again.

The phrasing of the title also echoes the Feast of the Epiphany, January 6th, the first day of the play, and a celebration referenced in the play as a symbol of traditional Puerto Rican religious and cultural values in decline. Epiphany, or Three Kings Day, when the three kings of the east came to Bethlehem to bring gifts to Jesus, is referred to as Adoration of the Magi in descriptions of visual works dating from 15th century Italy. And it is worth remembering that this timing echoes the end of Maria's visit in *La Gringa*, suggesting Rivera's play as an alternative future to the relatively happy resolution implied by the re-connection in Carmen's play. José also introduces Cheo, Kevin Alejandro Betances, the mainland educated advocate for independence, as a poorly assembled figure of one of the Three Kings. Cheo claims, in the aftermath of a failure to generate community involvement, that people "would rather be watching *Bonanza* reruns" rather than participate in this residual practice that no longer has significant cultural appeal.[56]

Cheo's invocation suggests that the primary vector of resistance from the point of view of independence is contemporary concern with US colonial practices and a desire to return to Puerto Rican traditions, naturalizing the influence of Spanish heritage Catholicism in the establishment of these traditions. Cheo's frustration with the dismissal of tradition is presented as a continued cultural shift away from independence toward domestic comfort and resignation, reflecting an attitude that emerged for many *independentistas* from the new colonial relationship of the Free Associated State in 1952.[57] This small moment also points to the larger concern about the practices of Americanization—the problematic imposition of American cultural values and practices—that have manifested in different guises from language and school curricular campaigns to the importation of US franchises and cultural practices.

Though there is a recognition of bilingualism and the domination of Spanish as a spoken language in Puerto Rico, José's lack of fluency in Spanish fits well with an institutional desire for audience comfort in regional theater in maintaining the conceptual fiction of bilinguality while not requiring a significant encounter with untranslated difference.[58] As with many plays operating in a space of bilingualism while trying to negotiate a presence in the US monolingual regional theater in the last 35 years, the play has only one sentence of untranslated Spanish, "pero todavia lleva la mancha de plátano,"[59] literally "but she still carries the mark of the plantain"—referencing the continued visible embodiment of Puerto Rican identity in Vanessa. This marker retains greater weight when we learn that Vanessa is Adoración's descendant, not Belén's, marking the continuing presence, despite attempted historical erasure of blackness, within Puerto Rican identity. The use of this untranslated phrase also directly references the poem by Luis Lloréns Torres, himself a supporter of independence, who insists that the mark persists through the ages as an authentic marker of jíbaro identity, here explicitly connected to the presence of blackness carried into the space of the diaspora.

All the other exchanges in the play are indicated by the quality of the articulation in the language, or in some cases when individuals are speaking their second language, English for Ismael and occasionally for Belén and Spanish for Vanessa, the language is marked in bold. Thus, the incapacity of speech and the development of Spanish becomes a way of marking both the challenges of communication between members of the same family as well as the ways in which they are moving closer to understanding.

Halting and stylistically problematic choices reflective of limited knowledge and practice are articulated in English but reflect the structure of the fictional underlying language. For example, in Vanessa's narratives in "Spanish" the language reflects challenges with both conjugation and vocabulary but is carefully pitched so that one can hear the broken Español through the English if one has a relative fluency in Spanish. For example, in expressing her sorrow after the death of Cheo, "**The body. It was. His hands, his kissings. His body was mine. Now it is the earth.**"[60] Through this strategy the audience operates in a position of bilingual privilege without actually earning the position through knowledge.[61] This access allows the audience to understand the difficulties of communication without in fact experiencing the visceral realities of ignorance and incomprehension.

A young woman of 17, Vanessa has her own challenges based on ignorance, a myopic understanding of the world shaped by her immediate surroundings, and at least, according to her elders, a selfish, close-minded, narrow focus on her own needs. Vanessa's visit to the island is intended to connect her with family and ideally delink her from a familiar set of urban challenges presented by mainland culture in Paterson, New Jersey.[62] While Vanessa follows a familiar path of consciousness raising within an awareness of the loss of political and cultural autonomy as a result of US colonial impacts, her evolution is negotiated through the competing attention of two young men, friends from youth, but separated by their current political attitudes. She has not meaningfully reflected (or consciously encountered) the larger question of politics that informs the condition of her island, and her relationship to it, and is presented as a self-absorbed adolescent whose pathway to thinking through the politics is based on shifting desire. Her presence as an uninformed member of the diaspora also strategically allows the play to rehearse positions potentially new to a regional theater audience, which would have been exhausted repetitions for a more politically aware, presumptively Puerto Rican audience.

Her detailed introduction to the persistent tensions between Cheo's nationalist advocacy for independence (an increasingly small minority on the island) and Ismael's desire for full incorporation as a state (whose numbers have historically increased) in the second half of scene two is performed using familiar frames of tradition and modernization. Both men believe in their positions as the most positive outcome for Puerto Rico, with Cheo presented as an idealist actively working for political change and Ismael as a pragmatic realist focused on the best economic outcome for himself and for the island. Neither expresses interest in the status quo.

This rhetorical competition's function as a courting ritual for Vanessa's attention justifies the heavy expositional background on the question of Puerto Rican status. Vanessa, like the implied mainland regional theater audience (specifically the La Jolla, California audience at the premiere) begins in ignorance of the realities of life on the island, of the long-standing political debate on status, of the history that Doña Belén embodies, and of fluent Spanish.[63]

The reviews of the INTAR production appreciated the acting and set but were concerned with both the direction and the play, claiming the work was stilted and overexplanatory, which could on the one hand be a result of the movement from a less visibly Puerto Rican space to one in which much of the history, in a Latine space in New York, is more viscerally present and immediate for members of the audience. And yet, it is important to consider that this talking is doing what it is intended to do: trapping itself in the awkwardness of explanatory dialogue because this is the only way to move forward. The stilted awkwardness of the presentation highlights the trauma and ugly patches that serve as a connective glue around which the politics of relation can and should be understood. In doing so we must keep in mind Malavet's claim about "the carefully constructed general ignorance of [the US/Puerto Rico] relationship among most citizens of the United States."[64] If indeed the experience of this question around status is presented without a halting and difficult structure then the conditions of the work itself work as a means of erasing the complexity, and even though in its rhetorical performance the conversation has been reduced to a very simple mode of thinking in terms of the binaries of radical states of independence and statehood, this fantasy is itself a falsehood that is exposed by the awkward lumbering quality of the work itself.

This debate about Puerto Rican status has existed as long as Puerto Rico has had an explicit political relationship to the United States, with the desire for autonomy pre-dating the transfer enacted by the Treaty of Paris in 1898 when criollo elites were willing to side with Spain and not advocate for revolutionary action in Puerto Rico because a form of local autonomy was poised to take effect on the island.[65] Most would argue that status is the basic horizon for Puerto Rican politics, though in the 1998 referendum, the closest preceding the play's premiere, the unique structure of the ballot resulted in a situation in which the most popular choice was "none of the above." This clear evidence of a populace frustrated with the problematic structural and institutional terms of this political framework of choice provided has been accompanied by significant work by scholars in cultural and literary studies increasingly questioning the structure of this question, arguing through various lenses that traditional models of using attitude toward status as a primary lens of political division is not a productive model for contesting the colonial status of Puerto Rico.[66]

Rivera acknowledges the then current and continuing reality that independence is only explicitly supported by 3% in a typical referendum and rehearses many of the concerns that would emerge in a move to independence.[67] Ismael's belief in the possibility of statehood has not been treated seriously by the US federal government worried about shifting the economic balance of the states and federally enfranchising a dominantly Spanish speaking population.[68] Ismael's position ironically reflects more limited experience in the US, explicitly marked by his heavily accented use of English.

Despite his unaccented English and Vanessa's claim that he is not very Puerto Rican, Cheo centers his identity in Puerto Rican traditional culture and as the voice of revolutionary independence; his attempted Epiphany performance also uses the cuatro, reflecting his clear investment in cultural history. Educated on the mainland, Cheo's rejection of this social trajectory and resistance to capitalist privatization interrupts his fast-track trajectory toward a job with the state department and the continuation of status quo politics. This self-styled figure of "Che" Guevara, even Ismael jokingly marks the similarity in nickname, is also highly educated and from relative privilege.[69]

Cheo's rhetorical investments in loss extend beyond the cultural to the ecological, both in terms of the silence of the coqui and his account of the privatization and enclosure of a formerly public beach at La Posa, which provides the first strong emotional connection with Vanessa. He and rival Ismael swam as boys in La Posa beach, whose transformation symbolizes the incursion of US private capital and consequent practices of exclusion: a fence now protects the privacy of the beach for tourists staying at a luxury hotel. Ironically, Cheo, condemns the loss of public access through private enclosure of natural resources in the direct service of a tourist economy, but at the same time, he accepts the conditions of this separation as something that is "lost," an oddly fatalistic capitulation that ignores the real and ongoing history of attempts to reclaim Puerto Rican land, from Monchi's fictional work in *La Gringa* to Cotto-Morales's accounts of historical land rescue and other strategies discussed in scholarship.[70] Even Vanessa is more willing to perform a subversive act of embodied occupation to momentarily disrupt colonial capitalism, though her strategy coincides with a sexualized thrill of taboo transgression. Cheo, reflecting a specific nostalgic claim that self-sufficiency has been lost in the structures of US imperialism's narrative of loss, offers a return to an idealized liberalism based in a romanticized traditional Puerto Rico prior to a gringo invasion. Temporally anachronistic in terms of its visceral immediacy, his position echoes the language of resistance to active

Americanization in the 1940s and 1950s. Prior to Ismael's arrival Cheo presents his case to Vanessa with the full support of Belén. Cheo's performance typically results in him being labeled "crazy" or "ignored" even as he insists "the sad truth is in five hundred years, we've been a free people for only a week and a day. And that has to change."[71] He repeats his speech to her in which he insists "If Puerto Rico votes to become a state of the United States, forget it! We will be shitting on our past, dishonoring the dead, lobotomizing the future and performing in an absurdest [sic] tragedy worthy of Jean Genet!"[72] Cheo's heightened rhetoric is intended for public persuasion and reveals much about the logic underlying independence claims in the play. His last set of claims suggest that thinking and meaning are fundamentally contingent upon national autonomy, and that incorporation into the United States not only moves away from Puerto Rican values but toward an unthinking incoherence.[73] He follows with a claim about exposing revolutionary leader Pedro Albizu Campos to radiation during his incarceration and then Ismael enters to dismiss this as bullshit, proceeding to make an economic argument about the need for statehood and the lack of political and economic feasibility of an independent Puerto Rico.[74] They have staged this conflict before, so often they can anticipate each other's contributions.

Nevertheless, because of a new audience, Vanessa, their clear desire to impress her, and the impending referendum, their argument perhaps moves to a more combative and rhetorically violent language than normal. Most importantly, perhaps, there is a question around respect and disrespect as a grounding point. If the desire is for incorporation and validation, then the many Puerto Ricans who gave their lives to the United States to US military campaigns would be shat on in Ismael's mind, whereas the relevant dead for Cheo are those who have fought for independence. In both cases the devaluation of ideological sacrifice is presented in brutal scatological terms. The ultimate question is whether US intervention ultimately had any sustained beneficial impact. Although the play emotionally invests in Cheo's desire for independence, it constrains this idealism within the pragmatic reality of probable outcomes.

Ismael's desire for statehood is presented in rational, though ultimately commercial terms, but his claim that "any pig-faced red-neck senator from Mississippi can decide what life in Puerto Rico should be like. I'd love to see a Puerto Rican senator changing life in Mississippi"[75] inspires Vanessa, who at this early stage in the play is more comfortable with Ismael's rhetoric. Following this example, it is interesting to consider where allegiances might initially emerge for an audience new to this debate—toward traditional Puerto Rican resistance to the destructive forces of Americanization or toward desire for a particular kind of federal power to control its own destiny.

What is most important to remember, however, is the performance of Doña Belén's strategic act of de-escalation staged as anxiety about the heightened intensity of the conflict. As the argument moves into a more intense space of affect and there is real danger of a familiar argument shifting into violent rupture, Doña Belén's cries and crying derail the trajectory and shift focus to the need to care for an elder and it is crucial to note that she is recalling her grandfather's meaningless death at the hands of "gringo soldiers" to whom the people provided "almost no resistance."[76] Only her grandfather shot, and managed to hit himself in the foot, but was killed anyway. This moment of failure of violent resistance combined with a rhetorical desire for freedom becomes one pathway through which the weight of history provides a possibility for sustaining pragmatic unity in the face of conflict. It offers a way of thinking through the relationship of belonging that echoes the expanded familial metaphor.

José extends his play to a future that has "still" not yet happened, but in the play's fictional future referendum, statehood is selected with 52% of the vote while only 3% of the vote goes toward independence.[77] The other 45%, unaccounted for in the play's narrative, is presumably devoted toward the status quo, as it has been historically, based on the inertia provided by a fear of loss despite the difficulties of contemporary conditions. Cheo cannot accept this blow to his dreams of independence and vows to shift from non-violent organizing to join the New Nationalists, a group willing to embrace violence to work toward liberation. These events echo from a historical distance the shift that occurred in the thinking and practice of independence movements on the island soon after the establishment of the first locally elected governor, Luis Muñoz Marín, in 1948. In this shift, we witness a temporally compressed reprise of the events of 1950 when the nationalist independent movement was betrayed to the authorities. Just like the 1950s, as seen in *REVOLT!* in Chapter 1, the FBI informant gives away the location of revolutionary spaces. However, instead of the pre-emptive strikes and moments of armed resistance that occurred historically, with the longest lasting resistance about a week in the town of Jayuya (and is called by some El Grito de Jayuya) there is no meaningful violent resistance. They are surrounded, and despite attempts to negotiate, slaughtered in what is labeled in the play "The Massacre of Arecibo."[78]

With the referendum over, Belén can pass on, and forgive Adoración, in part because the island is no longer her island—the shift to the 51st state changes the nature of her relationship to history, indicating that she represents a particular account of colonial history and that a future course now must be charted. And Kevin Alejandro Betances, Cheo, who holds the last name of the revolutionary leader of El Grito del Lares is brought back to Vanessa's bed, the same one haunted by Adoración for so many years. The bed itself is a figure of trauma,[79] but it is at the same time an altar of sorts. There is a great deal of attention paid to both the nature of its beauty and the simple materiality of concrete blocks and wooden pallet frame. While initially Belén wants Cheo to destroy the bed to expiate the ghost, it survives to become a space of alternate possibilities at the end of the work.

Vanessa changes the haunted bed, one that holds and produces the spirits of a dead past, into a positive space of dreams and possibilities where Vanessa can connect with the man she loved and lost. Crucially, she invites the body of the revolutionary man to her space as a woman whose desire and interest is in maintaining a Puerto Rican lineage, despite the more formal looming incorporation into the United States. This action takes place only after Vanessa recognizes the power and wisdom contained in Belén— "I learned about birth and death and war and power by studying the lines in your face"[80] and her newly revealed decision to remain and go to university in Puerto Rico, to remain connected to what she has learned, and to understand her history.

Vanessa's movement toward radical consciousness raising carries on a particular legacy of history and maintains the flame of independence connected with a desire for a deep knowledge of Puerto Rico not only as culture but as political geography; however, it refuses to directly engage the material shift in conditions arising from the speculative future of a completed referendum and Puerto Rico's transition from territory to state. As such, her ability to call Cheo's spirit might be read as an overtly magical ending, empowered by Belén's bed; but it is also authorized by the Puerto Rican eco-system as the coqui returns to sing at the play's conclusion. This aural shift, echoing Maria's experience at the end of *La Gringa*, stresses that despite the violence and the impending political transition, Puerto Rico is still materially and spiritually present.[81] Vanessa's surrogation of Belén's historical function marks a shift from liberatory exhortation and radicalization toward violent resistance toward a different educational path invested in individual self-development moving toward a larger ecology of knowledge.[82] In José's world, the change, such as it is, involves moving past a static history without removing cultural ties. From a political point of view, this resolution could be read liberal capitulation to the conditions of individual solace, but Vanessa's decision is deeply imbedded in her desire for education. Like his work in *School of the Americas*, José moves to an ending that does not advocate for moments of violent revolution, but rather a scene of education and gradual transformation.[83] But this is not the play's only conclusion.

Crucially, the FBI's act of repression also crystallizes a new attitude in an unexpected place—Ismael. He lets Vanessa and Belén know he is "holding a vigil" for Cheo and "And when it's over, I promise I'll do everything to make sure the actions of the police and FBI are investigated. Hear me? Then we'll see how good this gringo justice really is."[84] While potentially still trusting in the possibility of an ethical incorporation into the US, Ismael nonetheless reclaims cultural investment in Puerto Rico itself: "If you need anything else, I'm the house with the Puerto Rican flag on the second floor."[85] The invocation of the Puerto Rican flag is always heightened because of the repressive history of Ley de la Mordaza. Restricting the public display of the Puerto Rican flag was one of the most prominent suspensions of First Amendment rights during the crackdown on nationalist expression during the transition to ELA status. Though this is on one hand a casual synecdoche/metonymy, the fact that Ismael "is" the house with the Puerto Rican flag reclaims home in a particular way in this moment of transition to future fictional statehood. His notion of Puerto Rico is predicated on giving the benefit of the doubt to the operations of official justice of the United States. While on the one hand a potentially too easy capitulation to new forms of capitalism and incorporated Federalism (and in the space of increasing calls for police abolition and anxieties about the presence of federal troops as a means of cracking down on primarily peaceful protest this may seem to be a naive claim), on the other hand Ismael is beginning to express Puerto Rican solidarity, which was Doña Belén's dream from the beginning.

Though with its own melodramatic threads in terms of the immediate and radical shift that emerges in Ismael, the explication that sustains this change, along with an audience desire for some kind of conventional movement away from conditions of injustice, is the idea that Ismael's consciousness raising parallels Cheo's in recognizing the failure of the United States to live up to their implied promises. This is more than borne out in recent experience with the continued failure to provide sufficient investment for the victims of natural disasters in Puerto Rico and the continued debilitating work of PROMESA. The identity of Puerto Rico as a nation is too imbricated in its ambiguity with the US to disentangle in any singular moment of revolution.

It is precisely in the space between the rhetoric of revolution and the reality of meaningful social and political change that pragmatic liberation emerges. This is not an argument for capitulation or compromise as such, but rather a recognition that in any conflict the ability to sustain the white-hot anger or passion or sense of fundamental right is difficult outside the space of complete confidence, or at least a performance of confidence, that one is acting in opposition to injustice and has a clear pathway for resolution. While many violent and non-violent revolutions, and other social movements and armed conflicts have managed to crystallize investment precisely through this logic, it is much easier to accomplish in spaces constructed by faith (in creed, institution, or transcendent individual) or, more familiarly, a melodramatic world in which the conditions of good and evil are explicit and defined, in which there are sides that can and should be taken, and in which there is clear rhetorical and affective support for a right action or pathway.

Without the convenient and comfortable framing of melodrama, moral certitude is explicitly open to question. The palpability of the realist aesthetic, expanded both by a capacious sense of history and the existence of a ghost, insists that in the lived experience in this dramatic world the ghosts of history can in fact haunt the very beds in which we sleep. In doing so, they shift our connection with those closest to us and offer a spectral embodiment of the affective weight of history. The political ambiguity of the dramaturgy invested in a diverse conception of injustice provides a useful lens through which the structures of opposition and conflict can be engaged in their full, polyphonic, complexity and inconsistency, rather than in rigid formal oppositions enabled by the scripting of melodramatic evil. In this space there is an implicit gesture toward new possibility but always within a pragmatic lens, which may already exist or emerge alongside the situation. In this sense pragmatic liberation involves a revolution of the imagination in which a reframing of the conditions of the real provides a different mode of thinking about the world as it is, and in doing so, points to the possibility of a world as it could be. But the rhetorical force of such an assertion is predicated on motivating the possibility of believable change, recognizing the impact of consistent, causal logic, and the inertia of the everyday. To do so we must establish the conditions under which this form of thinking becomes its own form of possibility.

In the next chapter we will look at the ways in which individual self-development and transformation shifts relationships to revolutionary consciousness in multiple spaces of the diaspora. In doing so we will also encounter a deep investment in forms of artistic practice as related to notions of liberatory practice, insisting on the necessity of art making in community while questioning the idealization of its impact toward liberation. We do so through two plays by Quiara Alegría Hudes, *The Happiest Song Plays Last* and *Daphne's Dive*, as well as Nelson Diaz-Marcano's *Paper Towels*.

CHAPTER 4

Before Revolution, Honesty?

THE EVERYDAY PRAGMATICS OF ACTIVIST WORK

In "Pausing and Breathing," a keynote address at the 2018 Association for Theatre in Higher Education (ATHE) Conference delivered dialogically with her younger sister and fellow theater artist Gabriela Sanchez, Pulitzer-Prize winning Puerto Rican diasporic playwright Quiara Alegría Hudes jokingly addressed the theme of revolution by listing self-care products with "revolutionary design" before positing that "Maybe you gotta turn back on yourself for real revolution to be possible"[1] and then reframing her mandate as "Before revolution, honesty. That is my first step."[2] Her claim that revolutionary action in and through the theater requires introspection and honesty resonates with the practice of acknowledging given circumstances, an honest appraisal of current contexts that too rarely precedes transformative action. Honest self-reflection and analysis are a necessary precursor to discovering a sustainable path to move forward. Reflecting on her experience, Hudes highlights the micro and macro aggressions she encountered while being celebrated in mainstream theatrical spaces, while implicitly contrasting the relative invisibility of her sister's significant work in community-based theater in Philadelphia. Hudes's portion of the talk highlights problems in the current environment and a need for changes in value and practice while Sanchez celebrates her own work and invites the audience to move forward with her. The call to think about what we are doing, where, how, and why we intervene, is heightened by their dialogic speech where construction by, for, and near a community is reasserted as a central value. Community engagement is at the heart of an investment in activism through and beyond art as a means of working toward personal and collective liberation.

In her commentary and response theater historian Patricia A. Ybarra draws attention to what was left out in published documentation of the event, highlighting the elision of both art and art makers that refuse capitalist logics of success. *American Theatre*, Theatre Communication Group's national magazine centered on regional theater in the US, entirely elided Sánchez's material, replicating its historical lack of investment in community-based work, while the more comprehensive reproduction in *Theatre Topics*, ATHE's journal, focused on pedagogy and practice, but left out a performed excerpt from Hudes's MFA thesis play *Adventures of a Barrio Girl: Lulu's Golden Shoes*, albeit at Hudes's request. Following Hudes's claims of critical misunderstandings of her work when it does not meet racially and class coded expectations, Ybarra invokes reviews of Hudes's musical *Miss You Like Hell*, insisting on this rupture with the intersection of white supremacy and capitalism:[3]

> That critical confusion reveals the cultural incompetence of critics who cannot fathom how nonwhite non-middle-class people, whose enemies are things other than their own middle-class white capitalist family members, live. But, to my larger point, the absence of plays like *Lulu's Golden Shoes* from commercial stages also reveals a discomfort with art that refuses or rejects capitalist success as an end.[4]

As Ybarra crucially notes in her brief reading of *Lulu's Golden Shoes*, the characters' "value here is not accrued through being transformed into liberal subjects, but through the theatrical rendering of a system that kills them and does not accede them their value *even as the play does*."[5] Ybarra's insistence that Hudes's play "advocates for the survival of the ordinary"[6] reinforces a pragmatic liberatory gesture of moving forward as necessary, incorporating possibilities of joy and hope. This acknowledgement that the protagonists are always "*aqui, en la brega*," offers a lived pragmatism central to the sustained survival of Hudes's committed activist figures, as they struggle to realize their dreams while surviving and experiencing joy in the present.

Like Hudes's plenary, this chapter explores real challenges in everyday life activism by exploring gaps between intention and action, as well as the challenges of activist work at moments when others are not yet ready. It moves beyond political thinking on the Puerto Rican archipelago to think critically and carefully about how pragmatic liberation can intervene within the practices of theater making and activism. Looking first at "Pausing and Breathing" and her memoir *My Broken Language*, the chapter argues that Hudes's critique recognizes the clear dangers of individual, familial, and communal harm generated by existing structures, but crucially refuses to accept these given circumstances. Instead, she works toward a sustainable pathway forward at the intersections of art and political activism. Moving into a reading of her plays *The Happiest Song Plays Last* and *Daphne's Dive*, the chapter examines the challenges of sustaining activism in the face of resistance in the immediate environment of ostensibly supportive communities. These works recognize multiple paths forward for different individuals, all of which retain some possibility of truth and progress toward a desired political outcome. They simultaneously acknowledge the ongoing struggle between the necessity to act and the real challenges of transformative change that generate tension around activism in the community. This exploration of pragmatic liberation in drama allows us to carefully explore a different model of thinking about relation, responsibility, art making, and the power of politics. The chapter concludes with a reading of Nelson Diaz-Marcano's one-act *Paper Towels*, which explores the invocation of revolution, the limits of violence, and the need to call attention to the thousands of unacknowledged victims of Hurricane Maria. Diaz-Marcano's climate refugee protagonist combines an art installation critiquing the brutal dismissal of climate disaster with a planned mass shooting as a way of drawing attention to the ongoing neglect of Puerto Rico; in so doing, his play calls attention to violence as a potential end to transformative storytelling. Tragically, both *Daphne's Dive* and *Paper Towels* highlight the lost potential of an artist who is convinced the only way to generate meaningful change is terminal violence; these plays remind us that despite crucial urgency, working through conflicts takes time, and the path forward is complex.

Hudes's reflection in "Pausing and Breathing" questions deliberately perpetuated institutional limits of theater making, and the necessary struggle that exists under these conditions. She asks a series of pointed questions emerging from her own opening night anxiety that reflect larger presumptions of audience reception and demography:

> How will the audience view my Latinx stories, and if they are mostly white, does that mean my cast is performing race, and doesn't that injure our pride, our self-determination? How will it feel to go out onstage and once again not be afforded the luxury of neutrality? Will all the community outreach I've done in the Latinx community, saying Hey, you know that huge theatre downtown? I'm here to say, you are welcome there, I invite you inside! Will all that community outreach lead to two percent Latinxs in the audience or hopefully dear god maybe fifteen percent? Will the audience be mostly wealthy, and so will my characters' poverty seem monstrous? Is my play cultural tourism?[7]

Her rhetorical questions clearly establish the ongoing challenges of intervening in the traditional demographics and political economies of regional theater. They make clear the additional labor involved in attempts to transform the audience make up and the persistent stasis of the status quo which translates into forms of marginalization. The self-reflexive questioning also places into question the extent to which the intention of the playwright is subsumed within the institutional frameworks of representation that reduce diversity to consumable tropes. And while progressive voices and artists are actively attempting to shift these trends, they continue to perpetuate in limited access to production and other resources.

Despite Hudes's broad nationally recognized success, the more Puerto Rican her play's aesthetics, the more it is presumed to be in the service of, and therefore displayed in, a space associated with Latine theater audiences. This presumption was visible in the Latino Theater Company and Center Theatre Group co-production of Hudes's Elliot trilogy in Los Angeles in 2018. While the desire and collaborative effort to stage the trilogy so the city's theater audiences could access all three plays simultaneously is noteworthy, so are the choices of production venues.[8] *Water by the Spoonful*, the Pulitzer-Prize-winning second installment with a broadly diverse cast was presented at the Mark Taper Forum at the Music Center in Downtown Los Angeles with an audience capacity of 739, while *Elliot, A Soldier's Fugue*, a Pulitzer finalist with a completely Puerto Rican cast played at the Kirk Douglas Theatre venue in Culver City, where they "take risks," and with an audience capacity of 319.[9] *The Happiest Song Plays Last*, not recognized by the Pulitzer committee, incorporates Puerto Rican and Arab/American characters and the musical vocabulary of both the Puerto Rican cuatro and Middle Eastern oud, and was produced by the Latino Theater Company at the Los Angeles Theatre Center.[10] Clearly, assumptions about taste, demand, and accessibility shape placement, as well as conceptions about the function and necessity of art making.

These placements reflect not only the presumed habits of upper-middle-class white regional theater audiences, but more insidiously the critical presumptions of institutional gatekeepers who limit the kinds of stories made accessible to their audiences. Too often these gatekeepers practice static institutional curation, acknowledging only the limited frameworks of their own given circumstances rather than truly exploring the shifting conditions of the world around them.[11] Their practiced refusal perpetuates limited political horizons, resulting in homogenized theatrical programming and dramaturgical flattening that runs the risk of erasing experiential complexities, perpetuating the continued obscuration of unpalatable political realities.

The danger of smoothing the contours of story, so palpable in Hudes's plenary, is also eloquently explored in her prose work *My Broken Language: A Memoir*. This autobiography, while providing insight into her complex familial relationships, argues for storytelling forms that move audiences toward understanding without reducing into conventional structures in the service of palatable coherence. In exploring her extended maternal Puerto Rican family, the Perezes, Hudes highlights the ongoing plagues of violence, addiction, and what she refers to as the "unnamed"[12] HIV culling the family. She highlights her need for a frame to understand the circumstances, a story structure that could shape the experience to enable "the bearing of witness," since she has "[n]o title pages or final paragraphs to name it, no opening sequences or final shots to help me see."[13] This sense of death, omnipresent and hungry, robbing us of potential artists and cultural workers is reflected in Hudes's plays from the period where she charts the loss of crucial figures who maintain forms of community-based artistic activism, but who cannot find an audience. The presence of a meaningfully engaged and respectful audience offering support, a true community, can sustain activist agency, and its absence, real or perceived, can, at its most extreme moments, lead to self-annihilation.

The Happiest Song Plays Last and the Limits of Activism

The Happiest Song Plays Last (*THSPL*) has received significantly less critical attention and fewer productions than the first two plays of Hudes's Elliot Trilogy. While all three are brilliantly structured, each focused on a central musical practice, Puerto Rican cuatro music is less immediately recognizable to a regional theater audience than Bach fugues or Coltrane's free jazz.[14] Crucially for our purposes, *THSPL* explicitly discusses revolutionary change through the Tahrir Square protests in Egypt, a local protest in Philadelphia, and in the premiere production at the Goodman Theatre in Chicago, a framing invocation of the 2009 protests in Arizona advocating for Latine immigrant rights and the importance of ethnic studies (briefly referenced in the text itself). By drawing these events together, the local and the global, *THSPL* inaugurates a thinking of the Puerto Rican diaspora in a different set of global terms.

THSPL centers on two figures from *Water*, Elliot and his cousin Yazmin (Yaz), charting their course after their transformative decisions in Puerto Rico following the scattering of Mama Ginny's ashes (the activist family matriarch and aunt who raised Elliot) that sends Elliot to Hollywood in order to avoid hurting himself and others, and Yaz to purchase Mama Ginny's house and imbed herself more deeply as the next generation activist in the North Philly community.[15] At the start of *THSPL* in January 2011 Elliot is in Jordan starring in a movie he was originally a consultant for (about Marines in the 2003 invasion of Iraq), while negotiating relationships with his Arab American co-star Shar, and Ali, the Iraqi "Consultant on Arab Culture *and* Number One Gofer."[16] Ali volunteers to share the true Middle East, to provide access to his family, to try and establish a very different interpersonal connection than Elliot experienced as a soldier. Over the course of the play and the filming Elliot and Shar become increasingly intimate and in our final encounter with them she is pregnant. Meanwhile, Yazmin struggles with the reality of her role as neighborhood activist; her two primary neighborhood interlocutors are Agustín, an older community music teacher who teaches the cuatro, and Lefty, an unhoused man she pro-actively feeds who sees his responsibility to mark pedestrian fatalities and to protect children from dying by vehicular traffic. Yaz and Elliot have separate scenes in their individual geographies and spend a few scenes connecting through Skype calls, except for the final scene where they are physically reunited at Yaz's house in Philadelphia. The play centers the varied work of quotidian and reparative activism that is necessary but never as simple or as effective as we would wish it to be. By reparative activism I am presuming a concept of civic engagement paralleling the best work of careful inquiry and attention to genuine needs that can be met in their specific contexts rather than a generic sense of progressive intervention. While some might choose to dismiss this as a form of voluntarism that perpetuates systemic inequities, it is simultaneously a form of taking action that insists on the small practices of the everyday in a sustainable form.

THSPL's reference to moments of Egyptian protest in 2011 in Tahrir Square crucially serves as a model of "in the moment" political transformation through a relatively non-violent protest practice. Elliot wants to be a part of this, to witness this social transformation, as an alternative to his participation in military invasion and regime change, as well as potential exoneration from his personal ghost. This evolving revolutionary space is crucially located outside the United States, which changes both its dynamics and potential. This difference is clear as Shar reads from a Facebook post of a protest organizer "When you arrive at Tahrir Square tonight, do not provoke the infantry. No screaming, throwing or insults. Hug a soldier. Bring your sons and daughters, have your child hug the soldier, too. They will not shoot the protestors if they are part of the protestors."[17] Though the protests are a source of aspiration and hope, Ali is reluctant to take them to Egypt because of the potential danger. This difficult ambivalence, of a middle-class interest in revolutionary change combined with the weight of inertia establishes the challenge of sustaining authentic participation in genuine change. The space of Tahrir Square is viewed as dangerous and inaccessible, where the stakes of conflict and resistance pose a higher individual risk than many contemporary liberation movements in the US, where assault, arrest and incarceration are more likely than death; there is also a key question about the extent to which anyone entering from the outside is merely practicing a safe form of allyship that does not account for the true material risks.

This is a difficult question that highlights the knife edge between pragmatic liberation and a form of "safe activism," between measured strategic choices made with significant reflection on consequences and acceptable risk, and mere virtue signaling or avoidance of struggle. There is a genuine doubled sense of aspirational desire and middle-class limits in the exchange that highlights Hudes's recognition of the desires for, and the limits of activism, within specific spaces, as well as a concern about the ease with which such a position can be used to justify non-action or non-participation.

SHAR: Can a gal from Beverly Hills friend the Egyptian revolution?
ELLIOT: Join them. March with them.
SHAR: How? We're two countries away.
. . . .

(Elliot takes the phone, clicks a button.)

ELLIOT: There. You just friended them.
ALI: Congratulations. You are revolutionary! I am, too.[18]

In this moment Shar, Ali, and Elliot are not simply performing an armchair investment in liberation struggles, they are struggling with the meaning of allyship and the ways connectivity is possible and allowed; in doing so, the play also connects an Iraqi refugee in the same mediated revolutionary relationship, despite a presumed greater immediacy of belonging to the geography and political concerns. In response to Shar's ethical question about her geographic, cultural, and potential class differences from the majority of the protestors, Elliot's immediate and simple answer, logistically untenable because of distance, is nonetheless astute about how to sustain revolutionary protest—make the choice to join.

The question of activist involvement requires recognition of which bodies hold higher risk or privilege in the space. Rather than an easy virtue signaling allying to the revolution by accepting the limited virtual "be longing" associated with being a Facebook friend, Shar is empowered both individually and politically by accepting her ethnic/cultural identity through a willingness to accept (and earn) her name.[19] As Hudes asserts, "before revolution, honesty." Eager to experience the revolution in person, Elliot tries to convince Shar to fly from Jordan to Egypt on February 11th, the night of Egyptian President Hosni Mubarak's resignation, cajoling that she is "the one friending them. You're the online revolutionary. But not in the flesh, huh?"[20] "In the flesh" not only evokes a powerful feminist genealogy of material accounts of embodied racial difference in the movement from theory to practice, it also heightens the material embodiment valorized through shared co-presence that makes the energetic potential of revolution palpable. Ignoring the basic fact that Elliot himself clicked the button, his attempt to involve her is genuine, demonstrating a comfortable impurity of motive in the act of political persuasion. In response to his call to "earn your name" she reminds him "People died there, those protestors haven't slept, they've prayed as bullets flew, they held hands to protect each other's prayers, they shouted things their parents were terrified to whisper. I don't get to waltz in and claim that."[21] At the same time, the ethical refusal of connection is problematic because it eliminates the possibility of engagement, the chance that one's political horizon can be shifted to better comprehend the given circumstances and behave accordingly.

After more cajoling and Elliot's insistence that "you do have a choice, and you choose to be nothing" Shar bursts out "Fuck off and do not lecture me! I will be pragmatic, I will self preserve, and I will not apologize for it, especially not to you."[22] Her response highlights the necessity of individual choice, the connections between pragmatism and self-preservation, insisting on structural limits. However, part of the ongoing discomfort with this claim in progressive circles is the extent that these are self-imposed by custom, habitus, or conventional forms of hegemony, rather than generated from the genuine necessity of survival. The expectations for participation within the spaces of struggle for US democracy may indeed be built on unnecessarily artificial restrictions that need to be disrupted, as opposed to the real material violence of spaces working against authoritarian or colonial structures abroad.[23] Yet, the latter clearly exist as well and are the cold hard realities of given circumstances. Hudes's presentation of Shar's negotiation centers a useful ethical dilemma that critiques the easy presumption of efficacy and allyship in the act of participation.

Meanwhile, in North Philly, Yaz struggles to hold a space of ordinary life for her community but constantly encounters the difficult erosion of her soul. Agustín, guidance counselor, traditional music teacher, and Yaz's lover dies from a heart attack in an emergency clinic waiting room, unnoticed until he does not react to the theft of his watch. In addition to highlighting underfunded and overburdened health care in poor communities of color in the US, Agustín's death points to one end of activism with the untimely and unnoticed death of a community leader. The lack of recognition of Agustín's humanity and his fundamental role in the community brings home Yaz's struggle to maintain belief in her position as a community activist in the face of selfish expectation and apathy. While we see her initial call to action, we don't necessarily witness the failure of her protest—it is merely reported in conversation.

This thread also explicitly places the efficacy of community-based service and labor into question as a generative source of revolutionary change within the US. It is important to repeat that this act of questioning is not a refusal of the possibility of efficacy, utility, or importance, but rather a demand for concrete change rather than comfortable reliance on the assumption that activist work will inherently generate political change. This is especially true when faced with empty promises and protestations of solidarity that may be no more than virtue signaling labeled "performative activism." Yet, as theater scholar Michelle Liu Carriger suggests,

> The transformation of performative into an anti-theatrical slur indexes a very reasonable exhaustion and a very correct recognition that representations and statements are unstably attached to action; but to suggest that the verdict of performative is the end of an inquiry, instead of its beginning, would be to cede a vast territory wherein although we can't clearly understand what is happening, things are clearly happening.[24]

Hudes highlights that in this gap between representational calls for change and the snail pace of substantive institutional change, the collective struggle of individuals working to move things forward still matters, as painful and slow and unsatisfying as it too often is. Doing the work matters.

In the press conference that opens the second act Yaz names both the corporate silence and continuing structural failures while narrating Agustín's many community contributions before calling for a protest and boycott. Despite the injustice of this preventable loss and the importance of his impact on the community, only eleven people show up for her protest, a reflection of the inertia against this form of political action, placing into question its presumed efficacy. It is worth noting that both the media and the police show up, indicating the potential for an event with a greater possibility of impact, even though this went unrealized in the world of the play. It is not a failure of advocacy or planning—Yaz has done the necessary work to generate awareness and visibility, contacted potential supporters, done all the right things—yet the protest is much too small to have an impact.

> Guess how many people showed up to *my* protest? . . . . Eleven. There were flyers in every church. *Al Dia* published the details online and in print. Spanish radio announced it. Consilio and Aspira did e-blasts. Everyone I cook for said they would be there. But it drizzled, two drops of water . . . .[25]

Her disappointment surfaces the ongoing challenges of initiating and sustaining change, and even generating protest, in a US context where there is minimal tolerance for risk or even personal discomfort.

This revelation to the audience of an unwitnessed poor protest turnout in the penultimate scene is part of a deliberate juxtaposition with Elliot's report on the revolutionary events in Egypt. Yaz and Elliot Skype from their own global locations, indicated in their stage separation on either side of the stage, which continues until they are interrupted on Elliot's side by Ali's entrance. Elliot shares that he and Shar made it "twenty minutes outside of Cairo" where they assist in tearing down a billboard with Mubarak's face: "Everyone was just calm, just breathing together. Then you could hear the paper of the billboard start to rip. Everyone wanted to cheer, but you can't or else we'll fall down and crush each other. So people were just breathing without cheering, Yazmin, electric."[26] His narration highlights one form of real community efficacy. Rather than joy and cheering, the power of this collective emerges from an ability to "breathe together," a deep sense of ensemble attentiveness combined with a willingness to defer audible celebration until their collective task is complete. The absence of comparable meaningful collective action in her neighborhood triggers a crisis of faith for Yaz who decides to quit her servicial[27] relationship to the community, a decision marked by locking her front door following a refusal to accept Elliot's suggestion that she merely needs a break to recover from her disappointment. Her struggle to function as surrogate community center places into question the extent to which such a position can be constructed in a sustainable way in the current environment. Her choice also reinforces the power of refusal as a means of changing one's circumstances as opposed to perpetuating a cycle of harm and recuperation.

Yaz's abrupt virtual departure at Ali's physical entrance also establishes a productive contrast between the stakes of protest and resistance for even marginalized citizens in the US when compared to undocumented individuals in other geographies. Dramaturgically the visual replacement of two bodies sharing the same real stage space but completely different virtual spaces highlights the difference between US middle class citizens protesting with some minimal faith in institutions protecting their free speech and activism in the Global South in less democratic conditions. And, ironically, in her disappointed emotional state Yaz announces she's "gotta go lock her front door" before "*log[ging] off unceremoniously*" immediately after Ali enters the physical space, posing a question as to whether or not he is an additional provocation toward this reaction (and what this could imply about the racial and cultural politics of her gesture). Ali informs Elliot that he needs to go away for a while as his undocumented Iraqi identity is on the verge of discovery, highlighting his precarity. But despite immediate personal concerns about his safety, Ali is just as worried about the film, something that makes little sense to Elliot in the moment.

> ALI: Do me favor. Tell Nigel I am sick. If he does not know, better. Maybe Nigel hires new Iraqi expert. Here. Phone number of university professor who knows good detail, real Iraqi. Movie should be accurate.
> ELLIOT: Fuck the movie. That's the last thing on my mind right now.
> ALI: Elliot, don't be crazy. Always you are crazy.[28]

For Ali, the risks inherent in discovery are subordinated to the importance of the veracity of the story he is helping craft, and Elliot's craziness is his dismissal of this potential in the face of an immediate crisis. Though his individual story will draw little or no attention, Ali recognizes the movie's inherent potential to access a broader platform and present a more accurate account, which it indeed succeeds in doing in the year-long gap before the play's final scene. Their interaction ends with an exchange of favors. Despite his troubles, Ali has already fulfilled his promise to help Elliot return an Iraqi passport, the key to his personal haunting, by sending it to his "basketball cousin"[29] Nasser to return it to the family. Elliot honors his promise by

"pull[ing] a plastic baggie out of his pocket. It is full of dirt. He gives it to Ali.)

ALI: Good-luck charm. Egypt freedom dirt.
ELLIOT: Revolution in a bag, bro.[30]

Elliot's gift is material remains of the geography of revolution, the land, but also hints at the ease with which such a symbol could be transformed into a commodified sign of allyship without real investment (though such a change is not manifest in this moment).

The play's final scene, one year after the previously sequential scenes, gathers the protagonists into shared co-presence in North Philly to model a process for moving forward, for surviving, and negotiating the difficult realities of the world. This model of daily struggle emphasizes the crucial role of forgiveness despite the complications of moving forward—no one is free of obligation; no one gets away clean. With Elliot's arrival, Yaz forgives Lefty and welcomes him back to her home, indicating her renewed commitment to the community. Rather than being exculpated from the ghost that has haunted him since *Water by the Spoonful*, Elliot finds out that his attempt to return the passport of the first man he killed in Iraq has failed, not because Ali's cousin was unable to find the family, but because in the encounter Nasser learns the horrific truth of Elliot's encounter. A child who witnessed his father's murder at the hands of an American soldier no longer speaks and Elliot must keep carrying the burden of violence. As Ali explains, "I understand rule of soldier. Man makes ghost, man keeps ghost. You cannot give your ghost for someone else's shoulders."[31] There is no exculpation in Ali's words, only the need to take responsibility. There is an understanding of Elliot's humanity and the power of context—following orders—but that cannot justify absolution; instead, the text acknowledges that military and colonial evil are perpetrated by complex individual humans capable of love and sacrifice along with horrific violence. The path forward, never simple, involves Elliot burying the passport in Yaz's garden while Shar watches, pregnant with their child.

Hudes's ending insists that we must maintain our burdens and live with and through them while continuing to strive for change, recognizing it as the sustained slow labor of a lifetime, not a moment of enlightenment or absolution. Burying the passport with his blood in Yaz's garden in Philadelphia opens Elliot up to forgiveness of a particular sort, a necessity arising from the constant introduction of new life coming into the world which is simultaneously predicated on the acceptance of a history whose burden can be managed if it is shared. This possibility of hope, healing, potential growth, a new ecology is always possible in Hudes's gardens, which always explicitly offer an alternative geography of hope in the local space of organic growth.

(Un)timely Activism in *Daphne's Dive*

Hudes's *Daphne's Dive*, which premiered in 2016, initially appears geographically and thematically removed from questions of pragmatic liberation and Puerto Rican status, but Puerto Rico is present in the music and the plants, and the play shares many of the questions that haunt *The Happiest Song Plays Last*. Dedicated to the Chinese American performance artist Kathy Chang(e), it is about the function of art making, politics, and the necessary compromises of survival, ways of making family and negotiating connections in a shared communal space that welcomes and accepts disagreement. It argues implicitly for the joy and possibility of sacrifice in spite of challenges when embraced by an individual's choice and supported by a voluntarist community. Storytelling here is once again a primary mode of sustaining family history and forming community. *Daphne's Dive* insists on "the survival of the ordinary," foregrounding questions of relationality and responsibility as forms of "be longing," as well as modes of art making and politics within a pragmatic framework. It invites us to consider the ways in which everyday life can enable revolutionary change over time on both smaller and larger scales, from sustaining individuals, to shifting electoral landscapes and the built environment, highlighting both present possibility and the personal and collective challenges of transformation.

Set primarily in the titular dive bar in northwest Philadelphia, the Puerto Rican area of the city, *Daphne's Dive* reminds us of the expanded landscape of diaspora. The bar setting enables collective community and networking to support artists through engagement by both laborers and entrepreneurs, an active form of negotiating within the struggle. At the center of this play is a set of contrasts of personal choice in terms of political action and art making illustrated through the starting attitudes and practices as well as the evolution of the characters. The historical scope allows Hudes to dramatize shifting allegiances and political attitudes through shared time in the space, which constitutes its own form of "be longing."[32] Brief statements marking the passage of time and her shifting age from 1994–2011 through the five scenes of the play enable protagonist Ruby to narratively frame events which, like Diaz-Marcano's young female narrator in *REVOLT!* (Chapter 1), explicitly connects the play to precise historical given circumstances and a particular historical trajectory. Over seventeen years we witness evolving relationships and a generational cycle beginning with Ruby's discovery and adoption by Daphne and ending with her behind the bar anticipating Daphne's impending departure to Puerto Rico.

Along the way, the careful juxtaposition of characters' political/artistic journeys emphasizes the limits and the possibilities of being in community. Puerto Rican Acosta is married to, and then later divorced from, Daphne's sister Inez; a member of the entrepreneurial upper middle class, he moves into politics during the play, rising from city councilman to state senator with aspirations. Based on Asian American radical performance artist Jenn's comments, Acosta was once a social activist working the streets and calling for reform in solidarity and co-presence with her protests ("Don't act like we never got arrested together. For blocking rush-hour traffic on Market Street").[33] But the audience tracks him through a familiar model of entrepreneurial capitalist self-hood, moving further and further away from his activist roots. Other regulars criticize this choice, though they tolerate his ambition; but some recognize the importance of his transformation of the neighborhood. His business develops in parallel, from working in an informal economy with his laborers, to formal city contracts, and from bricks to glass. Pablo, the Cuban-born conceptual artist creating art from trash and later the remains of fires, considers Acosta's development work his own form of artistic practice, but refuses to engage in the lucrative but mundane task of painting roadway lines while Rey, the motorcycle riding highly skilled construction worker insists on continuing his life as a day laborer and hires Pablo to do a custom paint job on his bike. While there is an ongoing line of humor about him getting access to the bar's trash, Pablo's collage work is an important means of documenting history. As he suggests to Acosta, "There's decay in the world. Broken pipes, shattered windows. You fix them, I record them."[34] Pablo's insistence on exploring the dumpster for materials for his work enables Ruby's discovery—she had fallen through a glass window into a dumpster during her parents' violent encounter with government officials.

Jenn, the character most explicitly advocating for and working toward the possibility of revolution, is an avatar of Kathy Chang(e), the Chinese American performance artist who spent her last fifteen years staging nearly daily protests on the University of Pennsylvania campus hoping to raise students' consciousness before immolating herself in her most violent act of practice, an act that also ended her life.[35] Jenn first enters the play in a flag inspired bikini with a torn flag calling for "PEACE LIBERTY ECOLOGY DEMOCRACY"—as a counter to Newt Gingrich's contract with America.[36] This revolutionary artist commits suicide by self-immolation as a political act to draw attention to causes that she supports; also a sex worker, she struggles with addiction, over time losing some connections with those who have moved further mainstream with their politics and capitulated to a normative construct of political action. Hudes deliberately shifts the temporality to situate the performance activist in a different historical context and her fictional avatar has a different configuration of compatriots, but nonetheless strongly resonates with Chang(e) through a close adherence to many elements of the biography. But the play extends beyond both her model's lived history and the character's life to reflect on questions of commitment and belief, the personal violence that sometimes accompanies the call for immediate change, and the choices one makes for survival.

Ruby interacts with both artists, curating Pablo's works for her college senior thesis and supporting Jenn in her various protests as a younger child and teenager. The only scene that leaves the space of the bar presents this curation, the first time that Pablo succeeds in selling his artwork, moving forward into more mainstream recognition in European galleries. This moment of recognition is paralleled by Jenn's self-immolation, presented in the play as both a cry for help and a clear political and artistic act of resistance. This convergence contrasts two very different forms of revolutionary action, only one of which allows for survival.

Daphne's primary point of contrast is her sister Inez, a suburban trauma counselor interspersing entrepreneurial capitalist aspiration and traditional grassroots power along with an insistence on her Boricua identity. Inez begins the play married to Acosta, not because of any shared values, but because of their ability to dance well together—in the play's backstory they met at the bar while resolving a brewing conflict through dance. Daphne and

Inez's sibling rivalry and different class experiences are predicated on their experiences growing up in Puerto Rico where Inez was insulated from the incestual sexual violence Daphne lived through, including a caesarian section to remove the offspring. We learn this history in the second scene, in conjunction with the revelation of Ruby's own experience of familial abuse and Daphne's brief, unfulfilling marriage she accepted to get away from her family in Puerto Rico. The sense of a differentially classed experience of sexualized violence resonates throughout Hudes's work and sustains its grounding in everyday struggle.

Jenn's call at her suicide is to wake up, and Pablo and Daphne want to keep Ruby from entering that space of awareness to protect her during a moment of celebration, her impending graduation, and the successful curation of her thesis. Jenn's self-immolation is a fundamentally troubling and ambivalent gesture that cannot be rewound, and in which everyone is complicit. However, instead of being placed in the conventional penultimate moment leading to a comfortably recuperative transformation, it is instead positioned in the middle of the play, followed by two different moments of memorialization of her death which avoid the too easy resolution without giving up on the possibility of change.

At the last, Jenn appears as first Ruby, then both of them, and then Jenn alone reads a poem which ends,

> You are revolution.
> But you need a louder alarm clock
> to shake the cobwebs from your eyes
> Armageddon isn't D-days or mushroom clouds
> it's the moment the tree forgets the soil
> And so I will be your sunrise awakening
> And so I will be your torch for liberty
> And so I will try to spark the discussion
> I'll light the match of your human memory
> and come ablaze with transformation
> Wake up[37]

This poem claims an inherently revolutionary consciousness in everyone that needs to be awakened or remembered, asserting that the apocalypse is not nihilistic violence but rather a stripping away of one's connections to the earth. While the repeated imagery of light and fire are resonant with Jenn's performative act, the decision to serve as a spark exhibits tremendous faith in the untapped potential of humanity. There is an immense trust in the capacity for transformation and a level of optimism that should be celebrated but not overly simplified. The tension between transformative consciousness raising and pragmatic liberation is not necessarily the opposition of optimism and pessimism, but rather an acknowledgement of given circumstances. If, in fact, the human conditions contain an untapped revolutionary potential, then moving to access it would be a logical step in the right direction. The question is whether such a conclusion is grounded in attentive experience or untested optimism.

This call to wake up also has echoes in other places. On one hand it recalls the first images of Jose Rivera's *Marisol* where acts of immolation are acts of neo-Nazi violence against the homeless and not forms of artistic and political resistance.

Spray-painted on the wall is this graffiti-poem.

The moon carries the souls of dead people to heaven.
The new moon is dark and empty.
It fills up every month
with new glowing souls
then it carries its silent burden to God. WAKE UP.

The "WAKE UP" looks like it was added to the poem by someone else.[38]

The poem also echoes the language of Chang(e)'s Final Statement in which she uses the term "Armageddon" and offers herself as "a torch for liberty." Jenn's poem becomes a call that can only ever be a memorialization because she made the choice to absent herself physically from the space; in this moment in the play the group moves off to celebrate her during an occupy event with Angela Davis, mourning the presumed necessity of personal violence as the grounds of revolution.

In her "final statement" intended to define her suicide, Chang(e) herself wrote,

> I want to protest the present government and economic system and the cynicism and passivity of the people in general. I want to protest this entirely shameful state of affairs as emphatically as possible. But primarily, I

want to get publicity in order to draw attention to my proposal for immediate social transformation. To do this I plan to end my own life. The attention of the media is only caught by acts of violence. My moral principles prevent me from doing harm to anyone else or their property, so I must perform this act of violence against myself . . .[39]

An explicit advocate for the possibility of "transformation now," her history reinforces both the appeal and the dangers of this political platform. Her fervent belief in immediate transformation was predicated on capitalism's failure and dangerous association with freedom, as well as her recognition of an encroaching authoritarian sensibility, all political concerns that have continued and accelerated in the 21st century. While she was not successful in generating sustained support for her political position, she was able to continue her practice until she decided that the only reasonable catalyst was self-destruction. There is clear evidence that Chang(e) had been thinking about this for a long time as she had been experimenting with different accelerants for more than a year; performance scholar Joseph Shahadi reminds us that,

She made a strategic decision to use her death for a larger purpose, which removes her actions from the merely personal and places them back in the world—a world that acted upon her, to be sure, but one that she, with her spectacular public suicide, also acted upon. If Change was mentally ill she was also a political activist and performance artist and these identities do not preclude one another.[40]

She fundamentally believed in an instinctual human goodness that needed to be released and encouraged to allow radical transformation, and while many of her claims can be argued as familiar forms of paranoia, others clearly echo the careful thinking of anti-multinational corporate activists whose visibility Chang(e) predated and anticipated.[41]

Shahadi's argument is that Chang(e) performed radical disappearance and while her stated intent was to free herself from her body to enter the spirits of students in a position to transform the world, her death disseminated her presence and ideas through emerging forms of digital distribution. While the work of Friends of Change, and the continued presence of the website www.kathychange.org supports his argument, the increasing fragility of the internet as archive means that even some of Shahadi's references have become inaccessible. At the same time, since the publication of his article, her life has been theatricalized in Soomi Kim's one woman show *Chang(e)* in addition to her presence in Hudes's play.[42]

In Hudes's play Jenn's choice to self-immolate forces Ruby to negotiate her own meaningful path through art, politics, and activism. Changing the historical chronology, Hudes moves the play into a virtual present and places Jenn's suicide in 2003 simultaneously with Ruby's college graduation. The characters of the play are recipients of her final message and do not engage in time (if that was ever even a possibility); though in Hudes's play there has been a gradual drifting apart as Jenn's mental state and addiction along with her ruthless critique of others' choices become increasingly difficult to engage with. But she importantly evades the strong pull of servicial conditions that haunt so many of Hudes's protagonists.

Ruby is at the center of *Daphne's Dive*, not only because of her framing voice, but by the symbolic pragmatism of the "lucky shoe" nailed to the bar that symbolically and actively holds this group together after Scene 1. The shoe's story is a necessary improvisation that solidifies into a lucky charm materially and figuratively keeping people in this place. To understand this, we begin with the last scene of the play, a return to the beginning but not quite the earliest moment, as Ruby had not yet entered the space at the chronological start of the play. In this scene, Ruby has been with Daphne a brief time and her biological mother is now free from jail and wants to see her. Ruby is hesitant to see her mother but doesn't have a good enough reason to justify temporarily staying with Daphne, so Daphne improvises by setting up a situation in which Ruby has supposedly stepped on a nail and ruined her shoe. She intends to make this fiction real by nailing a hole in Ruby's shoe, but instead of placing a nail hole in the shoe, she nails the shoe to the bar, connecting the object firmly to the space, generating simultaneously a material synecdoche for Ruby's presence as well as an accidental, necessary, generous, and mildly problematic irrevocable gesture that becomes part of history. The shoe cannot and will not go away. Omnipresent in the play, only at the end do we learn its origin story, shifting our understanding of an idiosyncratic icon into a fundamental reminder of Daphne's determined commitment to Ruby. It reflects love, connection, and basic human responsibility, a sense of "be longing" that maintains Ruby's fundamental place in the bar. It symbolically and materially illustrates the ambivalent ties that hold us in place as other things which may have once kept us together shift underneath.[43]

Though from one point of view Jenn's revolutionary act fails, this concept of failure is based on idealized effects; Jenn's act does generate a memorial legacy that catalyzes different forms of pragmatic activism in everyday life. While confirming that revolutions are too often out of time or out of place, her act epitomizes the desire for an imminent future moment of transformation that drives revolutionary action. However, *Daphne's Dive* crucially avoids this utopic futurity by situating radical sacrifice not as an ultimate gesture, but as one act in an ongoing path of life. In doing so it insists on the need to honor acts of struggle while still viewing them through unvarnished lenses that recognize both artists' intention and labor, as well as real material and communal attitudinal change—acts of everyday survival.

Genealogy and legacy, both personally and politically, serve as connective tissue beyond the everyday norm, suggesting the additive weight of lived continuity. This is briefly illustrated in Acosta's suit passed from man to man to serve for important occasions, and more thoroughly in the connections of mothers and daughters. Daphne, like Yaz in *THSPL*, has voluntarily accepted the role of motherhood without a partner, and she treats Ruby better than her own mother did. The intimate relationship of the family related first by blood is renegotiated as a family by choice which serves as another mode of everyday survival. The legacy of familial rape becomes clear, along with a child that was given up because she was only 12 when she gave birth by C-section, almost the same age Ruby is when she hears the story from Daphne at the end of the play. It is important to end with this connection after the departure to memorialize Jenn once more, because it highlights choice and necessity, need and gaps, offering a model of everyday survival and choice that acknowledges trauma but also personal strength. The need for survival is crucial despite the truth that part of life must occur among other people whose actions and points of view one struggles to accept.

For Daphne's survival it is crucial not to fall into the trap of being "servicial." She must draw the line between being of service and being ground down by an externally mandated and destructive selflessness, and she shares this understanding early on with Ruby.

> DAPHNE: Mami was servicial. Always serving the men first, pouring orange soda for the kids.
> RUBY: Same like you.
> DAPHNE: No, that's my nightmare. There's a line where being humble isn't cool. Her back was so hunched from waiting on my father, her eyelashes grazed the damn ground.[44]

While Ruby sees parallels, Daphne has established a clear and conscious limit of the presumed and traditionally accepted gender asymmetry of the world and the ways in which this asymmetry can be crushing. Charting this alternative possibility requires maintaining a line in the sand; through the frame of bartending her acts of service become professional rather than personal. But even her mother demonstrated resistance. A powerful anecdote of her mother's walk across the island in only one shoe to participate in a cooking contest despite her husband's opposition reflects both personal power, and pride in suffering. The difficulty of proceeding in one shoe leads to the idea of keeping Ruby a little longer, but Daphne's desire to generate material evidence ends up nailing the shoe to the bar, enabling her to accept Ruby's necessary presence despite the fact she "[makes her] raw, like Mami's bloody foot."[45] Rather than taking pleasure in the pain, Daphne understands this as a necessary personal and political act that enables survival in the everyday, and eventually the continued lineage for curating a necessary space of community building and artistic patronage, as Ruby takes over as tender for the dive bar.

Paper Towels and the Further Limits of Activist Violence

Nelson Diaz-Marcano's one act play *Paper Towels* charts an unsuccessful attempt to draw attention to the human cost of the failed response to Hurricane Maria; its artist protagonist Toño even commits suicide in his desperate desire for recognition.[46] Official death tolls at the time of the play in 2019 counted less than one hundred people killed in the violence of the storm and its immediate aftermath, rather than the more than 3000 killed due to lack of medical care, exposure, hunger, and other factors, deaths that could have easily been prevented by the kind of attention reserved for white mainland citizens.[47] Investigative journalists and artists were at the forefront of calling for an acknowledgement of the losses and the differential size and speed of investments in providing emergency aid to displaced US citizens. Regular comparisons were made with the travesty of black bodies trapped and suffering in the aftermath of Hurricane Katrina in Louisiana with insufficient federal aid resources.[48]

The play's title stems from a widely circulated moment of colonial callousness when then President Donald Trump, in a visit to San Juan, purportedly to more fully grasp the effects of the natural disaster and the subsequent human tragedy, was captured on video throwing rolls of paper towels into a crowd.[49]

To allow for such an event presumably someone conceived of this distribution method as a sign of personal engagement, compassion, and meaningful assistance. Instead, it was recognized and vilified as a clear symbol of the federal government's continuing failure to meaningfully address the impact of natural disasters when the primary recipients of violence are black, brown, and/or colonial citizens who do not necessarily speak English, despite their equal rights to access assistance. To be clear, the catastrophic damage was not merely a result of the violence of wind and rain, but also a decrepit power system and an economy, already devastated by unconstitutional mandated austerities[50] that also suffers the logistical challenges of being predicated on the importation of basic food while relying on a single port for most of its imports. In addition, because of the continuation of colonial administrative practices more than 100 years old, the legal designation of Puerto Rico as a coastwise property, Puerto Rico is only allowed to receive ships from New Orleans and New York and not directly from foreign governments.[51] While this law was briefly suspended to enable some direct aid to reach the island by ship, corruption in procurement and hiring of contractors to repair the grid, as well as insufficient appropriation of funds to insure necessary shipments of supplies, including basic food and water and the construction materials to re-roof houses, delayed productive aid. Only in October 2020, more than 3 years after the disaster, did President Trump finally release $12 billion of relief money to Puerto Rico in what some saw as a gesture to garner votes in the November election. While some individuals evacuated in the immediate aftermath, the corruption and delayed aid meant that there was a mass exodus of those, like Toño, who had family or other resources or connections on the mainland. For some the archipelago became a blank slate for new forms of elitist capitalist investment, a rapidly encroaching future dystopia masquerading as benign investment.[52]

Set on the mainland, *Paper Towels* does not explicitly address the forces of finance capitalism and the rapacious consumption of cryptocurrency in its libertarian environmental violence, instead focusing on an acknowledgement of the loss of life, infrastructure, and the refusal of US federal politicians to act to provide meaningful aid. A two-hander, *Paper Towels* deliberately engages with the revolutionary politics of violence—specifically why and how a shooting can or should meaningfully enact change. The play addresses political questions of generating visibility, seeking redress, and working through the seduction of spectacular violence and its limits in relation to highlighting the colonial condition of Puerto Rico.

A climate refugee displaced from the island and living with his cousin Mariel, Toño is desperate to draw attention to the real scope of the devastation, the losses, and the continued lack of intervention to Hurricane Maria. He combines Taíno myth and Puerto Rican revolutionary figures as touchstones for a potential revolutionary action framed within artistic practice to call out the scale of human loss, economic disenfranchisement, and environmental refugees. The play explores performance as an (im)possible source of political resistance, accounting for specific histories and cultural transmissions across the transit from archipelago to diaspora.

Set in his cousin Mariel's dance studio, the play tracks the completion of Toño's installation memorializing the Puerto Rican dead and the debate over his intention to raise awareness of the Puerto Rican situation by shooting a Senator. Conversational exchange between Mariel and Toño is the heart of this play, taking place almost entirely in real time except for brief introspective monologues that temporarily suspend time. Toño's interests help focus attention, not only on the trauma of loss but also on the material effects on the living and the dead, on the fact that bodies were unburied by the storm. Diaz-Marcano activates the cousins' bodies through dance and games, opening up the structure of "be longing" as a necessary human act even as Toño tries to refuse the fundamental power of creating material human connection between one and another made palpable through physical connection. The negotiation of embodied art through dance and games serves a physical supplement to the verbal argument over the utility of his proposed action.[53] Much of the physical action of the play is taken up initially with his art project, his struggle with his gun, moments of dancing together and separately, and a game to determine the outcome. In the end, Toño shoots himself instead of committing his intended act of violence against the Senator. And the media repeating of the aftermath elevates and amplifies Mariel as a hero stopping a terrorist attack rather than directing attention to Toño's real grief and grievances, something Mariel had anticipated and tried to use as evidence to dissuade him from his plan.

Their arguments span issues of racism, colorism, and the cultural function of dance forms in relation to connections of knowledge and culture. In doing so, the play explores expectations about language and knowledge and the ways in which histories circulate as particular forms of truth in a variety of forms. This map of ambivalent tensions paints the contours and fault lines of conceptions of Puerto Rican culture on the island and the mainland. Toño's outsider position is reflected in his inability to get Alexa to understand his

Before Revolution, Honesty?   147

voice commands, "Alexa, mi amor play Aguanile de Hector Lavoe," but the stage directions inform us that *"Alexa does her schtick "Now playing," but what coms [sic]out is anything but. A catchy but terrible pop song like Aqua's "Barbie Girl" starts blasting.*[54] Positioned outside the programmed consumer demographic, Toño's language practice eludes Alexa's, humorously highlighting his distance from certain forms of popular musical culture. In Mariel's attempts to get Toño to see the relative irrationality of his position, she insists he explain how he broke the Echo, in a sense asking him to work through his assumptions and to begin to understand how things actually function in this environment. His humorously frustrating interaction with the device illustrates both Alexa's homogenizing and conventional responses as referenced earlier, but also Mariel's different taste in music.

> TOÑO: Alexa No, fo que es eso! Alexa stop. (Beat) Play Aguanile . . . Hector Lavoe!

> *A reggaeton song from the 90's comes through. The kind that only real life booty droppers know.*

> TOÑO: Que jodienda. Alexa stop! Me quitas la concentracion and that's not the song I asked for. (Beat) Se nota that you are Mariel's echo with that music. Y que reaggaeton?[55]

Toño's choice of Héctor Lavoe as a subject for his installation and as background music is important because of Lavoe's role within Puerto Rican culture. Mariel's first critique of his unsanctioned occupation of her dance studio is his choice of Lavoe for his installation. Toño's desired song choice, "Aguanile," is particularly poignant because, as Frances R. Aparicio suggests, in an interwoven reading of the song and a short story of the same title about the impact of listening to it,

> A current reading of "Aguanile" as both sonic and literary text allows us to find a language for mourning after María and, possibly, a space for relationality between the island and the diaspora, between gender subjectivities . . . and among Puerto Ricans of diverse generational identities.[56]

Lavoe's song and his overall practice are read differently in generational and gendered terms, with feminist scholars critiquing the problematic masculinity of the work even though for (primarily male) listeners of past generations he creates affective community. Mariel's resistance is precisely along these lines, as is, presumably Toño's slightly anachronistic attraction. The strong sense of healing and mourning, and the failure to get access to this potential balm, adds to the poignancy of the technological disconnect.

Diaz-Marcano establishes a strong sense of "almost . . . reverence" for the gun and its "power"[57] through Toño's physical relationship with it, which in the 2019 INTAR production was visually similar to an AR-15 automatic rifle fully capable of carrying out a massacre (the title given to any mass casualty event in Puerto Rico). The gun is quick access to a recognizable form of power that in the end is ubiquitous enough to work against the intended political specificity of its project—shooting does not draw attention to a political cause. His cousin Mariel makes this argument, and the play agrees that despite the seductive possibility of power, a gun in a BIPOC hand is not recognized as an act of political resistance or necessary survival. Calling on "Lolita" "Albizu" and "Betances"[58] Toño situates himself within a revolutionary axis of Puerto Rican history, his own physical fear and uncertainty manifest in a shaking reaction that requires his own personal pep talk to begin to move into the mind set where it might be possible to commit murder in the service of political action.

Mariel's return to stop Toño is nearly cut short when he points the gun at her and pulls the trigger. They are both saved from this intrafamilial horror by his failure to release the safety, setting up both a point of dramatic tension as well as reinforcing Toño's lack of familiarity with firearms:

> And what exactly are you doing, hermanito? Cause I'm confused right now. I see you got a gun, so you shooting them folks out there, but there you got that pretty installation there, and then you tell me is a necessary step . . . So you promoting your art while taking the necessary step of killing innocents, is that what it is?[59]

Mariel recognizes his idealism as equally selfish narcissism—a need and desire to do something because of the ways that grief and loss have made him feel disempowered.

Toño struggles to find a justification for his actions in his own language. He quotes various historical figures, from Betances, to Albizu to Lebrón to justify his action, and yet he also recognizes the potential violence of his intention. The son of a military man, his actions are also a reflection of the betrayal of the US; his recognition of the ways in which the US does not live up to its responsibilities in Puerto Rico sets the groundwork for his personal resistance. While not overt, there is a potential critique of militarized masculinist violence implied by Diaz-Marcano's sustained belief in the futility of gun violence as a source of transformation. When Toño cannot find another answer to justify his actions, he settles on labeling himself "the hurricane"[60] calling on the Taíno God and the impact of his presence on the island in an increasingly surreal moment. Taíno invocation is once again deployed here as a way of stepping outside of colonial legacies and starting anew. Toño's voicing of the familiar intersection of love of Puerto Rico as a geography, its natural beauty, is tinged with anger at the degradations and destruction of hundreds of years of colonialism. But whereas before his anger at the impact of colonialism was assuaged by his love for the beauty of the island, Hurricane Maria's devastation, the explicit visual record of destruction, has taken away that balance point, forcing him to directly face his anger and pain. Directly encountering these emotions accelerates him toward the sloppy power of a trigger. And the play seems to both ask for a slowing down and implicitly to reassert the necessary step of storytelling—of making others fully aware, something that happens even to Mariel as she learns about the effects of the hurricane on cemeteries.

Paper Towels clearly exists in a historical moment (2019) whose politics reflect both a heightened attention to the fact that Black Lives Matter and careful attention to the realities of how acts of violence get read based on the skin color of the perpetrator. This explicit acknowledgment of both systemic racism that exists on the island and the mainland, and the related but not equivalent violence of colonialism, come together in the dialogue about how Toño's actions will be read. Mariel questions the feasibility of his action as a means of raising consciousness. His defense is based on a recitation of famous sayings from various failed revolutionaries, asserting a need to act despite the blood, despite the shame that it will bring to his family because something must be done. This revolutionary exuberance is ultimately unsuccessful, and the power of the play is a celebration of this desire for necessary action, while recognizing that spectacular acts cannot in and of themselves transform thinking and engagement. Unlike Jenn in *Daphne's Dive*, who sees self-violence as a catalyst to energize existing potentials, oddly enough because of her inherent optimism in human potential, Toño's clearly problematic and desperate solution is the use of violence against others. Ironically, though, he also echoes Pablo and Ruby's artistic curation through his desire to simultaneously offer an art installation as a different form of consciousness raising.

Toño's attempts to legitimize his action by establishing a clear legacy end with him invoking a Taíno story that conceives violence as a double cut, beginning one thing but ending another.

> MARIEL: Fucking mass shooting? Best thing you can come up with?
> TOÑO: Violence is always the start of something.
> MARIEL: Because it ends something else.
> TOÑO: You know that one of the Taino myths had to do with a father killing a son cause he didn't trust him?
> MARIEL: En serio?
> TOÑO: Y despues, he put that head on some gourd, and from there the fish were created. We got our food, from a family member killing another.[61]

Here. Toño relies on a Taíno myth that suggests the ancestral roots of internecine violence are at the heart of community survival. His story reiterates the intimacy of conflicts about the best path forward, while serving as a basic decolonial gesture, shifting away from received histories to offer an alternative story.

Their conflict also reflects an alternative embodied thinking—that forms of dance itself can be a kind of rebellion and at minimum serve as an argument for the advancement of a different form of holistic identity away from "bullshit boricua duality . . . the duality of dropping ass or standing straight"[62] as Mariel asserts. She refuses Toño's parroting of an older generation's moral concerns about particular forms, insisting instead on the importance of joy as an act of rebellion. This rejection of imposed morality asserts the crucial power of dance as embodied action and reflects consideration of dance forms and their cultural, identitarian, and political positioning. While each form exists in multiple iterations that have their own racial, political, and cultural histories, dance itself writ large also operates as an effective metaphor. If one takes seriously José Ramón Sánchez's understanding of Puerto Rican political practice in New York as a dance, it becomes crucial to recognize not only how one leads or follows or is given proper cues or wears the proper costume or performs the choreography, but where the impulse initiates and how it travels through the body.[63] In the literal and metaphorical exploration of this travel we can see how the sequencing of movement through the body is a lived practice of corporeal politics that requires significant time to develop. As such, it allows us to look anew at the way dramatists have formed networks of articulation, through language and bodies, that change the configuration of relationality. The location of this play in a dance studio, and the negotiation of dancing bodies, highlights the physical and intimately material nature of their engagement.

Mariel insists that the revolutionary history that Toño cites is a history of failed attempts, but that does not change his thinking. She has no delusions about an idealistic revolutionary action—she knows he will be seen only as a terrorist and dismissed as such—that his reasons will not become visible in the media accounts of what occurred, whether he is successful or not. And it is this gap between the imagined action of rebellion that might change the world and the desire to do something, anything, that helps clarify the stakes and heighten the sense of entrapment and futility.

If such a revolutionary action were to work, Diaz-Marcano would be writing us into a utopian future precisely because we would have entered another world, one in which the complexities of the current world have been elided. Instead, he keeps us firmly situated in a present very much like our own, where the admirable desire for action is tempered by a sense of impossibility that nonetheless points toward an alternative. At the same time the level of horror of Maria's impact is reiterated through a recognition that is not only the number of dead from the hurricane and its collateral impacts, but the flooding and erosion that have exposed corpses to the sun; the previously buried are now unearthed and baking in the sun, a moment of horror that revisits historical death.

There is no convincing argument for revolutionary violence in this play; instead, the son is destroyed by his own hand, and it is from this act that a modicum of change arises, much like the Taíno myth but in a different form. The importance of dancing together establishes a different mode of relationality. If power is a dance and attention is drawn to the interrelationships that must be negotiated, then the dancing between Mariel and Toño becomes a form of knowing one another, potentially as well, offering a different way of being in the world. In the longest extended sequence, the stage directions indicate:

> The lights dim as he holsters the gun on the side of his pants, the room feels like a club. Toño grabs Mariel and they dance Salsa like they are experts. They twirl, they have fun. The song is now louder than anything. They rally

each other. At one moment they break out and they dance off. Then she gets close again and they dance. This is the most fun they had, this is them challenging each other as kid and seeing how they do as adults.[64]

Like *REVOLT!* there is a contest based on a childhood game that determines, in this case, the ultimate outcome for the characters, reflecting Diaz-Marcano's investment in the power of play for personal and political decision making, and for consciousness raising. The game "1,2,3 pescao colorao,"[65] will determine who gets the gun, as Mariel is unwilling to leave but Toño will not back down on his intended path. The game, performed in a heightened space of narrative action with a shift in lighting to reflect the physicalized intensity of the stakes, offers an alternative model to the previous contestation manifest in and through dancing bodies.

Unlike the cooperative competition of dancing bodies responding and building from one another while still set in dialogue and competition, the game 1,2,3 pescao is about surveillance and control. The one in control generates pauses, containing and constraining movement in exact opposition to the freedom proposed by the dancing body. There is evasion and concealment, determining ways of moving without being caught, and adjusting one's personal rhythm of movement to work with and against the figure who calls out and constrains action. On the stage, sound and lighting heighten the deliberately "slow motion" effect to raise the stakes for both players and audience. In doing so, it establishes a specific slow rhythm of heightened attention in which one's actions are scrutinized to a much higher level than in everyday life. In this space of game, the contest itself has taken on a ritual or ceremonial quality, and the nature of attention has shifted from the easy dialogic realism of political debate to a consensual decision-making process enabled through moving bodies.

Rather than committing homicide, Toño instead commits suicide; in doing so, he allows for the fully intended consequence of uplifting his cousin, while failing to enact the change and draw attention to the specific plight of those suffering on the island of Puerto Rico. We see this clearly as Mariel counts through the steps of the game. Her increasing intimacy, both through physical proximity and through her narration of multiple acts of kindness she has received, clarifies the ability of a single life to lift up another. Even though Toño can never realize his dream of a single life serving to draw attention to the plight of a people, the play itself is intended in this direction. The paper towels, a symbolic comment on the ineffectual way of engaging with the aftermath, end up being used to clean the aftermath he creates, something that he in fact anticipates and sees as an ironically "considerate"[66] action. This gesture reiterates from the fundamental anger that injustice cannot simply be wiped away like the blood generated by the offering of his own life staged in front of an altar of memory and revolutionary history.

And this offering has a second function that Mariel is unable to grasp until it manifests. As Toño anticipates, Mariel is celebrated because no one understands or wants to know the complexity of the real story. In her final monologue she insists:

> It didn't matter, by the time I told them the story they had twisted and turn everything for their political gains. The liberals ask "How come he had a gun? How did he get that", the conservatives said "They are obviously dangerous people, maybe we should reconsider citizenship" but nobody ask or said anything about him. His sweetness. His care. Nobody talked about the Toño we knew. Nobody talk about how had he lost his island and his faith had gone with it. How he couldn't see anything else despite all his life being able to see far beyond all of us. How a tragedy had broke down the best of us. No, all they gave a shit about was how they could use his actions. And all I care about was what he told me at the end. He said that he knew our people had problems to fix within our own society, but how can we fix it if we cease to be here. Cease to be here? . . . . I guess he was right about Salsa it might not be ours, but it let people knew we existed. He was right. He usually was (*A moment, a painful moment*) But the thing he missed to tell me was what am I supposed to do now that he, himself, ceased to exist?[67]

Her insistence on the fact that both sides of the political debate had no space for his action clarifies the ways in which his version of politics is impossible in the currently bifurcated and oversimplified world of US politics. No one really wants to know his story, which on a simple level shows the crucial importance of drama to embody stories in their full complexity in a way journalism, and especially popular media accounts, constrain. The danger, though, remains the encounter with a story that we already presume to know. Toño imagines a world where his use of a gun can step outside the reductive binaries of politics and the pre-determined structures of storytelling and end with something new. The play itself, as many do, is an attempt to provide this complex back story, to fill in the given circumstances to such an extent that the familiar dramaturgy is no longer satisfying, showing the potential for erasure that asks the audience to learn differently.

Of course, whether the audience can in fact be moved to action by the play (and it offers the clearly paradoxical conclusion that Toño's art within it is unsuccessful), the specificity of the story now has material presence; it has been spoken. While there are precise rhetorical mechanisms of power in place to try and reconfigure these events into a more sympathetic narrative that aligns with pre-existing structures, the play itself stages the more complex narrative as a counter to the US erasure of Puerto Rican realities. In doing so, we at a minimum move from metaphorical claims about the work of colonial racism to an impassioned manifestation of palpable violence that reinvokes the intensity of the material impact of Hurricane Maria as an ongoing symptom of colonial neglect. Not that such awareness will bring change, but with repetition, perhaps we can begin to expand the conditions of story for those trapped within a myopic liberal history of the United States. We can provide new stories that offer a starting place and further steps forward in the process of practicing new forms of education in our interrelationality, our potentially transformative connection to others.

As Mariel reminds Toño and the audience "You forget once your skin is a different color the cause do not matter. Your act will get attention alright, but not the one you want. A different culture means you don't get the mental health excuse. You get a label. A label that shouldn't be yours."[68] The explanations collapse precisely because there is the historical weight of white supremacy that no longer allows individual stories to be told; forms are compressed because of pre-existing assumptions about both race and culture. In this case, the "mental health" excuse is not available, despite the insanity of unfreedom and colonial violence. The play itself, and the story of one life is precisely that which begins to draw attention to the complexity of what has been lived and erased. By structuring his call to arms as an artistic intervention, Toño presents a version of the power and the limits of the installation itself. It can be transformative for those in a position ready to learn, to encounter the terms of governmental neglect and the erasure of lived experience. It is supposed to be his legacy, but it is only legible to those who have been taught how to read it. And the final call, like the end of *REVOLT!*, is a refusal of martyrdom, because the continued present struggle allows for the possibility of dancing, of moving, of changing, and making the story more complex.

One of Mariel's last admissions in her final monologue that "he was right about Salsa it might not be ours, but it let people know we existed,"[69] opens the potential for thinking and transformation within pre-existing constraints. This shifting question about the appropriateness of history and the ways in which colonial stories take on their own rhetorical force seems crucial to carefully articulating the connective limits of logic. On the one hand it is an act of capitulation that perhaps is unnecessary, but it nonetheless demonstrates a need to connect to the audience, to move from a space of existing knowledge, assumptions, and projected identities on a pathway toward new forms of thinking. In the next chapter we are presented with the possibility of revolution enacted, and importantly the problematic limits that emerge in the moment of this interaction through two plays that engage the aftermath of revolutionary action, José Rivera's *Massacre: Sing to Your Children*, and Kristoffer Diaz's *#therevolution*.

CHAPTER 5

After the Revolution

MASSACRES, COLLATERAL DAMAGE, AND MOVING FORWARD

While moments in the previous chapters have explored the ambivalent potential of individual acts of resistance and revolution, collective revolutionary action has primarily appeared as an unrealized (and sometimes unrealizable) possibility, reaffirming the need for alternative models of thinking about emancipatory practice. Taking up this possibility, it is worth considering what a transformational revolutionary future looks like in dramatic terms. Within the framework of pragmatic liberation, such a vision needs to be presented on a realistic basis, acknowledging the potential unintended impacts on those closest to us and the ways in which personal relationships impact and are impacted by the practice of revolution, as well as the capacity for sustaining revolution. While there are historical examples of successful revolutions, in the contemporary period most of the references to revolution are to instances which have failed, been unsustainable, lost their way, or are under constant threat. Beginning with the famous authoritarian co-optation of the communist impulse there are ongoing threats to movements for popular democracy by militaries and the global forces of neoliberal capitalism, as well as populist movements invested in maintaining forms of national identity that retain inequitable status quo governance structures. But despite the difficulty of beginning and sustaining revolution, there is still a strong imaginative desire and need for concerted collective action to transform the status quo.

To examine the paradoxical tension between the necessity and desirability of revolution on one hand, and the real practical challenges engaged in insuring and sustaining meaningful change, we return to the work of José Rivera and Kristoffer Diaz, who have, in *Adoration of the Old Woman* and *All Ears*, demonstrated a necessary suspicion of the rhetoric of easy transformation. This chapter explores the potential critique offered by and through the logics of pragmatic liberation in relation to revolutionary action that has already taken place. The two plays under examination, José Rivera's *Massacre: Sing to Your Children* and Kristoffer Diaz's *#therevolution*, both question the efficacy of revolution, exploring the complex challenges that emerge in the aftermath of revolution, and the necessary intentional and unintentional messiness of revolt. Rather than presenting a future fictional moment of Puerto Rican revolt, these plays figure their actions within an immediate present/future in the mainland US: Rivera's play in Granville, New Hampshire, and Diaz in any of a list of hipster neighborhoods, including Silver Lake, Los Angeles. Both plays expand the conceptual scope of our investigation of pragmatic liberation as we move into geographies less explicitly shaped by legislatively mandated structural differences of US and Puerto Rico. In extending beyond the explicit framework of coloniality into questions of authoritarianism and inequality, Diasporic Puerto Rican playwrights move away from the specific history of Puerto Rico but retain a deep investment in explicating and critiquing the persistence of inequities of power. Both plays chart the emergence of revolution from a small or intimate group, the necessity for action based on the collapse of the politics of relation in the face of a sustained inegalitarian structure of power, and the complex deeply personal and contested aftermath of revolutionary action. Through both plays there is an important growing realization of post-revolutionary interpersonal challenges even within the very terms of radical political resistance. This general resistance to representing the easy premise of revolutionary action, and the sustained suspicion of utopic transformation and change, reflect both the minor and major degradations of the conditions of everyday life through the obscured colonial condition as well as the implied necessity to consider questions of sustainability prior to action.

The Challenge of Revolutionary Change in *Massacre (Sing to Your Children)*

In his political allegory *Massacre (Sing to Your Children)* José Rivera foregrounds the difficulty of sustaining a revolutionary project in the face of fear, self-interest, and the contemporary US political climate. The play, which premiered in 2007, eerily echoes more recent concerns with the seductive, charismatic rhetoric of a populist leader shifting the very conditions of our lived environment. *Massacre* begins with the aftermath of a tiny revolutionary purge—seven people rushing into a room with an assortment of bloodied weapons, having just killed a monster, Joe, who has dominated their community, manipulated them, and destroyed loved ones; they have come together communally, despite their fear, to commit a violent murder to restore their community. *Massacre* stays within the single confined space of this event, asking how does one move forward into the future? Is it possible to sustain a coalition of like-minded individuals once an authoritarian threat has been defeated? What are the conditions that allow such a structure to emerge? And what can actually keep the horror from returning?

Massacre insists on coalition building; even in its single action of gathering together to collectively murder an authoritarian figure. A provisional assemblage of individuals invest in a shared goal for their own specific needs and logics. Their level of commitment to the goal and to each other ranges from fragile to resilient. Erik, the *"philosophical leader"* of the group articulates the nature of Joe's dominance and their liberation as follows:

> Think of all the ways he uncoupled words from their natural meanings. All the savage mind-games he played on a population of sheep. Remember how we reacted with all the stupid impulses he landscaped for us. How we walked his roads the way he *twisted* them. The laws our parents trusted: that gravity pulls them down, that the sun precedes daylight, that hearts are designed for loving, that night is for rest and stars for focusing desire... you couldn't trust those laws 'cause he subverted them and told us exactly what he would do and we didn't listen 'cause we stopped trusting the sound of our instincts.[1]

This shift away from instinctual knowledge is symptomatic of a broadly environmental transformation of human experience within a distorted world. Joe, who reflects in part the interventionist policies of the two Bush presidential administrations, has transformed the conditions of everyday life, warped the function of language, and shifted lived experience into a realm of fearful uncertainty. The ultimate spin doctor, he "landscaped" their entire political geography, making it extremely difficult to think or act outside the borders he installed. The medium is language, the act of communication, and this suggests a problem with individual communication as a potential site for political resistance—if the very terms of language have shifted, then the articulation of resistance may not be possible. This notion of lived experience and the work of politics as an environmental and geographic shift palpably illustrates the permeation of the political into all aspects of material life. The reconsideration of the total experience of the shift in the political, a sea change that has become increasingly visible in 21st century US politics, has a direct impact on the conditions within both states and territories. The colonization of language itself results in the transformation of physical laws, insisting on the necessity of a poetic voice, of the work of art and music, as elements lost in this world. But recognizing the source of this loss, the nature of this entrapment is itself a challenge. Rivera quotes Gore Vidal in one of the play's epigraphs, "We hate this system we are trapped in, but we don't know who has trapped us or how. We don't even know what our cage looks like because we have never seen it from the outside."[2] Vidal's commentary on the US political situation resonates strongly with Rivera's own passion about politics referenced in an interview with Latine playwright Caridad Svich describing the evolution of *Massacre*:

> Since the 2000 election I had wondered what kind of response would be appropriate to the outrageous political madness that seemed to be occurring in the US. . . . I remember thinking how happy I was when President Bill Clinton was elected—it felt as if we had finally 'killed' Bush and his kind. Then, 2000, and the resurrected son haunts the landscape, avenging and revenging. The play deals with resurrected fear—how we tame our fear more through amnesia than through actual struggle with the fear itself.[3]

The conversations that emerge in these spaces become particularly interesting when they attend to the conditions of revolution or radical transformation. José Rivera here builds upon his sense of the inescapable connections to the US and moves into the perpetuation of authoritarian structures that reshape the very environment and geography of a small town. While the violent actions of these seven seem to question such a conclusion, the larger concern with the return and the ways in which they have to deal with the aftermath is central to the Puerto Rican experience of aftershocks. This concept extends from the relationship to a singular natural disaster, to the ongoing structural damage of a geography of "landscaped impulses," or a sustained colonial framework where the absence of sovereign autonomy restricts the capacity to make changes for a sustainable future.

The resurrection becomes clear in the play through an ominous knock at the end of Act 1: Joe, has not yet been destroyed. His subsequent conversation through the door begins a process of self-doubt, the return of fear, the internalization of guilt and self-implication, and the general dissolution of the revolutionary cadre. Joe leaves behind multiple trails of blood and two women still willing to hunt him down. The others have talked themselves out of further action—believing resistance to be a dream, though the two who remain still have faith. The play ends, however, not with the blackout suggesting that "[t]he fight continues,"[4] but with a scene from five years ago when the group waits eagerly for the arrival of this new inhabitant of their small New England town who knocks to announce his arrival.

While repeatedly critiqued as overwrought and over talky, as failing to follow through on the ideas hinted at and generated in the conversational threads, I argue this is not a failing of the play but rather a symptom of our difficulty in witnessing the complex and messy aftermath of revolutionary action. The work of manipulation through the operation of power and the presentation of the unjust conditions are dramatically compelling; the melodramatic movement toward the possibility of justice is moving; but the collapse into the confused ambivalence of real reflective consideration about how to move forward in a space in which the current conditions of politics have fundamentally shifted is consistently seen as overwritten and problematic. This reaction persists even in conditions of meaningful struggle. The desire for a heroic aesthetic to connect to the transformational temporality of the possibility of a new future means that any careful pragmatic account of the work is likely unsatisfying. While the claim is always about the writing, it is to a large extent the constraints of generic expectation on the possibilities of both the heroic and the human connection—the stakes of the conflict must be at the center of the character in order to generate effective conflict and sufficient stakes, but this framework for proper dramaturgy and writing is perhaps too embedded in an aesthetic practice that demands particular forms of action and conflict.

Massacre examines both the potential of revolutionary violent action, its success and failure, and the realities of the aftermath. To the extent to which these actions can be imagined as necessary to move the world forward, the gesture of coming together to destroy a tyrant is necessary. At the same time the question of what it takes to move forward, how easily humans can adapt to a new normal, especially in the face of risk, and the ways in which we are complicit in our destruction is built on forgetting. The call for reckoning, and revolutionary freedom, is difficult to sustain, and the aftermath often breaks down the group that brought the revolution into place.

The play's seven revolutionaries, connected socially and personally within this small-town space, but holding their own tensions and demons, come together for this massacre in part because of the all-encompassing nature of the threat.[5] They have all been directly harmed by Joe and agree that the five years of his presence in their community have created a destructive and unsustainable environment. Even the house where they commit the act is "in a depression."[6] Despite their social and personal bonds, the fractures among them are only sutured temporarily by the commitment to this act of violence necessary to restore their lives.

Following off-stage sounds of violence, pain and terror, the play begins with the seven, armed, blood-drenched revolutionaries stumbling into the room, beginning to process what they have accomplished. Amid their adrenaline stoked commentary on their success and the transgressions that justified their violence, cracks begin to emerge in the group. In addition to the resurfacing of interpersonal tension and conflict, there is also a fundamentally lingering fear (later justified) that their triumph is naïve and short lived. As Lila remarks, "I know nobody wants to hear this question but if it was so easy, how come no one did it five years ago?"[7] The belatedness of the revolutionary activity acknowledges what no one wants to truly admit, that it is neither as easy nor as clean as the rhetoric of revolutionary action would like us to imagine. Even this short-lived action is extremely difficult, reflected in the regret and uncertainty that accompany the liberatory act of violence.

It is clear from their conversation that there are material and immaterial forces of evil that have already enabled horrific forms of physical and mental violence, fundamentally transformed everyday life to make meaningful communication impossible, and separated, silenced, and divided them through fear. The destructive forces that shape the community, unspoken and irrational, are viscerally witnessed as random violence against bodies to maintain conditions of terror; but what is crucial is that even these conditions are barely sufficient to assemble a collective willing to rebel to restore social order. US contemporary consciousness of revolution is typically articulated from marginal positions, as a rhetorical provocation, and/or as a historical phenomenon. And even in spaces of radical protest calling for revolutionary change, there has yet to be a critical mass of individuals in the 20th or 21st century willing to radically restructure US democracy. I am not suggesting or diminishing the impact of civil rights activism, uprisings in Los Angeles, the Occupy movement, #BLM, the Capitol insurrection, and other actions historically in the service of change, but rather acknowledging the absence of successful revolution. Unlike Cuban and Mexican diaspora populations whose family histories often center on the displacing work of revolution in the home country as an impetus for immigration, Puerto Ricans have not experienced sustained or successful guerrilla military revolutions that have resulted in massive population displacement, despite an independence movement that pre-dates US control.

After the emotional immediacy diminishes slightly, the revolutionaries' task is to find their new place in the world and to restructure relationships now that the organizing principle of resistance no longer holds them together. Part of the necessary transformation is the re-emergence of creativity and the ability to repair language, to reintroduce energy and vigor and excitement—freedom from forms of self-constraint. An act of intimacy, *"VIVY kiss[ing] HECTOR . . . a public display of passion they haven't seen in five years,"*[8] catalyzes other emotional releases of joy and grief. The pervasive degradation of their material and affective lives is captured in Lila's comment "When you're afraid to close your eyes, even a kiss is dangerous and political."[9] The reclamation of the biological as the political heightens the material embodiment of political forces and action, reinforcing the sense of the necessity of everyday forms of resistance in *la brega* and implicitly suggesting the level of authoritarian constraint that had been naturalized under the previously existing authority. To a large extent, the death of the autocrat has transformed both the possibility of imagining a future and the way they move through everyday life, reclaiming "our time, our land and our laws"[10] along with the autonomy of self-definition.

The participants recognize the power of revolutionary action to enter one into the historical narrative and generate new possibilities for liberation. Eliseo's speech near the end of Act 1 in the last minutes of belief in a successful revolution, reflects on the transformational possibility of participation:

> No one ever asks me, 'yo, Eliseo, what do you think of this and that? Politics, the economy, what's your take, my sexy, Latin brother?' Being a key part of the force for liberation, the whole world's gonna wanna know my story. . . . I DON'T HAVE TO SHUT UP NO MORE. I'M GONNA ROAR AND SHRIEK AND EVERYONE CAN JUST KISS MY FINE BORICUA ASS.[11]

Participation in radical action implies access to special knowledge since the implied commitment and willingness to act moves beyond the everyday. This change invites a search to understand how to begin to walk the path, to understand the terms of commitment, to grasp how such a thing becomes possible. Eliseo implicitly invokes the potential cult of personality attached to revolution leaders through the construction of story. Beyond his shift in status, he also self-authorizes his own elevated vocal status, moving beyond the constrained silencing of his current policed position into a different register of self-expression. This shift into voice echoes a more profound embodied liberation where expectations of social comportment shift into a much more aggressive presence, enabling the possibility of action of what is crucially named as "roar and shriek" which echoes the liberatory sensibility of the grito, or yell.

This restoration of palpable embodied presence is followed by the culminating performance of Janis's original song, "*a lovely melody born of suffering, dreams postponed, and survival,*"[12] immediately interrupted by the not-actually-dead Joe's knocking on the door. The emotional celebration of liberation is ephemeral, but Janis's intention is to craft a song that both crystallizes momentary experience and constellates a community. The function of music is the source of the play's subtitle, and in a cyclical return to the past, one of her last actions in the play, in a scene set five years previous, her stated intention is to craft a song that will exist alongside the life of her child, from birth to death, and disappear with it. This notion of song as fundamentally connected with all the relational threads of a single life offers a model of intersecting life and artistic expression.

Of course, completely refusing the possibility of melodramatic success, the alliance collapses at the very moment it has settled. This dramaturgical gesture, which highlights the (im)possibility of sustaining a successful revolution and the immense difficulty attached to maintaining one's real commitment to incipient revolution, is structurally echoed at the end of the play with the knock anticipating Joe's first introduction. The desire for song, which is often a life blood catalyst for revolutionary change, is intimately attached to the celebration of a life well-lived, but too easily subject to the harsh interruption of percussive contact. The fragility of this ideal is carefully balanced with its temporary efficacy—a song is transformative but ephemeral. Janis's call to "sing to your children" is a move away from the singular ephemerality of a song to a ritual repetition that integrates song throughout a life. In doing so she offers a path for art making to create conditions in which the community holds shared responsibility over time.

The end of the first act is Joe's aural return through the wall—creating emotional distress, expanding relational fractures, and engineering the collapse of the revolutionary alliance. Ending both the first act and the entire play with Joe's return establishes a contrast between the contemporary horror he represents and the world that existed prior to his arrival. The name Joe, average Joe, places him outside of the cultural configurations of the existing group. His description also suggests wealth beyond the access of this small group of professionals, small business owners and service workers. He is clearly an outsider, and his initial arrival coincides with "the first crime in Granville since the Revolutionary War."[13] They explicitly reference an obligation of inclusion, a clear reminder that a small town is not necessarily always open to the new.

This explicit exploration of inviting and welcoming a new neighbor into the space at the end of the play anticipates the possibility of seeing Joe in person, which never happens in the original production, but does in the 2012 Rattlestick Playwrights Theater production. According to critic David Rooney,

> The second act becomes more compelling, primarily because Mr. Yusef brings snaky poetry and insidious power to Joe. To his panicked attackers, he remains a tormenting voice outside the slaughterhouse. But to the audience, he is a vivid presence, weaving among the vigilantes and exposing their own sins, one by one.[14]

This invocation of critically satisfying "vivid presence" is offered as a contrast to the otherwise less comprehensible structure of the work. Michael Feingold's negative review of the production suggests,

> *Massacre* is a play in which every assertion turns out to be either an evasion or a lie, shortly to be rebuked by somebody else's assertion . . . Joe, whose ostensible slaughter doesn't prevent him from having a lot to say in reply, provides plenty of evidence that his opponents' faults lie in their own dishonestly mixed motives. Ideas, revelations, and confrontations zing by . . . The tonal incoherence doesn't help Rivera's provocative, but maddeningly shapeless, play.[15]

Though the audience gets to witness him in the second act, Rooney is perfectly clear that Joe's status is not,

> Who or what the oppressor is, in this case, is open to interpretation. While he appears as an eloquent Englishman named Joe (Anatol Yusef), wearing pristine white with a red poppy in his lapel, he may be real or unreal,

dead or alive. He may also be an abstract force rooted in politics, religion, commerce, in contemporary culture or in the history of bloodshed and injustice embedded deep in the land.[16]

Critics found Joe's presence compelling, and their conventional reaction reinforces the need for a particular form of concrete melodrama in which we can place a face and a body on evil to manage it, rather than allowing it free reign within the disembodied world of the voice. Audiences are fascinated by the unbridled assertion of power and control and seem to enjoy the opportunity to see evil embodied in order to be comfortably secure in self-righteousness, to be convinced of the necessity of the massacre. Despite the introduction of a visual presence, Rooney suggests the nature of the oppressor is multiple and open to interpretation, and this I would argue is precisely the challenge and the power of the play. The inability to fully mark the role of the oppressor, or to free the revolutionaries from their own historical culpability, deftly and frustratingly illustrates the fundamental absence of simple moral equations in the face of the necessity of survival.

In the original text and production, though, there is no mention of an apparition for the audience to consume—Joe is only ever a voice through the wall, but that voice has immense emotional and psychological power. And the voice's disorienting lack of fixity in a visible body could be even more threatening, suggesting the abstraction of a condition of oppression that could easily be paralleled with the structural logic of coloniality. Joe knows things about all the characters, revealing their flaws and past transgressions, their inevitable interweaving with each other and with the violence within the community. Just the sound of his voice is capable of driving one of the women toward self-harm, and there is the palpable question of the nature of his power—how much is granted by the townspeople themselves. Yet this rumination, never fully settled, is not intended as an indictment but as an acknowledgment of the immense difficulty of scripting an accurate account of the multiple forces that engender and sustain revolution without devolving into a clear, comforting but ultimately perniciously melodramatic framing of revolutionary action. In other words, it is the "maddeningly shapeless"[17] quality that provides a more palpable sense of the difficult process of sustaining revolutionary action. Unlike social media activism, the revolutionary actions here are violent, intended to end life, and operate at the highest level of risk. As Malcolm Gladwell's popular article reminds us about social media activism in contrast to more embodied forms of activism, "Facebook activism succeeds not by motivating people to make a real sacrifice but by motivating them to do the things that people do when they are not motivated enough to make a real sacrifice."[18] Here, instead, the community has managed to come together to act, to make a real sacrifice in the interest of making their town a better place.

And yet, in addition to undercutting any comfortable resolution, Rivera's play insists on not freeing anyone from their actions, including the long history of settler colonialism that marks the very space of this theoretically idyllic town. He accomplishes this in Joe's extended incrimination which moves from the conceptual, "we all know how strong our thoughts can be. How our thoughts make the world"[19] to the historical,

> I bet you people never wonder about this town and all the massacres that made it possible. Bet you never asked yourself: who's haunting the walls of my house? Whose bones are holding up its foundation? Whose tears are pouring through the faucet to thicken my coffee? Whose betrayal made my freedom possible? Whose food supply is fattening my kids? Whose myths have I stolen to write my story?[20]

The language of massacre is very invested in colonial violence and the subsequent structures of inequality whose presence is continuously obscured. Since this is Joe's indictment, it serves a clear rhetorical purpose to situate their actions, both violent and quotidian, within an inescapable history. This totalizing model of culpability, intended to paralyze radical action, must be taken seriously (it is not untrue), but it also cannot serve as a deterrent to action. Here, a local choice in the current context is necessary, but its difficulty must first be established.

The chronological end[21] of the play offers a crucial look at the potential responses to a failed revolution, watching the frenetic positivity engendered by the group's imagined success fade into the dread realization of the potential continuation of the status quo. Crucially, Rivera's reintroduction of Joe enables a taxonomy of responses to the acknowledgment of the given circumstances of a failed attempt. And the choices made based on this acknowledgment, the forms of acceptance, offer a disheartening account of pragmatic survival. The majority choose to run or hide, to stay quiet and argue that the situation is not as bad as they thought, that things are getting better, that they can endure, and that this act of peaceful endurance becomes its own form of sacrifice. One of the leaders, Panama, suggests that he could serve as a physical sacrifice to appease Joe's wrath, but he is also refused—no form of sacrifice will serve as a meaningful heroic act engendering political change in this play. With people hiding or running, Vivy and Lila, the two women who first manifest interpersonal tension in the group, pick up their weapons with the intent to continue the fight. Not only were they the first to suspect that the conflict was not over based on affect or instinct, but they also believe it is close to the end, that the act of resistance is itself a necessary beginning. They are willing to continue the fight "cause now he knows we'll hit back. And that's got to freak him out. On some level, he knows we're not the same scared, little people we used to be."[22] But their departure, weapons in hand, is the last we see of them, leaving an uncertain future to the revolution, especially given how quickly failure results in capitulation for the majority. Sustaining the revolution is a conscious act of will that still requires collective support and the necessary conditions to emerge.

This post-revolutionary play predicates both the need for and the difficulties of revolutionary action in part in the self—a logic of internal colonialism predicated as the easy submission to a comfortable dictatorial presence and the need to struggle against these instincts. While Rivera sets this conflict in a small town in New Hampshire, it still resonates with the operations of coloniality, the historical structures of unequal power, and the ways in which the operations of power transform the very environment and the conditions for life. The need for life is poignantly touched on in Panama's final chronological comments about his own house, the site of the massacre, "For a couple of minutes, it felt good to live here again, felt like it used to."[23] This momentary shift in the environment suggests both the power of hope within an environment and the ways in which the operations of power work to erode the affective and material qualities of life. While the play's geography does not explicitly address the obscured colonial condition, its fixation on the ease with which the return of a repressed form of violent authoritarianism is allowed into our spaces, the contemporary shifts in the Puerto Rican experience, and the collapse of even the façade of local sovereignty with the imposition of PROMESA, reinforces the need for a critique of charismatic authoritarian paternalism as well as the need to find the individual resources to work against it. While not a reaction to these events, their very presence emphasizes the violent predictability of the repetition of colonial power.

From Witnessing to Listening:
Sustaining Meaningful Revolution in *#therevolution*

"I remember when this all started. And I remember why it started. And it didn't start because you killed someone. See, that's where I think we've gone wrong. I didn't follow you because you killed someone. I wasn't waiting for someone to kill someone. People killed—and kill, still—people all the time. No, I followed you because that killing was, weird as it sounds, the first positive step I had seen someone take in, I don't know, forever. It was a step. I was waiting for someone to take a step. And then you did, and I was excited, so were a lot of other people, and we didn't even stop to think if it was even a halfway decent kind of step that you had taken. And now, shit. It totally wasn't."[24]

The Witness, #therevolution

"You know very well I am not in principle opposed to violence or destruction. But the constant negation of the theatre from within itself, obtained, in what is finally a monotonous manner, by a sort of excessive appetite for the real, for pure presence, for the naked, torn, and tortured body exposed onstage in the very violence of its presence, all of this combined with spectacular lights, shocking images, and a powerful sound system, cannot and must not constitute the whole of the theatre. It's a problem we know well in politics: negation, doctrinally reduced to itself, never on its own brings about affirmation. Destruction destroys the old world, which is necessary, but its own means run aground when it comes to construction. In the twentieth century, in the enthusiasm of the first victorious revolutions, we were able to believe that the destruction of the old world would extend itself to the advent of the New Man, but we know today, at the cost of terrible experiences, that this is not true."[25] Alain Badiou, *In Praise of Theatre*

Philosopher Alain Badiou's recognition of theater's specific fantasy, emerging out of a desire for "pure presence," exemplified by the work of French Surrealist Antonin Artaud (whose profound influence on US theater was central to the embodied experiments of off-off-Broadway theater in the 1960s), is here used as an example of the repeated illusion that something new and better will emerge from the destruction of the old. He insists that theater's revelation of self as manifest through an adherence to an Artaudian logic of presence, of cruelty or terror, visceral, embodied experience as the epitome of the experience of the real, is only one of its facets. The extreme affects and effects of Artaud's theatrical aesthetics are often figured as a shift away from the exhausted limits of realist theater, enticing and transformative, insisting on the primacy of the theatrical experience rather than the materiality of everyday life. This reference to theatrical aesthetics invested in an idealized transformation serves to echo the challenges of a revolutionary impulse primarily centered on removal of the stale remainders of a flawed system, while also insisting on the difficult and much less intense but sustained self-transformation that might be involved in making a better world, not merely invoking it into being. In the service of a pragmatic model of liberation, transformation premised through cruelty seems counter to an affirmational structure of theatrical poesis and world building engaged in the process of recognizing what must be done to create meaningful and sustainable revolutionary transformation.

As evidenced in the examination of *All Ears* in the introduction, playwright Kristoffer Diaz recognizes the fundamental necessity to think about the complex factors that enter into consideration in any political action, including human fallibility, ego, emotional exhaustion, and focus on immediate necessity to the sometimes exclusion of long-term planning. Deeply invested in dismantling easy ideas about community solidarity and politics he simultaneously insists on their fundamental importance to transformation in plays, like *Welcome to Arroyo's* and *The Elaborate Entrance of Chad Deity*, that illustrate the power and challenges of storytelling as a means of understanding complex histories. Instead of allowing easy platitudes about affiliation and collaboration to stand, he insists on personal responsibility for measured and reflective choices. However, rather than modelling this behavior in a pragmatic revolution, his 2014 play *#therevolution* takes the opposite position, satirizing the destruction wrought by an unreflective uprising, one driven and sustained by the self-interest of the instigators and subsequent leaders.[26] Diaz's play explores the promise and collapse of revolution, demonstrating the powerful seduction of a willingness to act on conviction as a catalyst while reminding us that conviction is insufficient to transform individual radical action into meaningfully sustained collective work. In doing so, he provides a picture of authoritarian power emerging in the absence of collective vision as an overcorrection to the complexities of interpersonal understanding and the daily challenges that arise in the attempt to sustain revolution.

The play follows the evolution of a revolution catalyzed by The Witness's social media dissemination of The Revolution's act of violence. Over a series of scenes primarily framed as public service announcements taped in front of a wall that serves as a revolutionary symbol, the two of them try and fail to negotiate their relationship, devolving into forms of cruel authoritarianism. As the addition of The Muscle moves The Revolution toward slicker, more spectacular presentation, The Witness tries to step away from this movement gone awry. Underneath the satire is a clear recognition of complex human desire for both change and connection that catalyzes action but does not always provide a simple path forward.

The desire for, and refusal of, a simple positive movement toward futurity is a necessary part of a model of pragmatic liberation that acknowledges the difficult work of sustaining revolutionary change. It is not that the world does not require revision or that speculative world building needs to go away, but rather that energy needs to be devoted to achieving and sustaining a mode of affiliative politics, of working together toward a common end. Historically, some of the efficient ways of initiating an impactful and rapid revolutionary transformation are a) under the auspices of a military coup, enacted by members of the military or invoked by a civilian leader invoking their close affiliative relationship with the needs and values, often conservative, of the military authorities, whose access to the resources of spaces of confinement, weapons and the necessary training for efficient elimination of threats, including the death and disappearance of resistant civilians or b) driven by a charismatic individual leading the way, perhaps of a named movement that establishes recognizable ideological opposition. In both cases, these intense revolutionary forms often operate in contradistinction to a liberatory logic in which greater autonomy or sovereignty is enabled for a larger section of the population, because although the initial conditions of violence serve to eliminate the existing structures of power, their replacement is often not structurally dissimilar or is caught up in the idiosyncratic ideological limits of a single figure of authority.

Diaz takes up the aftermath of an unintentional revolution using the second form of a charismatic leader figure unwittingly cast in the role of The Revolution by The Witness's dissemination of her inciting incident, a murder, via social media. By beginning after the initial revolutionary action, Diaz's premise situates us squarely in the question of transitioning from revolutionary violence to the establishment and maintenance of a more egalitarian state in a condition of peace. The play operates on one hand as a humorous critique of middle-class anxieties about conditions of "oppression" as an individuated limit on one's opportunities, and an often-naïve belief that we know how to make meaningful change simply because we are aware of conditions of oppression and understand many of the existing forms of inequality of power despite our continued historical lack of access to forms of high-level institutional power.[27] While moving toward entropy is easier than moving toward order, Diaz is also invested in poking at the comfortable structure of progressive and liberal piety, a kind of armchair revolution akin to the problematic practice of virtue signaling. In this vein the play can easily be read as a response to hearing once too many times complaints in a conversation in a bar or café about the state of the world and the need and pathways to make a change, to "fix" it. It is the daydream construction of one person calling out—if I ran the world and letting that scenario play itself out, learning on the fly the implication of one's decisions and the resultant potential chaos that is asserted when the moral compass of a revolution is located in principles held and spoken by one individual, rather than trans-individual values.

The premise of *#therevolution* is a hipster liberal actor's daydream gone amuck, in which an actor's violent solution to their failure to get roles—kill some of the people in their way—leads to societal revolution through large-scale imitation resulting in a "New State of the World."[28] Rather than carefully planning and preparing the way for transformation, the revolution rapidly goes viral over social media. *#therevolution* begins after the initial revolutionary action has resulted in a change of power and is starting to shift the conduct of life, though it is clearly in the initial stages of violence and establishing a consistent order of power.

While acknowledging the importance of individual ties and self-interest in the generation of revolutionary action, it also highlights the challenge of establishing a more egalitarian state after the cessation of revolutionary violence due to the initial impulse of immediate, impassioned, and affective resistance that never fully considers the complexities of human psychology, lived histories, and comfortable habits. Here it is important to keep in mind the specific origin of this unconsidered revolution, one Diaz explicitly locates in a neighborhood such as "Silver Lake, Los Angeles. Or maybe Williamsburg, Brooklyn. Or Uptown, Minneapolis. You get the idea."[29] His choices are rapidly gentrifying spaces with a demographic shifting toward young, often white, educated professionals, with a general sense of liberal politics and a problematically comfortable relationship with the benefits of neoliberal capitalism. These hipster[30] spaces of upper middle class privilege are full of youth decrying the failure of status quo institutions to sufficiently acknowledge their contributions, replicating narcissistic, class-blind demands for change deliberately ignorant of the economic violence of liberal gentrification. This deliberate ignorance serves as a product parallel to the sustained practices of obscuring Puerto Rico's colonial condition. And of course, in marking the time Diaz suggests: "The future. The really, really, really near future. Like so near it may have already happened."[31]

His insistence on the cultural and temporal specificity of the now, which for him is at least in part the 2014 of the play's composition (though obviously extending beyond that), suggests a contemporary reflection on the persistent concerns with conditions of inequality framed within the bubble conversations in upper-middle-class spaces of privilege. This is not a call for inclusion and access to power from those who have been fundamentally denied rights, live in food and housing insecurity, and are struggling to eat on a daily basis, this is a revolution from and for those whose sense of exclusion is predicated on differential access to representational power, casting choices, and being cool enough to feel comfortable in a café. The intentional irony, coming from outside the space of this youthful discontent, is an implicit indictment of its lack of vision, its inability to see beyond the petty concerns of the bourgeoisie. Part of the play's critique is that while some of the political shifts emerging with potentially revolutionary force in our shared reality are real issues of the abuse of power, they are less invested in changing the nature of power than shifting who wields it. On a literal level, the revolution is pragmatic and liberatory in the sense of engaging with immediate material concerns resulting in specific improvement (from their point of view), but Diaz quickly makes clear that a lack of structural understanding ensures the ultimate failure to achieve any sustainable form of individual or collective liberation. The play walks a dangerous knife edge because the satirical treatment of revolution and transformative change could easily become an argument for maintaining and sustaining the status quo, not because of acceptance, but because of the lack of any meaningful alternative. This concern is one of the basic critiques of incremental resistance to substantive change, except that in Diaz's play he is much too cognizant of this concern. While on the one hand there is a danger that the reduction of revolution to the product of an accidental tweet that inadvertently leads to radical social upheaval sets up the very sense of revolutionary action as something problematically arbitrary, Diaz's play is not interested in shutting down the meaning or possibility of revolution. Having crafted a number of careful political critiques of easy liberalism that also insist on the unsustainability of inequality, he is not refusing the possibility of a real revolution, well prepared by people consciously thinking about the means to prepare the way so that the world and society are ready for the change. Rather, he acknowledges many people deeply invested in critiquing their position in the status quo are not necessarily versed in determining root systemic causes or meaningfully considering functional structural alternatives.

Importantly, Diaz's play attends to the impact of individual and collective desire, engaging Deleuze's critique of revolution as replicating structures of power and not fully attending to the power of desire. A great deal of the momentum of this revolution is predicated on desire, both a cathexis on the pleasure of seeing someone commit to radical action to change one's conditions, and a desire for physically intimate relational configurations between, most clearly, The Witness and The Revolution. Humorously but not inaccurately, the amount and nature of sexual encounters are highlighted as a part of the purview of the revolutionary authorities even as they stumble through their confused edicts about individual choice, appropriate comportment, and the appropriate deployment of power.

The basic structural design premise for the work, of increasingly sophisticated internet broadcasts from a wall which represents the force of the revolution, charts the progression of the revolution in its course from emergent uprising to established power structure. During the play videos from the wall become increasingly spectacular and authoritarian, and eventually The Witness and The Revolution are joined by The Muscle, who has no patience for The Witness's moral questioning of their action nor the sidebar distraction (motivation?) of her status as object of desire for The Revolution. The use of the wall as revolutionary symbol allows Diaz to play with audience associations with the built architecture dividing Berlin, putting into question the nature of revolution as a form of rupture and creating dissonance in its own right. The play's other location, a café, creates a more private space for intimate engagement but maintains the visibility of issues of gentrification and inclusion shaped by the worst forms of privileged liberalism—those who are cool enough to be there, an access granted by social capital theoretically available across intersectional lines, but certainly not open to all.

#therevolution also confronts the fascistic power of the spectacle as a dangerous epiphenomenon of the capitalist status quo, fully engaging the dangers contained in Debord's critique in *Society of the Spectacle*. It is important to note that this series of declamatory scenes are most often framed by an increasing technical sophistication in the video transition and introduction framing the majority of scenes. What begins as a grassroot broadcast by The

Revolution and The Witness progresses toward slicker visuals and clearer evidence of an increasingly sophisticated propaganda department reflected in explicit changes to the spectacular quality of the videos themselves. Diaz marks the shift to hegemonic/mainstream production sources and the increasing centrality of the revolutionary message with specific attention to the increasing production values of the introductory spectacles. The language also begins to reflect an increasingly fascistic and authoritarian model, especially following the entrance of The Muscle, who serves as a kind of shift to a more brazen assertion of power and defined modes of behavior; her introduction brings into relief a breakdown in attitude and vision between the instigators, which in part is implicitly driven by a failed reciprocation of individual desire and the need for validation.

Echoing conventional critiques of the collapse of revolutionary movements into authoritarian structures, and the ironies of the collapse of the poorly considered horizontality of the post-revolutionary space, the problems that accompany this revolution exist because of lack of theory and a lack of planning. This violent overthrow of the old guard is against the concrete structures of the past, the old way of doing things, only ever referenced as abstractions. The only concrete manifestation of specific change is increased access to roles for The Revolution in her everyday life as an actor and her assertion first as the head of the American Theater and later of Art, an ironic claim accompanied by an increasing reduction in creativity and compassion. Ironically, of course, the entire need to control the representational machinery of the American Theater is undermined by the premise of the play itself in which the representational power of theater disappears within the more effective frame of digital content creation. While it's possible that in addition to a humorous unreflective megalomania infecting The Revolution, her desire to control all "Art" reflects the very limits to her ambition that her unexpected success has exposed, this concrete assertion is also a nice self-reflexive moment for liberal theater goers (and Diaz loves to create them) to examine their own assumptions and ideals about representational power.

In the process, the critique extends to unthinking reform in the legislation of art. While Revolution's initial self-serving gesture unintentionally struck a chord resonating with the pent-up frustration of many people who witnessed her murderous act in the digital realm, she maintains a self-serving, myopic political framework that increases her authority without any increase in understanding. As part of asserting control over "art" she offers a familiar critique of the militarist structure of the national anthem, before offering a replacement, "I Love It" by Icona Pop, which was a #1 hit in two different dance charts in the US in 2012, but which is also not a US product. She goes on to assert when and where the song should be used, providing an implicit mockery of political decorum through the heightened juxtaposition of the song's dance club popularity.

The song's catchy hook, "I don't care, I love it" is a peculiar impetus on which to ground a movement toward radical change. The lyrics set up a model for action, but it is action in response to individual betrayal in issues of love, fixated on the individual personal with zero systemic analysis or broader understanding. It offers elements of anarchic glee and the joy of human movement as a kind of breaking down and breaking apart of things in the world. While the play explicitly focuses on the hook, the repetition of "I don't care, I love it" as a cry toward freedom and a repudiation of respectable conventional behavior, it is important to think about the open-ended catalyst for the anarchic spur of destructive feelings and action in the actual verses, one of which goes, "I got this feeling on a summer day when you were gone I crashed my car into the bridge/I watched/I let it burn." This anarchic witnessing of the destruction of the status quo by destroying one's own personal property without remorse offers a release from societal obligation that could arguably be called revolutionary. However, it is presenting this as a nihilistic individuated affective response rather than a considered reaction. And more disturbingly, although she wants everyone to learn the new anthem, she has made the selection without actually knowing all the words herself, one more example of abusive power.

More insidiously, the introduction of the anthem is an opportunity to shoot Harvey, a temporary character who is named precisely because he is disposable. A servant of the revolution, Harvey is killed to remind those who had power and those questioning the operations of the revolution that while they are in the process of generating a new world with new modes of action and engagement, the new leaders are still fully capable of asserting power through the traditional revolutionary mode of gun violence (and relatively arbitrary gun violence intended to generate repressive fear and reinforce positions of traditional authority). The anthem functions effectively as a foreshadowing of the emergent relationship between The Revolution's sense of betrayal over The Witness's relative lack of personal investment in their relationship. The song itself talks about the way that "You're on a different road." And that "We gotta kill the switch" as a means of implying the basic grounds for the original destructive act. While this may have been a failed suicide attempt, the song's narrative highlights deliberate distancing from a productive relationship with an outdated individual holding one back and dragging one down. This conventional reading of a relationship's collapse is echoed in the collapse of revolution. There is an established parallel between personal action predicated on desire, and sustained revolutionary action predicated on the desirability of new forms of social relations. Unsurprisingly, the anthem sounds increasingly martial and militaristic within the evolving aesthetics of the revolution's media broadcasts.

While there are theoretically claims about reform in different ways coming out of hipster practices of consumption, understanding the play as an example of a particular form of hipster revolution also fits it within a particular global phenomenon in which there is a complete lack of awareness of what is and is not happening within the space of revolution. In this particular case, the introduction of the figure of Aurora in the play crystallizes the discontent and disconnect between The Revolution and The Witness in terms of their relationships to sex and sexuality; but in her accidental encounter with them in a coffee shop where the normal operations of retail and commercial action have been displaced (The Witness is serving coffee to herself and The Revolution) there is a telling comment that the work of revolution in creating chaos has also had the productive effect of changing the atmosphere of the place in a positive way from Aurora's point of view. The revolution has created a world in which she no longer feels like she is not cool enough to belong.

The evolution over time presents increasing comfort with holding power in a new form of hierarchy without any meaningful organizational change (except the displacement of the original authorities). The emerging conditions appear to be as bad or potentially even worse than before—with the leaders replicating rather than transforming power relations. The concrete example of this "shift" is the indictment of the violence of sexual assault followed by an assumption that authority and power grants sexual access and implied consent. While for The Revolution, sexual liberation is initially exciting, she is specifically interested in The Witness, a feeling either unacknowledged or unshared, and the implied catalyst for her turn to The Muscle as a means of both "furthering" the aims of the revolution and satisfying her own libido. The Muscle is a realist interested in shaping and maintaining the structure and trappings of power as well as speaking the unvarnished truth; it is clear from her introduction that the aesthetic and ethos of the performance of revolution must change to reflect this new reality.

The play's relation to the revolutionary power of social media is crucial since it was crafted in the aftermath of the highly publicized Twitter activism connected to 2011 events in Tahrir Square and the much broader revolutionary movements within the Middle East, initially labeled the Arab Spring (which we saw a version of in Chapter 4). The hashtag as title itself forces a consideration of both the power of Twitter as a micro-blogging site and the expansion of Twitter vocabulary within the larger universe of social media. In many ways this revolution could be viewed as employing media scholar Zeynep Tufekci's concept of "adhocracy" which

> allows for the organization . . . of big protests or major online campaigns with minimal effort and advance work, but this empowerment can come along with a seemingly paradoxical weakness. . . . [M]any such movements lose out on *network internalities* or the gains in resilience and collective decision-making and acting capacity that emerge from the long-term work of negotiation and interaction required to maintain the networks as functioning and durable social and political structures.[32]

The unspoken elephant in the room is the #BLM movement which emerges concurrently with this play and is also catalyzed by women integrating their protest over social media. #BLM started a year before the final draft of Diaz's play was completed and offers a precise alternative to the failures of this revolution as presented by Diaz precisely by insisting on a communal and collective attachment to a particular principle, Black Lives Matter, which organizes and informs the movement. As Bunyasi and Smith describe in *Stay Woke: A People's Guide to Making All Black Lives Matter*, "The Black Lives Matter (BLM) movement . . . is broadly concerned with raising awareness of ongoing racial disparities, developing empathy for Black life and ending anti-black racism."[33] This clear focus for a movement, initially conceived in the commons structure without a hierarchy of leadership, was an intentional structure to sustain revolutionary momentum for the people. BLM was invested in not centering individual leaders and in doing so is an example of more carefully considered forms of revolution enabled by and through the structures of digital space and communal gathering, whose weight of interest can in fact result in meaningful, transformative cultural and political change. Performance Studies scholar Marcela A. Fuentes "offer[s] the concept of performance constellations as a theoretical lens to define tactics of disruption and worldmaking enabled by activist articulations of body-based protest performances and digital networking."[34]

Instead of offering transformative performance constellations, Diaz's revolutionaries move along a too familiar path in the evolution of power from good intentions and a rhetoric of radical structural change to increasingly unapologetic authoritarianism. The Witness's gradual displacement from the structures of power, along with a retroactive claim about the intentionality of the structural acts of power, sets up a system of self-justification that moves from a level of qualified moral uncertainty to a place of seamless, spectacular authority and toward new revolutionary storytelling in which the myth of the revolution can successfully move beyond a singular cult of personality and the individual investments in a leader into a larger model. This relatively easy satire of the challenges of revolutionary thinking matters when it is considered as a kind of serious theatrical opening calling for specific and sustained analyses that recognize substantive structural change that can only occur through careful consideration. Scholars and activists thinking much more carefully about revolutionary action than Diaz's protagonists chide even more cognizant left activists for operating in a space of denial about the real conditions of, and useful structures for, revolutionary change. In *The Last Day of Oppression and the First Day of the Same: The Politics and Economics of the New American Left* Jeffrey E. Webber "demonstrate[s] . . . the ways . . . Weberian historical sociology and limited liberal conceptualization of democracy are unable to comprehend the totalizing power of capital and its multifaceted forms of coercion and exploitation."[35] He goes on to argue the need for

> popular power in the economic sphere [that] would necessarily entail much more than a passive paternalism of the welfare state (itself under dramatic retrenchment in most of the world in the age of austerity). It would also entail more than merely a moral condemnation of poverty and inequality; rather, a renewal of the other tradition of democracy, as literally popular power, would require a recognition of, and resistance to, the inbuilt exploitative basis of class relations under capitalism and their internal relations with other forms of social oppression.[36]

This last phrase is crucially important as Webber carefully acknowledges the imbrication of multiple forms of oppression in the structures of the politics of relation, the sense of "be longing" (though he would never use that logic). This sense of the power of the people, referencing Wood's *Democracy against Capitalism*, also calls us back to Enrique Dussel's *Twenty Theses on Politics* and the centrality of the people as the basis for politics.[37] What these projects share in my reading is a form of hope predicated in large part on attentive quotidian action within a radical framework rather than idealized conceptions of radical action. Naomi Klein also suggests this model of local activism as a strong alternative, manifest in practical terms for example by self-sustained solar micro grids.[38]

The built environment of the wall, emblem of the initial revolutionary change, also charts resistance to the power and authority of revolution. Emerging as cracks in the wall that are increasingly destabilizing, these visual signs prompt both The Muscle and The Witness to caution against action that undermines the wall in different ways. Unsurprisingly, in the end The Witness performs the dangerous anti-revolutionary action of taking down the wall, not as an intentional calculation but as a product of frustration. However, rather than insisting on maintaining authority and further fracturing relations, the play instead transitions into a new, more hopeful politics of relation. The leaders explicitly name themselves and invite collaboration, actively promising to listen. The Witness catalyzes the transition reframing the course of revolution as

> You took a step. And I came with you. And so did a whole lot of other folks, like your friend here, and Aurora, and even Harvey. And most of those people waiting outside to kill you, they started out taking steps with you too. And I think the walking, that was a good idea. And I think the all of us walking together, shit. That was a really good idea. And so I think we should walk together again. . . . We're going to walk outside, Veronica and Aurora and Josephine and Emily or you can call her Emmy, either one. And I don't know exactly what we're going to do, but we're not going to kill anyone, and if you want to talk about what we should do next, we'd more than love to listen.[39]

Moving into a space of listening, acknowledging the given circumstances, that they do not know what to do, effectively derails the disturbingly familiar trajectory from radical intervention to authoritarianism. Instead, the play suggests they begin the process of talking and listening carefully, engaging in an honest and personal discussion to begin to determine what to do next. In making this provisionally hopeful conclusion, Diaz recognizes that change is both easier and harder than we think. If we can take our assumptions and egos out of the way and recognize that we share a desire for change with others, that the change must be material and broadly acceptable, and that we need to listen to each other carefully and walk slowly enough to understand, then we have a chance. In her conclusion to *Twitter and Tear Gas* Zeynep Tufekci relates a conversation with a young Spanish activist that resonates powerfully with this ending, suggesting that Diaz is very much imagining invoking the sustaining revolutionary practice of the Zapatistas in these final moments of his play. As Zeynep recalls,

> She tried to ponder some scenarios but too many unprecedented things had already happened. Prediction was difficult. "I don't know," she said. "We will keep walking, and keep asking questions," she continued, talking mostly in English but occasionally switching to Spanish. I was startled. It was a phrase ... I had heard almost two decades earlier in the mountains of Chiapas from the indigenous peasants of the Zapatista rebellion: "Preguntando caminamos" or "Asking, we walk"—we make our path, questioning it as we go along. I first thought that she had consciously evoked the phrase, but then I realized that she might have been too young to have known any details about the Zapatistas. I was about to bring it up, but then I changed my mind. It was important to learn from the past, no doubt. But maybe it was better to keep walking forward and to keep asking questions.[40]

Though like Tufekci I do not know for sure if Diaz was directly referencing the Zapatistas, the constellation of resonance matters more in the thinking of pragmatic liberation as we continue along the path.

Conclusion

THE LABYRINTH OF FREE ASSOCIATION AND SUSTAINABLE PRAGMATIC LIBERATION

> Puerto Ricans do not look back on a place as a home nor can we return to a golden, innocent time, when we were whole—we are still waiting to become. We haven't been offered the luxury of looking back—so we must look into the future, longing for a place to belong. In the meantime we exist as people in diaspora and that place of belonging resides within us.
> CARMEN RIVERA[1]

As I end this book, I try to imagine a future, not where this book is celebrated for providing a mode of understanding, but where it is forgotten, because both the problems and the modes of resistance explored in its pages are now historical figures that reflect past horrors unthinkable in the logics of the present. And yet as I write even that I hear the dangerous call of the romantic, utopic ideal of change for the future, possibly imaginable yet not fully attainable. So, in the spirit of what has come before, we must figure out which steps to take next.

And it gets that much harder when Hurricane Fiona, hitting Puerto Rico on the 5th anniversary of Hurricane Maria, amplified the ongoing coloniality of power in the US media, reminding those with the luxury of partial forgetting of the colonial violence enabled by current law and precedent, and the legislative validation of action fostering extractive misuse of human lives and land.

Pragmatic Liberation Now

In composing this conclusion and assembling examples of the ongoing work of pragmatic liberation, I came across the following in the concluding chapter of *From #BlackLivesMatter to Black Liberation* by Keeanga-Yamahtta Taylor: "radical Michael Dawson argues for 'pragmatic utopianism' that 'starts here we are but imagines where we want to be . . . based on the utopian imaginings of a much different America—one we are repeatedly told was impossible to obtain—combined with the hardheaded political realism that generated the strategies and tactics necessary to achieve their goals.'"[2] In the fourth chapter of Dawson's *Blacks In and Out of the Left* he argues the need for utopia in order to restore the possibility of imagining the world otherwise. Building on cultural theorist Lauren Berlant's idea of cruel optimism and philosopher Alain Badiou's recognition in *The Communist Hypothesis* that we need to reclaim the language necessary to imagine a more egalitarian world outside the space of capitalism, Dawson expresses concern that "Blacks no longer have anywhere near the ideological resources they had during the last century for productive utopian thinking and debate."[3] Centering the civil rights movement as one space where transformation occurred, Dawson lists seven suggestions to move toward a sustainable practice of pragmatic utopianism. The one that resonated most strongly with the world of Puerto Rican politics and its intimate familial imbrications as well as the continued destruction of Puerto Rican political economy is his call,

> to renew our commitment to the value of meaningful work that can actually support oneself and one's loved ones, and to education for all that not only makes it possible to acquire meaningful and rewarding work but allows each person to discover for themselves what it means to flourish while contributing to society.[4]

This form of practical idealism in relation to the structure of labor is particularly compelling in relation to the experience of Puerto Rico and its diasporas, where the question of access to meaningful labor has been a central crisis of the political economy of the operation of US colonial power in Puerto Rico.

But Diasporicans and their island networks have never been naïve about the realities under which they operate. Despite moments of apparent success, including the withdrawal of the US military from Vieques and a successful resistance to gubernatorial corruption, the Obama administration's imposition of PROMESA continues to lay bare the fundamentally colonial condition of territorial status underlying the ostensibly "free associated state." In his 2021 essay "Puerto Rico: The Ascent and Decline of an American Colony" Pedro Cabán constructs a parallel between the first few years of US control from 1898–1900 and the impact of Hurricane San Ciricao with the recent events of 2016–2019 including PROMESA and the failed response to Hurricane Maria. While he ends on the potentiality of a "cross-generational movement that inexplicably rose to renounce the instrumentalities and agents of colonial oppression"[5] he frames the comparison within "Puerto Rico's early conversion into a lucrative commercial and strategically significant asset of the evolving American empire and its subsequent descent into a debt-ridden, poverty-stricken, ecologically damaged territorial possession of questionable value to the United States."[6]

Ironically, the intensification of this mistreatment and the subsequent collective action consistently serves as a point of possibility for future transformation. The success of Puerto Rican activism on the island in the wake of Hurricane Maria is seen as inspirational for a range of scholars, historians, and activists, and while a detailed reading of the success of this event is a different project already being conducted by a range of committed scholars, I wanted to draw attention to a connection with the question of pragmatic liberation. Remember, the catalyst for #RickyRenuncia was in part the release of disparaging emails from the political class that established a fundamental disrespect for the people of Puerto Rico. The release of emails functioned in practical terms as a form of unintended honesty, and while I am playing a bit here, remember Quiara Alegría Hudes's phrase which forms the title of Chapter 4—"Before revolution, honesty." For me this is a crucial step in the process of recognizing and acknowledging our given circumstances in such a way as to begin taking steps on the pathway forward, even if they are very often sideways.

While this seems like an odd lesson to pull from this event, there is a crucial consideration in acknowledging the recognition of shared interest in whatever form they manifest, as well as considering the ways in which strong ties can lead to more committed acts which can in turn reinforce belief. In a problematic distinction very much reflecting the cultural moment of its creation, there is an extended passage in Gordon K. Lewis's 1974 book *Notes on the Puerto Rican Revolution* in which he suggests,

> The divided Puerto Rican nation is a nation divided against itself. That can clearly be seen in the prototypical difference between the island nationalist and the mainland nationalist. The first is warm, tolerant, indecisive, almost happy-go-lucky. The second is harsh, tough, and determined. The first talks theoretically of revolution. The second acts as a revolutionary,

because he has been forced to do so by the humiliating discrimination of the ghetto.[7]

While there are huge problems with Lewis's claim, and it is very much a part of the civil rights praxis of power manifest in political groups such as the Young Lords, this sense of a differential experience of the idea of revolution and political change is still necessary to consider, in large part because these questions continue to actively manifest both explicitly and through allegorical structurations of power and space that clearly reflect a conscious or unconscious understanding of the complex politics of "free association."

Puerto Rican philosopher Rocío Zambrana's recent *Colonial Debts* explores the concepts of "interruption" and "operation" in the coloniality of power within the Puerto Rican context focusing on the structure of debt, "In the case of Puerto Rico, coloniality posits the colony anew. As a form of coloniality, debt posits the colony anew—within and through the strictures of financialized neoliberal capitalism."[8] Her incisive reading of the conditions of coloniality that have stripped away any illusions of local authority after the imposition of the PROMESA board present a focus that resonates with the immediate practicality of the basic claims of pragmatic liberation, through language in a different register:

> Rather than liberation or freedom, however, I argue that decoloniality is a praxis that seeks to unbind the world of capital/coloniality, intervening in material conditions to dislocate modes of power, being, knowing, and sensing. Notions of liberation or freedom must also be unbound from the image of the capitalist/colonial world. Hence, I focus on variations of material praxis that attend to present material conditions. Many of these practices deploy the language of freedom, sovereignty, and solidarity, but the content of those terms is prefigured, rather than stated, by the reorganization of life itself. The content is articulated in and by a material praxis that alters the relation to land, the city, the coast, the ocean, the body, the other.[9]

Zambrana's concept of unbinding and new relationality echoes the interruption of habitual readerly consumption to enable the possibility of different forms of thinking and engagement. In this context it seems useful to consider the profoundly not quite quotidian gesture of slowing down to shift the quality of attention. While there is a level of privilege attached in many cases to the capacity to slow down, especially in spaces of industrialization and neoliberal service labor, and I don't intend to naively idealize a voluntarist practice of the slow, there is a mode of thinking in which shifting conceptions and experiences of temporality are themselves forms of interruption that might unproductively (in the best sense of the word) open up alternative modes of, in the terms I have been repeating throughout the text following Aimee Carrillo Rowe, "be longing," or perhaps in the language of Zambrana above "material praxis that alters the relation." I am not claiming an equivalency of these terms or processes but rather placing them in a larger model of relationality and acknowledgment that starts with an honest understanding of where we are, and the forces arrayed in opposition, as a means of embarking on a journey of liberation. The language here, of "present material conditions" points at a re-recognition of the need to work in the moment on the concrete that has stemmed from the collective success of various Puerto Rican activist projects. And, in the questioning of prefiguration and structural framing of terms of power and liberation, Zambrana highlights their "prefigur[ation] . . . by the reorganization of life itself," a process that generates fundamental change, and when figured in pragmatic liberatory terms, toward the good.

In an earlier draft of this conclusion, I posed myself several questions, and I have learned over the years more and more intensely the value and accessibility of questions as a heuristic and reflective tool. What is the future that is offered by these versions of emancipation? What is the work on the ground in Puerto Rico doing this and where is the urgency in this moment? How much does this mode of poesis offer a way of thinking otherwise? These questions seem more immediately to emerge in the on-the-ground activist work of the last few years than in the dramatic writing of Diasporic playwrights, and yet the persistent, consistent questioning of the need for change on a realistic basis suggests these are on-going questions with a longer durations in which structural and legislative change along the path become touchstones, but in which everyday modes of survival practice are a necessity. We are humans, surrounded by humans, and that is thrilling and depressing. The question becomes how to sustain long term versions of transformation, of a long durée of hope outside of already commodified and captured institutional rhetorics of ostensibly progressive change to generate a better life.

And part of the challenge of real meaningful change is the ways in which institutional power structures can so easily reframe the terms of engagement to halt what otherwise might be a radically empowering action. Guillermo Rebollo Gil tells such a story in his chapter "Regarding the Future" in his compact 2018 book *Writing Puerto Rico*,[10]

> on April 24, 2014, Christina Victoria Pasquinucci—accompanied by her son and daughter . . .—trespassed into a Walgreens construction site to protest the chain pharmacy's hyperbolic expansion in Puerto Rico . . . the woman perpetrated an act of civil disobedience by blocking the entrance to the construction site with a van . . . . She also planted what was meant to be the first of many trees. In her words, the protest was directed "against the American monopoly in pharmacies. On behalf of the local economy and natural medicine" (Quintero 2014). Her plan was to set up camp there for several weeks.[11]

But, as Gil immediately continues, "Unfortunately, she ended up abandoning the site the very same day"[12] because of the threat by authorities to take away her children. Drawing on the journalism of Laura Quintero, Gil makes clear that the participation of her children was "not out of necessity" but "*desired*"[13] by the activist and uses this as a jumping off point to address both the challenges of activism and a call to consider the ways in which any action can have impact. He suggests,

> instead of each protest serving as more or less fertile ground for one's speculation about movement building in present-day Puerto Rico, one can simply show up or look at each individual protest with a willingness to be moved. With the vulnerability and vision of that lone female protestor, whose singular act of dissent illustrates that, in the realm of the political, desire, will, and optimism—however uncalculated the risk, however frustrated the goals—trump objective living conditions time and again. I mean, honestly, how else is one to stay pumped with the revolution?[14]

The political labor comes in large part from the affective work of the gesture whether or not it is sustainably successful. This is perhaps the most optimistic view of the pragmatic challenges of modulating institutional resistances designed to target individuals where they are most vulnerable. And, I would argue, this capability is intensified by the continuing perpetuated grounds of coloniality in the relational structure of power.

On the Challenges of the Labyrinth

I want to a take a moment here to invoke a metaphorical phrase that has haunted my thinking on this project from its earliest transformations from a project on the challenge of middle-class revolution in Latine theater to a work centered on Puerto Rican diasporic drama—the labyrinth of free association. While for most the term free association may immediately invoke the unconscious practice of psychological discovery, in this study it contains the complex relational tension of the ELA, the Estado Libre Asociado, which is almost never translated into English as the Free Associated State, in large part because that anomalous construction suggests a relationship that is in fact not real given the continued and intensified territorial status of Puerto Rico within US political economy. The labyrinth seems an apt metaphor for the continued difficulty of negotiating the given circumstances of US and Puerto Rico in the face of a deliberately obscured colonialism.

While there are hints of the complex ruminations of Octavio Paz and Jorge Luis Borges in my musings, my only idiosyncratic image is predominant here—the question of how we know how to move forward. A crossroads metaphor could work equally well, but I tend to think more about the lack of comprehensive vision generated by the walls that shape the paths. The question of not and not quite is a consistent lingering reality for me as a scholar in the world of Latine studies where anticipated admonitions to stay in your lane are premised by lack of access to particular forms of authenticity. But more crucial than this manifestation of insecurity are the ongoing challenges of achieving a dense, complex, specific understanding in the face of received narratives deliberately structured to sustain ignorance.

How do we remember and honor the difficulty of clearing and walking the path without constraining the imagination pressing us toward necessary transformation? There are two directions I can imagine; no, there are many directions we can imagine; wait, how many directions are practically constrained? Many fewer than we are allowed to see. Walking the road carefully—what you see is constrained by the limits of what we are insistently informed are the sensorial and conceptual limits of the relatable, a stand in for the acceptable cultural logics of capitalism, coloniality, and persistent inequality.

The material metaphor of the labyrinth as a built structure is fascinating as something intended to trap, contain, or defer arrival and slow the path of progress despite continual movement. Is this the unending line at a theme park where the crowd retains a level of docility because of the frequent, intermittent reinforcement of ostensible progress? Certainly, the last several years have done a great deal to strip away a comfortable assumption that the eventual ride will be worth it. And this form of deferral is precisely a sign of the essential need to establish new forms of relationship, new built spaces through which to move, and perhaps to elevate our awareness to another level to consider whether following the path of the labyrinth is worth our time.

The pragmatic in pragmatic liberation is not about refusing change or deliberate deferral. It is, fundamentally, about ways in which we can begin to generate sustainable long term successful change that transforms the environmental expectations into a space where justice and equity are inherent parts of life. And this work, reliant on the immense creativity and honesty of playwrights, points to what is too often overlooked as a site for meaningfully encountering the terms of our given circumstances and exploring creative possibilities for transformation. I hope this work becomes increasingly recognizable as a source for thinking through and with challenges inherent in real, sustainable processes of meaningful transformation that can occur. This is ideally a book that reminds us to consider the next step in the path that shifts the terms of structural power inequities, moving us from spaces demanding endurance and resilience to spaces inviting joy and affective transformation along the slow path to change.

Choosing a Sustainable Path of Pragmatic Liberation

Ideally at the end of a book one would like to imagine that the way forward is clearer, but in this case, it is not so much a path as the emergence of a quality of attention and movement as a means of re-conceptualizing and re-imagining relationships, paying attention to our steps as we go. It is important to think carefully and honestly about our forms of liberation. In doing so it is important at the end to acknowledge the crucial work of the theaters, the teatros, the institutions, ensembles and collectives, the artistic collaborators, that generate the opportunities for performers and audiences to spend time with and experience these works. Given the consistently challenging contexts for thinking making, institutions that actively champion the work of Latine dramatists are crucial resources that need to be celebrated and acknowledged, encouraged, and supported to move steadily, with an awareness of their given circumstances, so that they can sustain their presence over the long arc of transformative change. Repertorio Español and INTAR have often been a home for Diasporican dramatists, along with many other Latine centered regional and university sponsored theater spaces, but Pregones/PRTT is the most important institution supporting their cultural production.[15] And an updated scholarly account of their work is more than overdue, as the existing comprehensive accounts do not meaningfully go past the 1990s. As emergent 21st century spaces the Latinx Theatre Commons is a crucial producer of Latine theater, but I want to specifically highlight UrbanTheater Company (UTC) in Chicago, which has produced Diasporican plays from its start with Miguel Piñero's *Short Eyes* and other Piñero plays, and moving through *La Gringa*, *Adoration of the Old Woman*, and other Rivera plays, *Lolita de Lares*, and Desi Moreno-Penson's *Devil Land*. In a 2019 interview with Amanda Finn in relation to their production of Guadalís Del Carmen's play *Not for Sale*, co-founder Ivan Vega shared the following:

> "It's one thing to be a theater company *in* a community [but] that isn't what UTC is all about," Vega says. UTC is much more interested in being part of "the fabric of the community," he says, not just existing within it. "How do we connect in a way that becomes an extension of what this community is about?" he asks. "It's about preservation of cultural space and preservation of identity. We are not *just* a theater." A big part of what UTC does for its community is focus on the concept of a legacy. What can they contribute to make a lasting impact?[16]

As Quiara Alegría Hudes reminds us in comparing her struggles in the creation of work within the US regional theater and its dismissal of contributions of Latine dramatists:

> My great-grandmother, now she was the actual revolutionary. She fought for Puerto Rico's right to self-governance and self-determination. Her left breast was blown off *en el grito de lares* fighting for independence for her island. Perhaps I will gird myself and get back into the fray. Perhaps I will lose both breasts if necessary. But it will hurt. I may sacrifice my breasts, but I demand the right to say "ouch" when doing so.[17]

Hudes's invocation of an actual revolutionary ancestor acknowledges the material difference between actively stepping forward into a violent fight and other forms of activism, while still acknowledging the genuine physical and emotional risks attached to each form of liberatory action.

As a next step in our path, I want to close with a final example of worldmaking, a brief look at one moment from Hudes's Pulitzer Prize-winning drama *Water by the Spoonful*. At the center of the play is a sense of connection through physical distance and difference; many characters share an experience of addiction but do not in fact encounter each other in real life. The space of *Water by the Spoonful* is doubled, a real space which "is populated with chairs of different sorts from many locations" and an online "space that connects the chairs."[18] The play centers around reactions to the loss of the community engaged matriarch Ginny, and Odessa's work as the moderator for an online chat room for recovering crack addicts. Puerto Rico and its diaspora are very present in the work as is the concept of liberation, but in this play, it is understood as a form of self-definition and a manifesto that can sustain you through challenges and bring you to a place where questions of dissonance can be asked and not necessarily resolved. If we understand dissonance as conflict, then conventional expectations of resolution should result in a highly conventional structure of writing and thinking that demands resolution and clarity of change.

But Hudes's work does something profound and necessarily different, insisting on the challenges of reaching toward connection and staying in connection, the sense of honesty that leads to potential change and revolution and the danger of avoiding the truth, acknowledging the reality of our given circumstances, especially those truths sparked by those closest to us. In dealing with a community of recovering crack addicts there is a profound recognition that community is necessary for preserving life, but also that brutal honesty is necessary to move forward, though only at the pace and to the extent one can sustain their sobriety.

I want to look closely at the end of the journey for two members of the group, both known to the audience and each other by their screen names rather than their given names. Chutes&Ladders, a middle aged Black IRS call center employee, cautions Orangutan, a much younger Japanese American woman in her twenties who grew up in Maine, that she cannot afford to take the emotional risk of seeking out her birth parents while she is in Japan because any disappointment could derail her sobriety.[19] While Chutes&Ladders' admonition suggests that in some cases, it is better and safer not to reach out, the play refuses to reduce the world to only virtual connections. In a powerful moment of connection, we witness the physical encounter of Chutes&Ladders and Orangutan in an airport in Japan, after a man has sold his car and flown halfway around the world to join a young friend whose real name he will only learn after their first face to face encounter. This moment near the close of the play exemplifies a safe and necessary form of connection for two characters struggling to stay afloat, but in need of assistance to do so. The genuine need for help, and the necessity of being prompted to ask and receive, is exemplified by chat room moderator Odessa's symbolic (and real) gift of water wings to keep Chutes&Ladders from drowning and prompt him to embrace the risk of friendship and expanding horizons in an environment that is safe enough to maintain his sobriety.

The pleasure that emerges in this moment becomes one means of thinking with the specific material conditions of pragmatic survival. Hudes describes their coming together as "[a] hug of basic survival and necessary friendship,"[20] the conjunction insisting on both elements as essential—a recognition of human connection as a basic element of survival, not as a cynically pragmatic act, but as a fundamental necessity that is deeply affective and precisely specific to the labor of developing the connection emerging between these two. The intimacy in this moment has become something radically different than has come before, and somehow, this simple hug now contains the world, at least for me when I have read or witnessed it. This moment of genuine authentic connection represents one potential image for the thinking of another politics—two humans, exhausted, clinging to one another for physical and structural support in an intimacy that engages the whole of the self. What happens in this moment, and in the future I hope for, is full acceptance of the other in their lived complexity, a profoundly different form of free association.

How does one name this connection? How can one find it? I would like to believe it emerges in a space of hope that is still beyond profound acknowledgement of the real, though I worry even as I write this that the insistent desire for hopeful resolution is already shifting, moving me too far away from the quotidian material realities that ground pragmatic liberation. And yet, I want to believe in a path forward that allows an honest accounting of the relationship between self and other at all scalar levels, that begins to allow the space for thinking new configurations and stepping out of our labyrinths.

Notes

Introduction

1. In invoking the hero's journey, I am referencing the broad practice in both playwriting and screenwriting of using Joseph Campbell's Jungian inspired schematization of mythic storytelling as a model for dramatic structure. While I believe this is an effective form, I also believe its hegemonic standardization does not leave space for other forms of story. According to Lance Lee, "Thus the most curious thing about the consonance between Campbell and drama is the structural nature of that resemblance. This is a critical point. Campbell points out myths rarely tell the entire hero story, concentrating often enough on some aspect of it. But the fundamental story pattern is always the same, while simultaneously infinitely varied in actual story content. It is the underlying pattern of dramatic structure that echoes Campbell's full hero's quest, which every screenplay thus carries through structurally: we could say, drama is the story with a thousand faces." Lance Lee, *The Death and Life of Drama: Reflections on Writing and Human Nature* (Austin: University of Texas Press, 2005), 112. For one reading of the connections and a detailed account of Campbell in this light see Lee's Chapter 10, "The Nature of the Hero's Journey."

2. There is an interesting parallel formulation in a recent *Chronicle of Higher Education* article discussing the challenges of the rhetoric of wokeness. In it, philosopher Regina Rini concludes, "Here are two thoughts we ought to be able to hold in our heads at the same time. First: Our institutions are still riven with centuries-old inequalities. Second: Sometimes well-intentioned people respond to this problem by overcorrecting and inflicting unfairness on others. Keeping both thoughts active at once is difficult. Finding actual solutions is even harder. But we make no progress by imaginatively exchanging real life for the superhero Götterdämmerung of Woke vs. anti-Woke. Fight scenes are entertaining; they don't save the world." Regina Rini, "Why I'm Tired of Hearing About 'Wokeism': Overblown rhetoric doesn't advance social justice," *Chronicle of Higher Education Review*, 15 November 2021, https://www.chronicle.com/article/why-im-tired-of-hearing-about-wokeism

3. José Rivera, *Marisol and Other Plays* (New York: Theatre Communications Group, 1997), 67.

4. Rivera, *Marisol*, 68.

5. Rivera, *Marisol*, 68.

6. Rivera, *Marisol*, 68.

7. Jill Dolan, "Performance, Utopia, and the 'Utopian Performative,'" *Theatre Journal* 53, no. 3 (2001): 455–79.

8. Aimee Carrillo Rowe, "Be Longing: Toward a Feminist Politics of Relation," *NWSA Journal* 17, no. 2 (Summer 2005): 15–46.

9. Carrillo Rowe, "Be Longing," 28.

10. Carrillo Rowe, "Be Longing," 40.

11. Chantal Mouffe, "For a Politics of Nomadic Identity," in *Chantal Mouffe: Hegemony, Radical Democracy, and the Political*, ed. James Martin (New York: Routledge, 2013), 150. She goes on to suggest "Identity cannot, therefore, belong to one person alone, and no one belongs to a single identity. . . . For an appropriate definition of identity, we need to take into account both the multiplicity of discourses and the power structure that affects it, as well as the complex dynamic of complicity and resistance which underlies the practices in which this identity is implicated. Instead of seeing the different forms of identity as allegiances to a place or as a property, we ought to realise that they are the stake of a power struggle" (150).

12. In addition to the discussion in Dorinne Kondo, *Worldmaking: Race, Performance, and the Work of Creativity* (Durham: Duke University Press, 2018), Tony Fisher is also particularly interested in exploring these dynamics in relation to what he understands to be a politics of tragedy. See Tony Fisher, "Introduction: Performance and the Tragic Politics of the *Agōn*," in *Performing Antagonism: Theatre, Performance & Radical Democracy*, ed. Tony Fisher and Eve Katsouraki (London: Palgrave Macmillan, 2017), 1–23.

13. Kondo, *Worldmaking*, Kindle, Location 2882–2890.

14. Carmen R. Lugo-Lugo goes further and calls it invisibility in her essay, "U.S. Congress and the Invisibility of Coloniality: The case of Puerto Rico's political status revisited," *Centro Journal* 18, no. 2 (Fall 2006): 125–45. In their "Introduction: Beyond Nationalist and Colonialist Discourses: The *Jaiba* Politics of the Puerto Rican Ethno-Nation," in *Puerto Rican Jam: Rethinking Colonialism and Nationalism*, ed. Frances Negrón-Muntaner and Ramón Grosfoguel (Minneapolis: University of Minnesota Press, 1997), Ramón Grosfoguel, Frances Negrón-Muntaner, and Chloé S. Georas suggest "Just as the creation of the ELA produced national subjects without a state, it also produced a context of illusory autonomy from the metropolitan center. We call Puerto Rico's autonomy 'illusory' not because there is no Puerto Rican agency in this process but because the cultural and political discourses of autonomy have obscured how (subordinately) integrated Puerto Ricans are to the United States' economic and political structures (e.g., Puerto Ricans on the island cannot elect congressional representation or vote for the president and are under the territorial clause). The U.S. Congress has absolute authority over Puerto Rico's local political structures." 12.

15. For a comprehensive education in the contemporary Puerto Rican situation, visit the Puerto Rico Syllabus at https://puertoricosyllabus.com

16. Rivera, *Marisol*, 17. The word endure is particularly powerful here as it is both a key term for Sandra Ruiz's understanding of the lived condition of Puerto Ricans under the conditions of colonial time in her work *Ricanness* and is also importantly invoked as a counter to resilience as a description of Puerto Ricans, because resilience implicitly validates ongoing structural violence.

17. Patricia Ybarra also highlights the prescience of this play in "For Whom is Apocalypse a New Idea?: Thoughts on Staging the End," in *Life in the Posthuman Condition*, ed. Stephen Wilmer and Audrone Zukauskaite (Edinburgh University Press, 2023). As I have argued in "José Rivera, Neoliberalism, and the Outside of Politics," *Latin American Theatre Review* 43, no. 1 (Fall 2009): 41–56, Rivera is very much aware of contemporary challenges, but his political horizon is often compressed to a liberal viewpoint.

18. In writing about the Zapatistas Diana Taylor reminds us that they are as invested in the practices of government and of tradition as the nationally elected officials,

but they retain an awareness and an ability to speak evaluatively and act on the difference between good and bad government. And I believe that the same ethical judgment can and should be applied when thinking with and through and acting inside a pragmatic structure. See Diana Taylor, ¡Presente!: *The Politics of Presence* (Durham: Duke University Press, 2020).

19. "During the decade in which some began to talk about Puerto Ricans' struggles in the United States in terms of 'recognition' instead of simply in terms of equality as citizens, young activists made a definitive contribution to the language of their community's various political claims. Rather than asking for recognition in a liberal discourse of inclusion-as-equals, militant youth and even some of their more mainstream counterparts framed their demands for recognition in American society in more challenging terms, insisting on the legitimacy of their claims for sovereignty—'self-determination' and 'liberation'—both for Puerto Ricans in the metropole and for their homeland itself." Lorrin Thomas, *Puerto Rican Citizen: History and Political Identity in Twentieth-Century New York City* (Chicago: University of Chicago Press, 2010), 7.

20. Kondo, *Worldmaking*, Kindle Edition, Location 619-20.

21. Michael Mark Chemers, *Ghost Light: An Introductory Handbook for Dramaturgy* (Carbondale: Southern Illinois University Press, 2010), 77.

22. Chemers, *Ghost Light*, 80.

23. Fornés's contributions are considerable and are slowly receiving a resurgence of interest through a range of scholarly and creative projects, including the Fornés Institute (https://fornesinstitute.com). While it is true that Fornés is of Cuban and not Puerto Rican heritage, she argued in many spaces for a broader Hispanic aesthetic in playwriting.

24. Anne García-Romero in *The Fornes Frame: Contemporary Latina Playwrights and the Legacy of Maria Irene Fornes* (Tucson: University of Arizona Press, 2016), reads Quiara Alegría Hudes as one playwright influenced by the Fornes frame and certainly elements of her work resonate with other writers in the work.

25. García-Romero, *The Fornes Frame*, 46.

26. García-Romero, *The Fornes Frame*, 52.

27. José Rivera, "36 Assumptions about Writing Plays," in *References to Salvador Dali Make Me Hot and Other Plays* (New York: Theatre Communications Group, 2003), 253.

28. Acting teacher Stella Adler reminds us that it is the work of the imagination within the fictional circumstances taken as truth that shape our ability to understand and act within the world (of the play). In *The Technique of Acting* (New York: Bantam, 1990), Adler quotes Stanislavski: "The truth in art is the truth of your circumstances." She suggests not beginning with words but beginning with place and reminds her students that "Onstage you are never actually in lifelike circumstances, but you have to accept them as such. . . . You must understand that the first rule is that you accept that the circumstances the playwright gives you as the truth. If you work for twenty years on a play without knowing your circumstances, you will fail. If you go first to the words, you will not be a modern actor—just a bad one. As an actor you are always in given circumstances. It is your responsibility to fill that place. Take the fiction out of the circumstances by letting the place tell you what to do" (31).

29. Elinor Fuchs, "EF's Visit to a Small Planet: Some Questions to Ask a Play," *Theater* 34, no. 2 (Summer 2004): 4-9.

30. Patricia A. Ybarra reminds us in *Latinx Theater in the Times of Neoliberalism*

(Evanston: Northwestern University Press, 2018), that "These artists' experiences have inevitably revealed the limitations of certain U.S.-based conceptions of identification and dramaturgies of belonging that depend on mainstream conceptions of the frameworks of Latinx identity: unidirectional migration, an emphasis on cultural authenticity, and the assumption of the stability of national sovereignties and national identities. Nonetheless, these plays and the world in which they were born also show that Latinx subjects are certainly not post-identity, post-ethnic, or post-racial in any sense of the words. Racism and neocolonialism clearly persist" (4).

31. Luis Alfaro, "La Maestra Fornés Has Left the Room, But What a Room!," *American Theatre*, October 31, 2018.

32. Raymond Williams, "A Lecture on Realism," *Afterall: A Journal of Art, Context and Enquiry*, no. 5 (2002), 106–15.

33. Walter Kerr, *How NOT to Write a Play* (New York: Dramatic Publishing, 1998), 40. Original publication 1955.

34. Gabriela Serena Sanchez and Quiara Alegría Hudes, "Pausing and Breathing: Two Sisters Deliver the ATHE 2018 Conference Keynote Address," *Theatre Topics* 29, no. 1 (March 2019): 4.

35. I am indirectly referring here to the manifesto "We See You, White American Theater," https://www.weseeyouwat.com

36. Dorinne Kondo's extended explorations of her dramaturgical collaborations in Worldmaking strongly echo this.

37. And yet beyond just a mere call for thinking otherwise is a recognition of Enrique Dussel's claims around the axis of feasibility as a means of engaging the political real by engaging with the people as the center of power. Dussel provides an important and useful critique for thinking through the political beginning with his basic claim that "the primary and ultimate collective subject of power is always the political community, or the people" (18). "In this *twentieth thesis* on feasibility, I would like to point out that this sphere of possible transformations (including revolutions) is situated within the strict space of *liberation* from an oppressive or exclusionary state of affairs. As such, these transformations are in accordance with a praxis of liberation. It is true that bourgeois Revolution spoke of *liberty*, but what is necessary now is to subsume that liberty and speak instead of *liberation* (as in North American pragmatism, one does not speak of *truth* but rather of veri-*fication*). So now we do not refer to liberty but instead to liber-*ation* as a process, as the negation of a point of departure, and a tension pressing toward a point of arrival." Enrique Dussel, *Twenty Theses on Politics*, trans. George Ciccariello-Maher (Durham: Duke University Press, 2008), 137.

38. This is a very different intent from that of the other major conflict deliberately manufactured for territorial acquisition, the North American Intervention, known to most US historians traditionally as the Mexican American War. For most historians who have more accurately labeled the conflict the Spanish Cuban American War, the US intervention on the side of Cuban independence fighters was generated not only out of a sense of democratic patriotism in the face of European colonialism, but was also considered a calculated move to ensure the US was negotiating influence not with Cuban independence fighters flush with victory, but with a Spain struggling to hold global territories in the face of increasing local opposition. The Spanish Cuban American War was also manufactured based on a strategic investment in naval security and military presence in the Caribbean, given the intent to create a canal in Panama to reduce shipping costs. It also served to protect US interests in coffee, tobacco, and sugar cultivation given the looming potential of Cuban independence.

39. Avalon Project, "Treaty of Peace Between the United States and Spain; December 10, 1898," https://avalon.law.yale.edu/19th_century/sp1898.asp

40. See for example, Edgardo Meléndez, "Citizenship and the Alien Exclusion in the Insular Cases: Puerto Ricans in the Periphery of American Empire," *Centro Journal* 25, no. 1 (Spring 2013): 106–45.

41. Meléndez, "Citizenship," 119.

42. For more information on the insular cases see Juan R. Torruella, "Ruling America's Colonies: The 'Insular Cases,'" *Yale Law & Policy Review* 32, no. 1 (Fall 2013): 57–95.

43. Sam Erman, *Almost Citizens: Puerto Rico, the U.S. Constitution and Empire* (Cambridge: Cambridge University Press, 2019), 144.

44. The relative lack of sovereignty was made palpable in the US Congress removal of Article II Section 20 from the Puerto Rican Constitution prior to approval, which was simply a restating of the UN Declaration of Human Rights, but which presented a crisis of face for the US because these claims of rights exceeded those accessible through the constitution. The article was removed from the Puerto Rican Constitution with the acceptance of the non-voting Resident Commissioner from Puerto Rico who, according to the Congressional Record, did not want any confrontation.

45. Pedro A. Malavet, *America's Colony: The Political and Cultural Conflict Between the United States and Puerto Rico* (New York: New York University Press, 2004), 10. Malavet outlines the key issues existing in the US Puerto Rico relationship from his position within LatCrit scholarship, acknowledging the intersectional tensions with questions of reparations in relation to structures and histories of US anti-black racism, insisting these same structures are at the root of the sustained colonial relationship with Puerto Rico, a politics of race too often elided in playwrights' dramatic accounts that run the risk of inscribing the desire of the criollo elites for an autonomy of power that does not radically reimagine the status quo.

46. Malavet, *America's Colony*, 9.

47. Malavet, *America's Colony*, 10.

48. Ramón E. Soto-Crespo, *Mainland Passage: The Cultural Anomaly of Puerto Rico* (Minneapolis: University of Minnesota Press, 2009).

49. This quote is presented in many ways, but here I am directly quoting Desi Moreno-Penson's play manuscript of *Beige* discussed in detail in Chapter 2 (New Play Network Exchange), 44.

50. Grosfoguel, Negrón-Muntaner, and Georas, "Beyond Nationalist," 4. See also Ramón Grosfoguel, *Colonial Subjects: Puerto Ricans in a Global Perspective* (Berkeley: University of California Press, 2003).

51. Maria Acosta Cruz, *Dream Nation: Puerto Rican Culture and the Fictions of Independence* (Camden: Rutgers University Press, 2014).

52. Yarimar Bonilla, "Nonsovereign Futures? French Caribbean Politics in the Wake of Disenchantment," in *Caribbean Sovereignty, Development and Democracy in an Age of Globalization*, ed. Linden Lewis (New York: Routledge, 2012), 215.

53. Bonilla, "Nonsovereign Futures?," 219.

54. Juan Manuel García Passalacqua, *Dignidad y Jaibería: Temer y Ser Puertorriqueño*, (Puerto Rico: Editorial Cultural, 2003), 58.

55. García Passalacqua, *Dignidad*, 61.

56. Grosfoguel, Negrón-Muntaner, and Georas, "Beyond Nationalist," 30.

57. Grosfoguel, Negrón-Muntaner, and Georas, "Beyond Nationalist," 30–31.

58. He was the second local governor and the first to be democratically elected.

59. State agricultural and grower groups in the Northeast were more interested in finding populations whose presence in the US was not based on citizenship and was contingent on employment so as to undermine any labor organizing around wages or working conditions. See Edgardo Meléndez, *Sponsored Migration: The State and Puerto Rican Postwar Migration to the United States* (Columbus: The Ohio State University Press, 2017).

60. This concept seems closely allied to the Chicanx *rasquachi* aesthetic. See Tomás Ybarra-Frausto, "*Rasquachismo*: A Chicano Sensibility." Marc Zimmerman, *Defending Their Own in the Cold: The Cultural Turns of U.S. Puerto Ricans* (Champaign: University of Illinois Press, 2020) importantly recognizes Soto-Crespo's exploration of *bregar* as fundamentally ending the debate over Marqués's docility thesis.

61. Arcadio Díaz Quiñones, *El Arte de Bregar: Ensayos* (San Juan: Ediciones Callejón, 2003), 20.

62. This translation is mine. I am unhappy with the phrase "appears like a forced rhyme" which is translated literally but does not convey the specific nature of the shape of the phrase but do not have a better solution.

63. Quiñones, *El Arte*, 54–57.

64. Quiñones, *El Arte*, 22. The translation is my own.

65. Of course, this most recent migratory movement after Hurricane Maria is part of a larger practice of cyclical migration and of shifting language use (moving between English and Spanish depending upon age and location).

66. More information about the history and impact of this powerful project, including the plays themselves, is available at https://every28hoursplays.org/about-2/. Alick began a project entitled The Ferguson Moment with several artist collaborators and continued this work forward with the assistance of the Oregon Shakespeare Festival in dialogue with Dominic D'Andrea and the One Minute Play Festival.

67. Kristoffer Diaz, *All Ears* in *Every 28 Hours Plays* https://every28hoursplays.org/the-plays-2/

68. See, for example, HowlRound's collection of essays at https://howlround.com/series/ferguson-moment

69. In a cursory glance at the history of revolutionary movements in the Caribbean, Central and South America (as well as Southeast Asia, the Middle East and North Africa), there is an ongoing question as to the sustainability of post-revolutionary transformation. While the majority of the failures can be attributed to explicit or covert intervention of other international actors with strong economic and political self interest in resisting or undermining movements toward egalitarianism, I am concerned here with the utility of engaging the failures and necessary compromises that occur in the trajectory toward an aspirational ideal. Even more insidiously, the limits of individual political horizons and ideological structures propagate impediments to thinking clearly and openly about both the radical reconceptualized possibilities and the entrenched limits of egalitarianism that some clusters within the global assemblage of humanity comfortably cohabit.

Chapter 1

1. John V. Antush, ed., *Nuestro New York: An Anthology of Puerto Rican Plays* (New York: Penguin, 1994), xi–xii. Note that despite the translated title, this first production was in Spanish. The English translation is René Marqués, *La Carreta*, trans. Charles Pilditch (New York: Scribner's, 1972).

2. After merging with another major Puerto Rican theater company, Pregones, in 2014, the PRTT continues to this day.

3. Jason Ramírez, "Miriam Colón: Puerto Rican Icon and Theatrical Traveler," *Latin American Theatre Review* 50, no. 2 (2017): 235-36.

4. Ramírez, "Miriam Colón," 234.

5. See the beginning of Chapter 2 for a brief discussion of this.

6. Elisa de la Roche, ¡*Teatro Hispano!: Three Major New York Companies* (New York: Garland, 1995), 62.

7. This language manifests "in 1939 [in] Emilio S. Belaval's essay 'Lo que podria ser un teatro puertorriqueño' (What a Puerto Rican Theatre Could Be). In his essay, Belaval calls for a theatre in which every element addressed the Puerto Rican reality: choice of themes, means of production, playwrights, actors, directors and designers, in other words, a theatre for Puerto Ricans by Puerto Ricans." Eva C. Vásquez, *Pregones Theatre: A Theatre for Social Change in the South Bronx* (New York: Routledge, 2003), 9.

8. Krigwa Players. "Krigwa Players Little Negro Theatre." Manuscript. New York (N.Y.), 1926. *Digital Commonwealth*, https://www.digitalcommonwealth.org/search/commonwealth-oai:z603r832h (accessed August 23, 2021).

9. The 1964 Civil Rights Act and the 1965 Immigration Act also set an expectation for social justice reforms while providing clearer pathways for immigration from Latin America, increasing the presence of Latin American immigrants in major US urban centers. The influx of new immigrants and migrants along with the long present communities of Puerto Rican migrants and Mexican immigrants increased the population of "Hispanic New York," fomented frustration with the slow pace of reform, and provided growing synergies with other social movements.

10. Sanchez and Hudes, "Pausing and Breathing," 4-5.

11. De la Roche, ¡*Teatro Hispano!*, 62.

12. This language emerged in the 1940s and 1950s in New York, primarily in response to intensified migration and challenges generated for these new migrants. See, for example, Thomas, *Puerto Rican Citizen*, Chapters 4 and 5.

13. Nowhere is this increasing awareness seen more prominently than in the PRTT's collaboration with New York-based Puerto Rican playwright Jaime Carrero.

14. Vásquez, *Pregones*, 13, translating Lydia Milagros González, *Libretos para El Tajo del Alacrán*. San Juan, P.R.: Instituto de Cultura Puertorriqueña, 1980, 10.

15. Vásquez, *Pregones*, 157.

16. Vásquez, *Pregones*, 120.

17. Vásquez, *Pregones*, 120-21.

18. Frances Negrón-Muntaner, ed. *None of the Above: Puerto Ricans in the Global Era* (New York: Palgrave Macmillan, 2008), 13.

19. Negrón-Muntaner, *None of the Above*, 14.

20. Scholar Nicolás Kanellos, for example, while arguing for more careful delineation between second and third generation ethnic literature and immigrant literature, nonetheless places René Marqués's play *La Carreta* within an immigrant framework because of its structure and thematic investments. Nicolás Kanellos, *Hispanic Immigrant Literature: El Sueño Del Retorno* (Austin: University of Texas Press, 2011), 24.

21. Antush, *Nuestro*, xi-xii.

22. Carmen Haydee Rivera and Jose L. Torres-Padilla, eds., *Writing off the Hyphen: New Perspectives on the Literature of the Puerto Rican Diaspora* (Seattle: University of Washington Press, 2008). (Page 5 and Note 17 on page 21.) There are a number of

more contemporary Puerto Rican playwrights who also fit into this structure, many of whom also had graduate academic training in the United States and, while working in Puerto Rico, also actively collaborate with institutions in New York and elsewhere. Prominent examples include Aravind Enrique Adyanthaya, Sylvia Bofill, and Jorge González. Also consider the ways in which Camilla Stevens thinks through the transnational Dominican experience in *Aquí y Allá: Transnational Dominican Theater and Performance* (Pittsburgh: University of Pittsburgh Press, 2019).

23. Rosalina Perales, *Me Llaman Desde Allá: Teatro y Performance de la Diáspora Puertorriqueña* (Santo Domingo: Impresora Soto Castillo, 2010). Perales draws attention to Miguel Piñero, Pedro Pietri, Jaime Carrero and Roberto Rodriguez Súarez, Eduardo Gallardo, Cándido Tirado, Migdalia Cruz, Juan Shamsul Alam, and John Jesurun. Her work was published in book form in 2010 and draws on materials originally crafted as articles beginning in the mid-1990s. Also writing from Puerto Rico, Lowell Fiet's "Preguntas Paradigmáticas Sobre El Teatro Hispanocaribeño Isleño y La Diáspora," *Latin American Theatre Review* 37, no. 2 (March 1, 2004): 7–24 provides one important framing document. A crucial but often overlooked history of diasporic work is Felix Cortes, Angel Falcón, and Juan Flores, "The Cultural Expression of Puerto Ricans in New York: A Theoretical Perspective and Critical Review," *Latin American Perspectives* 3, no. 3 (1976): 117–52, which contains a unique and substantial section on drama. In addition to their seminal anthology *Nuevos Pasos: Chicano and Puerto Rican Drama* (Houston: Arte Público Press, 1989), Nicolás Kanellos and Jorge Huerta have been central figures in the dissemination and study of Latine drama. Other major scholars that laid substantial groundwork include Alicia Arrizón, Tiffany Ana Lopez, Elisabeth Ramirez, Lillian Manzor, and Alberto Sandoval-Sanchez. Recent major works that touch on Puerto Rican drama in the diaspora and/or Latine drama that form a necessary background not mentioned elsewhere include José Muñoz's posthumously published *The Sense of Brown*, edited by Joshua Chambers-Letson and Tavia Nyong'o (Durham: Duke University Press, 2020); Brian Eugenio Herrera, *Latin Numbers: Playing Latino in Twentieth Century U.S. Popular Performance* (Ann Arbor: University of Michigan Press, 2015); Israel Reyes, *Embodied Economies: Diaspora and Transcultural Capital in Latin Theater and Fiction* (New Brunswick, NJ: Rutgers University Press, 2022); Carla Della Gatta, *Latinx Shakespeares: Staging U.S. Intracultural Theater* (Ann Arbor: University of Michigan Press, 2023); Trevor Boffone, Teresa Marrero and Chantal Rodriguez's edited collections, *Encuentro: Latinx Performance for the New American Theater* (Evanston: Northwestern University Press, 2019) and *Seeking Common Ground: Latinx and Latin American Theatre and Performance* (New York: Methuen, 2022).

24. Jorge Duany, *The Puerto Rican Nation on the Move: Identities on the Island and in the United States* (Chapel Hill: University of North Carolina Press, 2002).

25. The quality of movement and the inapplicability of the transnational is an important context. For a parallel discussion in Dominican drama see Stevens's *Aquí y Allá*.

26. Lawrence La Fountain-Stokes, Translocas: *The Politics of Puerto Rican Drag and Trans Performance* (Ann Arbor: University of Michigan Press, 2021), 16–17.

27. See, for example, the reading of Nelson Diaz-Marcano's *REVOLT!* New Play Exchange Network, manuscript. https://newplayexchange.org/plays/104965/revolt in the second half of this chapter as well as the plays in Chapter 3 that engage diasporic return as a central trope.

28. Meléndez, *Sponsored*, 18.
29. Meléndez, *Sponsored*, 29.
30. Patricia Herrera, *Nuyorican Feminist Performance: From the Café to Hip Hop Theater* (Ann Arbor: University of Michigan Press, 2020), 48. Another crucial work on Nuyorican poetry is Urayoán Noel, *In Visible Movement: Nuyorican Poetry from the Sixties to Slam* (University of Iowa Press, 2014).
31. Herrera, *Nuyorican Feminist*, 50.
32. Herrera, *Nuyorican Feminist*, 52.
33. For a study and critique of this issue see Marisel C. Moreno, *Family Matters: Puerto Rican Women Authors on the Island and the Mainland* (Charlottesville: University of Virginia Press, 2012).
34. While in *The Diaspora Strikes Back: Caribeño Tales of Learning and Turning* (New York: Routledge, 2009) Juan Flores highlights the "cultural remittances" that move from the diaspora to the mainland, this is more visible in poetry, performance, fashion, and music than in theater. Certainly, Diasporican drama has been produced, but typically through Spanish translation that implicitly highlights forms of mainland language play that differ aesthetically from some traditional formalities of island practice more inflected by Latin American synergies than local, individuated resistance to the specificities of US racism and discrimination.
35. Moreno, *Family Matters*, 29.
36. This experience is different from the experiences of integration of the Cuban American population, whose economic and educational conditions were not only better prior to the mass immigration caused by the Revolution of 1959, but the subsequent seizing of private companies by Castro made accepting and supporting Cuban refugees a prime goal of the US, extending its interest in "doing the democratic thing" in a global platform by offering an alternative to state sponsored socialism by ensuring the economic success of the new Cuban immigrant through aggressive and unprecedented access to capital through small business administration loans. See Grosfoguel, *Colonial* for an extended discussion of this differential treatment.
37. Grosfoguel, Negron-Muntaner, and Georas, "Beyond Nationalist," 18.
38. Also known as the Gag Law, it essentially made it illegal to advocate for independence by banning, among other things, flying the Puerto Rican flag. It was repealed in 1957.
39. In this sense, the practical issue of both a lingua franca and the necessary challenges to understanding that emerge out of this condition of writing in English despite a central sense of independence as fundamentally anti-US, which can result in a desire for a return to a culture associated with forms of Spanish colonialism, but rather fundamentally decolonial, which allows for an autonomous articulation of the diversity of Puerto Rican identity. In doing so, we can both acknowledge English as a language in which some work of migration and intersectional understanding manifests and recognize that the diasporic condition provides a unique lens and space for the writing of drama that reflects on the complexity of the complex forms of Puerto Rican nationalism.
40. Camilla Stevens "demonstrate[s] how a series of plays staged between 1958 and 1960 . . . participate in a public discussion on Puerto Rico's failure to gain independence and on what constitutes the island's identity. [She argues] that . . . a desire to found the nation through a national family romance characterizes Puerto Rico's search for identity. The family quarrels and failed romances portrayed in these plays

evoke the contrasting stances on Puerto Rican political and cultural identity debated on a national level and the use of the space of the house raises questions about what kind of family should embody the nation." Camilla Stevens, *Family and Identity in Contemporary Cuban and Puerto Rican Drama* (Gainesville: University Press of Florida, 2004), 12.

41. Nelson A. Denis, *War Against All Puerto Ricans* (New York: Nation Books, 2015), 52.

42. For a detailed account of the misrepresentation see Denis, *War*, and Garfield Hays "Report of the Commission of Inquiry on Civil Rights in Puerto Rico, May 22, 1937" Part III pages 28 and following.

43. Hays, "Report" 41.

44. Hays, "Report." 7.

45. The investigation extends further into examining the limits placed on university professors and students, which rather than separating their professional weight from their personal action (which is a practice continued in many spaces today) it completely disallows any political action on the part of individuals affiliated with the university, thus reducing the capacity for political dissent. In "Pedro Albizu Campos and the Ponce Massacre," a 1965 Marxist pamphlet by Juan Antonio Corretjer, Albizu Campos's revolutionary colleague, there is a clear desire to indict the highest reaches of the US government for their culpability and in doing so to confirm the limits and collapse of the idea of US liberal ideology in relation to the colony of Puerto Rico. It also paralleled this with another problematic action in relation to questions of labor and the power of capital, of then President Roosevelt, when rather than condemning outright the shooting of striking steel workers in the same year 1937, in a repressive action against the strike, he blamed both sides for their intransigence leading to violence.

46. Corretjer argues "In Puerto Rico itself, the American residents, some 1500, with the exception of half a dozen, were solidly behind Winship and joyful for the massacre. It is good to keep this in mind, because there are 65,000 U.S. residents in Puerto Rico today, who are here only as exploiters and agents of exploiters. In a similar event, one can venture to say that the half dozen of 1937 would not be much bigger now. A portent of this was given ten years ago when Americans at the Teatro Tapia fanatically cheered the police during the presentation of Rene Marqués 'PALM SUNDAY,' a drama on the Ponce Massacre" (np).

47. René Marqués, *Teatro Basada en la Masacre de Ponce 1937*, Edición Centenario. (Ediciones Mágica. Puerto Rico, 2019), 39. "Al estar ubicada en la segunda planta de una estructura típica de la arquitectura española colonial, la residencia de los Winfield funge como palco desde el que se aprecian la parada y matanza final, lo que reproduce espacialmente la jerarquización de la sociedad." [Located on the 2nd floor of a structure typical of Spanish colonial architecture, the Winfield residence serves as a box from which the parade and final slaughter are appreciated. It reproduces spatially the hierarchy of society], Maribel Acosta Lugo, "Prologo," Marqués, *Palm Sunday*, 26, author translation.

48. Marqués, *Palm Sunday*, 39. The American flag remains present throughout the play, while the Puerto Rican flag only gets a brief reference regarding how it is treated during the massacre itself. It is important to consider this within the framework of the Ley de la Mordaza.

49. Marqués, *Palm Sunday*, 40. Following patriarchal conventions, Marqués's

speech prefixes for the older male characters are their last names or profession, whereas the younger men and the one woman are referred to by first name.

50. Marqués, *Palm Sunday*, 39. De Diego's "Songs of Rebellion" is a famous collection of poetic exhortations for Puerto Rican liberty first published in 1916.

51. "Independentamente de todo esto, sin embargo, creo que un empleado de nuestro gobierno que se abstenga de actuar en una obra teatral por temor a represalias de sus jefes le está imputando a este gobierno prácticas y actitudes que confío sólo existen en su imaginación y que repudio enérgicamente." [Independently of all this, without a doubt, I believe that an employee of our government that abstains from acting in a work of theater for fear of reprisals from their bosses is accusing this government of practices and attitude that only exist in their imagination and which I strongly repudiate.] Carta de Luis Muñoz Marín a René Marqués, 26 de junio de 1956 in René Marqués, *Palm Sunday*, 129, author translation.

52. Marqués, *Palm Sunday*, 69, 114.
53. Marqués, *Palm Sunday*, 70–71.
54. Marqués, *Palm Sunday*, 56.
55. Marqués, *Palm Sunday*, 89.
56. See for example Ronald Fernandez, *The Disenchanted Island: Puerto Rico and the United States*, 2nd ed. (Westport: Praeger, 1996), 111–12 and Chapter 5 as a whole for a longer revolutionary context.
57. Gavin Arnall, *Subterranean Fanon: An Underground Theory of Radical Change* (New York: Columbia University Press), 208.
58. Arnall, *Subterranean Fanon*, 207.
59. Nelson Maldonado-Torres, "Outline of Ten Theses on Coloniality and Decoloniality." 2016. http://caribbeanstudiesassociation.org/docs/Maldonado-Torres_Outline_Ten_Theses-10.23.16.pdf, 21.
60. Nelson Maldonado-Torres, "Outline," 22.
61. This is not intended to overlook the crucial role of women within the work of the independentistas and Albizu Campos's own conceptions of the pathway to independence, but rather highlights Marqués's overwrought dismissal of the value of the intervention of strong women even as he himself crafts them.
62. Marqués, *Palm Sunday*, 91.
63. Marqués, *Palm Sunday*, 92.
64. Marqués, *Palm Sunday*, 96.
65. Marqués, *Palm Sunday*, 96.
66. Marqués, *Palm Sunday*, 97.
67. This enduring coloniality echoes broadly throughout Latine drama as a mode of policing boundaries and difference, often manifest in explicit discussions of militarized borders.
68. Marqués, *Palm Sunday*, 92.
69. Louis Althusser, "Ideology and Ideological State Apparatuses," in *Lenin and Philosophy and Other Essays*, trans. Ben Brewster (New York: Monthly Review Press, 1971), 127–86.
70. The desire to keep the flag raised shows up in the Hays Report, though in the history it is members of the nurse corps who carry and raise it again. Note that we never actually see the Puerto Rican flag as the Ley de la Mordaza is in effect at the time of the production in 1956.
71. René Marqués, *The Docile Puerto Rican: Essays*, ed. and trans. Barbara Bockus

Aponte (Philadelphia: Temple University Press, 1976), 37. Aponte clarifies that aplatanado means "[c]rushed in a moral sense; submissive" (124).

72. Marqués, *Docile*, 41.

73. Marqués, *Docile*, 44.

74. For a powerful refutation of Marqués's concept of docility see the introduction to Soto-Crespo.

75. Bonnie Hildebrand Reynolds, *Space, Time and Crisis: The Theatre of René Marqués*, (York, S.C.: Spanish Literature Publishing Company, 1988).

76. Marqués, *Palm Sunday*, 124.

77. The world premiere was presented by Visión Latino Theatre Company (https://www.visionlatino.com) at Chicago Dramatists from April-May 2018, directed by Xavier M. Custodio with set design by Nicholas Schwartz. As of May 2023, you could get direct access to the full script through the playwright's website: www.ndmstrikes.com

78. The 1950 revolt was also the catalyst for the assassination attempt on Harry Truman in the following days.

79. This fictional retelling of the history from one observer's position echoes the sense of intimate betrayal and the ongoing influence of the weight of history shared in a play like José Rivera's *Adoration of the Old Woman* discussed in Chapter 3. The play can be found in José Rivera, *Boleros for the Disenchanted and Other Plays* (New York: Theatre Communications Group, 2012).

80. The HBO short film *Yo Soy Taino* makes the claim that this game actually dates back to the Taíno, the indigenous inhabitants of Borinken (their name for the archipelago) when Europeans first began their violent incursion and indicates a clear sign of cultural continuity.

81. Diaz-Marcano, *REVOLT!*, 25.

82. Diaz-Marcano, *REVOLT!*, 25.

83. Yarimar Bonilla and Marisol LeBrón, eds. *Aftershocks of Disaster: Puerto Rico Before and After the Storm* (Chicago: Haymarket Books, 2019).

84. There is also an interesting parallel here with the Young Lords' decision to go to Puerto Rico discussed at the beginning of Chapter 3.

85. As Nelson Denis makes clear "With the two-thirds rule waived in November 1953, the U.S. petition for acceptance of Puerto Rico's "new status" was approved over the opposition of Socialist states, recently liberated countries, and the Latin American nations of Mexico, Uruguay, and Guatemala" (Denis, *War*, 268).

86. Denis, *War*, 269.

87. A deliberate result of Luis Muñoz Marín's increasing strategy of garnering US economic investment, the 1940s saw an increasing Americanization coupled with industrial investment and an active program of migration to reduce unemployment and the concomitant economic discontent, while conveniently providing a source of cheap "immigrant" labor as needed for various places in the US, coordinated with the official Office of Migration. See Meléndez, *Sponsored Migration* for a detailed account of the challenges and interrelations of this situation.

88. Diaz-Marcano, *REVOLT!*, 42.

89. The Cerro Maravilla incident has received recent theatrical attention through Jonathan Marcantoni, *Puerto Rican Nocturne: Bilingual Edition*, (Self-published, 2019).

90. The Young Lords emerged in the late 1960s as an evolution in practice and purpose from a Chicago street gang and in their initial organizing work drew attention to failure to provide social services to the Puerto Rican diasporic community in New

York. For an incisive reading of their history see Johanna Fernández, *The Young Lords: A Radical History* (Chapel Hill: The University of North Carolina Press, 2020).

A brief discussion of their work on the island can be found in the beginning of Chapter 3.

91. Diaz-Marcano, *REVOLT!*, 91.
92. Diaz-Marcano, *REVOLT!*, 91.
93. Diaz-Marcano, *REVOLT!*, 94.

Chapter 2

1. They were labeled terrorists in media accounts of the event and in the language within the courts. They considered themselves to be nationalist freedom fighters. This tension is a significant part of Desi Moreno-Penson's thinking about *Beige*, the second play analyzed in this chapter.
2. Reading the actual Congressional Record is fascinating because you have intersecting vectors of interest in a moment where there was no bilateral agreement between the US and Mexico because of Mexican concerns about workers' rights not being protected under the Bracero program.
3. "Would-Be Assassins Grimly Cry: Not Sorry for What We Did," *Newsday* (1940–1991); Mar 2, 1954, 21.
4. Miranda was the person who provided her the weapon.
5. For extended coverage of this see Sherrie L. Baver, "'Peace Is More Than the End of Bombing': The Second Stage of the Vieques Struggle," *Latin American Perspectives* 33, no. 1 (2006), 102–15.
6. Diana Taylor, "Brecht and Latin America's 'Theatre of Revolution,'" in *Brecht Sourcebook*, eds. Henry Bial and Carol Martin (New York: Routledge, 2000), 173–84.
7. Mady Schutzman, "Activism, Therapy, or Nostalgia? Theatre of the Oppressed in NYC," *TDR* 34, no. 3 (Autumn 1990): 80.
8. Sandra Ruiz, *Ricanness: Enduring Time in Anticolonial Performance* (New York: New York University Press, 2019), 39. Ruiz offers the following definition of her neologism: "[a]s a *via negative* through the living death of colonialism, *Ricanness* is an intersubjective relational type of dreaming of an otherwise" (20).
9. Ruiz, *Ricanness*, 61.
10. It is worth noting that "[t]he evidence against them came, in large part, from an FBI informant within the NP as well as Lebrón's brother, a Nationalist leader in Chicago who cooperated with the prosecution." Andrea Friedman, *Citizenship in Cold War America: The National Security State and the Possibilities of Dissent* (Amherst: University of Massachusetts Press, 2014), 119.
11. Migdalia Cruz, *Lolita de Lares*, Latino Literature: Poetry, Drama, and Fiction. ProQuest, 11. For more on El Grito de Lares see Olga Jiménez de Wagenheim, *Puerto Rico's Revolt for Independence: El Grito de Lares* (Boulder: Westview Press, 1985).
12. Cruz, *Lolita*, 11.
13. Cruz, *Lolita*, 11.
14. See, for example, Friedman, *Citizenship*.
15. Cruz, *Lolita*, 55.
16. Priscilla M. Page, "Charting the Terrain of Latina/o/x Theater in Chicago" (2018). Doctoral Dissertations.1453. https://doi.org/10.7275/12328595, 139.
17. Alberto Sandoval-Sánchez, "Introduction: I Don't Consciously Set Out to Write

About Blood," in *El Grito del Bronx and Other Plays* by Migdalia Cruz (NoPassport Press, 2010), 15.

18. Sandoval-Sánchez, "Introduction," 17–18.

19. Sandoval-Sánchez, "Introduction," 19.

20. Migdalia Cruz, "Searching for Home in All the Wrong Places: Why My Nuyorican Reality is Stateless," in *Theatre and Cartographies of Power: Repositioning the Latina/o Americas*, eds. Jimmy A. Noriega and Analola Santana (Carbondale: Southern Illinois University Press, 2018), 107.

21. Maldonado-Torres, Nelson. "Outline of Ten Theses on Coloniality and Decoloniality." 2016. http://caribbeanstudiesassociation.org/docs/Maldonado-Torres_Outline_Ten_Theses-10.23.16.pdf

22. Cruz, *Lolita*, 5.

23. https://urbantheater.tumblr.com/post/147847869907/get-to-know-our-lolita-de-lares-cast-tamika

24. Page, "Charting," 148. Page goes further claiming "Lolita de Lares by Migdalia Cruz is key to understanding the continuity of Latina/o/x theater in Chicago. It was produced by two different companies: Latino Chicago and Urban Theater, two decades apart, and it exemplifies the re-mapping of Chicago through theater that is the wider focus on my current research. From the Firehouse theater on Damien Ave in Wicker Park, where Latina/o/x artists literally transformed an abandoned space and ultimately a neighborhood to Humboldt Park where Puerto Rican cultural pride thrives in many forms of public expression, this play moved from one space to the other as a part of the claiming of space and the articulation of Latina/o/x culture and identity" (121).

25. Page, "Charting," 137.

26. Priscilla Page, "Afterword: My World Made Real," in *El Grito del Bronx and Other Plays*, Migdalia Cruz, (NoPassport Press, 2010), 488.

27. And Vejigante Estrella is also revealed as the Virgin of Providence, the patron saint of Puerto Rico.

28. https://tallerpr.org/vejigantes-of-puerto/

29. Cruz, *Lolita*, front matter.

30. Cruz, *Lolita*, 23. For some the jíbaro functions as a repository of Taino histories and knowledges. See, for example, Tony Castanha, *The Myth of Indigenous Caribbean Extinction: Continuity and Reclamation in Borikén (Puerto Rico)* (New York: Palgrave Macmillan, 2011).

31. Cruz, *Lolita*, 23

32. Seen most explicitly in a different branch of Latine theater in the El Teatro Campesino acto *Las Dos Caras del Patroncito* where the boss expresses a desire to change places with his workers because they don't have a care in the world, the unstated reality being because in the abusive labor conditions of migrant farm work they are carefully positioned to have nothing to lose since they have little or no resources. See Luis Valdez and El Teatro Campesino, *Luis Valdez—Early Works: Actos, Bernabé and Pensamiento Serpentino* (Houston: Arte Público Press, 1994).

33. Armando Garcia, "Freedom as Praxis: Migdalia Cruz's *Fur* and the Emancipation of Caliban's Woman," *Modern Drama* 59, no. 3 (2016): 345.

34. Garcia, "Freedom," 348.

35. Trevor Boffone, 50 Playwrights Project, https://50playwrights.org/2017/04/10/desi-moreno-penson/ and Desi Moreno-Penson, *Devil Land*, National New Play Exchange, manuscript.

36. Desi Moreno-Penson and Noemi de la Puente, *Not Like Us*, National New Play Exchange, manuscript.

37. Moreno-Penson, *Beige*, 3.

38. The issue of colorism in Puerto Rican society is a frequent and important topic in Diasporic drama. Two of the clearest examples are *Ariano* by Richard V. Irizarry, in *Recent Puerto Rican Theater: Five Plays from New York*, edited by John V. Antush, 167–226 (Houston: Arte Público Press, 1991) and Charles Rice-Gonzalez's *I Just Love Andy Gobb: A Play in One Act*, in *Blacktino Queer Performance*, edited by Ramón H. Rivera-Servera and E. Patrick Johnson, 509–41 (Durham: Duke University Press, 2016). Lawrence La-Fountain Stokes has a critical essay on the play in the same volume.

39. Trevor Boffone, 50 Playwrights Project, https://50playwrights.org/2017/04/10/desi-moreno-penson/

40. Moreno-Penson, *Beige*, 7.

41. Moreno-Penson, *Beige*, 74.

42. The question of direct military violence has a long history for Lebrón, as Migdalia Cruz provides an anecdote of a child who dies from biting a misplaced bullet and the subsequent and the clear devaluation of Puerto Rican life based on the level of compensation and emotional remorse in *Lolita de Lares*.

43. Though the period of incarceration she endured was substantial, and in fact directly non-proportional to the actual crime she was convicted for, part of the shift emerged out of a willingness on the part of the judge and jury to recognize her explicitly stated mission to draw attention to the situation in Puerto Rico rather than to actually kill anyone—I came here to die, not to kill.

44. Moreno-Penson, *Beige*, 24.

45. And this language of Solitude cannot help but indicate a connection with Octavio Paz's meditation on identity, emerging from his position as a Mexican man writing at the time in the United States in *The Labyrinth of Solitude: Life and Thought in Mexico* (New York: Grove Press, 1962).

46. Moreno-Penson, *Beige*, 34.

47. Moreno-Penson, *Beige*, 39.

48. Moreno-Penson, *Beige*, 58.

49. Moreno-Penson, *Beige*, 32.

50. Moreno-Penson, *Beige*, 8.

51. Moreno-Penson, *Beige*, 14.

52. The argument is not hard to see. The US provided both industrial investment and increased autonomy for Puerto Ricans, allowing domestic elections for a Puerto Rican government, and while voting representation on the Federal level was not achieved, and continues to place Puerto Ricans in a space of diminished political representation, the second investment in this moment was building an industrial infrastructure, in part funded through a dress rehearsal for the maquiladoras in the free trade zones of the US/Mexico border beginning in the mid-1960s with the border industrial program. This particular program was insidious because it reduced the local tax base by creating ridiculous levels of tax exemption that only invited investment as long as the exemptions were sustained; they were dismantled immediately with the change in the tax code.

53. Irene Vilar, *A Message from God in the Atomic Age*, trans. Gregory Rabassa (New York: Pantheon, 1996), 8.

54. This structure and logic also echoes elements of Argentinian Guillermo Gentile's aesthetic of fantastic realism, which deeply influenced the practice and thinking of Carmen Rivera (see Chapter 3).

55. Interestingly, at one point she was a subject of negotiation between President Carter and Fidel Castro, who was offering the possibility of freeing her and the other Puerto Rican political prisoners in exchange for returning four CIA operatives held by Cuba. Lebrón was disgusted by this and did not want her freedom exchanged for that of the CIA men, but ultimately the deal was not considered because in the eyes of the federal government, the United States does not hold political prisoners, only criminals.

56. The actual political site of conflict is not the general relationship of the US to Puerto Rico but the policies, in this case the legacy of the military influence in the administration of Puerto Rico, which, following Ramón Grosfoguel's model, military issues were predominant in the initial intervention brought on by the Spanish American War. In fact, the strategic importance of Puerto Rico as a point to protect the imagined transcontinental canal was already part of US military thinking several years before the US intervention, and the war itself is clearly framed by some historians as a logical strategy to secure US territorial interests. As mentioned before in discussing the initial framing of the relationship, the logic of "foreign in a domestic sense" emerged from rulings in the insular cases.

57. Mario Murillo, *Islands of Resistance: Puerto Rico, Vieques, and U.S. Policy* (New York: Seven Stories Press, 2001), 18.

58. Moreno-Penson, *Beige*, 72.

59. Moreno-Penson, *Beige*, 79.

60. While the invocation of the Taino runs the risk of functioning as a kind of romanticization of the indigenous, there is a thread of political thinking, and a controversial line of scholarly investigation, that affiliates rural elders with indigenous knowledge forms to reclaim jibaro identity as a continuation of extended authentic Puerto Rican culture—that the nationalist symbol of the jibaro as a particular form of Puerto Rican culture is precisely the present day manifestation through a direct line of Taino knowledge. Moreno-Penson makes her knowledge of Taíno cultural legacy and spiritual cosmology clear in her play *Devil Land*. And this situation is in deeply powerful consonance with the invocation of the opening poetry reimagining the function of jíbara identity as a particular kind of connected empowerment in opposition to an overly simplified thinking that associates rural spaces with naïve poverty, or the basic strength of agricultural labor, both celebrated and denigrated in the double movement toward the re-invention of a national culture during the 20th century, especially in the face of rapid industrialization driven by external forces.

61. "The production of Latinos as easily digestible and marketable within the larger structures of corporate America is therefore revealing of the global bases of contemporary processes of identity formation and of how notions of place, nation, and race that are at play in the United States and in Latin America come to bear on these representations." Arlene Dávila, *Latinos, Inc.: The Marketing and Making of a People* (Berkeley: University of California Press, 2001), 3–4.

62. Charles Taylor, *Multiculturalism and "The Politics of Recognition": An Essay*, ed. Amy Gutmann (Princeton: Princeton University Press, 1992), 66.

63. Taylor, *Multiculturalism*, 67.

64. Judith Butler, "Recognition and the Social Bond: A Response to Axel Honneth," in *Recognition and Ambivalence*, eds. Heikki Ikäheimo, Kristina Lepold, and Titus Stahl (New York: Columbia University Press, 2021), 46–47.

65. Lois McNay, "Historicizing Recognition: From Ontology to Teleology," in *Rec-*

ognition and Ambivalence, eds. Heikki Ikäheimo, Kristina Lepold, and Titus Stahl (New York: Columbia University Press, 2021), 89.

66. Judith Butler, *Notes Toward a Performative Theory of Assembly* (Cambridge: Harvard University Press, 2015).

67. Moreno-Penson, *Beige*, 45.

68. Moreno-Penson, *Beige*, 54.

69. David Gonzalez, "Vieques Advocate Turns From Violence of Her Past," *New York Times*, June 18, 2001, https://www.nytimes.com/2001/06/18/us/vieques-advocate-turns-from-violence-of-her-past.html?smid=url-share

70. For a history of the US relationship with Vieques and the continuing environmental problems see Andrew Rice Kerr's dissertation "A Disembodied Shade: Vieques, Puerto Rico at the intersection of Empire and Environmentalism in the Twentieth Century," (PhD, University of California, Davis), https://www.proquest.com/docview/1519305523/abstract/F7E52FA2558B4CBDPQ/1

71. John Holloway, *Change the World Without Taking Power: The Meaning of Revolution Today* (Pluto Press, 2019) Kindle, Location 4493–4502.

72. Rose Muzio, *Radical Imagination, Radical Humanity: Puerto Rican Political Activism in New York* (Albany: State University of New York Press, 2017), 141.

73. Juan Duchesne Winter, "Vieques: Protest as Consensual Spectacle," in *None of the Above: Puerto Ricans in the Global Era*, ed. Frances Negrón-Muntaner (New York: Palgrave Macmillan, 2008), 87.

74. Alexis Soloski, "'Notes on Killing' Review: For These Puerto Ricans, Promises Never Kept," *New York Times* May 30, 2022. https://www.nytimes.com/2022/05/30/theater/notes-on-killing-review.html. PROMESA, tasked with reducing Puerto Rican debt, primarily through austerity, was imposed without the consent of the Puerto Rican people. Broadly condemned, PROMESA is considered by some to be illegal and a violation of the Puerto Rican constitution, and by others as problematically addressing a debt that itself is the product of the ongoing colonialist economic machinations of the United States. PROMESA and its austerity plans are just one salvo in a larger project of ensuring the economic functionality of Puerto Rico for wealthy US citizens, explored, and contested in journalist and film-maker Naomi Klein's recent short work on disaster capitalism in Puerto Rico, *The Battle for Paradise* (Chicago: Haymarket Books, 2018).

75. Raven Snook, "Notes on Killing Seven Oversight, Management and Economic Stability Board Members," *Time Out*, https://www.timeout.com/newyork/theater/notes-on-killing-seven-oversight-management-and-economic-stability-board-members

76. Jed Ryan, "Notes on Killing Seven Oversight, Management and Economic Stability Board Members" at Soho Rep: A Review," *Lavender After Dark*, May 31, 2022, https://lavenderafterdark.com/2022/05/31/notes-on-killing-seven-oversight-management-and-economic-stability-board-members-at-soho-rep-a-review/

77. Soloski, "'Notes on Killing.'"

Chapter 3

1. Though not traditional practice, because the key playwrights in this chapter share a surname, I will refer to them at times by first name to maintain clarity.

2. This is already clearly visible in *REVOLT!* in Chapter 1 and *Beige* in Chapter 2.

3. Fernández, *Young Lords*, 344.

4. Fernández, *Young Lords*, 352.

5. The only other play given this treatment is *Barrio Hollywood* by Chicana playwright Elaine Romero.

6. A streaming taped production in Spanish directed by longtime artistic director René Buch is available from Repertorio Español's website at https://repertorio.secure.force.com/ticket/#/events/a0S0h00000UpdejEAB

7. Jason Ramirez, "Carmen Rivera: Theatre of Latinidad" (PhD Diss., City University of New York, 2009), ProQuest, 18.

8. Ramirez, "Carmen," 35.

9. https://international.ucla.edu/lai/article/248568

10. Juan Flores, *The Diaspora Strikes Back*: Caribeño *Tales of Learning and Turning* (New York: Routledge, 2009).

11. Carmen Rivera, *La Gringa*, English Version (New York: Samuel French, 2008), 8.

12. Sherina Feliciano-Santos, *A Contested Caribbean Indigeneity: Language, Social Practice, and Identity within Puerto Rican Taíno Activism* (New Brunswick: Rutgers University Press, 2021), 180.

13. Feliciano-Santos, *Contested*, 182.

14. Rivera, *La Gringa*, 10.

15. This jacket was interestingly used as part of the promotional materials for the production, at one time even using a photograph of the playwright herself wearing it when she temporarily stepped into the production. Ramirez, "Carmen," 10.

16. The persistent power and danger of the servicial ideology for women is also discussed in relation to Quiara Alegría Hudes's *Daphne's Dive* (New York: Theatre Communications Group, 2017) in Chapter 4.

17. In the popular Repertorio Español production, director René Buch decided to use a suggestive minimalism with chairs, fabric and lighting shifts suggesting movement between locations.

18. Néstor David Pastor, "25 Years of La Gringa: An Interview with Carmen Rivera," The Latinx Project, New York University, https://www.latinxproject.nyu.edu/intervenxions/25-years-of-la-gringa-an-interview-with-carmen-rivera

19. This self-imposed constraint in many ways echoes the struggle of Soledad Iglesias in Chapter 2 in her attempts to free herself from the conventional constraints of her liberal existence.

20. Rivera, *La Gringa*, 21.

21. Rivera, *La Gringa*, 21.

22. Rivera, *La Gringa*, 29.

23. Rivera, *La Gringa*, 35.

24. In the conclusion to *Colonial Debts: The Case of Puerto Rico* (Durham: Duke University Press, 2021) Rocío Zambrana provides a brief interlacing of several movements including land rescue: "While Cotto-Morales focuses on the impact of the long-standing land rescue movement for social movements in Puerto Rico, Fontánez-Torres discusses juridical theory and practice at the center of dispossession and its resistance. Muñiz-Varela, in turn, conceptualizes these interventions as modes of "interruption" that rather than seeking to restore the proper when rescuing land or subverting private property, build "infrastructures" for binding life anew. Variations of autogestión ("autonomous organizing or mutual aid") within economic downturn, hurricane disaster and recovery, and post #RickyRenuncia protests are important in this context" (153). The reference here to #RickyRenuncia is to the activist movement which launched on the island in 2019 in response to chat messages by then Governor

Ricardo Rosselló and his cronies that widely criticized and disparaged individuals and demonstrated disrespect for the function of government. See Yadira Nieves-Pizarro and Juan Mundel, "#RickyRenuncia: The Hashtag That Took Collective Outrage from Social Media to the Streets," in *Latin American Diasporas in Public Diplomacy*, edited by Vanessa Bravo and Maria De Moya (Palgrave Macmillan, 2021), 169–87.

25. Rivera, *La Gringa*, 34.

26. Rivera, *La Gringa*, 53.

27. As Rivera explains, "I don't know what made this play 'the one.' I know it's a hero's journey and I was very conscious of following mythology when I wrote this. I had the mythology maps around me as I was working on this. Every character is someone. I wrote a Threshold Guardian who became Norma. Iris is the Trickster. Manolo is the Mentor. There's María, the reluctant hero, who says, 'I'm here . . . I'm Puerto Rican!' I think that when Rollo May talks about mythology and how it works, I followed his formula and it works." Ramirez, "Carmen," 93–94.

28. Mary Beth, "Episode 43: Cándido Tirado." Beyond The Lights: A Conversation with Theater Professionals. Podcast. https://beyondthelightspodcast.com/episodes/episode-43-cndido-tirado

29. Her previous ventures into San Juan are all merely reported after the fact in expositional fashion.

30. Rivera, *La Gringa*, 68.

31. Rivera, *La Gringa*, 71, 73.

32. Rivera, *La Gringa*, 75.

33. According to Ramirez, "in her play *La Gringa* . . . the use of Latin music, instruments and salsa will help identify many of the basic core arguments regarding the hybridization of Nuyorican and Puerto Rican culture through music" ("Carmen," 38).

34. In Hudes's play *Daphne's Dive* the character Inez says "A güiro is a gourd, a calabash. More Puerto Rican than a crucifix on the rearview. Más Boricua que un parakeet in the kitchen" (12).

35. Jade Power-Sotomayor, "Corporeal Sounding: Listening to Bomba Dance, Listening to Puertorriqueñxs," *Performance Matters* 6, no. 2 (2020): 43.

36. Power-Sotomayor, "Corporeal," 44.

37. Power-Sotomayor, "Corporeal," 45.

38. The focus on sound also resonates with Ren Ellis Neyra's claims about the power of the cry in *The Cry of the Senses: Listening to Latinx and Caribbean Poetics* (Durham: Duke University Press, 2020). In a brief accounting of *bomba* in Chapter 1 they layer on the Haitian revolutionary history of the musical form along with the more materially explosive condition of the revolutionary bomb which they explore in Chapter 3.

39. It was first published in *Boleros for the Disenchanted and Other Plays* (New York: Theatre Communications Group, 2012) which includes the three hander *Brainpeople*, which explores identity and connection in a dystopic future, where power cannot provide connection, but wealth can serve as a proximate substitute, and the titular play that deals directly with questions of migration and the evolution over time of a love story inflected by Rivera's own family history.

40. While still at times centered in US spaces (*Massacre: Sing to Your Children*), he does expand to think with larger global patterns of inequality, identity, and loss (*Brainpeople*), and revolution (*School of the Americas*).

41. José Rivera, *Adoration of the Old Woman*, in *Boleros for the Disenchanted and Other Plays* (New York: Theatre Communications Group, 2012), 166.

42. Rivera, *Adoration*, 227.

43. Rivera, *Adoration*, 226.
44. Rivera, *Adoration*, 226.
45. Rivera, *Adoration*, 227.
46. Perhaps extending the same practice of exclusion toward North African influence in the history of Spain in the practice of Al-Andaluz. For more on this see the introduction of Lisa Jackson-Schebetta, *Traveler, There is No Road: Theatre, the Spanish Civil War, and the Decolonial Imagination in the Americas* (Iowa City: University of Iowa Press, 2017).
47. See Meléndez, *Sponsored*.
48. Rivera, *Adoration*, 225.
49. Castanha, *Myth*.
50. See Feliciano-Santos, *Contested*.
51. This resonates with Anishinaabe scholar and novelist Gerald Vizenor's concept of survivance "Native survivance is an active sense of presence over historical absence, the dominance of cultural simulations, and manifest manners. Native survivance is a continuance of stories." Gerald Vizenor, *Native Liberty: Natural Reason and Cultural Survivance* (Omaha: University of Nebraska Press, 2009), 1.
52. J. Rivera, *Adoration*, 225.
53. This is most explicitly represented in US dramatic literature in Dion Boucicault's *The Octoroon*, the subject of a powerful contemporary revisionist adaptation, *An Octoroon*, by African American playwright Branden Jacobs-Jenkins which centers on the compelling, affective power of melodrama as form.
54. This image serves as an ironic connection to the kinds of ghosts of a play like Tennessee Williams's *Cat on a Hot Tin Roof* where the haunting absence of homosexual lovers is only a stage direction suggestion and a designer's atmospheric invitation, but where in Rivera's world the ghost has as much materiality and reality as anyone else in the space, albeit the ghosts are visually imperceptible to the men.
55. This is my translation of the definition in Spanish from https://dle.rae.es/adorar?m=form
56. Rivera, *Adoration*, 181. It is important to note as well that he is playing the cuatro as he sings traditional ballads, a musical genre and instrument that is central to the work of Quiara Alegría Hudes's *The Happiest Song Plays Last* (New York: Theatre Communications Group, 2014) in Chapter 4.
57. The collapse of the attention to the Three Kings is framed here as a loss of Puerto Rican cultural identity, and while from one radical point of view this is itself an issue of lost indigenous identity, the conditions of Spanish rule were in the process of shifting just as the US took over control, which is in fact one of the arguments as to why the US intervened when it did. The argument is that the US, fearing Cuban success in their fight from independence, intervened to deal with Spain, who would be more willing to grant concessions on behalf of their territories, than the Cubans would on their newly acquired homeland. As always, the driving force was both military and economic.
58. Rivera himself does not speak Spanish fluently and has worked with translators to help him develop passages in Spanish.
59. Rivera, *Adoration*, 195.
60. Rivera, *Adoration*, 223. Bold in the original.
61. Of course, one of the ironies of the language, besides the fact that Cheo has unaccented English based on his time spent in educational institutions in the United

States, is that the use of Spanish (and even the invocation of the Three Kings) is a direct result of the previous forces of colonialism—the Spanish, and a call for liberation does not reach that far into the indigenous histories of the Taíno, whose living heritage is potentially disrupted but whose practice of areíto is a means of recuperating this history and heritage.

62. It also echoes the playwright's own visits to his grandmother in Las Arenas. The precise use of the word "delink" here is intended to deliberately echo the work of Walter D. Mignolo, *The Darker Side of Western Modernity: Global Futures, Decolonial Options* (Durham: Duke University Press, 2011) in his expanded engagement with Aníbal Quijano's concept of coloniality and the colonial matrix of power in "Coloniality and Modernity/Rationality," *Cultural Studies* 21, nos. 2–3 (March 1, 2007): 168–78. The intended use of rural Puerto Rico as a site of redemption interestingly reinforces a shared communal reading of René Marqués's account of the loss of traditional values accompanying the migration into urban spaces and away from the island in *La Carreta, The Ox-Cart*, whose bilingual productions by the Puerto Rican Traveling Theater Company in the 1960s in New York were both foundational for that company and for the emergence of Puerto Rican theater in its US diaspora (see Chapter 1).

63. It's worth noting that Rivera is not fluently bilingual and has had others do the translation for the Spanish language elements in his play. And, while one might assume a community so close to the US/Mexico border would have more familiarity with Spanish, La Jolla as a neighborhood, despite the presence of UC San Diego, is often presented as a bastion of conservative whiteness. The fact that this piece premiered in San Diego offers its own interesting interconnectivity in the sense that it is in a different space of intentional forgetting, in which the proximity of the border and the question of Mexican and, increasingly in the present tense, Central American migration, are palpable subjects of everyday life. While the US relationship with Mexico is not obscured, it is the subject of heightened political rhetoric that reveals the fundamental political and economic interrelationality that has only heightened with the post-revolutionary intensification of border attention. However, the shifting attitudes toward immigration, especially in forms that lack state documentation, serve as an oddly equivalent proxy toward questions of political autonomy and forms of liberation, as well as a desire for incorporation and a juxtaposed resentment and resistance that frame the arguments around Puerto Rican status in the play.

64. Malavet, *America's Colony*, 10.

65. See Frances Negrón-Muntaner, *Boricua Pop: Puerto Ricans and the Latinization of American Culture* (New York: New York University Press, 2004), 9–12.

66. See, for example, Soto-Crespo, *Mainland Passage*; Grosfoguel and Negrón-Muntaner, *Puerto Rican Jam*; and Grosfoguel, *Colonial Subjects*.

67. Something Malavet addresses in the context of a necessity for reparations, a move that opens up critical tension with the extent to which the primary sites of economic reparation are in relation to the legacies of African chattel slavery and the continued systemic anti-black racism as well as the betrayals of indigenous sovereignty and treaty violations. Pedro A. Malavet, "Reparations Theory and Postcolonial Puerto Rico: Some Preliminary Thoughts," *Berkeley La Raza Law Journal* 13, no. 2 (2002): 387.

68. Interestingly prescient in terms of the increasing interest in statehood, Rivera's play is oddly more optimistic about the weight of the elections for status, ignoring the multiple times that there has been an apparent "victory" for statehood based sheerly on the number of explicit votes for a particular status. Of course, while the interest in

statehood grew significantly in parts of the island, what Rivera's play does not attend to is the complex issues of participation and unique and interesting forms of ballot resistance, done as a particular form of voting in which one either participates in the process in such a way as to place the process in question. Up until 2017 this was a continuous part of status electoral politics, indicating a strong preference for forms of resistance and reimagination working within the institutional form of voting to demand an alternate form of determination, suggesting the limits of strict electoral decisions as a means of negotiating the complexly historically imbricated conditions of status attitudes and understandings of past and present status quo, as well as possible imagined futures. This process collapsed in the June 11, 2017, plebiscite with the pro-statehood legislative impatience with this murky contestation, setting up a strict positivist structure in which a blank ballot was not allowed to hold representational weight and in which the choices of status are rejected by the non-statehood parties, with specific calls to boycott the election. This led to a participation rate of 23% in that election, much lower than in previous status votes, but did clearly indicate that close to a quarter of the voting populace do strongly support the idea of statehood. This sense of division is of course seen as problematic to the extent that it impedes actions taken to improve the quality of life for Puerto Ricans in their daily patterns. It is also important to note that the vote in 2017 happened prior to Hurricane Maria.

69. An additional irony of Cheo's initial investment in the non-violent advocacy is that he recognizes himself that he has never walked the dirt of Puerto Rico. He also explicitly models Che's motorcycle trip through Argentina as a consciousness raising activity, riding his bicycle from one side of the island to the other which, according to Cheo, took more than a year and left his butt feeling sore rather than necessarily providing any radical consciousness raising. This reference to Che's motorcycle trip likely stems from Rivera's work on the screenplay for *Motorcycle Diaries*.

70. See the conclusion of Rocío Zambrana, *Colonial Debts*.

71. Rivera, *Adoration*, 184.

72. Rivera, *Adoration*, 184.

73. As mentioned elsewhere, one of Muñoz Marín's political triumphs rested in disaggregate cultural and political nationalism in order to enable the continuity of the past regardless of status as a way of defusing one leg of the nationalist argument. The dishonoring of the dead is of course related to *Adoration*'s sense of the dead in Puerto Rico that have historically fought for freedom at different times.

74. A long ongoing belief that he was subject to illegal radiation treatments has actually received some relatively recent documentary support in Denis's passionately *independentista* history of revolutionary Puerto Rico, *The War Against All Puerto Ricans*. Of course, this claim remains controversial, but many people strongly believe it, and the ongoing history of treating Puerto Rican bodies as subjects for experimentation as evidenced both by the historical sterilization campaigns and the long-standing practicing of bombing in Vieques reinforces belief in this possibility.

75. J. Rivera, *Adoration*, 187.

76. J. Rivera, *Adoration*, 188.

77. In 2006, there was a legislative shift to dominance by a pro-statehood party and additional referendums have gained increased support for the idea of Puerto Rican statehood; more recent movement in Congress has occurred in H.R. 8393, The Puerto Rican Status Act, which calls for a binding plebiscite, passed by roll call vote in the House in December 2022. However, the effort died in the Senate. Puerto Rico is

still represented in Congress by a non-voting member, a Resident Commissioner, who despite their explicit and active investment issues of Puerto Rican sovereignty, have not been able to advance significant changes in the treatment of Puerto Rico.

78. Referencing both the violent end to the conflict in Jayuya and the Palm Sunday Massacre in Ponce in 1937.

79. A connection here to the dominance of the bed in *Cat on a Hot Tin Roof* is revealing insofar as the centrality of the bed is about both the challenges of sexual intimacy and loss of love, but also reflects the difficulty of negotiating legacy, genealogy, and history. Of course, in all material aspects this is a radically different bed.

80. Rivera, *Adoration*, 224.

81. Also, though it is unlikely that José was aware of this, his ending shifts the terms of martyrdom and violence that historically emerged in the plays of dramatists on the island, such as Marqués's *La Casa Sin Reloj* in which the woman kills her revolutionary lover as an act of preservation, and a similar gesture is presented at the end of Puerto Rican playwright Roberto Ramos-Perea's *Cry of the Moon*, in which Teresa kills her brother Pepe as a means of preserving the future possibility of revolution, at least in my reading of the text.

82. See Jon D. Rossini and Patricia Ybarra, "Neoliberalism, Historiography, Identity Politics: Toward a New Historiography of Latino Theater," *Radical History Review*, no. 112 (January 2012): 162–72.

83. This is very similar to a conclusion Rivera reaches at the end of his 2007 play about Che Guevara's last days, *School of the Americas*. I write about this in a different framework, one in which I am less focused on the pragmatic possibility and more concerned about the collapse of radical possibility in the face of neoliberalism in "José Rivera, Neoliberalism, and the Outside of Politics," *Latin American Theatre Review* 43, no. 1 (Fall 2009): 41–56.

84. Rivera, *Adoration*, 221.

85. Rivera, *Adoration*, 221.

Chapter 4

1. Gabriela Serena Sanchez and Quiara Alegría Hudes, "Pausing and Breathing: Two Sisters Deliver the ATHE 2018 Conference Keynote Address," *Theatre Topics* 29, no.1 (2019): E-2.

2. Sanchez and Hudes, E-7.

3. Another language for this is racial capitalism.

4. Martine Kei Green-Rogers, Shawn LaCount, Patricia Ybarra, and Harvey Young, "Continuing the Conversation: Responses to Gabriela Serena Sanchez and Quiara Alegría Hudes," *Theatre Topics* 29, no.1 (2019): E19. Ybarra's response was internally titled "Pa'Lante: A Response to Pausing and Breathing." Another example of this same dynamic is described explicitly in an account of Quiara's experiences in high school English in her memoir: "What do you think, Quiara? You wrote this in your reading response: 'The roots of the grass lawn are rotting.' Say more." "It just annoys me how Loman thinks he's tragic. Two sons healthy enough to throw the pigskin. A marriage intact. Like, what's so awful?" "You tell me. What's his problem?" The teacher trained his eyes on me. "Well . . . Loman's a Brady Bunch guy, the kind of patriarch smiling in an insurance ad. The billboards and TV shows make him out to be some kingly provider archetype. And I guess he drank the Kool-Aid and then, like, eventually had

to face the fact that he's average. So that's his tragedy. Being average. Which I don't find tragic." Quiara Alegría Hudes, *My Broken Language: A Memoir* (New York: Random House, 2021), 64.

5. Ybarra, "Pa'Lante," E-18.

6. Ybarra, "Pa'Lante," E-19. Patricia A. Ybarra, "How to Read a Latinx Play in the Twenty-First Century: Learning from Quiara Hudes," *Theatre Topics* 27, no. 1 (2017) also provides an excellent view of Hudes's work.

7. Sanchez and Hudes, E-3.

8. I certainly availed myself of the opportunity, driving down from Sacramento to see all three plays in two days.

9. "The Mark Taper Forum, located at The Music Center, is where we think about how art sheds a light on society. It's where we produce plays—whether they're world premieres, second productions, or the remounting of important works—that provoke conversations." https://www.centertheatregroup.org/visit/mark-taper-forum/ "The Kirk Douglas Theatre, located in Downtown Culver City, is our home for adventurous new work. It's where we do the most world premieres, play with conventions, and take risks, fueling an all-encompassing experience." https://www.centertheatregroup.org/visit/kirk-douglas-theatre/

10. "The Los Angeles Theatre Center is a facility of the City of Los Angeles, Department of Cultural Affairs and is operated by the Latino Theater Company, a 501(c)3 non-profit organization. The Los Angeles Theatre Center produces theater, dance, and music programming, along with creating summits and artistic discussions for peoples of all cultures. Accordingly, LATC is committed to commissioning new plays, training young actors, writers, and theater artists, providing arts education, and creating international cultural exchange with artists and audiences from around the globe." https://culturela.org/cultural-centers/los-angeles-theatre-center-latc/

11. This is part of the larger question about access to representation and whose work is heard and seen, a problem manifest by a dominance of male voices despite a majority of female playwrights, and a predominance of particular kinds of voices of stories, which has only recently begun to meaningfully shift. As Ybarra's argument reminds us, even when different voices are introduced and listened to, they are often invited in to replicate familiar stories of growth and transformation and not to upset the dominant ideology of the space.

12. Hudes, *My Broken Language*, 70.

13. "Those books had title pages and final paragraphs. Spielberg's film had an opening sequence and final shot. The horror of history, made slightly less unbearable through the telling, the forensic understanding, the bearing of witness. But whatever beast stalked the Perezes was present-tense and its appetite was peaking. No title pages or final paragraphs to name it, no opening sequences or final shots to help me see. This reaper nipping at our heels, pulling up a chair at our Thanksgiving table." Hudes, *My Broken Language*, 72–73.

14. The musical forms referenced in the first two plays.

15. "If I stay in Philly, I'm gonna turn into it. I'm gonna become one of them." Quiara Alegría Hudes, *Water by the Spoonful* (New York: Theatre Communications Group, 2017), 92.

16. Quiara Alegría Hudes, *The Happiest Song Plays Last* (New York: Theatre Communications Group, 2014), 12. Hereafter, *THSPL*.

17. Hudes, *THSPL*, 16.

18. Hudes, *THSPL*, 16–17. This is echoed in Zeynep Tufekci's comment in *Twitter and Tear Gas: The Power and Fragility of Networked Protest* (New Haven: Yale University Press, 2017), "An Egyptian friend of mine would later joke that this must have been the first time in history when a person could actually join a revolution by clicking on 'I'm Attending' in response to a Facebook e-vite. But such social media sites were important to audiences beyond the protesters; the world also followed the uprising" (22).

19. There are useful parallels between Shar and Soledad Iglesias in *Beige* (Chapter 2) who ultimately traces a journey of political consciousness raising and subsequent action.

20. Hudes, *THSPL*, 64.

21. Hudes, *THSPL*, 66.

22. Hudes, *THSPL*, 66.

23. This is not to deny the murder of activist protestors in the US, but rather to highlight the level of shock and outrage associated with such events as opposed to their parallel occurrences elsewhere.

24. Michelle Liu Carriger, "Of Affects, Effects, Acts, and X," *Journal of Dramatic Theory and Criticism* 35, no. 2 (2021): 10. This is from Carriger's introduction to a special section of this issue which she edited entitled "#Performative X" that engages 17 contributions relating to this current slippage.

25. Hudes, *THSPL*, 75.

26. Hudes, *THSPL*, 74.

27. This word choice is deliberate, reflecting the language Daphne uses to describe her mother in *Daphne's Dive*.

28. Hudes, *THSPL*, 77.

29. Hudes, *THSPL*, 85.

30. Hudes, *THSPL*, 78.

31. Hudes, *THSPL*, 85.

32. This play has powerful parallels to Lynn Nottage's *Sweat* as a similar place in which people both connect and grow apart based on their politics and their ways of addressing the world, in a world transformed by the shifting of relationships with the retrenchment of capitalism following the global collapse of 2008.

33. Hudes, *Daphne's Dive*, 21

34. Hudes, *Daphne's Dive*, 17.

35. Unsurprisingly Christopher Isherwood's review completely misses this connection. https://www.nytimes.com/2016/05/16/theater/review-daphnes-dive-where-everybody-knows-youre-broke.html?_r=0

36. Hudes, *Daphne's Dive*, 10.

37. Hudes, *Daphne's Dive*, 67.

38. Rivera, *Marisol*, 5.

39. Joseph Shahadi, "Burn: The Radical Disappearance of Kathy Change," *TDR: The Drama Review* 55, no. 2 (2011): 52–53.

40. Shahadi, 61.

41. Think about the parallels between Kathy Chang(e)'s vision and Yarimar Bonilla's description of a powerful general strike in Guadeloupe in the context of nonsovereign resistance. "In many ways this alliance resembles the kind of 'network politics' that are said to typify contemporary social movements (particularly international anticorporate globalization movements). This new form of political action, which

came to national attention after the 1999 anti-WTO protests in Seattle, is known for its ability to rally a wide range of political actors and agendas (agricultural workers, labor unions, environmentalists, etc.) against a common enemy (global corporate capitalism and its regulatory institutions) and for its decentralized forms of organization and consensus-based decision making (Juris 2008; Graeber 2002)" (Bonilla, "Non-Sovereign," 217).

42. Vivian L. Huang, "'What Shall We Do?': Kathy Change, Soomi Kim, and Asian Feminist Performance on Campus," *TDR* 62, no. 3 (2018).

43. Casting Samira Wiley as Ruby in the premiere production of *Daphne's Dive* situates her both within and outside the legacy of Puerto Rican identity as her specific identity and origin are never named while ensuring a black presence central to Puerto Rican history. In contrast see the June 2021 controversy about the casting of the film version of *In the Heights* where Lin Manuel Miranda has tweeted an apology for a lack of color diversity in his cast and was initially defended by Rita Moreno for being someone who has at least made Puerto Rico visible. On a different note, there is a crucial reminder of the limits of intervention as Ruby's disabled brother does not experience the same level of care and individualized attention and despite Ruby's demands, Daphne refuses to take on this responsibility, recognizing her own limits.

44. Hudes, *Daphne's Dive*, 69.

45. Hudes, *Daphne's Dive*, 69.

46. Performed in 2019 at INTAR; Directed by Charlie Chauca; Scenic Design by Holden Gunster: Lighting Design by Nicholas Palatella.

47. The more than 3000 was the more common progressive number at the time of the play. It is now up to 4695 in the most recent scholarly works, though interestingly media coverage of Hurricane Fiona in September 2022 was still using the more than 3000 number.

48. See, for example, Yarimar Bonilla and Marisol LeBrón, eds., *Aftershocks of Disaster: Puerto Rico Before and After the Storm* (Chicago: Haymarket Books, 2019).

49. Caroline Kenny, "Trump tosses paper towels into Puerto Rico crowd," Oct 3, 2017, https://www.cnn.com/2017/10/03/politics/donald-trump-paper-towels-puerto-rico

50. This extends further into the 21st century with the work of PROMESA, which some figures consider to be illegally appointed based on the Puerto Rican constitution, and whose job it is to address the debt conditions of Puerto Rico, a debt generated by an external practice of authorizing investment in a way that did not serve the interests of the Puerto Rican people, because as structures encouraging investment and development were suspended, the existing industries would simply shift global locations to new spaces where better possibilities existed.

51. For more details see the introduction of Robert McGreevey, *Borderline Citizens: The United States, Puerto Rico, and the Politics of Colonial Migration* (Ithaca, NY: Cornell University Press, 2018).

52. Being sold as a tax shelter and block chain paradise according to Naomi Klein, in her short work on disaster capitalism in Puerto Rico. Instead, she contrasts the progressive, local responses of diverse organic farming and solar powered microgrids. Naomi Klein, *The Battle for Paradise: Puerto Rico Takes on the Disaster Capitalists* (Chicago: Haymarket Books, 2018).

53. There is a whole potential discussion of the politics of the history of salsa in relation to Puerto Rico.

54. Nelson Diaz-Marcano, *Paper Towels*, manuscript, New Play Exchange Network, 1.
55. Diaz-Marcano, *Paper Towels*, 1.
56. Frances R. Aparicio, "*Aguanile* Critical Listening, Mourning, and Decolonial Healing," in *Critical Dialogues in Latinx Studies: A Reader*, ed. Ana Y. Ramos-Zayas and Mérida M. Rúa (New York: New York University Press, 2021), 478. See also Wilson Valentín-Escobar, "'Nothing Connects Us All but Imagined Sounds': Performing Trans-Boricua Memories, Identities, and Nationalisms Through the Death of Héctor Lavoe." In *Mambo Montage: The Latinization of New York*, ed. by Arlene Dávila and Agustín Laó-Montes (New York: Columbia University Press, 2001).
57. Diaz-Marcano, *Paper Towels*, 4.
58. Diaz-Marcano, *Paper Towels*, 4.
59. Diaz-Marcano, *Paper Towels*, 17.
60. Diaz-Marcano, *Paper Towels*, 35.
61. Diaz-Marcano, *Paper Towels*, 10.
62. Diaz-Marcano, *Paper Towels*, 16.
63. José Ramón Sánchez, *Boricua Power: A Political History of Puerto Ricans in the United States* (New York: New York University Press, 2007). Ramón H. Rivera-Servera's *Performing Queer Latinidad: Dance, Sexuality, Politics* (Ann Arbor: University of Michigan Press, 2012) offers a very different picture of the political work of dance.
64. Diaz-Marcano, *Paper Towels*, 28.
65. As Toño says, "In America they get to be cars, we are just fishermen. We are just tools for resources and now we have none." Diaz-Marcano, *Paper Towels*, 37.
66. Diaz-Marcano, *Paper Towels*, 32.
67. Diaz-Marcano, *Paper Towels*, 41.
68. Diaz-Marcano, *Paper Towels*, 32.
69. Diaz-Marcano, *Paper Towels*, 41.

Chapter 5

1. José Rivera, *Massacre (Sing to Your Children)* (New York: Broadway Play Publishing, 2007), 28.
2. Gore Vidal, *Imperial America: Reflections on the United States of Amnesia* (New York: Nation Books, 2005), 12.
3. Caridad Svich, "'An Urgent Voice for Our Times': An Interview with José Rivera," *Contemporary Theatre Review* 14(4): 2010, 87.
4. Rivera, *Massacre*, 61.
5. Erik and Janis are married, Hector owns a restaurant, Panama is a mechanic, Vivy, Lila a tarot card reader, Eliseo a bar tender who is younger and works for the others.
6. Rivera, *Massacre*, 1.
7. Rivera, *Massacre*, 14.
8. Rivera, *Massacre*, 31.
9. Rivera, *Massacre*, 34.
10. Rivera, *Massacre*, 16.
11. Rivera, *Massacre*, 37.
12. Rivera, *Massacre*, 37.
13. Rivera, *Massacre*, 66.

14. David Rooney. "They Kill the Tyrant but Can't Seem to Bury Him," *New York Times*, April 16, 2012, https://www.nytimes.com/2012/04/17/theater/reviews/massacre-sing-to-your-children-at-rattlestick.html

15. Michael Feingold, "Congealed Weapons in Massacre (Sing to Your Children)—The Village Voice," https://www.villagevoice.com/2012/04/18/congealed-weapons-in-massacre-sing-to-your-children/

16. Rooney, "They Kill."

17. Feingold, "Congealed."

18. Malcolm Gladwell, "Small Change," *The New Yorker*, October 4, 2010.

19. Rivera, *Massacre*, 48.

20. Rivera, *Massacre*, 48.

21. Act 2 Scene 1 is the chronological end of the play. Act 2 Scene flashes back 5 years and ends the performance.

22. Rivera, *Massacre*, 60.

23. Rivera, *Massacre*, 61.

24. Kristoffer Diaz, *#therevolution*, National New Play Exchange, manuscript, 83.

25. Alain Badiou with Nicolas Truong, *In Praise of Theatre*, trans. Andrew Bielski (Cambridge: Polity, 2015), 18–19.

26. Premiered by InterAct Theatre Company in 2016 directed by Seth Rozin. https://www.interacttheatre.org/season-archive

27. The radical action of a desperate actor to transform one's career is a familiar part of political rhetoric in Latine theatrical comedy, in which the attempt is often problematically tied to more ostensibly virtuous, collective political action.

28. Diaz, *#therevolution*, 1.

29. Diaz, *#therevolution*, np.

30. Diaz doesn't use this term himself.

31. Diaz, *#therevolution*, np.

32. Tufekci, *Twitter*, 269–70.

33. Tehama Lopez Bunyasi and Candis Watts Smith, *Stay Woke: A People's Guide to Making All Black Lives Matter* (New York: New York University Press, 2019), 13–14.

34. Marcela A. Fuentes, *Performance Constellations: Networks of Protest and Activism in Latin America*. (Ann Arbor: University of Michigan Press, 2019), 3.

35. Jeffrey R. Webber, *The Last Day of Oppression, and the First Day of the Same: The Politics and Economics of the New Latin American Left* (Chicago: Haymarket, 2017), 94.

36. Webber, 94.

37. See as well, Judith Butler, *Performative Theory of Assembly*.

38. See Klein, *Battle*.

39. Diaz, *#therevolution*, 85.

40. Tufekci, *Twitter*, 277.

Conclusion

1. Ramirez, "Carmen," 148.

2. Keeanga-Yamahtta Taylor, *From #BlackLivesMatter to Black Liberation* (Chicago: Haymarket Books, 2016), 217.

3. Michael C. Dawson, *Blacks In and Out of the Left* (Cambridge: Harvard University Press, 2013), 186.

4. Dawson, *Blacks*, 200–201.

5. Pedro Cabán, "Puerto Rico: The Ascent and Decline of an American Colony," in *Critical Dialogues in Latinx Studies: A Reader*, edited by Ana Y. Ramos-Zayas and Mérida M. Rúa (New York: New York University Press, 2021), 24.

6. Cabán, "Puerto Rico," 13.

7. Gordon K. Lewis, *Notes on the Puerto Rican Revolution: An Essay on American Dominance and Caribbean Resistance* (New York: Monthly Review Press, 1974), 256.

8. Rocío Zambrana, *Colonial Debts: The Case of Puerto Rico* (Durham: Duke University Press, 2021), 14.

9. Zambrana, *Colonial Debts*, 14.

10. Guillermo Rebollo Gil, "Regarding the Future," in *Writing Puerto Rico: Our Decolonial Moment* (Springer International Publishing, 2018).

11. Rebollo Gil, "Regarding," 64.

12. Rebollo Gil, "Regarding," 64.

13. Rebollo Gil, "Regarding," 65.

14. Rebollo Gil, "Regarding," 67.

15. The Latinx Theatre Commons is also a hugely supportive and incredibly crucial space, though they do not directly hold any resources.

16. Amanda Finn, "Not For Sale: UrbanTheater Company Co-Founder Ivan Vega on Community, Gentrification and the Next Generation of Theater Makers," *Newcity Stage*, April 17, 2019. https://www.newcitystage.com/2019/04/17/not-for-sale-urbantheater-company-co-founder-ivan-vega-on-community-gentrification-and-the-next-generation-of-theater-makers/

17. Sanchez and Hudes, "Pausing and Breathing," E-7.

18. Hudes, *Water by the Spoonful*, 6

19. Note that none of these details are available to the participants of the chat room in the interest of protecting personal anonymity and privacy.

20. Hudes, *Water*, 88.

References

Adler, Stella. *The Technique of Acting*. New York: Bantam, 1990.
Alfaro, Luis. "La Maestra Fornés Has Left the Room, But What a Room!" *American Theatre* (October 31, 2018).
Althusser, Louis. "Ideology and Ideological State Apparatuses." In *Lenin and Philosophy and Other Essays*, translated by Ben Brewster, 127–86. New York: Monthly Review Press, 1971.
Antush, John V. *Recent Puerto Rican Theater: Five Plays from New York*. Houston: Arte Público Press, 1991.
Antush, John V., ed. *Nuestro New York: An Anthology of Puerto Rican Plays*. New York: Penguin, 1994.
Aparicio, Frances R. "*Aguanile*: Critical Listening, Mourning, and Decolonial Healing." In *Critical Dialogues in Latinx Studies: A Reader*, edited by Ana Y. Ramos-Zayas and Mérida M. Rúa, 476–88. New York: New York University Press, 2021.
Arnall, Gavin. *Subterranean Fanon: An Underground Theory of Radical Change*. New York: Columbia University Press, 2020.
"Avalon Project—Treaty of Peace Between the United States and Spain; December 10, 1898." Accessed November 11, 2020. https://avalon.law.yale.edu/19th_century/sp1898.asp
Ayala, César J. "Puerto Rico and Its Diaspora," blog. https://international.ucla.edu/lai/article/248568
Badiou, Alain, with Nicolas Truong. *In Praise of Theatre*. Translated by Andrew Bielski. Cambridge: Polity, 2015.
Baver, Sherrie L. "'Peace Is More Than the End of Bombing': The Second Stage of the Vieques Struggle." *Latin American Perspectives* 33, no. 1 (January 1, 2006): 102–15.
Beth, Mary. "Episode 43: Cándido Tirado." Beyond The Lights: A Conversation with Theater Professionals. Podcast. https://beyondthelightspodcast.com/episodes/episode-43-cndido-tirado
Boffone, Trevor. 50 Playwrights Project. https://50playwrights.org/2017/04/10/desi-moreno-penson/
Boffone, Trevor, Teresa Marrero and Chantal Rodriguez, eds. *Encuentro: Latinx Performance for the New American Theater*. Evanston: Northwestern University Press, 2019.
Boffone, Trevor, Teresa Marrero and Chantal Rodriguez, eds. *Seeking Common Ground: Latinx and Latin American Theatre and Performance*. New York: Methuen, 2022.
Bonilla, Yarimar. "Nonsovereign Futures? French Caribbean Politics in the Wake of Disenchantment." In *Caribbean Sovereignty, Development and Democracy in an Age of Globalization*, edited by Linden Lewis, 208–27. New York: Routledge, 2012.

Bonilla, Yarimar, and Marisol LeBrón, eds. *Aftershocks of Disaster: Puerto Rico Before and After the Storm*. Chicago: Haymarket Books, 2019.

Bunyasi, Tehama Lopez, and Candis Watts Smith. *Stay Woke: A People's Guide to Making All Black Lives Matter*. New York: New York University Press, 2019.

Butler, Judith. *Notes Toward a Performative Theory of Assembly*. Cambridge: Harvard University Press, 2015.

Butler, Judith. "Recognition and the Social Bond: A Response to Axel Honneth." In *Recognition and Ambivalence*, edited by Heikki Ikäheimo, Kristina Lepold, and Titus Stahl, 31–53. New York: Columbia University Press, 2021.

Cabán, Pedro. "Puerto Rico: The Ascent and Decline of an American Colony," In *Critical Dialogues in Latinx Studies: A Reader*, edited by Ana Y. Ramos-Zayas and Mérida M. Rúa, 13–24. New York: New York University Press, 2021.

Carriger, Michelle Liu. "Of Affects, Effects, Acts, and X." *Journal of Dramatic Theory and Criticism* 35, no. 2 (2021): 9–11.

Carrillo Rowe, Aimee. "Be Longing: Toward a Feminist Politics of Relation." *NWSA Journal* 17, no. 2 (Summer 2005): 15–46.

Castanha, Tony. *The Myth of Indigenous Caribbean Extinction: Continuity and Reclamation in Borikén—Puerto Rico*. New York: Palgrave Macmillan, 2011.

Chemers, Michael Mark. *Ghost Light: An Introductory Handbook for Dramaturgy*. Carbondale: Southern Illinois University Press, 2010.

Corretjer, Juan Antonio. "Pedro Albizu Campos and the Ponce Massacre." New York: 1965, pamphlet. http://hdl.handle.net/2027/mdp.39015074201214

Cortes, Felix, Angel Falcón, and Juan Flores. "The Cultural Expression of Puerto Ricans in New York: A Theoretical Perspective and Critical Review." *Latin American Perspectives* 3, no. 3 (1976): 117–52.

Cruz, María Acosta. *Dream Nation: Puerto Rican Culture and the Fictions of Independence*. Camden: Rutgers University Press, 2014.

Cruz, Migdalia. *Lolita de Lares*. Latino Literature: Poetry, Drama, and Fiction. ProQuest. Accessed September 28, 2020.

Cruz, Migdalia. "Searching for Home in All the Wrong Places: Why My Nuyorican Reality is Stateless." In *Theatre and Cartographies of Power: Repositioning the Latina/o Americas*, edited by Jimmy A. Noriega and Analola Santana, 106–8. Carbondale: Southern Illinois University Press, 2018.

Dávila, Arlene. *Latinos, Inc.: The Marketing and Making of a People*. Berkeley: University of California Press, 2001.

Dawson, Michael C. *Blacks In and Out of the Left*. Cambridge: Harvard University Press, 2013.

De la Roche, Elisa. *¡Teatro Hispano!: Three Major New York Companies*. New York: Garland, 1995.

Della Gatta, Carla. *Latinx Shakespeares: Staging U.S. Intracultural Theater*. Ann Arbor: University of Michigan Press, 2023.

Denis, Nelson A. *War Against All Puerto Ricans*. New York: Nation Books, 2015.

Diaz, Kristoffer. *#therevolution*, National New Play Network/New Play Exchange, manuscript.

Diaz, Kristoffer. *All Ears. Every 28 Hours Plays*. https://every28hoursplays.org/the-plays-2/

Diaz-Marcano, Nelson. *Paper Towels*, National New Play Network/New Play Exchange, manuscript.

Diaz-Marcano, Nelson. *REVOLT!* National New Play Network/New Play Exchange, manuscript. https://newplayexchange.org/plays/104965/revolt

Dolan, Jill. "Performance, Utopia, and the 'Utopian Performative.'" *Theatre Journal* 53, no. 3 (2001): 455–79.

Duany, Jorge. *The Puerto Rican Nation on the Move: Identities on the Island and in the United States.* Chapel Hill: University of North Carolina Press, 2002.

Dussel, Enrique. *Twenty Theses on Politics.* Translated by George Ciccariello-Maher. Durham: Duke University Press, 2008.

Ellis Neyra, Ren. *The Cry of the Senses: Listening to Latinx and Caribbean Poetics.* Durham: Duke University Press, 2020.

Erman, Sam. *Almost Citizens: Puerto Rico, the U.S. Constitution, and Empire.* Cambridge: Cambridge University Press, 2018.

Every 28 Hours Plays: About Us https://every28hoursplays.org/about-2/

Every 28 Hours Plays: The Plays https://every28hoursplays.org/the-plays-2/

Feingold, Michael. "Congealed Weapons in Massacre (Sing to Your Children)—The Village Voice." Accessed September 26, 2022. https://www.villagevoice.com/2012/04/18/congealed-weapons-in-massacre-sing-to-your-children/

Feliciano-Santos, Sherina. *A Contested Caribbean Indigeneity: Language, Social Practice, and Identity within Puerto Rican Taíno Activism.* New Brunswick: Rutgers University Press, 2021.

Fernández, Johanna. *The Young Lords: A Radical History.* Chapel Hill: The University of North Carolina Press, 2020.

Fernandez, Ronald. *The Disenchanted Island: Puerto Rico and the United States in the Twentieth Century,* 2nd ed. Westport: Praeger, 1996.

Fiet, Lowell. "Preguntas Paradigmáticas Sobre El Teatro Hispanocaribeño Isleño y La Diáspora." *Latin American Theatre Review* 37, no. 2 (March 1, 2004): 7–24.

Finn, Amanda. "Not For Sale: UrbanTheater Company Co-Founder Ivan Vega on Community, Gentrification and the Next Generation of Theater Makers." Newcity Stage, April 17, 2019. https://www.newcitystage.com/2019/04/17/not-for-sale-urbantheater-company-co-founder-ivan-vega-on-community-gentrification-and-the-next-generation-of-theater-makers/

Fisher, Tony. "Introduction: Performance and the Tragic Politics of the *Agôn.*" In *Performing Antagonism: Theatre, Performance & Radical Democracy,* edited by Tony Fisher and Eve Katsouraki, 1–23. London: Palgrave Macmillan UK, 2017.

Flores, Juan. *The Diaspora Strikes Back: Caribeño Tales of Learning and Turning.* New York: Routledge, 2009.

Fornes Institute, The. https://fornesinstitute.com

Friedman, Andrea. *Citizenship in Cold War America: The National Security State and the Possibilities of Dissent.* Amherst: University of Massachusetts Press, 2014.

Fuchs, Elinor. "EF's Visit to a Small Planet: Some Questions to Ask a Play." *Theater* 34, no. 2 (January 1, 2004): 4–9.

Fuentes, Marcela A. *Performance Constellations: Networks of Protest and Activism in Latin America.* Ann Arbor: University of Michigan Press, 2019.

García, Armando. "Freedom as Praxis: Migdalia Cruz's *Fur* and the Emancipation of Caliban's Woman." *Modern Drama* 59, no. 3 (2016): 343–62.

García Passalacqua, Juan Manuel. *Dignidad y Jaibería: Temer y Ser Puertorriqueño.* Puerto Rico: Editorial Cultural, 2003.

García-Romero, Anne. *The Fornes Frame: Contemporary Latina Playwrights and the Legacy of Maria Irene Fornes.* Tucson: University of Arizona Press, 2016.

Gladwell, Malcolm. "Small Change." *The New Yorker*, October 4, 2010.

Gonzalez, David. "Vieques Advocate Turns From Violence of Her Past," *New York Times*, June 18, 2001. https://www.nytimes.com/2001/06/18/us/vieques-advocate-turns-from-violence-of-her-past.html?smid=url-share

González, Lydia Milagros. *Libretos para El Tajo del Alacrán*. San Juan, P.R.: Instituto de Cultura Puertorriqueña, 1980.

Green-Rogers, Martine Kei, Shawn LaCount, Patricia Ybarra, and Harvey Young. "Continuing the Conversation: Responses to Gabriela Serena Sanchez and Quiara Alegría Hudes." *Theatre Topics* 29, no. 1 (March 2019): E-15–E-21.

Grosfoguel, Ramón. *Colonial Subjects: Puerto Ricans in a Global Perspective*. Berkeley: University of California Press, 2003.

Grosfoguel, Ramón, Frances Negrón-Muntaner and Chloé S. Goeras. "Introduction: Beyond Nationalist and Colonialist Discourses: The *Jaiba* Politics of the Puerto Rican Ethno-Nation." In *Puerto Rican Jam: Rethinking Colonialism and Nationalism*, edited by Frances Negrón-Muntaner and Ramón Grosfoguel, 1–36. Minneapolis: University of Minnesota Press, 1997.

Hays, Garfield. Commission of Inquiry on Civil Rights in Puerto Rico. *Report of the Commission of Inquiry on Civil Rights in Puerto Rico, May 22, 1937*. New York, 1937. "1937, Ponce Massacre, Legislative Commission of Inquiry." Accessed January 11, 2021. http://llmc.com/titledescfull.aspx?type=6&coll=58&div=231&set=08149

Herrera, Brian Eugenio. *Latin Numbers: Playing Latino in Twentieth Century U.S. Popular Performance*. Ann Arbor: University of Michigan Press, 2015.

Herrera, Patricia. *Nuyorican Feminist Performance: From the Café to Hip Hop Theater*. Ann Arbor: University of Michigan Press, 2020.

Holloway, John. *Change the World Without Taking Power: The Meaning of Revolution Today*. Pluto Press, 2019. Kindle.

HowlRound: The Ferguson Moment, https://howlround.com/series/ferguson-moment

Huang, Vivian L. "'What Shall We Do?': Kathy Change, Soomi Kim, and Asian Feminist Performance on Campus." *TDR: The Drama Review* 62, no. 3 (2018): 168–74.

Hudes, Quiara Alegría. *The Happiest Song Plays Last*. New York: Theatre Communications Group, 2014.

Hudes, Quiara Alegría. *My Broken Language: A Memoir*. New York: Random House, 2021. Kindle.

Hudes, Quiara Alegría. *Daphne's Dive*. New York: Theatre Communications Group, 2017. Kindle.

Hudes, Quiara Alegría. *Water by the Spoonful*. New York: Theatre Communications Group, 2017.

Isherwood, Christopher. "Daphne's Dive: Where Everybody Knows You're Broke." *New York Times*, May 5, 2016. https://www.nytimes.com/2016/05/16/theater/review-daphnes-dive-where-everybody-knows-youre-broke.html?_

Jackson-Schebetta, Lisa. *Traveler, There Is No Road: Theatre, the Spanish Civil War, and the Decolonial Imagination in the Americas*. Iowa City: University of Iowa Press, 2017.

Kanellos, Nicolás. *Hispanic Immigrant Literature: El Sueño Del Retorno*. Austin: University of Texas Press, 2011.

Kanellos, Nicolás, and Jorge Huerta, eds. *Nuevos Pasos: Chicano and Puerto Rican Drama*. Houston: Arte Público Press, 1989.

Kenny, Caroline. "Trump Tosses Paper Towels into Puerto Rico Crowd." CNN. Oct 3,

2017, https://www.cnn.com/2017/10/03/politics/donald-trump-paper-towels-pu erto-rico

Kerr, Andrew Rice. "A Disembodied Shade: Vieques, Puerto Rico at the Intersection of Empire and Environmentalism in the Twentieth Century." Ph.D., University of California, Davis. Accessed June 17, 2021. https://www.proquest.com/docview/15 19305523/abstract/F7E52FA2558B4CBDPQ/

Kerr, Walter. *How NOT to Write a Play*. New York: Dramatic Publishing, 1955.

Klein, Naomi. *The Battle for Paradise: Puerto Rico Takes on the Disaster Capitalists*. Chicago: Haymarket Books, 2018.

Kondo, Dorinne K. *Worldmaking: Race, Performance, and the Work of Creativity*. Durham: Duke University Press, 2018. Kindle.

Krigwa Players. "Krigwa Players Little Negro Theatre." Manuscript. New York (N.Y.), 1926. Digital Commonwealth. https://www.digitalcommonwealth.org/search/com monwealth-oai:z603r832h (accessed August 23, 2021).

La Fountain-Stokes, Lawrence. *Translocas: The Politics of Puerto Rican Drag and Trans Performance*. Ann Arbor: University of Michigan Press, 2021.

Lee, Lance. *The Death and Life of Drama: Reflections on Writing and Human Nature*. Austin: University of Texas Press, 2005.

Lewis, Gordon K. *Notes on the Puerto Rican Revolution: An Essay on American Dominance and Caribbean Resistance*. New York: Monthly Review Press, 1974.

Lugo-Lugo, Carmen R. "U.S. Congress and the Invisibility of Coloniality: The Case of Puerto Rico's Political Status Revisited." *Centro Journal* 18, no. 2 (Fall 2006): 124–45.

Malavet, Pedro A. *America's Colony: The Political and Cultural Conflict Between the United States and Puerto Rico*. New York: New York University Press, 2004.

Malavet, Pedro A. "Reparations Theory and Postcolonial Puerto Rico: Some Preliminary Thoughts." *Berkeley La Raza Law Journal* 13, no. 2 (2002): 387.

Maldonado-Torres, Nelson. "Outline of Ten Theses on Coloniality and Decoloniality." 2016. http://caribbeanstudiesassociation.org/docs/Maldonado-Torres_Outline _Ten_Theses-10.23.16.pdf

Marcantoni, Jonathan. *Puerto Rican Nocturne: Bilingual Edition*. Self-published, 2019.

Marqués, René. *The Docile Puerto Rican: Essays*. Edited and translated by Barbara Bockus Aponte. Philadelphia: Temple University Press, 1976.

Marqués, René. *Palm Sunday: Teatro Basada en la Masacre de Ponce 1937*. Edición Centenario. Ediciones Mágica. Puerto Rico, 2019.

Marqués, René. *La Carreta*. Río Piedras: Editorial Cultural, 1955. Translated by Charles Pilditch. New York: Scribner's, 1972.

McGreevey, Robert. *Borderline Citizens: The United States, Puerto Rico, and the Politics of Colonial Migration*. Ithaca: Cornell University Press, 2018.

McNay, Lois. "Historicizing Recognition: From Ontology to Teleology." In *Recognition and Ambivalence*, edited by Heikki Ikäheimo, Kristina Lepold, and Titus Stahl, 69–97. New York: Columbia University Press, 2021.

Meléndez, Edgardo. "Citizenship and the Alien Exclusion in the Insular Cases: Puerto Ricans in the Periphery of American Empire." *Centro Journal* 25, no. 1 (Spring 2013): 106–45.

Meléndez, Edgardo. *Sponsored Migration: The State and Puerto Rican Postwar Migration to the United States*. Columbus: The Ohio State University Press, 2017.

Mignolo, Walter D. *The Darker Side of Western Modernity: Global Futures, Decolonial Options*. Durham: Duke University Press, 2011.

Moreno, Marisel C. *Family Matters: Puerto Rican Women Authors on the Island and the Mainland*. Charlottesville: University of Virginia Press, 2012.
Moreno-Penson, Desi. *Beige*. National New Play Network/New Play Exchange, manuscript.
Moreno-Penson, Desi. *Devil Land*. National New Play Network/New Play Exchange, manuscript.
Moreno-Penson, Desi, and Noemi de la Puente. *Just Like Us*. National New Play Exchange, manuscript.
Mouffe, Chantal. "For a Politics of Nomadic Identity." In *Chantal Mouffe: Hegemony, Radical Democracy, and the Political*, edited by James Martin, 146–53. New York: Routledge, 2013.
Muñoz, José. *The Sense of Brown*. Edited by Joshua Chambers-Letson and Tavia Nyong'o. Durham: Duke University Press, 2020.
Murillo, Mario. *Islands of Resistance: Puerto Rico, Vieques, and U.S. Policy*. New York: Seven Stories Press, 2001.
Muzio, Rose. *Radical Imagination, Radical Humanity: Puerto Rican Political Activism in New York*. Albany: State University of New York Press, 2017.
Negrón-Muntaner, Frances. *Boricua Pop: Puerto Ricans and the Latinization of American Culture*. New York: New York University Press, 2004.
Negrón-Muntaner, Frances, ed. *None of the Above: Puerto Ricans in the Global Era*. New York: Palgrave Macmillan, 2008.
Negrón-Muntaner, Frances, and Ramón Grosfoguel. *Puerto Rican Jam: Rethinking Colonialism and Nationalism*. Minneapolis: University of Minnesota Press, 1997.
Neyra, Ren Ellis. *The Cry of the Senses: Listening to Latinx and Caribbean Poetics*. Durham: Duke University Press, 2020.
Nieves-Pizarro, Yadira, and Juan Mundel. "#RickyRenuncia: The Hashtag That Took Collective Outrage from Social Media to the Streets." In *Latin American Diasporas in Public Diplomacy*, edited by Vanessa Bravo and Maria De Moya, 169–87. Palgrave Macmillan, 2021.
Noel, Urayoán. *In Visible Movement: Nuyorican Poetry from the Sixties to Slam*. Iowa City: University of Iowa Press, 2014.
Noriega, Jimmy A., and Analola Santana, eds. *Theatre and Cartographies of Power: Repositioning the Latina/o Americas*. Carbondale: Southern Illinois University Press, 2018.
Page, Priscilla. "Afterword: My World Made Real." In *El Grito del Bronx and Other Plays* by Migdalia Cruz, 479–90. NoPassport Press, 2010.
Page, Priscilla M., "Charting the Terrain of Latina/o/x Theater in Chicago" (2018). Doctoral Dissertations.1453. https://doi.org/10.7275/12328595 https://scholarworks.umass.edu/dissertations_2/1453
Pastor, Néstor David. "25 Years of La Gringa: An Interview with Carmen Rivera." The Latinx Project. New York University. https://www.latinxproject.nyu.edu/intervenxions/25-years-of-la-gringa-an-interview-with-carmen-rivera
Paz, Octavio. *The Labyrinth of Solitude: Life and Thought in Mexico*. Translated by Lysander Kemp, Yara Milos, and Rachel Phillips Belash. New York: Grove Press, 1962.
Perales, Rosalina. *Me Llaman Desde Allá: Teatro y Performance de la Diáspora Puertorriqueña*. Santo Domingo: Impresora Soto Castillo, 2010.
Power-Sotomayor, Jade. "Corporeal Sounding: Listening to Bomba Dance, Listening to Puertorriqueñxs." *Performance Matters* 6, no. 2 (2020): 43–59.

Quijano, Aníbal. "Coloniality and Modernity/Rationality." *Cultural Studies* 21, nos. 2–3 (March 1, 2007): 168–78. https://doi.org/10.1080/09502380601164353

Quiñones, Arcadio Díaz. *El Arte de Bregar: Ensayos*. San Juan: Ediciones Callejón, 2003.

Ramírez, Jason. "Carmen Rivera: Theatre of Latinidad." PhD Diss., City University of New York, 2009. ProQuest.

Ramírez, Jason. "Miriam Colón: Puerto Rican Icon and Theatrical Traveler." *Latin American Theatre Review* 50, no. 2 (2017): 233–37.

Ramos-Zayas, Ana Y., and Mérida M. Rúa. *Critical Dialogues in Latinx Studies: A Reader*. New York: New York University Press, 2021.

Rebollo Gil, Guillermo. "Regarding the Future." In *Writing Puerto Rico: Our Decolonial Moment*, edited by Guillermo Rebollo Gil, 63–69. Springer International Publishing, 2018. https://doi.org/10.1007/978-3-319-92976-7_9

Reyes, Israel. *Embodied Economies: Diaspora and Transcultural Capital in Latin Theater and Fiction*. New Brunswick, NJ: Rutgers University Press, 2022.

Reynolds, Bonnie Hildebrand. *Space, Time and Crisis: The Theatre of René Marqués*. York, S.C.: Spanish Literature Publishing Company, 1988.

Rini, Regina. "Why I'm Tired of Hearing About 'Wokeism': Overblown rhetoric doesn't advance social justice." *Chronicle of Higher Education Review*. 15 November 2021.

Rivera, Carmen. *La Gringa*. English Version. New York: Samuel French, 2008.

Rivera, Carmen Haydée, and Jose L. Torres-Padilla, eds. *Writing Off the Hyphen: New Perspectives on the Literature of the Puerto Rican Diaspora*. Seattle: University of Washington Press, 2008.

Rivera, José. "36 Assumptions about Writing Plays." In *References to Salvador Dali Make Me Hot and Other Plays*, 251–56. New York: Theatre Communications Group, 2003.

Rivera, José. *Adoration of the Old Woman*. In *Boleros for the Disenchanted and Other Plays*. New York: Theatre Communications Group, 2012.

Rivera, José. *Marisol and Other Plays*. New York: Theatre Communications Group, 1997.

Rivera, José. *Massacre (Sing to Your Children)*. New York: Broadway Play Publishing, 2007.

Rivera, José. *School of the Americas*. New York: Broadway Play Publishing, 2007.

Rivera-Servera, Ramón H. *Performing Queer Latinidad: Dance, Sexuality, Politics*. Ann Arbor: University of Michigan Press, 2012.

Rivera-Servera, Ramón H., and E. Patrick Johnson, eds. *Blacktino Queer Performance*. Durham: Duke University Press, 2016.

Rooney, David. "They Kill the Tyrant but Can't Seem to Bury Him." *New York Times*, April 16, 2012, sec. Theater. https://www.nytimes.com/2012/04/17/theater/reviews/massacre-sing-to-your-children-at-rattlestick.html

Rossini, Jon D., and Patricia Ybarra. "Neoliberalism, Historiography, Identity Politics: Toward a New Historiography of Latino Theater." *Radical History Review* 2012, no. 112 (January 2012): 162–72. https://doi.org/10.1215/01636545-1416223

Rossini, Jon D. "José Rivera, Neoliberalism, and the Outside of Politics," *Latin American Theatre Review* 43, no. 1 (Fall 2009): 41–56.

Ruiz, Sandra. *Ricanness: Enduring Time in Anticolonial Performance*. New York: New York University Press, 2019.

Sanchez, Gabriela Serena, and Quiara Alegría Hudes. "Pausing and Breathing: Two Sisters Deliver the ATHE 2018 Conference Keynote Address." *Theatre Topics* 29, no. 1 (2019): 1–13.

Sánchez, José Ramón. *Boricua Power: A Political History of Puerto Ricans in the United States*. New York: New York University Press, 2007.

Sandoval-Sánchez, Alberto. "Introduction: I Don't Consciously Set Out to Write About Blood." In *El Grito del Bronx and Other Plays by Migdalia Cruz*, 4–28. NoPassport Press, 2010.

Schutzman, Mady. "Activism, Therapy, or Nostalgia? Theatre of the Oppressed in NYC." *TDR* 34, no. 3 (Autumn 1990): 77–83.

Shahadi, Joseph. "Burn: The Radical Disappearance of Kathy Change." *TDR: The Drama Review* 55, no. 2 (2011): 52–72.

Snook, Raven. "Notes on Killing Seven Oversight, Management and Economic Stability Board Members." *Time Out*. https://www.timeout.com/newyork/theater/notes-on-killing-seven-oversight-management-and-economic-stability-board-members

Soloski, Alexis. "'Notes on Killing' Review: For These Puerto Ricans, Promises Never Kept." *New York Times*, May 30, 2022. https://www.nytimes.com/2022/05/30/theater/notes-on-killing-review.html

Soto-Crespo, Ramón E. *Mainland Passage: The Cultural Anomaly of Puerto Rico*. Minneapolis: University of Minnesota Press, 2009.

Stevens, Camilla. *Family and Identity in Contemporary Cuban and Puerto Rican Drama*. Gainesville: University Press of Florida, 2004.

Stevens, Camilla. *Aquí and Allá: Transnational Dominican Theater and Performance*. Pittsburgh: University of Pittsburgh Press, 2019.

Svich, Caridad. "'An Urgent Voice for Our Times': An Interview with José Rivera." *Contemporary Theatre Review* 14(4) (2010): 83–89.

Taller Puertorriqueño https://tallerpr.org/vejigantes-of-puerto/

Taylor, Charles. *Multiculturalism and "The Politics of Recognition": An Essay*. Edited by Amy Gutmann. Princeton: Princeton University Press, 1992.

Taylor, Diana. "Brecht and Latin America's 'Theatre of Revolution.'" In *Brecht Sourcebook*, edited by Henry Bial and Carol Martin, 173–84. New York: Routledge, 2000.

Taylor, Diana. *¡Presente!: The Politics of Presence*. Durham: Duke University Press, 2020.

Taylor, Keeanga-Yamahtta. *From #BlackLivesMatter to Black Liberation*. Chicago: Haymarket Books, 2016.

Thomas, Lorrin. *Puerto Rican Citizen: History and Political Identity in Twentieth-Century New York City*. Chicago: University of Chicago Press, 2010.

Torruella, Juan R. "Ruling America's Colonies: The 'Insular Cases.'" *Yale Law & Policy Review* 32, no. 1 (Fall 2013): 57–95.

Tufekci, Zeynep. *Twitter and Tear Gas: The Power and Fragility of Networked Protest*. New Haven: Yale University Press, 2017.

UrbanTheater Tumblr https://urbantheater.tumblr.com/post/147847869907/get-to-know-our-lolita-de-lares-cast-tamika

Valdez, Luis, and El Teatro Campesino. *Luis Valdez—Early Works: Actos, Bernabé and Pensamiento Serpentino*. Houston: Arte Público Press, 1994.

Valentín-Escobar, Wilson. "'Nothing Connects Us All but Imagined Sounds': Performing Trans-Boricua Memories, Identities, and Nationalisms through the Death of Héctor Lavoe." In *Mambo Montage: The Latinization of New York*, edited by Arlene Dávila and Agustín Laó-Montes, 207–34. New York: Columbia University Press, 2001.

Vásquez, Eva C. *Pregones Theatre: A Theatre for Social Change in the South Bronx*. New York: Routledge, 2003.

Vidal, Gore. *Imperial America: Reflections on the United States of Amnesia*. New York: Nation Books, 2005.

Vilar, Irene. *A Message from God in the Atomic Age*. Translated by Gregory Rabassa. New York: Pantheon, 1996.

Visión Latino Theatre Company https://www.visionlatino.com

Vizenor, Gerald. *Native Liberty: Natural Reason and Cultural Survivance*. Omaha: University of Nebraska Press, 2009.

Wagenheim, Olga Jiménez de. *Puerto Rico's Revolt for Independence: El Grito de Lares*. Westview Special Studies on Latin America and the Caribbean. Boulder: Westview Press, 1985.

Webber, Jeffrey R. *The Last Day of Oppression, and the First Day of the Same: The Politics and Economics of the New Latin American Left*. Chicago: Haymarket, 2017.

"We See You, White American Theater," https://www.weseeyouwat.com

Williams, Raymond. "A Lecture on Realism." *Afterall: A Journal of Art, Context and Enquiry*, no. 5 (2002): 106–15.

Winter, Juan Duchesne. "Vieques: Protest as Consensual Spectacle." In *None of the Above: Puerto Ricans in the Global Era*, edited by Frances Negrón-Muntaner, 87–98. New York: Palgrave Macmillan, 2008.

"Would-Be Assassins Grimly Cry: Not Sorry for What We Did," *Newsday* (1940–1991); Mar 2, 1954; ProQuest Historical Newspapers: *Newsday*, 21.

Ybarra, Patricia A. "For Whom is Apocalypse a New Idea?: Thoughts on Staging the End." In *Life in the Posthuman Condition*, edited by Stephen Wilmer and Audrone Zukauskaite, 53–70. Edinburgh: Edinburgh University Press, 2023.

Ybarra, Patricia A. "How to Read a Latinx Play in the Twenty-First Century: Learning from Quiara Hudes." *Theatre Topics* 27, no. 1 (2017): 49–59.

Ybarra, Patricia A. *Latinx Theater in the Times of Neoliberalism*. Evanston: Northwestern University Press, 2018.

Ybarra-Frausto, Tomás. "Rasquachismo: A Chicano Sensibility." In *Chicano Art: Resistance and Affirmation, 1965–1985*, edited by Richard Griswold del Castillo, Teresa McKenna, and Yvonne Yarbro-Bejarano, 155–61. Los Angeles: Wight Art Gallery, University of California, 1991.

Zambrana, Rocío. *Colonial Debts: The Case of Puerto Rico*. Durham: Duke University Press, 2021.

Zimmerman, Marc. *Defending Their Own in the Cold: The Cultural Turns of U.S. Puerto Ricans*. Champaign: University of Illinois Press, 2020.

Index

9/11, 80
#RickyRenuncia, 98, 183, 210–11n24

absolutism, 46, 52; absolutist, 47, 50, 101
absurdist, 42
activism, 29, 35, 36, 77, 80, 91, 93, 95, 100, 124, 125, 126, 128, 129, 132, 134, 136, 165, 166, 179, 183, 186, 189; activist, 88, 131, 137, 141, 142, 143, 161, 177, 185
Adler, Stella, 195n28
Adyanthaya, Aravind Enrique, 200n22
African, 17, 23, 73, 85, 109, 111, 212n46, 213n67; Afrodiasporic, 106
aftermath, 30, 155, 157, 159, 160
Afro-Latina, 112
agonistic, 4, 23
Alam, Juan Shamsul, 200n23
Albizu Campos, Pedro, 42, 46, 57, 68, 69, 72, 81, 109, 118, 148, 203n61
Algarín, Miguel, 38
Alfaro, Luis, 12–13
Alick, Claudia, 25
allyship, 130, 132, 135
American Theatre, 124
Americanization, 69, 114, 118, 119
anagnorisis, 85
Antush, John V., 31, 36
Aparicio, Frances R., 147
Apstein, Theodore, 41
archipelago, 21, 37, 38, 56, 84, 94, 97, 145, 146
Arnall, Gavin, 46–47
Arrizón, Alicia, 200n23
art, 148, 150, 154, 159, 163, 174; artist, 141, 144; artistic, 188; practices, 137, 146; act, 138; patronage, 144
Artaud, Antonin, 168–69

Association for Theatre in Higher Education (ATHE), 124, 125
Ateneo Puertorriqueño, El, 97
audience(s), 2, 14, 61, 115, 116, 119, 126, 127, 128, 154, 155, 165, 173, 188; implied audiences, 9
authoritarian, 30, 64, 132, 141, 156, 158, 159, 162, 167, 169, 173, 174; authoritarianism, 157, 170, 179
autonomy, 39, 56, 57, 69, 104, 118, 159, 162, 170, 194n14; autonomous, 88
Ayala, César J., 97

Badiou, Alain, 168, 182
Belaval, Emilio S., 199n7
belonging, 18, 24, 34, 37, 78, 119, 181. *See also* Rowe: "be-longing"
Betances, Ramon, 68, 69, 72, 148
Black Lives Matter, 149, 177, 182; #BLM, 161
Black Panther Party, 95
blackness, 107, 112, 114
Boal, Augusto, 65
Boffone, Trevor, 200n23, 206n36
Bofill, Sylvia, 200n22
bomba, 106
Bonilla, Yarima, 19, 56, 217–18n41
border(s), 2, 21, 40, 158, 203n67, 207n52, 213n63
Borges, Jorge Luis, 187
Boricua, 56, 77, 78, 81, 99, 100, 103, 138, 150, 162
Bracetti, Mariana, 68
Brecht, Bertolt, 65
bregar, 19, 21, 22, 23, 34, 35, 66, 102, 198n60; *aquí en la brega*, 21, 22, 23, 125; *la brega*, 39, 40, 106, 162; *bregando*, 52, 93

233

Index

Buch, René, 210n6, 210n17
Buenaventura, Enrique, 65
Bunyasi, Tehama Lopez, 177
Butler, Judith 86, 87, 88, 220n37

Cabán, Pedro, 182–83
cannibalism, 75–76
Cantos de Rebeldía, 44, 203n50
capitalism, 28, 86, 117, 121, 125, 141, 145, 156, 171, 178, 182, 184, 187, 217n32; capitalist, 103, 138
Carballido, Emilio, 65
carpetas, 57. *See also* secret files
Carrero, Jaime, 38, 199n13
Carriger, Micelle Liu, 132
Castanha, Tony, 110
Ceiba, 109, 110
Chemers, Michael, 8
Chicanx, 12, 32
Cerro Maravilla, 58, 204n89
Chang(e), Kathy, 138, 140, 141, 217n41
Chauca, Charlie, 218n43
Chicago Dramatists, 204n77
Chicago Latino Theatre Company, 68, 70, 72, 206n24
citizen(s), 15, 17, 21, 63, 116, 134, 144, 145, 195n19; citizenship, 36, 38, 41, 84, 98, 153, 198n59; colonial, 16, 36, 84
climate, 5, 23, 96, 103, 126, 146, 157
coastwise property, 145
code-switching, 38, 44
coffee, 6, 22, 68, 73, 81, 109, 166, 176, 196n38
collateral, 11, 30, 64, 151, 156
Collazo, Oscar, 63
Colón, Miriam, 31, 41
colonial, 4, 19, 24, 33, 34, 37, 38, 41, 42, 45, 55, 56, 58, 74, 75, 76, 78, 83, 94, 99, 100, 102, 103, 106, 107, 108, 110, 113, 115, 116, 132, 135, 144, 145, 154, 155, 157, 159, 167, 172, 182; colonialism, 11, 15, 18, 19, 21, 23, 24, 29, 44, 45, 46, 48, 49, 50, 63, 66, 105, 111, 114, 149, 166, 187; colonialist, 16, 48, 68, 77, 209n73; anti-colonialist, 88, 182; coloniality, 6, 19, 28, 36, 47, 53, 71, 76, 77, 104, 157, 164, 181, 184, 186, 187
colorism, 146, 207n38; colorist, 109; lack of color diversity, 218n43; color semiotics, 112
commonwealth, 16, 18, 34, 56, 97
community-based, 31, 124, 125, 128, 132
consciousness, 113, 161; raising, 89, 90, 115, 120, 121, 140, 149, 150; revolutionary, 105, 123, 139; Puerto Rican, 107
coqui, 105, 106, 113, 117, 120
Cordero, Andreas Figueroa, 63
Corretjer, Juan Antonio, 202n45, 202n46
Cortes, Felix, 200n23
Cruz, Maria Acosta, 19
Cruz, Migdalia, 9, 29, 67, 68, 72, 190, 207n42; *Lolita de Lares*, 29, 67, 68–76; *Fur*, 75–76
cuatro, 117, 127, 128, 129, 212n56
Custodio, Xavier M., 204n77

dance, 74, 75, 110, 138, 146, 147, 150, 151; dancing, 106, 151, 152, 154
Davenport, Danielle, 112
Dávila, Arlene, 85, 208n61
Davis, Angela, 140
Dawson, Michael, 182
de la Puente, Noemi, 77; *Not Like Us*, 77–78
de la Roche, Elisa, 32
decolonial, 29, 41, 46, 68, 76, 86, 102, 105, 150; decoloniality, 47, 93, 103; decolonization, 93
Del Carmen, Guadalis, 189
Della Gatta, Carla, 200n23
Democracy Against Capitalism, 178
Denis, Nelson A., 42, 54, 55, 56, 204n85, 214n74
Deus ex machina, 3
diasporic, 1, 5, 14, 19, 22, 23, 24, 31, 34, 36, 37, 41, 94, 96, 98, 99, 107, 124, 157, 185, 187
diaspora, 21, 29, 36, 37, 39, 40, 42, 50, 94, 95, 98, 101, 114, 123, 128, 136, 146, 147, 181, 182, 190
Diasporican, 5, 14, 36, 40, 53, 66, 98, 99, 105, 106, 107, 182, 189, 201n34
Diaz, Kristoffer, 24–27, 30, 155, 156, 157; *#therevolution*, 30, 155, 157, 168–80; *All Ears*, 25–27, 156, 169; *The Elaborate*

Entrance of Chad Deity, 169; *Welcome to Arroyo's*, 169
Diaz-Marcano, Nelson, 29, 30, 54–62, 123, 126, 137, 144, 154; *Paper Towels*, 30, 123, 126, 144–55; *REVOLT!*, 29, 53–62, 68, 119, 137, 152, 154
dignidad, 19, 49; dignity, 70
docile, 34, 48, 51, 52; docility, 20, 102, 198n60
Dolan, Jill, 2; utopian performative, 2
Duany, Jorge, 37
dramatic worlds, 3, 11, 14, 27; worldmaking, 10; world building, 17
dramaturgy, 30, 86, 100, 122, 154, 160; dramaturgical, 3, 6, 110, 128, 163; dramaturgically, 134; dramaturgies, 12, 14, 196n30
Du Bois, W. E. B., 32
DuPrey, Melissa, 112
Dussel, Enrique, 178, 196n37

endure, 84, 167, 194n16, 207n43; endurance, 6, 20, 167, 188
English (language), 23, 38, 40, 82, 96, 99, 112, 114, 115, 117, 145, 201n39, 212–13n61
Estado Libre Asociado (ELA), 15, 16, 18, 21, 23, 41, 44, 48, 98, 121, 187, 194n14
Erman, Sam, 16
exceptionalism, 15, 16, 49, 50
expanded realisms, 10, 27, 61
estadolibrismo, 17, 20, 39, 98
Esteves, Sandra María, 39
Every 28 Hours Plays, 25, 198n66

Falcón, Angel, 200n23
family, 13, 20, 26, 29, 39, 41, 43, 53, 100, 136, 142, 149, 201n40; familial, 93, 98, 182; intra-familial, 53, 94, 96, 101, 147. See also *gran familia puertorriqueña*
Fanon, Franz, 46–47; Fanonian, 50
fantastic realism, 104–5, 207n54
FBI, 57, 58, 108, 119, 121, 205n10
Feingold, Michael, 164
Feliciano-Santos, Sharina, 100
Ferguson Moment, 27, 198n66
feminism, liberal, 79; feminist, 3, 39, 62, 88, 97, 131, 147

Fernández, Johanna, 95–96, 204–5n90
Fiet, Lowell, 200n23
Finn, Amanda, 189
Fisher, Tony, 194n12
flag, 51, 60, 61, 63, 68, 71–72, 78, 100, 121, 202n48, 203n70
Flores, Juan, 98, 200n23, 201n34
Fornés, Maria Irene, 9, 12–13, 195n23
Free Associated State, 15, 16, 20, 39, 86, 114, 182, 187
free association, 24, 63, 74, 90, 181, 184, 187, 191
freedom, 19, 23, 39, 56, 58, 64, 86, 101, 119, 141, 160, 162, 166, 175, 184
Friedman, Andrea, 205n11
Fuchs, Elinor, 11
Fuentes, Marcela A., 177

Gag Law, 57, 71–72
Gallardo, Eduardo, 200n23
Gallitos, 55
Garcia, Armando, 75–76
Gassner, John, 41
García-Romera, Anne, 9, n24 195
Garcia Passalacqua, Juan Manuel, 19, 20, 22
Gentile, Guillermo, 104–5, 207n54
geography, 27, 67, 98, 99, 102, 107, 135, 136, 149, 159, 167; political, 36, 120, 158; geographic, 131; geographies, 157
given circumstances, 1, 3, 6–7, 8–10, 11, 12, 15, 17, 23, 24, 27, 29, 30, 34, 39, 44, 48, 51, 53, 68, 91, 99, 103, 124, 125, 127, 131, 132, 137, 140, 153, 166, 179, 183, 187, 188, 190, 195n28
Gladwell, Malcolm, 165–66
Goeras, Chloé S., 18, 19–20, 40, 194n14
Goodman Theatre, 128
González, Jorge, 200n22
González, Lydia Milagros, 34
gran familia puertorriqueña, *la*, 20, 39, 54, 96, 97, 98, 102, 106
Grito de Jayuya 54, 64, 119; Jayuya Revolt, 17, 29
Grito de Lares, 17, 67, 68, 108, 120, 189, 205n11
Grosfoguel, Ramón, 18, 19–20, 40, 194n14, 201n36, 208n56

guiro, 106, 211n34
gun, 58, 89, 108, 146, 148, 149, 151, 152, 153, 175; pistol, 66, 92

Hays, Arthur Garfield, 42; report, 44, 45, 203n70
hero's journey, 1, 2, 193n1
Herrera, Brian Eugenio, 200n23
Herrera, Patricia, 38–39; pláticas, 39
hipster, 30, 157, 171, 176
Holloway, John, 90–91
home, 18, 34, 41, 54, 70, 71, 79, 121, 181; homeland, 97
Honneth, Axel, 86
horizon, political, 11–12, 13, 15, 27, 28, 29, 52, 61, 62, 74, 91, 116, 128, 131, 198n69; of activism, 80; of expectation, 81; fusion of, 86
Hudes, Quiara Alegría, 14, 29–30, 32–33, 123, 124, 125, 127, 128, 183, 189, 190, 195n24; *Adventures of a Barrio Girl: Lulu's Golden Shoes*, 125; *Daphne's Dive*, 30, 123, 126, 136–44, 149, 211n34; *Elliot, A Soldier's Fugue*, 127; *The Happiest Song Plays Last*, 29–30, 123, 126, 127, 128–36; *Miss You Like Hell*, 125; *My Broken Language*, 125, 215–16n4, 216n13; "Pausing and Breathing," 124, 126, 183; *Water by the Spoonful*, 127, 129, 135, 190–91, 216n15
Huerta, Jorge, 200n23
Hurricane Maria, 5, 15, 21, 23, 30, 56, 98, 144, 146, 147, 149, 151, 154, 181, 183, 198n65

idealism, 46, 70, 103, 118, 148; idealist, 115
identity, 3, 4, 18, 31, 41, 67, 73, 78, 79, 82, 83, 86, 89, 99, 100, 102, 103, 106, 114, 117, 122, 138, 150, 156, 194n11, 196n30; identities, 141, 155; identification, 36
immigrant, 36, 56; immigration, 213n63
immolation, 140; self-, 138, 139, 142
In the Heights (film), 218n43
independence, 16, 17, 18, 19, 42, 43, 48, 53, 54, 57, 58, 80, 93, 95, 112, 113, 114, 115, 116, 117, 118, 119, 162, 189
independentista, 45, 58, 114

indigenous cosmologies, 11, 100
insular cases, 15, 16, 208n56
INTAR, 9, 112, 116, 148, 188, 218n46
InterAct Theatre Company, 220n26
International Puerto Rican Theatre Festival, 97
Irizarry, Richard V., 207n38

Jackson-Schebetta, Lisa, 212n46
Jacob, Jenkins, Branden, 212n53
jaiberia, 19, 20, 22, 23, 51, 81
Jesurun, John, 200n23
jíbaro, 31, 74, 103, 110, 114, 206n30, 208n60

Kanellos, Nicolás, 199n20
Kerr, Andrew Rice, 209n70
Kerr, Walter, 14
Kim, Soomi, 142; *Chang(e)*, 142
Kirk Douglas Theatre, 127, 216n9
Klein, Naomi, 179, 218n52
Kondo, Dorinne, 4, 8

La Fountain-Stokes, Lawrence, 37, 98; translocality, 37, 98
La Jolla Playhouse, 107, 112
labyrinth, 24, 181, 187, 188, 191
land, 103, 104, 105, 117, 165
language, 38, 39, 44, 109, 110, 114, 146, 151, 158, 159, 162, 174, 201n39, 213n63
Latina/e/o/x, 12, 16, 32, 72, 73, 85, 116, 126, 127, 128, 159, 187, 188, 189, 206n55, 220n27
Latino Theatre Company, 127
Latinx Theatre Commons, 189, 221n15
Lavoe, Héctor, 147; *Aguanile*, 147
Lebrón, Lolita, 17, 29, 63, 64, 66, 67, 68–93, 148, 208n55
Lee, Lance, 193n1
Lewis, Gordon K., 183–84
Ley de la Mordaza (Law 53), 41, 60, 71–72, 121, 201n38, 203n70. *See also* Gag Law
liberal(s), 81, 84, 86, 90, 106, 121, 125, 153, 154, 171, 172, 174; liberalism, 14, 49, 76, 80, 85, 117, 173
liberation, 1, 2, 21, 25, 34, 35, 45, 76, 90, 105, 106, 107, 111, 123, 124, 130, 157, 162, 163, 172, 176, 184, 185, 190, 196n37

Lopez, Tiffany Ana, 200n23
Lugo, Maribel Acosta, 202n47
Lugo-Lugo, Carmen R., 194n14

magical realism, 112
Malavet, Pedro A., 16, 116, 197n45, 213n67
Maldonado-Torres, Nelson, 47, 71
Manzor, Lillian, 200n23
Marcantoni, Jonathan, 204n89
Mariposa, 98, 99
Mark Taper Forum, 127, 216n9
Marqués, René, 29, 34, 37, 41–45, 46, 48, 49, 50, 52, 53, 68, 198n60, 202n46, 203n61, 213n62; *La Casa Sin Reloj*, 215n81; *The Oxcart [La Carreta]*, 31, 36, 41, 199n20, 213n62; *Palm Sunday*, 29, 41–46, 48–53, 202n46; *The Docile Puerto Rican*, 8, 50–52
marquesina, 101
Marrero, Teresa, 200n23
martyr, 83, 112; martyrdom, 48, 51, 53, 64, 93, 101, 154; "martyr complex," 52
massacre(s), 43, 45, 49, 156, 161, 165, 166, 167
McGreevey, Robert, 218n51
McGregor, Patricia, 112
McNay, Lois, 86–87
Meléndez, Edgardo, 38, 198n59, 204n87; "sponsored migrations," 109
Meléndez, Mara Vélez, 29, 67, 92–93; *Notes on Killing Seven Oversight Management and Economic Stability Board Members*, 29, 67, 92–93
melodrama, 14, 24, 51, 52, 53, 54, 112, 122, 165, 212n53; melodramatic, 48, 97, 109, 121, 160, 163; melodramatic tableau, 44
mental health, 82, 154; disorders, 79; illness, 78, 83; imbalance, 89; state, 142; mentally ill, 90, 141
Message to God in the Atomic Age, A, 83
Mignolo, Walter, D., 213n62
migrants, 21; migration, 23, 29, 36, 38, 41, 101, 198n65, 199n9, 199n12, 204n87; migrate, 102; "sponsored migrations," 109; migratory, 31, 97
military, 36, 42, 54, 64, 69, 78, 80, 84, 88, 90, 118, 129, 135, 170, 182, 207n42, 208n56
Miranda, Lin Manuel, 218n43
Miranda, Rafael Cancel, 63
Mohr, Eugene, 37
Morales, Tamika Lecheé, 71–72
Moreno-Penson, Desi, 29, 67, 76, 77, 78, 189, 197n49, 205n1, 208n60; *Beige*, 29, 67, 76–91, 197n49, 217n19; *Devil Land*, 77, 189, 208n60; *Not Like Us*, 77–78
Moreno, Marisel, 39–40; transinsular, 39; *frontera intranacional*, 40
Moreno, Rita, 218n43
Mouffe, Chantal, 4, 194n11; "agonistic politics," 4
mulatta, 109, 111, 112
Mundel, Juan, 211n24
Muñoz, Jose, 200n23
Muñoz Marin, Luis, 20, 21, 22, 45, 57, 58, 119, 203n51
music, 102, 105, 129, 136, 147, 159, 163, 201n34, 211n33; musical, 106, 127, 128, 211n38

National Latino Playwriting Award, 76
nationalism, 18, 42, 54, 56, 74, 80, 95, 110; cultural, 97; nationalist, 45, 51, 52, 69, 75, 106, 115, 205n1
Nationalists, 43, 63, 64, 72, 81, 89, 119, 183
negotiate, 7, 14, 39, 94, 142; negotiated, 28, 71; negotiating, 3, 77, 136, 187; negotiation, 6, 20, 21, 22, 23, 29, 34, 44, 65, 97, 132, 146, 151
Negrón-Muntaner, Frances, 18, 19–20, 35, 40, 194n14
neoliberal, 12, 86, 93, 111, 156, 171, 184, 185; neoliberalism, 19, 80
Neyra, Ren Ellis, 211n38
Nieves-Pizarro, Yadira, 211n24
Noel, Urayoán, 201n30
Nottage, Lynn, 217n32
Nuyorican, 1, 36, 38, 39, 67, 76, 77, 92, 97, 98, 99, 104; aesthetic, 36, 38; Gothic, 77
Nuyorican Poets Café, 38

Oregon Shakespeare Festival, 25
oud, 127

Page, Priscilla, 72, 73, 206n24
Pasquinucci, Christina Victoria, 186
patriarchy, 28, 50, 77; patriarchal, 78, 80, 81, 85, 108
Paz, Octavio, 187, 207n45
Perales, Rosalina, 37, 200n23
performative assembly, 88
Pietri, Pedro, 38
Piñero, Miguel, 38, 189
Pop, Icona, 175
Ponce Massacre, 29, 41, 44, 53, 57, 95, 202n45, 202n46
Power-Sotomayor, Jade, 106
pragmatic, 1, 6–7, 19, 22, 24, 26, 38, 41, 51, 58, 63, 66, 67, 81, 102, 103, 107, 115, 118, 119, 160, 166, 172, 182, 186, 195n18; pragmatism, 6, 11, 34, 39, 40, 76, 101, 131, 142; liberal, 87
pragmatic liberation, 5, 11, 12, 21, 24, 25, 29, 34, 35, 47, 52, 53, 54, 57, 64, 77, 88, 91, 93, 94, 96, 104, 105, 108, 111, 122, 125, 126, 130, 140, 156, 157, 169, 170, 180, 181, 183, 184, 185, 188, 191
Pregones Theater, 35, 189, 199n2
premise(d), 1, 3, 10, 11, 14, 15, 17, 27, 44, 54, 57, 86, 157, 169, 170, 171, 173, 187
President Biden, 2; Bush, 158, 159; Carter, 57, 69, 84; Clinton, 159; Truman, 17, 204n78; Trump, 144, 145
PROMESA, 5, 21, 92, 98, 122, 167, 182, 183, 184, 209n74, 218n50
protest, 35, 42, 43, 48, 84, 108, 128, 130, 131, 132, 133, 134, 137, 138, 140, 161, 177, 186, 217n18, 217n23, 217n41
psychosis, 79, 82, 84
Puerto Rican Day Parade, 58, 61
Puerto Rican Traveling Theater (PRTT), 31, 35, 41, 189, 199n2, 199n13
"Puerto Rican Problem," 33, 55
Puerto Rican Syllabus, 194n15

Quijano, Aníbal, 213n63
Quiñones, Arcadio Diaz, 21, 22, 66
Quintero, Laura, 186

racism, 11, 15, 28, 40, 58, 81, 84, 146, 149, 154, 177, 196n30, 197n45, 213n67; racist, 78
Ramirez, Elisabeth, 200n23
Ramirez, Jason, 31, 96–97, 104, 211n33
Ramos-Perea, Roberto, 215n81
rasquachi, 198n60
Rattlestick Playwrights Theater, 164
realism, 10, 54, 68, 74, 78, 92, 97, 152, 182; realist, 122, 169
Rebello Gil, Guillermo, 186
recognition, 3, 11, 23, 29, 47, 48, 49, 51, 58, 60, 84, 85–88, 89, 90, 98, 103, 105, 108, 122, 130, 132, 138, 141, 144, 149, 151, 170, 178, 183, 185, 190, 191, 195n19
referendum, 16, 29, 58, 98, 107, 108, 116, 117, 119, 120; plebiscite, 213–14n68
relation, 22; politics of, 3, 19, 29, 37, 116, 157, 178, 179; social, 99, 176; relational, 3, 4, 7, 40, 163, 173, 186; choice, 46; praxis, 106; relationality, 8, 15, 23, 35, 47, 78, 94, 113, 151, 184, 185; inter-relationality, 8, 47, 48, 51, 52; relationally, 26; relationship, 79, 105; colonial, 17, 19, 21; political, 38, 56, 94
Repertorio Español, 96, 188, 210n6, 210n17
resilience, 194n16, 73, 177, 188; resiliency, 55–56
revolution 1, 8, 30, 46, 58, 64, 65, 69, 85, 92, 121, 122, 131, 135, 139, 155, 156, 157, 159, 160, 162, 163, 165, 166, 167, 168, 171, 172, 173, 176, 177, 179, 186, 198n69; revolutionary, 2, 3, 8, 12, 14, 26, 29, 30, 39, 53, 56, 58, 60, 61, 67, 68, 75, 76, 79, 84, 88, 90, 95, 105, 107, 118, 119, 120, 124, 128, 129, 130, 132, 133, 136, 140, 142, 143, 145, 146, 148, 149, 151, 153, 161, 164, 169, 170, 174, 175, 177, 189
Revolutionary Cadets, 42, 48, 55
Reyes, Israel, 200n23
Reynolds, Bonnie, 52
Rice-Gonzalez, Charles, 207n38
Rini, Regina, 193n2
Rivera, Carmen, 29, 93, 94, 96, 101, 104, 106–7, 113, 181, 211n27; *La Gringa*, 29, 93, 94, 96–107, 113, 117, 120, 189
Rivera, Carmen Haydeé, 37

Rivera, José, 1, 2, 3, 10, 29, 68, 93, 94, 107, 117, 121, 140, 155, 156, 157, 204n79, 211n39, 211n40; "36 Assumptions About Writing Plays," 10; *Adoration of the Old Woman*, 29, 68, 93, 94, 107–23, 156, 189; *Brainpeople*, 211n39; *Marisol*, 1–6, 140; *Massacre: Sing to Your Children*, 30, 155, 157–67; *Motorcycle Diaries*, 214n69; *School of the Americas*, 121, 211n40, 215n83
Rivera-Servera, Ramón, 207n38, 219n63
Rodriguez, Chantal, 200n23
Rodriguez, David Sanes, 64, 80, 84
Rodriguez, Irving Flores, 63
Rolón, Rosalba, 35
Rooney, David, 164–65
Rowe, Aimee Carrillo, 3, 11, 185; "be longing," 3, 11, 24, 37, 39, 131, 136, 137, 142, 146, 178, 185
Rozin, Seth, 220n26
Ruiz, Sandra, 66, 88, 194n16, 205n8; *Ricanness*, 66, 194n16, 205n8
Ryan, Jed, 92

sacrifice, 136, 142, 166, 167
Salsa, 151, 153, 154
Sanchez, Gabriel, 124
Sanchez, José Ramón, 150
Sandoval-Sánchez, Alberto, 70, 200n23
secret files, 58. *See also carpetas*
servicial, 101, 134, 142, 143, 210n15
Shahadi, Joseph, 141
Shutzman, Mady, 205n7
sideways, 91, 97, 99, 183. *See also jaibería*
Smith, Anna Deavere, 4; *Twilight: Los Angeles, 1992*, 4
Smith, Candis Watts, 177
Snook, Raven, 92
Society of the Spectacle, 173
Soho Rep, 92
sojourner, 37, 42
Soloski, Alexis, 93
Soto-Crespo, Ramon E., 17, 20, 21, 198n60
sovereign, 37, 159; sovereignty, 17, 19, 39, 84, 90, 93, 113, 170, 184, 197n44
Spanish (language), 38, 58, 80, 96, 99, 112, 114, 115, 116, 117, 180, 201n39, 212n58, 213n63

Spanish Cuban American War, 15, 80, 196n38, 208n56
spectacular, 62, 63, 170, 173, 174, 177
spiritual, 73, 88, 94, 102, 105, 106; spiritualism, 97; spiritualist, 77; spirituality, 67, 70; spiritually, 120
statehood, 16, 18, 93, 107, 116, 117, 118, 119, 121, 213–14n68; state, incorporation as, 115
status, 16, 18, 19, 24, 29, 34, 36, 58, 107, 112, 113, 115, 116, 136, 204n85
Stevens, Camilla, 41, 200n22, 200n25, 201–2n40
storytelling, 2, 3, 9, 10, 12, 19, 23, 24, 27, 38, 54, 58, 61, 62, 136, 149, 153, 169, 177
struggle(s), 22, 23, 27, 30, 34, 46, 53, 82, 102, 125, 126, 132, 135, 136, 139, 142, 146, 159, 160, 189, 194n11, 195n19
Suarez, Roberto Rodriguez, 31, 200n23
suicide, 139, 144, 152, 175
surrealism, 74
survival, 125, 131, 136, 138, 143, 144, 165, 166, 185, 191; surviving, 135
sustain, 122, 158, 160; sustainable, 26, 28, 60, 94, 96, 99, 111, 124, 129, 134, 159, 169, 181, 182, 186, 188; sustained, 71, 72, 93, 125, 136, 149, 157, 162, 172, 177, 179; sustaining, 29, 105, 119, 130, 156, 163, 167, 170
Svich, Caridad, 159
symbolic action, 63, 76, 88, 89, 90

Tahrir Square, 128, 129–30
Taíno, 17, 74, 77, 82, 84, 99–100, 102, 110, 146, 149, 150, 151, 206n30, 208n60, 213n61
Tajo del Alacran, El, 34
Taller Puertorriqueño, 73
Taylor, Charles, 85–86, 87
Taylor, Diana, 65, 194–95n18
Taylor, Keeanga-Yamahtta, 182
Teatro Campesino, El, 32, 65, 206n32
Teatro Nuevo Popular, 32
territory, 15, 16, 97, 108; territories, 159; territorial, 40, 208n56; territorial possession, 29, 183; territorial status, 182, 187

terrorism, 57; terrorist, 80, 90, 146, 205n1
Theatre Topics, 125
Thomas, Lorrin, 195n19
Tirado, Cándido, 104–5, 200n23
Toro, Vincent, 99–100
Torres, Luis Lloréns, 114
Torres-Padilla, Jose L., 37
Torresloa, Griselio, 63
transculturation, 65
transformation, 1, 2, 6, 20, 26, 27, 28, 30, 58, 71, 75, 94, 98, 105, 111, 129, 136, 137, 143, 155, 156, 157, 158, 159, 162, 169, 170, 171, 182, 183, 185, 187, 188; "transformation now," 7, 96, 141
transnational, 21, 37
trauma, 49, 110, 116, 120, 146
Treaty of Paris, 15, 116
Tufekci, Zeynep, 177, 180, 217n18

United Nations (UN), 16, 78, 84, 89, 197n44
UrbanTheater Company, 68, 72, 112, 189, 206n24
US regional theater, 14, 107, 115, 125, 127, 189

Valdez, Luis, 65
Vantín-Escobar, Wilson, 219n56
Vásquez, Eva C., 34, 35, 199n7
Vega, Ivan, 189
Vejigantes, 73, 74, 75, 76
Vieques, 35, 64, 78, 80, 81, 82, 84, 88, 90, 91,182, 209n70, 214n74
Vidal, Gore, 159
Vilar, Irene, 83–84

violence, 6, 23, 27, 30, 33, 40, 41, 43, 45, 46, 48, 49, 50, 51, 53, 54, 56, 58, 60, 61, 63, 64, 65, 74, 85, 89, 93, 109, 110, 111, 119, 120, 126, 132, 135, 138, 139, 140, 141, 144, 145, 149, 154, 161, 165, 166, 169, 170, 171, 172, 176, 181
virtue signaling, 132, 171
Vision Latino Theatre Company, 204n77
Vizenor, Gerald, 212n51

Wagenheim, Olga Jiménez de, 205n11
Webber, Jeffrey E., 178
Williams, Raymond, 13
Williams, Tennessee, 212n54, 215n79
Wiley, Samira, 218n43
Winter, Juan Duchesne, 91
world, another, 151; building, 8, 17, 40, 73, 169, 170; created, 176; dramatic, 9, 11, 14, 27, 61, 122; configuration, 7; creation, 3; generating, 175; imagines, 153, 182; making, 10, 15, 28, 34, 36, 67, 177, 189–90; of the play, 105, 107, 133; reimagine, 48, 65; revisioning, 12

Ybarra, Patricia, 124–25, 194n17, 195–96n30, 216n6, 216n11
Young Lords, 58, 95–96, 184, 204n84, 204–5n90
Yunque, El, 101, 105
Yusef, Anatol, 164
Yuyachkani, 65

Zambrana, Rocío, 184, 185, 210–11n24
Zapatistas, 180, 194–95n18
Zimmerman, Marc, 198n60